RICKY FLEET
INFERNAL
EMERGENCE

INFERNAL: Emergence
©2016 Ricky Fleet
First Edition
Edited by Christina Hargis Smith
Cover art by Jeffrey Kosh Graphics
Published by Optimus Maximus Publishing, LLC

ISBN-10: 1-944732-19-5
ISBN-13: 978-1-944732-19-6

DEDICATED TO

I would like to dedicate this novel to my best friend; Kevin. We may be miles apart, but you and the family are always in my thoughts.

I would also like to dedicate it to my three amazing children. You are my whole life and make me proud every single day.

Acknowledgements

I'm proud to include the 2 people who won the "Name a Demon" competition. Adam James Selby-Martin and Jason Morton who created suitably dastardly monikers for Hell's Generals.

My family, without whose support and patience I wouldn't be able to get these crazy dreams written down.

My friend, editor and publisher Christina. The journey is just beginning and long may our insane expedition continue.

Jeffrey Kosh, who never fails to create an incredible cover for my works.

And of course, all my friends and readers. Your support and kind messages keep me going through the niggling doubt.

A NOTE FROM THE AUTHOR

The Infernal series was borne of a nightmare I had one cold, winters night. Waking from the dream, I immediately drafted a storyline which follows Malachi on his incredible, and horrific, journey. He too suffers from inexplicable nightmares, but they have a far darker meaning than anything I experience.

I truly hope you enjoy the first installment of the Infernal series and will join me on the fraught path leading to the very gates of Hell itself. You haven't known true horror until seeing what lies in the darkness, waiting for our sins to summon them forth.

For upcoming news about future books, info about contests and prizes, or if you just want to chat, please follow me on my Facebook page at
www.facebook.com/Author Ricky Fleet
and on my publisher's page at
www.facebook.com/OptimusMaximusPublishing
and on Twitter @AuthorRickFleet and @Optimaxpublish

INFERNAL EMERGENCE

A Novel by
Ricky Fleet

OPTIMUS MAXIMUS PUBLISHING
Brick, New Jersey
∗ 2016 ∗

CHAPTER ONE

"So what do you think about the latest offensive by the Government against the Outlaws?" whispered Paul over the office dividing wall.

"It's about time they dealt with those bastards," replied his colleague Hector with a sneer.

"I know, right? How has one country managed to hold out against the Syndicate Nations for all this time?" asked Paul, returning his focus to the scrolling monitors. Three wide and three high, the screens showed the comings and goings of several shops and the surrounding streets in his surveillance district.

"We have just been toying with them, like a cat with a mouse. No, more like a lion and a mouse," said Hector, "But the Chosen have obviously become tired of trying to bring them into the fold. Now they pay the price."

Paul thought about the war taking place and how his brother was faring. He was part of an elite infantry platoon that had been airdropped into the thick of the fighting several days ago.

"Be safe, brother," he said to himself.

"He will be fine. They have the best tech and armor money can buy." Hector grinned and Paul knew he was right. Their equipment was impervious to bullets and most of the resistance were only armed with rudimentary machine guns.

There was a sense of euphoria growing in the office as the half hourly announcements over the tannoy detailed the gains of the Syndicate forces. City after city was falling to the brave soldiers and the Outlaws were in full retreat. A bank of TV screens showed in intimate detail the fighting from the reconnaissance drones, then switched to first person view of a squad of black clad troops as they breached a barricaded building. The smoke from the explosives curled around the aggressors as they rushed inside, raking the walls with fully automatic plasma weapons. Men, women, and children were cut down, flaring holes burned cleanly through their bodies. The soldiers were under orders to spare no one.

"Yes," whispered Paul with a fist pump, "Get those fuckers."

The scenes of death were arousing and he was glad to be seated at his desk or the telltale bulge would have betrayed him. Not that many people would have been judgmental about it; sexual freedom was one of the great betterments the Chosen Fathers had enshrined in the constitution. Disappointingly, the feed changed from the troops and switched to a heavily laden missile battery. The rockets streamed in blazing glory from rows of launching tubes into the distance, before the footage switched to the drone which was calling in the strike. Each missile impacted a concrete housing structure in quick succession and the screen lit up with righteous fire. Before the barrage was complete, the whole building crumbled into itself, but not before the aircraft zoomed in on the doomed people who begged for mercy on the rooftop.

"Did you see that? The pathetic scum don't even know what's hit them," Shelby purred, surprising Paul from behind. She reached down and cupped his balls, gently kneading them and then rubbing his throbbing erection.

"Later," Paul said breathlessly, pushing her hand away.

"I'll hold you to that," she gave him one more squeeze and walked away, looking back over her shoulder and blowing a kiss.

"You lucky bastard, I can't believe you get to bang that every night before going home. My wife still has issues about me touching other women, not that it's stopped her opening her legs to the gym instructor," Hector complained.

"It's law, she can't stop you. If she keeps refusing we will report her," Paul said, unable to look away from the TV screen and the incredible images.

Hector burst out laughing, "Can you imagine the look on her face if they took her away for reeducation?"

"Would serve her right. Selfish bitch."

"Hey, you need to get back to work, look at feed fourteen twelve."

Paul looked at the corresponding monitor and a woman was trying to sequester a loaf of bread into a child's stroller. He would have given her the benefit of the doubt, but the camera revealed her desperate eyes as they swiveled to and fro like a cornered animal. She carefully concealed the theft beneath another bag in the storage section under the seat. The blonde haired child was merrily kicking around and enjoying the bright colors on the food shelves, unaware his whole life was about to change.

"Security, this is operative Charlie, echo, three eight nine," Paul said into a small microphone mounted to his head.

"Go ahead, Paul," came a husky female voice.

"We have a possible theft in progress in the district four food dispensary. Request sentinels to apprehend the suspect upon exit. She is approximately five foot three inches tall, with shoulder length brown hair. Beige long sleeved top with a white skirt. Facial recognition is running her details to find a match," Paul explained.

"We have her on our screens now. Thank you, Paul, sentinels are on the way," said the erotic voice. What Paul wouldn't have given to have a chance to meet the source of the teasing tones.

Paul watched the target approach the payment machine and held his breath as she hesitated. If she had a change of heart and paid for the bread, the whole arrest would have to be called off. Looking around again, she decided to take the chance. After paying for the visible goods, she tried to calmly exit the building.

"Got you now, bitch!" spat Paul, reaching over to high five Hector.

The doors opened and four men pounced, throwing her to the ground with enough force to bounce her head from the pavement.

"Ouch, I felt that," giggled Hector, watching the blood start to stream from the head wound and pool on the pavement.

The guards were dressed in brilliant white; boots, armored suit, and reflective helmet. They were the vanguard of the Chosen Fathers, those picked for their purity and loyalty to the cause. The infant was thrown out of the stroller and went sprawling to the ground while the guard pulled the bread out. In a daze, the thief frantically shook her head in denial, causing drops of blood to fly in every direction. Some of the scarlet liquid splashed the gleaming uniform of one of her captors and her face went from frightened to terrified in an instant.

"That was silly," Paul said breathlessly; he knew what was coming.

The guard took out a small cartridge from his utility belt and barked an order over his shoulder. The small child was picked up by the back of his clothing and tossed like a rag doll into the holding cage of the waiting vehicle. Bones would have been broken by the savage throw, but as the child of a criminal, he no longer had any claim to rights. He would be brought up in the slave orphanage now. The woman shrieked and bucked under the sentinel who sat astride her and yanked her hair hard enough to tear some free of the scalp. The senior member of the team held the cartridge to the center of her forehead and pressed a button. A small flash of explosive drove the contents through the skull and into her brain.

"I hope I never do anything to warrant a visit from the sentinels," whispered Hector. The gadget was horrifying and he would often wake from nightmares where he had been caught committing subversive acts, the white guard reaching for him.

It had been designed to act as a device used for memory reclamation before the victim was summarily executed. The silver disc on her forehead was the size of a quarter, with four thin barbs buried in her skin to keep it in place. The probe had tendrils that bored through the brain tissue and attached to the different regions, allowing the mind to be picked clean of any information that might lead to co-conspirators. Her face was contorted in agony, but enough damage had been caused to render her immobile. The nerves were left unaffected to ensure every bit of pain was fully appreciated.

"Paul, look!" Hector cried, diverting his attention.

On the huge TV screen, a group of soldiers was cheering with jubilation and firing into the air. On his knees at their feet was an old man who had been severely beaten, blood running from his nose and dripping from the chin. Dressed in black, with a small, square white patch in the center of his collar which was rapidly turning red.

"The glorious forces of the Syndicated Nations have crushed the Outlaws. The head of the organization has been apprehended after surrendering following the use of small scale thermonuclear weapons on three of the larger cities. Reuben Marshall has been responsible for ordering innumerable incursions into Syndicate territory to steal the food of the hard working citizens of our great nation."

The figure swayed and nearly toppled to the side, but two burly, uniformed arms appeared at either side and held him roughly in place. Eyes rolling, he was drifting in and out of consciousness.

"For these crimes, you have been sentenced to death. This just punishment is to be carried out immediately to alleviate the risk of any remaining bandits attempting to secure your rescue."

A soldier stepped into view behind the elderly prisoner with a wickedly shaped ceremonial knife. The mirrored visor of his battle helmet reflected the camera operator and the gathered figures of the conquering troops. Taking the blade in both hands, the executioner raised it above his head. A smile appeared on the prisoner's lips and he started to recite a wrong-phrase.

"May God have mercy on…"

The knife was thrust downward with enough power to lift the soldier's feet from the floor. The sound of shank piercing skull bone with a crunch burst from the speakers and everyone in the office cringed. The soldier tried to twist the killing blade to inflict further damage and humiliation to the victim. The only result was a ghastly shake of the dead man's head, which made it look as if he was trying to deny his own demise. The commentator resumed the dialogue as the body slumped forward, displaying the vicious, gaping wound on the top of his cranium.

"This is a glorious day in our history and the Chosen Fathers have deemed it worthy of a celebration. All non-essential personnel will be permitted to leave their designated placements one hour early for today only."

A cheer erupted in the office at the death of their mortal enemy and the chance of leaving an hour before schedule. Paul caught the look that Shelby shot him from her desk and smiled at the debauched acts they would carry out on one another.

"Our forces will be continuing their efforts to liquidate the remaining pockets of resistance over the coming days. We know we can count on your continued vigilance and obedience as a new dawn approaches."

The TV screen showed the final seconds in the execution room as the remaining soldiers gathered around and shot the corpse indiscriminately, then blinked off to be replaced by the Syndicated Nations symbol.

"It's over, we have won!" shouted Hector, leaping from his chair. He grabbed Paul in a bear hug and swung him around, weeping with joy.

"My brother can come home now." Paul was crying with relief too.

A scowling female supervisor listened carefully to her earpiece. They were never happy with a change to the normal routine, not even one granted by the highest power in the world.

"All Class B operators are dismissed until tomorrow. Class A operators have been assigned essential and will finish as normal," she screeched.

"Fuck!" muttered Hector. As the senior surveillance operator in the pair he was to stay behind. Paul patted him on the back in commiseration and reached for his coat, intending to get to the hotel room early and prepare for Shelby's arrival.

"Did you want to meet up later at the pub for a drink?" Paul asked as he left.

"Damn right. I'm going to fuck someone tonight even if I have to pay for it," Hector chuckled at the thought of his wife smelling the scent of another woman on his clothing.

"I'll be there as soon as I am done with Shelby," Paul winked at his mistress and left the building, the anticipation building.

In the street the party had already started. Cars honked their horns in between the armored sentinel trucks who prowled the night looking for wrongdoers. Random strangers ran up and hugged him, caught up in the carnival atmosphere. In the sky, the dark clouds promised a heavy rain but not even this could dampen the spirits of the revelers. One woman threw herself at him, her eyes were dilated from obvious drug use.

"Are you coming?" said the beautiful brunette between sticking her tongue down his throat.

"Coming where?" Paul asked, reaching into her blouse and squeezing her breasts.

"There is a party in the square. Please say you'll come, I am so horny I want to dance for a while and then fuck all night long." She nibbled his ear and pushed his hand into her knickers, feeling the moist warmth within.

Paul was conflicted between meeting Shelby and trying out his new companion, but he had an hour until she was due to meet him at the hotel.

"I am supposed to be meeting someone," he muttered between more kisses.

"Bring him too."

"It's a her," Paul explained.

A mischievous smile spread on her lips, "Well that could make for an interesting night. Is she pretty?"

"Very."

"Would she be game for making love to me too?"

"I guess we will find out soon enough," Paul laughed and they linked arms.

Thunder rumbled in the distance and the first flashes of lightning jumped between the clouds.

"We are going to get wet," he said as they made their way towards the screams and shouts of the gathered partygoers.

"I'm already wet," she answered, biting the corner of her lip.

"I don't even know your name," Paul said.

"That makes it more fun," she giggled.

From a side street a young man stumbled out, clearly heavily under the influence of alcohol from his babblings and the way he swayed. He fell on the pair and started to harangue them, wagging a finger inches from Paul's face and hitting him accidentally several times.

"You don't understand…" he took an exaggerated, drunken pause, "I have seen them in my dreams. They are coming!"

"Fuck off, you moron," the woman snarled and pushed him away.

"But you must listen to me… the Chosen Fathers are evil, they have lied to us all!" he continued and fell forward, catching Paul in the face with his outstretched hand.

"You're dead!" shouted Paul, throwing a punch at the drunkard.

It connected with his nose and for a brief moment he sobered from the blinding pain. The woman took advantage of the shock and kicked him squarely between the legs causing a shrill squawk to escape his lips. He doubled over and fell to the ground clutching his damaged testes, mouth gaping like a fish out of water.

"What shall we do with him?" she asked.

"Kill him!" shouted one of the crowd who had seen the drunken outburst.

"Can I?"

"Well he did commit blasphemy against the Chosen which is punishable by death," Paul pondered.

"Won't the sentinels take me?" the mysterious woman looked worried and aroused at the same time.

"Not if you are with me," Paul declared, showing his security pass.

A chorus of; "do it, kill him, punish the unbeliever", gave her courage and she reached into her purse. Withdrawing a lethal looking flick knife, the razor sharp blade popped out and glinted in the neon lights of the shop displays. She seemed hypnotized by the weapon, staring at it with an unhealthy fascination that gave Paul the willies. Maybe he wouldn't take her back to the hotel after all.

"Miss, you have to believe me," begged the injured man as she knelt by his side.

"But I don't want to," she apologized and smiled.

"Then you are all damned," he whispered in resignation and lay his head down, exposing his neck.

"Damned fine ass you mean," she said, patting her rump.

Without hesitation, she drew the blade deeply across his throat, cutting skin, muscle, and arteries. A gargle of blood coughed from his mouth, covering his upturned face while a jet of crimson coated some of the morbid bystanders who leaned too close. Cheers and laughter roared from the gathered crowd as the feeble struggles ceased. The blood stopped flowing and Paul was sure the death rictus had a smirk turning one corner of the mouth up. It may have just been muscle damage though.

"Look, I have to go now. I'll see you around," Paul made his excuses and tried to merge with the crowd.

"You can't leave me now," smiled the woman, wiping the knife on her skirt. He wasn't sure if it was a plea or a threat.

"If the sentinels show, tell them it was Paul Atkinson who heard the sedition," he said, "I will file a report tomorrow."

The woman looked insane, teeth bared in a hideous smile. The crowd parted and Paul was nearly overcome with relief to put distance between himself and the beautiful murderer. The square was heaving with celebrations, with music blaring and people gyrating. Some were even having sex in the middle of the street, oblivious to all other stimulus. He looked at his watch and there was still plenty of time to have a shower and a couple of drinks before Shelby arrived, he just needed to fight through the crowd.

"Where do you think you are going?" called out the woman. She had cleared the group who still poked and prodded at the dead body, and looked completely normal again.

"Shit!" Paul muttered as she approached.

The street lights flickered and the music died, causing a massive groan of disappointment from the revelers. Rain started to fall and Paul was amazed to feel the warm drops hitting his exposed skin. Certain he must be imagining the temperature, he held out a hand and the rain was most definitely warm.

"What the fuck?" he said in confusion.

The clouds above started to swirl and meld together, like a force was churning them this way and that. No natural wind could cause such vivid undulations on the grey formations. The night seemed to lighten, and it was due to a growing mixture of reds, yellows, and oranges within the overhead vapor. The lightning danced around the moisture with a ferocity that made Paul duck down. This wasn't a thunderstorm.

"What the fuck?" gasped the woman as she reached Paul, echoing his earlier sentiments.

The sky was actually burning. Like a hovering pool of fuel, the clouds started to expel blazing balls of heated liquid. A few of the more drug addled party goers pointed and clapped, thinking it was a firework display in honor of the great victory in battle. Only when it impacted the ground, covering a group and turning them into a shrieking funeral pyre, did people start screaming and running.

"They must be fighting back, I thought we had beaten them?" wailed the murderess.

"I thought so too, I watched on the TV as they executed the leader," he replied, bewildered by the unfolding disaster. Whatever it was, the resistance didn't have access to thermobaric weapons.

"We need to…" she started but a voice silenced her protestations.

"It is time, my children. By your actions, you have given yourselves unto me."

The voice rasped from the sky and beyond all reasoning, from inside people's own minds. It was totally devoid of any humanity, the sound of a billion screams of agony and suffering given voice. Its source was something not of this world, an entity of unfathomable malevolence and hunger. It was so intensely evil that half of the people hearing the uttering vomited where they stood. The tone changed and the wails of the damned were replaced by clotted, gurgling laughter. It was the sound of a corpse long gone into putrescence, cackling from lungs brimming with the liquids of decay

"We are going to have so much fun, my children. I have cruelties to show you, such beautiful suffering to inflict, the likes of which you could never imagine. Until now."

Some of the crowd had started to claw at their own ears, ripping at the flesh to silence the malignance that was infecting their minds. The voice changed once more, now more akin to a serpent hissing as it prepared to strike.

"Your world is mine. Rise now, thralls of darkness. Teach my children the meaning of eternal torment."

Paul was frozen in terror and could only watch as the ground bulged impossibly in the middle of the square, throwing people from the rising mound as the earth cracked. Bursting forth was a creature unlike anything he could ever have created in his darkest nightmares. Six legged and the size of a large bus, with the body of a reptile, and a tail thick and heavily inlaid with razor sharp fins. Where the head should have been, was a mass of writhing tentacles and a toothless, sucking opening which could only be its mouth. Those closest were grabbed without mercy and fed into the greedy maw, their screams silenced by the crushing orifice. The tail thrashed around with the pleasure of feeding, rending bodies into pieces that still writhed on the ground in piles of their own innards and gore.

"We have to run!" shrieked the woman, dragging him backwards into a side alley.

"What is that thing?" Paul squealed louder and more feminine than even the woman could manage.

"I have no fucking idea, but we need to get away from it."

They hurried down the narrow path with one other man who had also managed to flee the unfolding horror. Ahead were several deep puddles of the collected rainwater, but Paul and his companion slowed down before reaching them. The stranger hurried on, oblivious of how the pools bubbled and seethed, giving off a poisonous smelling steam. Heedless of the danger as he splashed through, the liquid coated his leg and started to melt through the fabric. He dropped to the ground howling in pain as the corrosive substance caused flesh to peel away, dripping onto the tarmac in hissing blobs. A hand rose from the pool, then an arm, and finally a head which looked around, studying them. It had no eyes as it surveyed the three figures, only dark empty orbs that leaked acid in place of tears.

"Oh my God," gasped Paul, another wrong-phrase which would have surely cost him his liberty and life before this mayhem.

"God? Oh no, my son, they can't help you now. You are mine, for all time," the voice inside his head roared with laughter.

The child creature had impossibly pulled itself out of the inch-deep puddle and scurried on all fours to leap on the stricken man. The wet body soaked him even more and they watched aghast as he was slowly liquefied by the monster. Howls of intense agony bounced from the alley walls until the man's throat melted away into a sticky red puddle. More hands rose from the liquid and Paul hadn't noticed the increasing silence from their rear, so rapt were they on the prone man's plight.

"What the hell?" gasped the woman as shadows stretched without any light providing the cause. The shades thickened into firmer forms, roughly the size of people, but mobile.

"Hell? My daughter, you are about to find out how right you are," spoke the vile voice in her mind.

The wraiths reached out and plucked her from the ground as if they were corporeal. She thrashed in their translucent arms, but in spite of their ability to exert force upon her, the kicks passed through the dark forms as if they were nothing. Unformed faces moved in and started to feed, draining her of blood and vitality. Her body shriveled, aging her to a hundred years old in seconds. Her cheeks sunk and she took on the look of someone horrifically emaciated, finally culminating with her skin turning a leaden grey of death. The shades let her drop and the concrete was unforgiving of her brittle frame, cracking bones. Satiated, they made a noise like a dying exhalation and reformed into the nooks and crannies they had spawned from. Incredibly, the once beautiful woman who now resembled an arthritis riddled crone, reached for him imploringly.

"Get the fuck away from me!" he shrieked and kicked out at her gnarled fingers, breaking several.

Turning to flee back onto the street, he could only whimper as the huge reptilian amalgamation regarded him without eyes. Lightning quick, the tentacles lashed out and lassoed him before a scream could peal forth. Paul held out his hands defensively, but the mouth closed over him, mucus easing his passage down the crushing throat of the beast. His body was broken and, through the unspeakable pain, he couldn't understand why death hadn't claimed him. With a final movement, he was expelled into the pitch black stomach of the creature and splashed down into the gastric juices among other flailing bodies. His flesh started to soften as it was digested, and the acid filled his lungs, eating him from the inside. Gargled, melting moans echoed within the fleshy organ as other victims lamented their fate.

"Why am I not dead?" he screamed within his mind at the unbearable pain.

"You cannot die. You and all your kind are now mine. This is but a taste of the infinite ways you will suffer for my enjoyment. Eternity beckons, my son. Now is the time to despair!" the voice chuckled at their fate.

As Paul's eyeballs melted away, he did indeed despair; his suffering was just beginning and a billion deaths awaited.

Malachi woke with a start and a scream caught in his throat from the feeling of suffocation. Yanking at the bedcovers which had become entangled around his upper body, he slumped back down with exhaustion. Sweat ran from his fevered body, coating the bedspread. Why did the dreams always seem so vivid, so real that he could actually taste the sour flavor of vomit? It was then he realized the lumpy, sticky moisture on the bed wasn't all perspiration.

CHAPTER TWO

Malachi bowed his head, letting the water course over his scalp. The liquid was hot enough to sting, but it couldn't sear the haunting images from his mind. His legs still felt like jelly and that thought alone was enough to remind him of the melting victim on the dream street. Dry heaving in the small cubicle, only a little bile was brought up, with the rest of his stomach's contents being scoured clean by the washing machine which rattled in the kitchen area next door. Raising his head and opening his mouth, he let the scalding fluid flush some of the taste away.

"What the fuck is wrong with me?" he asked, slapping himself in the head to try and dislodge whatever misconnected neural pathway was causing the horrific visions.

Dreams were a normal part of the human psyche, an opportunity for the mind to catalogue and make sense of the day's happenings. Nightmares were the yin to common dreams yang, an interconnection of darkness and light which was essential. The slumbering terror gave release to subconscious fears and a chance to overcome them in safety. Malachi's fantasies were now manifesting in the physical world, an escalation that brought back long forgotten fears.

The darkness of his shuttered eyes triggered more memories of the corrosive bowels of the creature and he shuddered violently. Opening them to the morning light, the water swirled into the drain plug at his feet, carrying away the liquid just as surely as his sanity was being eroded by the awful imagination running rampant in his mind.

"Get a hold of yourself," he said, picking up the shower gel.

Washing thoroughly, the sudsy sponge followed the mounds of his taut body. The finely sculpted pectoral muscles flexed with each rotation and his firm stomach received extra attention. Pride was a balm to his frayed nerves and even though his mind seemed to be broken beyond repair, at least his physique was in peak condition.

Turning off the shower, the drain coughed and gurgled in protest, spitting a vile black sludge into the tray which needed to be wiped clean. It was just another issue with the tiny, dilapidated flat he called home.

"Mmm, delicious," Malachi grimaced as he held the blackened tissue at arm's length before tossing it into the toilet bowl and flushing.

Toweling dry, rubbing the skin with enough force to sting, some of the tension had evaporated along with the water. The mirror was blanketed with condensation as a result of the broken extractor fan, and he wiped it with his hand, the cold surface sending a chill up his arm after the heat of the shower. The face that returned his stare was in its early twenties and vaguely distorted by the rivulets of water that ran down the glass. His skin was smooth and bronzed from the time spent at the beach. Only the eyes betrayed the tortured soul within; red rimmed from torn capillaries in the orb itself, a sign of the mental pressure he felt during the visions. Those eyes had witnessed things no sane mind should see and it was fast approaching when the horror would prove too much to bear.

"Why me?" Malachi's voice broke and tears flowed unashamedly.

In the bedroom the alarm started to chime from his phone, a pointless exercise as the dreams tore him from sleep with increasing frequency. It was a welcome distraction from the self-pity, and with a final deep, shaky breath, he left the tiny bathroom and the disturbing visage in the mirror.

The flat wasn't even large enough to call a flat, more a bedsit. Comprising the bathroom, a small hallway and the bedroom which also doubled as the kitchen and lounge. Roughly two hundred square feet of cramped, mold creeping squalor. But it was home. The patterned wallpaper had started to curl away from the dampest parts of the room, and no amount of adhesive seemed to keep it in place. Malachi would paste the edge and, like clockwork, two days later he would wake and the paper would be sagging once more. He had always been taught to make the best of things and, despite the run down feel of the property, it was his sanctuary. Freshly changed linen adorned the paltry single bed, crisp and neatly turned down; until the next dream anyway. The meagre furniture would have been worthy of pity had it not been kept scrupulously clean. The armchair was accompanied by a small coffee table, coasters laid at perfect angles to the edges. On the TV screen a mix of the latest trance music played, crowds of revelers swaying to the melody and strobing lights.

"Shit!" cursed Malachi.

The celebrations were not unlike the nightmare and with a sigh of disappointment he silenced the tune with a press of a button. Music had a way of alleviating his distress, the bass and treble mingling into a structure that his own existence lacked. Praying the association between the loathsome events in his mind and the solace to be found in a vinyl melody would dissipate with the coming hours, he got dressed. The uniform had a faint scent of lavender from the fabric softener and as the t-shirt enveloped his head, he took several deep breaths. After the acrid smell of bile and partly digested food, the fragrance was heaven sent and lifted his spirits.

Looking at the toaster, the mere thought of food was enough to send his gut into spasms of protest so he ignored it and picked up his toothbrush instead. The minty foam and bristles dislodged the final remnants of the vomit that gargling in the shower could not. Finishing with mouthwash, the blue liquid set his tongue ablaze with alcohol and mixed chemicals. With a final swirl he spat it into the sink and rinsed the bowl with fresh water. The familiar belch came through from the bathroom drain and Malachi closed his eyes with growing frustration.

"You know you have to wait," he admonished himself.

Cleaning his teeth always caused the pipe to overflow, but in his distracted state he had forgotten. After cleaning it again, coupled with a pointless threat to the inanimate waste pipe for the constant aggravation, Malachi picked up his car keys. Pausing by the front door he glanced to the left and the picture of his parents that was hung there. A professionally shot image with a much younger Malachi dressed in his finest suit, seated at their feet. The beaming smiles spoke of a love so pure it could have eclipsed the sun. The term soul mate was often coined by people, but he had never seen a devotion as total as that shared by his folks.

"Love you, Mum. Love you, Dad," he said and planted a kiss on each mouth through the glass with his fingertips.

As his front door swung closed in his wake, the opposite entrance opened and Miss Cortez jumped in fright. She was as friendly as she was old, with a shock of white hair that no longer followed the guidance of her hairbrush.

"I'm sorry, Miss C, are you ok?" Malachi said, reaching out to steady the older woman.

"Yes, I'm fine. It's my own silly fault, I wasn't paying attention," she chuckled in reply, holding a hand to her chest.

"Do you want me to take that down for you?" Malachi enquired, seeing the heavy bag of rubbish clasped in her other hand.

"Would you mind? That would save these old knees from aching for the next few hours." She smiled with relief.

"Not at all. I will speak to the supervisor later and find out when the lift will be fixed, until then, you just shout if I can get you anything from the shops, ok?"

"You're an angel, Mal. If I was sixty years younger I would make an honest man out of you," she said and handed the bag over.

"I would have been honored," he laughed and started to walk away.

"When are you going to bring a beautiful young woman home for me to meet anyway?" she persisted, following him down the poorly lit hallway.

"You mean to see if she is good enough for me?" he chuckled.

"That too," she admitted, "I just hate the thought of you being alone night after night, suffering like you do."

"What do you mean?" Malachi paused and slowly turned, cheeks flushing red.

"I'm sorry. I didn't mean to be nosy, the walls are so thin here." She hurried over as fast as her twisted legs would allow to hold his face, stroking the shame from his skin.

"You've heard me?" he lowered his eyes with embarrassment. The genuine concern painted on her lined face was nearly enough to drive him to tears.

"I hear the night terrors you go through. The screams carry across the building," she explained.

"Oh God." He dropped the bag and rubbed at his temple as the first twinges of a stress migraine blossomed within his skull. The truth of why some of the other tenants regarded him with such disdain and mistrust was revealed.

"No, don't you fret," she continued, lifting his face, "I have set them straight. A couple of them asked me how I put up with it, so I gave them a piece of my mind!"

Malachi laughed at the image of the kindly old lady reading the riot act to their neighbors.

"Thanks for fighting my corner, Miss C." He caressed the gnarled hand at his cheek.

"Nonsense. You are like a grandson to me." She smiled, "Most people treat me as if I am invisible, but you always have a kind word or a helping hand when I need it."

"It's no trouble, honestly." Malachi felt awkward at the praise.

"You're a good boy, I want the best for you. You deserve some happiness after all you have been through."

"I really have to be going now," he politely dismissed himself. "Would you like me to bring you some fish and chips home for supper? We can eat together."

Sensing he was withdrawing she didn't push her concern, "That would be lovely, provided you don't mind spending time with a boring old woman."

"You are the most interesting person I know," he called back, "I will be home around seven so get the candles lit."

"It's a date," she replied with a smile, before hobbling home. It was clear the stairs would have been impossible in her debilitated condition and the knowledge that she would soon need a care home filled her with melancholy. Who would look out for Malachi then? Poor boy.

CHAPTER THREE

The car turned over with a cough of protest and more than a little black smoke from the rattling exhaust pipe. Instead of a gentle purr, the engine was more akin to the noise of an old man. Wheezing and groaning against any attempts at movement, the vehicle was not long for this world and would soon join all the others who had gone before in the great scrapyard in the sky. Repair costs were out of the question and with a looming rent bill, Malachi would be forced back onto the buses or cycling to reach work.

Gearbox crunching, he backed out of the parking space and merged into the passing traffic. A tune about drug use in Ibiza came on the radio and Malachi found himself singing along, tapping cheerfully on the steering wheel. Laughing at the absurdity of the only part of the car that actually worked properly was the stereo, his mood improved mile by mile.

A valiant battle was being fought between the morning sun and the stubborn cloud cover. Breaking through in places the beautiful rays looked like spotlights from heaven, perhaps illuminating people that bore God's graces on this day. It was unusual for Malachi to apportion religious significance to anything, especially the weather. He wasn't an atheist by any stretch, but neither was he prone to flights of fancy. If there was an omnipotent being sat on a pearly white throne waiting for him on judgement day, logic would be the backbone of his argument to achieve entry to the promised lands. Would a benevolent God allow the suffering of His subjects? Would He allow Malachi to descend the rabbit hole to insanity, or worse?

"We are going to have words when I get up there!" he growled, looking at the roof of the car and imagining God trembling at the coming confrontation.

Faces passed in a blur, going about their own lives and errands. At the final set of traffic lights before the turning for his gym, a woman was watching him intently from the neighboring car. Upon seeing the scrutiny, Malachi smiled and nodded a greeting. Instead of responding in kind she just scowled, looked away and wound the window up as if she feared he would attack her in broad daylight. Charming! He thought to himself until he looked in the rearview mirror and saw the reflection. Eyes still reddened, with dark bags settling beneath. Coupled with a wide grin it wasn't hard to imagine himself as a crazy person.

Giving it too much gas, the woman performed a screeching wheel spin before disappearing into the distance. Shaking his head in bewilderment, Malachi moved away and the parking lot of Jim's Gym was empty at this early hour. No one would be arriving for at least forty-five minutes and this provided an opportunity to have a quiet workout session before the rush of retirees, unemployed, and night workers who could exercise during the day. The blue lettered sign was accompanied by the customary flexing barbell of Olympic powerlifting notoriety. Unlike some poseur gyms, Jim's prided itself on catering to all markets without alienating certain demographics. The free weights were tucked to the rear for the 'grunt 'n groaners' who loved to watch their muscles flex. Bikes and rowing machines were also laid out against the side walls for warmup and cooldowns. In the main gym, mirrors were banned to spare people the sight of a red, sweaty, gasping image of themselves as they improved their fitness. The shaming culture of some establishments was forbidden by Jim, who had also lost over two hundred pounds before starting up his business. The upper floor was soundproofed and wide open for some of the classes that took place throughout the week; from kickboxing to Zumba dance.

Opening the main doors and disabling the impending alarm, Malachi stepped inside and turned on the lights from the large bank of switches behind the main reception desk. Normally comforted by the familiar surroundings, today the empty gym only reinforced the sense of loneliness he felt. The cavernous building with its rows of silent equipment seemed to mock him, highlighting how little he actually had in life. Close friends he could count on one hand with spare fingers left over, and financially his bank account was in the red more often than his eyeballs.

Finger hovering by the power button on the music system, Malachi opted to work out in silence. It would give him an opportunity to think on the future, about his next steps in combating the growing psychological damage that was destroying him as sure as drugs ravage an addict. Stepping onto the treadmill and placing his towel on the control console, he started out with a brisk walk. The slow rhythm of footfalls echoed back to him over the low hum of the expensive machine. The wall in front of the equipment was adorned with motivational posters that Jim had thought up after his own success. Frowning faces peered out, unhappiness evident at their physical condition. Side by side was their miraculous transformation which Malachi was heavily involved in. The support he provided wasn't limited to exercise regimes, but delved into personal issues and habits which could be the cause of the overeating. Nutritional plans were also provided for a small fixed fee to help the lifestyle adjustments. It was so rewarding to see the gradual change in both body and mind of his patrons, but this was quickly replaced by dark thoughts of his own situation.

Increasing the speed to compensate for his growing anger, the rotating belt turned into a blur beneath his feet. Leg muscles bunched and flexed with each stride and the lactic acid started to spread through the limb, burning ferociously. His lungs flared with ragged gasps and despite his own fitness, he was starting to struggle. The machine was at its limit and the motor whined as it tried to keep up with Malachi's sprinting form. Vision blurring and no longer able to keep up the pace, he pressed the emergency stop button and brought it to a standstill. Clutching his sides, the heat had spread to his lungs as he drew deep breaths in an attempt to alleviate the agonizing stitch.

"What the hell were you running from?" Kevin's voice came from the entrance and Malachi was too tired to even jump in surprise.

"Life," he gasped, "How long have you been standing there?"

"Long enough, buddy," Kevin admitted. "Shall I put the kettle on?"

Malachi nodded, wiped his brow and started the machine up again to cool down. Walking off the growing cramp and controlling his breathing, he thought about his closest friend. Kevin Boyns had been there for him all through school as a friend and confidante, never judging his strange habits and the fact Malachi often preferred solitude to larger groups.

"Want to talk about it?" Kevin offered as he handed the steaming mug of tea over.

"Maybe later, I need to get my head straight."

"I'm worried about you, dude," Kevin admitted, concern evident in his voice.

"Me too," admitted Malachi quietly.

"So talk to me. You know they say a problem shared is a problem halved," he pushed.

"Not this one, mate," Malachi replied.

"I hate seeing you like this. It's as if you are drifting away from us, becoming more isolated week by week. Have you been sleeping?"

"Not as much as I would like," he admitted.

"I thought so, your eyes look like you are on all sorts of drugs," Kevin said, partly serious and questioning.

"No, it's not drugs, don't worry."

"Then what?" Kevin asked with real pain in his voice.

Malachi put a reassuring hand on his shoulder, "Can we go for a beer after work? It will take a little while to explain it all."

"Yeah, of course," he replied with a smile of relief, "I will tell the missus I will be a bit late, she won't mind."

Malachi imitated the sound of a cracking whip and they both laughed, before Malachi enquired, "How is Laura anyway?"

"Oh you know women, always bitching and moaning. Telling me who I can see and can't see, what to wear, that I've gained a few pounds and need to lose weight. I said to her yesterday, *bitch, if you don't get off my back, I'm going to have to use my pimp hand on you!"* he answered, raising the back of his hand threateningly.

"Brave man. Did you really say that?" Malachi laughed.

"Fuck no!" Kevin chuckled, "She would wait until I fell asleep and then cut parts of me off that I would rather stay attached."

Malachi was jealous of their loving relationship; it was uncannily similar to that of his own parents. Lots of joking and laughing with, and at, each other. "She wouldn't ever try and control you anyway, she is an angel."

"She's a treasure," he agreed. "I fell on my feet when I found her."

"She's one in a million that's for sure."

An impatient banging came from the front door.

"Mr. Darlington," Mal and Kevin said in unison, shaking their heads.

The old man was hammering on the glass and attempting entry by pushing with all his might. A wagging finger of annoyance was thrust their way when they approached. Unlocking the front door, the older gentleman nearly fell on top of the pair.

"Listen, old timer," Malachi growled, grabbing him by the t-shirt, "If you don't get your watch fixed and stop disturbing us at ten to nine in the morning, I'm going to take you out to the car park and beat the shit out of you!"

"It's your fucking clocks that are slow!" he protested.

Kevin had taken the opportunity to phone the talking clock and the computer generated female voice chirped, "The time is now eight fifty-one and thirty-seven seconds."

The wrinkled face looked at the handset, then at the two young men. "She's wrong too."

Malachi burst out laughing and let the old man go, only to be clutched in a bear hug and lifted clean off the floor. It was a routine that played out every morning and each of them found some joy in it. Mr. Darlington knew that he was early but the bus always dropped him off at eight forty-eight and he didn't want to wait around outside. Mal and Kevin didn't mind the old gent using the facilities out of hours and they were always offered a crisp ten pound note at the end of each session. Honor meant they refused the kind offer, but every day the money would be pushed at them nonetheless.

"Did you want to step outside for a few rounds?" Mr. Darlington asked, raising his fists and throwing a couple of crisp jabs.

"Heavens no, you would take both our heads off," Kevin laughed, patting him on the back.

"Nah, you are both younger and more sprightly than this crooked old bastard," the old man chuckled.

"You're as old as the woman you feel!" called out Malachi.

"I need to pull myself a twenty-year-old lap dancer then don't I?" he replied with a roar of laughter, "I will be in with the free weights."

"Call if you want a spotter, we don't want you breaking a hip, old timer," Kevin added.

"Cheeky bastard," grinned Mr. D as the door closed.

On the CCTV screen that covered every inch of the building, they watched as the man started his warm up. Five minutes of shadow boxing before moving onto the bench press and various other items of equipment.

"Look at him go," Kevin nodded in approval.

He was over seventy, but the way his feet moved would have bettered a man half his age. The stringy muscles were covered with faded navy tattoos. The obligatory anchors and magpies on the hands told a story of bravery and service for ones' country. Their respect for the gnarled septuagenarian had grown into a deep fondness and when one of the other patrons had threatened Mr. D, they had raced to intercede before he could get hurt. It hadn't been necessary.

"Do you remember the time he knocked that wanker out?" Kevin laughed, reading Mal's mind.

"It was the funniest thing I've ever seen."

The young man, whose name they couldn't remember anymore, had tried to bully Mr. D aside from the bench. Being a gentleman, he had replied that as soon as the set of reps were finished it would be free. A born bully with slabs of steroid aided muscle, this hadn't been good enough, and he had thrown the old man from the machine and onto the, thankfully, soft matting. Unperturbed by the assault, he had calmly stood up and whirled the damp exercise towel, before expertly lashing it out with a crack. The tip of the fabric contacted the taut bottom of the thug and brought an agonizing sting of pain. As the weights room exploded with laughter and derision, the bully roared and tried to seize the man who had humiliated him, desperate to use his strength to rip him to pieces. The first mistake had been to assume that his bulk assured victory, the second had been to try and carry out his violence on a retired naval champion boxer. A lightning quick left hook followed by a right hook had stretched him out.

"Can you believe how we found him?" Kevin was crying with laughter at the memory.

"I don't think he had been trained in contortionism," Mal agreed, wiping his own tears away.

The punches had launched the hulk backwards and, as they burst in the room to help, he was already laid over the weight bench, twisted awkwardly and snoring.

"Still got it," Mr. D had beamed as the rest of the patrons congratulated him.

"Huh? Wha?" the thug had whimpered as he came to, eyes glazed from the knockout. His jaw sagged to the left, indicating a fracture, and the deep purple of bruising was already swelling.

"Hold still, you've had an accident," Kevin said, helping him move from his painful location.

"You're not wrong," chuckled Mr. D pointing at the dark wet patch on his light grey tracksuit trousers.

Tears of shame had flowed at the incontinence, followed by a ride in an ambulance. The man had cancelled his membership of the gym soon after. Mal had only seen him once on the street since, wearing a full head brace to hold the jaw in position as it healed. Rumor had it that following the humiliation of being sparked out by a pensioner, he had needed to attend a gym many miles outside of the city.

CHAPTER FOUR

The hours passed slowly and Malachi was glad for the constant interruptions from his macabre thoughts. Even the fainting of a gym goer who had overexerted herself had been a welcome distraction. The beams of light moved inexorably across the carpet of the reception, like a huge sundial counting down the moment where he would have to bare his soul to Kevin. Apprehension grew and on more than one occasion Malachi was going to call the drink off to spare his shame. The looks of support and hope that Kevin shot his way through the day were the only thing that held it in abeyance.

"How has the day been?" asked Jim merrily as he arrived.

"Apart from one faint, business as usual. I've counted the cash and left the chit in the office for you to check," Kevin replied.

"A faint?" Jim frowned, "How did that happen?"

"I set her normal routine but after two miles she came over all weak and passed out for a couple of seconds," Malachi explained.

"What went wrong? I don't want people thinking this place is unsafe." Jim had lost the smile and was all business.

"She admitted to drinking last night and had missed breakfast. It was just a case of running on empty," Kevin said.

"Did you fill out an accident form?"

"Of course, boss," Mal answered.

"And she was happy to sign it?" Jim pressed.

"Yeah, she was more embarrassed than hurt. I saw her eyes roll and caught her before she could do serious damage," Mal said.

"Her knight in shining red uniform," Jim chuckled, smile returning. "Ok, good work, boys. Did you manage to stop Mr. Darlington opening a can of whoop ass on any more customers?"

"He was chatting up a couple of the ladies from the local knitting club but no punches were thrown," Malachi replied laughing.

Jim studied the day's income and his smile grew.

"You've really been pushing the protein drinks, that's nearly two hundred pounds more than normal take."

"They don't taste like powdered shit anymore since we switched brand. With the new flavors, they sell themselves." Kevin shrugged.

"Don't be modest, they still don't taste that good," Jim added, taking out two twenty pound notes from the spring loaded compartment and offering them over the desk.

"You don't need to do that," Malachi took a step back.

"Look, I know you both don't like taking money. Mr. Darlington has told me about your moral code, but this is well deserved. I can't pay you as much in wages as I would like because the gym doesn't make a fortune, so this is just a little thank you." Jim wouldn't take no for an answer.

"Thanks, Jim," Malachi nodded in gratitude.

"Now get your asses out of here!" he barked, "You know I don't pay overtime!"

With a final thank you, the two young men gathered their belongings and left Jim to cater to the night customers. The sun had settled to the west as it continued its rotation, and the cloudless sky was awash with stunning blues and darkening magentas of twilight. The small scenes of beauty were a salve to the growing trepidation and Malachi hesitated long enough for Kevin to notice.

"Are you going to admire the scenery all night or are we going to get a drink?"

With a sigh of resignation, Malachi looked at his friend and begun walking towards the local bar. Not a word was spoken on the short walk, but their friendship had grown to a point where the silence wasn't awkward. Kevin knew the mental weight crushing his best friend would come out in time, like a boil filled with pus being lanced. The pressure had just grown too much to bear and he hoped to be the doctor who could aid in the healing process.

"What am I getting you boys tonight?" asked the bar owner in a heavy Jamaican accent.

Desmond DeCosta was the epitome of Jamaican heritage. A huge, welcoming grin showed rows of uneven teeth, and the thick dreadlocks hung most of the way down his broad back. His family had moved from the Caribbean when he was a teenager to take advantage of all that Britain had to offer. Fiercely patriotic to both his new home and the old country, their cultural pride had led to the opening of the 'Paradise Bar'. Desmond's parents had invested half of the capital, but kept away from the day to day running so they could enjoy a peaceful retirement.

"I'll just have a pineapple juice, Des. I still have to drive home," Malachi replied and sat down at the bar.

"Fuck that, man, you look like death. I'll make you a real drink, a Jamaican Zombie will do you the world of good." Desmond clapped his hands.

"Thanks, Des, but I have no other way of getting home. The buses stop running in two hours and I think we are going to be here a while longer than that," Malachi tried to dissuade him from the already half created cocktail.

"You leave that to me, I will call my cousin and he will take care of you," he said, adding the shots of rum. Desmond's cousin was even bigger, with longer dreadlocks all kept in place by a huge Rasta hat. He was a local celebrity for the big yellow and black taxi he drove with Bob Marley playing loudly on repeat.

"I can't afford it, mate," Malachi admitted with embarrassment.

"Shit, brudda, did I say anything about paying him?" Desmond looked hurt as he topped the gorgeous looking drink with a slice of orange and a cherry.

"I don't like taking charity," he replied quietly, knowing he meant well.

"I don't like giving it!" Desmond declared, putting the drink down on the coaster, "I call it investing in one of my best customers."

"I still have to get to work in the morning..." Malachi was still putting up a fight.

Pulling a face that said, *well damn I had never thought of that,* Desmond said, "I will come get you, I have a business proposition to make you anyway."

Handing over the extra twenty he had been given, Desmond dismissed it with a quick wave of the hand and moved off to another customer.

"The man doesn't like being told no," Malachi smiled as he put the money away.

"He's worried about you too," Kevin admitted.

"Let's take a booth, I want to have some privacy."

They seated themselves on the creaking red leather and faced each other. Still unwilling to unload his feelings, Malachi looked around at the brightly colored bar. Half a dozen Jamaican flags of varying sizes were mounted on the walls as well as the Union Jack flag of the United Kingdom. Barely anything within the establishment wasn't some shade of red, green, yellow or black. A lot of the locals had argued against the garish changes from the original Irish pub, but customers had flocked to drink here. The long bar was topped with a totally unnecessary grass roof and exotic plants stood in pots at regular intervals to bring a sense of nature. Murals on the walls were a mix of proud animals and icons from Jamaican history, with quotes about confidence and roots from Marcus Garvey; a prominent civil rights activist.

"This is really good," Malachi sighed in appreciation as the drink traced a warm glow down his throat from the rum.

"I know," Kevin replied bluntly, eager for the real conversation to begin.

"You aren't going to let this go are you?" Malachi slumped in the chair, his heart racing with anxiety.

Kevin only shook his head slowly, "It's for your own good."

"Fuck," Malachi spat, "Where do I begin?"

"At the beginning?" Kevin offered logically.

Stomach churning with apprehension, Malachi admitted defeat and began, "The first time it happened was when I was about twelve years old."

CHAPTER FIVE

"The orphanage I was moved into wasn't all that bad, certainly not what I had been expecting. The care givers were all motivated by love of the waifs and strays which came through their doors," Malachi said.

"I remember visiting you. It could have been worse," Kevin replied, then looked horrified. "Shit, I didn't mean it like that. I mean as a place to be put it was…"

Malachi smiled, "I know what you were getting at and you are right. There were far worse places I could have wound up. Anyway, the home was well funded which ensured we all had a clean bed and slept two to a room instead of being more crowded."

"So what happened?"

"I will never forget. It was early February and the day had gone from bad to worse," he started the story.

Malachi walked in and Pam, the senior caretaker rushed over to give him a hug. The orphanage had a no touch rule except in the case of restraining a violent child, but this occasion was different. Sporting a black eye and a split lip that had only recently stopped bleeding, his uniform was stained with droplets of claret.

"Are you ok?" Pam flustered around him and gathered some ice in a cloth to hold to the swollen eye.

"I'm sorry, Miss. I had a bad day and during lesson the teacher was talking about parent's evening," he said slowly, reluctant to use his painful lip more than necessary.

"Oh, honey," Pam cooed.

"I nearly made it out of the room before I started crying, but Jeff Lancaster had seen me and started laughing. I was in the toilet for a while trying to stop myself from being such a baby," Malachi said, voice wavering.

"It's not being a baby to miss the ones we love," she said, looking him in the eyes. *"The principal said that you got into a fight with the boy. How did it happen?"*

"He came in with a couple of friends during break and heard me in the cubicle. I tried to stay quiet but he knew I was in there because he looked over the top of the door," he answered, mind returning to the afternoon.

The flimsy door was weak from years of use and one good kick threw it inwards toward Malachi as he wiped away the tears. All three boys were laughing and pointing at the pitiful figure cowering inside.

"No wonder your parents killed themselves with a faggot of a son like you," Jeff taunted and the two accomplices slapped him on the back.

"They didn't kill themselves, just leave me alone!" Malachi shouted and tried to close the door.

Jeff stepped inside and blocked him, "Why don't you make me? Faggot!" He jabbed a finger into his chest.

"That hurt, get lost!" Malachi pushed the assaulting finger away.

"I don't listen to pussy faggots. What do you think we should do with him?" Jeff carried on pointing and looked over his shoulder for support.

"Make him lick the toilet," said one.

"Bog wash him," replied the other.

"Those sound like fine ideas," Jeff laughed.

The toilet was much the same as any in a high school, where the patrons were less concerned about hygiene than they should have been. Splashes of urine coated the floor and, inexplicably, so too did dried feces. Young boys could be disgusting creatures.

"Just leave me alone!"

"Just leave me alone, just leave me alone," mocked the boys as Jeff stepped forward.

Grabbing Malachi by the head and trying to hook a foot around behind his legs to topple him, he was astonished when his victim bared his teeth and snarled. Stamping down on the outstretched leg something tore in the limb, perhaps a tendon or ligament, and Jeff shrieked in pain. The fun was over and the two bullies looked unsure of themselves as the scrawny kid glared at them while forcing Jeff to the filthy floor.

"You like that then?" shouted Malachi into his ear, "How does it taste?"

"Mmmph, hrrmph," Jeff bawled as his lips were crushed against the crusted porcelain.

"Get off him!" cried one of the accomplices, stepping forward to swing a punch.

The angle was off and in the confines of the stall it caught Malachi a glancing blow in the eye. It had no effect and he didn't let go, the adrenaline and hatred were all consuming. The release of pent up grief was long overdue; like a pressure cooker it was bound to blow at some point. Unfortunately for the trio of bullies, they chose the wrong time to act tough and were now caught up in the explosion. With one final yell, he slammed Jeff's face into the bowl and chips of tooth flew from the bloodied mouth.

"What did you do that for?" squealed the third as he backed towards the door, hands raised in surrender.

"Obviously because I'm a pussy faggot whose parents killed themselves," Malachi laughed and it contained an unhealthy tone.

"You're fucking crazy!" yelled the bully, seeing his friend disappear through the exit.

More out of fear than spite, he threw another punch and Malachi's lip split open like an overfilled leech, blood streaming. A glare of pure malice contorted his face and the bully fell to the ground, begging for mercy.

"Get up!"

"Don't hurt me, I'm sorry. We were only doing it for a laugh," he sobbed as he was lifted to his feet by the shirt collar.

"If you ever look at me again. If you ever talk to me again. If I ever hear you have mentioned my name in conversation, I will wait until you are alone and I will do worse to you than I have done to him," Malachi said only an inch from the boy's face. Blood was running down his chin and coating both their shirts but terror had paralyzed his enemy.

"I won't," he gasped with terrified saucer eyes.

"You need to pick his teeth up," he finished and threw him into the cubicle on top of the wailing form of Jeff.

Walking from the restroom, the unshed tears of childhood innocence lost flowed and the sure knowledge that he was completely alone in the universe left his soul barren. Malachi was totally oblivious of the shouting teachers as they came to investigate the reports of an insane child killing another pupil. Opening the double doors of the fire exit, he sat down on the low wall outside and wept for the years of loneliness that awaited him.

"Yeah I remember that!" exclaimed Kevin. "You weren't in for a couple of days afterwards and we had an assembly about bullying and violence. The whole school knew your name."

"I wish they hadn't," Malachi admitted, "I never wanted to hurt anybody." The shame still burned brightly even to this day.

"Nobody ever messed with you again though, so it wasn't all bad. The rest of high school was a breeze."

"People did leave me alone," he conceded.

"So you had a fight, but I don't see what that has to do with your brooding and withdrawing from the world?"

"I said the day was bad, the night was so much worse."

Sat around the sprawling dinner table that was more suited to a medieval banquet hall, the other children had finished their dessert and moved off to play games on the computer. Malachi had offered to wash and dry the dishes, partly in self-atonement for the injuries he had inflicted, and partly because he enjoyed the feeling of making things tidy. It was a habit he had picked up from his parents; 'A clean home is a happy home'.

"You're being awfully quiet, Mal, are you worried about getting into trouble?" Pam asked, helping him with the chore.

"A little, Miss." He shrugged.

"Well don't worry about it. The principal has heard the story from the two other boys about how three of them attacked you and you only defended yourself. He has also taken into consideration your… troubled personal issues," she said, trying to be diplomatic.

"You mean my parents dying," he replied.

"Yes, honey," she said sadly.

"I don't want special treatment, that will just make things worse. Most of the kids probably hate me now anyway," Malachi said with worry. The fearful glances some of his housemates had shot him over dinner was eating at him.

Pam came close and lowered her tone conspiratorially, "Word is those boys have been causing a real nuisance for other children in the school for months. The principal said off the record he was glad to see them get their comeuppance. Rumor is you are being compared to a mixture between the Incredible Hulk and Mohammad Ali."

"But I didn't punch anyone," Malachi giggled at the overblown compliment.

"Well according to the gossip you went crazy and ripped your shirt off before beating all three of them up without mercy," Pam chuckled at the grossly exaggerated story doing the rounds from some of the other children in her care.

"I was the one that got beaten up," Malachi protested, pointing to his bruised face yet still smiling.

"I know, sweetie. How is it feeling?" Pam asked with genuine concern.

"It feels like my face is really tight?" he questioned, unable to express the strange feeling.

"That's the bruising, it will go down in a couple of days. Do you want some more medicine?"

"Nah, that's ok. Please, may I be excused to go and watch a bit of television?"

"Of course. Thank you for the help, Mal."

"No worries, Miss," he said and hurried off.

Pam smiled as he retreated. Her own boys were older and long flown the coop and it was a real shame her husband had refused to allow her to adopt. It was probably for the best, she was such a soft touch her home would look like something out of Lord of the Flies. Watching him leave the kitchen she still felt the old mothering instinct kick in, the need to protect the thin and gangly boy who she was so fond of.

The television couldn't hold his concentration, so halfway through his allotted time he passed over the controller to his younger roommate; Jack.

"Really? Wow, thanks, Malachi," he beamed as he changed the channel to his favorite cop chase show.

"You're welcome. Night, mate," Malachi gave a thumbs up and excused himself as the sound of sirens and shrieking rubber filled the room.

Closing the bedroom door quietly behind himself, Malachi quickly changed before brushing his teeth and using the toilet. The ensuite bathroom was another happy bonus of the generous funding and afforded the young men in the home some privacy. The bed was comfortable as he lay down and settled his aching head. The sporadic tick of contracting metal from the cooling radiator sounded like skeletal fingers tapping in the room and this triggered morbid thoughts of his beloved parents and their cold grave twenty miles away.

"I miss you both so much," he said to the empty room, hoping to solicit otherworldly contact and felt childish when, unsurprisingly, no answer came.

The pain in his eye was aggravated by the pressure of the goose down feather pillow so he turned over and faced the wall. Tracing his fingers in the patterns of his parent's names, tears came again but with less sobbing. The dwindling power of the emotional outpouring scared Malachi and he thought he was in danger of betraying their memory. Without any grief counselling so far, he was too young to understand the myriad paths in which acceptance of bereavement is reached.

"I'm so sorry, mate," Kevin patted the back of his hand.

"It's ok, you didn't even really know me at the time," Malachi appreciated the sentiment and scowled at Desmond in mock anger as he placed another free drink on their table with a wink.

"I think he is trying to get you to loosen up, you're like a coiled spring," Kevin chuckled as he picked up the glass.

"It isn't necessary; I have started the story so I will finish. I feel a little better already, but I don't think you will after you hear the next part."

"What happened?" Kevin whispered breathlessly, dreading the revelation to come.

The combination of stress and spent grief acted as a sedative and before Jack had returned to bed, Malachi drifted off into the dark recesses of his subconscious.

Pain. Such awful pain. Malachi found himself bound with his head bowed to the floor. The flaring sensation came from the bonds which held his arms and legs firmly in place against the upright post. Flexing the numb fingers and toes as much as the constraints allowed, blood started to flow and some small sensation returned. Opening his eyes, the ground was a mix of sand and small scrubby weeds. The purple leaves were wide stemmed and fluttered in the gentle breeze. It was unlike any plant he had ever seen.

"Ah, they awaken," came a deep cackle in a foreign language that for some unfathomable reason, Malachi could understand.

How long he had been unconscious was a mystery. A spasm in the contours of his spine from the slumped position and the pounding headache from the knockout blow would indicate a couple of hours at least. Looking up, the scene was totally surreal and confusion clouded his thoughts. The sky was totally cloudless and despite the hour being late, the darkness of night hadn't gained ascendency. Two moons lay overhead, one huge and close in orbit, the other more distant but the brighter of the pair. Backlit against the purple hued sky were huge moth type insects, glowing from their bodies like fireflies but the size of eagles. The strobing of their abdomens was a mating call, but how the hell did he know that?

"Focus his mind," came the familiar voice followed by a streak of white hot pain as a blade was drawn across his chest.

The shock of the cut broke the trance and Malachi looked around at the scene in panic.

"That's better," said the voice with satisfaction.

Mountains rose in the distance, mighty monoliths of rock from fractious shifting tectonic plates in the earth. The wailing forms of children were set against the majestic beauty, trussed and laid on a neatly stacked pile of strange timber which could only have one use. The sputtering torches of the villages attackers circled the unlit pyre and for the first time Malachi felt the gut wrenching terror within his heart.

"Thiassel!" Malachi cried in a voice not his own.

"Father!" came the sobbing reply.

"Let us go," someone demanded, "We are a peaceful people."

Glancing left and right, around twenty people were similarly bound to heavy wooden stakes, and all faced the spectacle in the village square. With a blood curdling realization, Malachi realized it was probably to ensure a captive audience for what was coming.

"You are indeed a fine and upstanding people who harbor no animosity toward other tribes," agreed the voice who Malachi still couldn't see, "And that is why you have been chosen."

Tribes? What was all this about wondered Malachi again. His shifting perspective from himself to the father of one of the captured children made his head swim. The poorly lit homes were basically stacked stones with a canvas of branches and leaves for roofs. His own attire was animal pelt and a rough, hessian type fabric that itched something fierce with the compression of the ropes. Their conquerors were clad in burnished jade armor, a metal which glimmered in the reflected firelight. The contradiction in technology was stark, with typical Neolithic features contrasting with the skilled metal working of the aggressors. Curved green swords hung from scabbards at the waist, so the metal was obviously resilient enough to face battle.

"We have never made war with you. Why have your Elders deemed us enemies?" asked a woman, never breaking eye contact with her infant son.

The source of the voice stepped into the meagre light and instead of the plated armor, he was adorned in a splendid cloak of gold trimmed black. His clothes were likewise dark in color and made of a much finer material than the villagers. Atop his head was a crown fashioned from four small, fire scorched skulls, bound together with twine and looking north, south, east and west with jaws gaping in silent screams.

45

"Compassion is your weakness. If you had been warriors, we could have used you. Your only purpose now is to become sacrifices for the empire."

The other captors started to shriek and wail, but firm hands appeared from hidden enemies behind and silenced the protests.

"Kay lowic morgel bar zoln diavol!" he cried into the night, arms held wide.

As one, the light from the gigantic bugs winked out and their wings could be heard carrying them away from the vicinity of the chanting. An oppressive pall fell over the area, as if the pressure was building from some unseen force making it difficult to draw breath.

"Thalon mer serlas pox quaan!"

The last word was drawn out in a sigh and the night darkened, as if the twin moons were losing their power to penetrate the thickening atmosphere. A light appeared at the feet of the man, small at first then growing in size until it was roughly two feet in diameter. The soil fell inward towards the pulsing illumination which alternated between red, yellow, and orange. Like a heatless fire the glow increased in intensity but didn't cause any discomfort to the swaying figure. A black tendril rose into the night from the pit, as thick as a snake it seemed to look around without eyes. An amorphous blob followed and the mass flowed together like sentient liquid.

"We have been answered," smiled the summoner as the vile creation started to climb his legs, small coils sprouting from the mass to gain purchase on the clothing.

When it reached his head the blob took on a shape of a face, humanoid in size but with features of nightmare. Many eyed and fangs of black, the visage studied the man and then smiled in a rictus of horror. The flowing mass melted once more and surged into the open mouth and throat of the willing host.

"What is happening?" someone screamed as the man started to gurgle and vibrate.

Almost as soon as it looked like he would die from the welcomed violation, his eyelids opened and the liquid churned within the sockets. He smiled and within, another, darker mouth smiled too. The other soldiers didn't make any sign of surprise or discomfort, this event was not new to them, nor was the subsequent order.

"Burn them!" croaked the man in a voice that was no longer his own.

Without complaint, the blazing torches were held to the piled brush and children. The fire took hold and climbed through the carefully slatted branches toward the tender flesh of the innocents atop the pyre. As the heat reached the poor infants, their screams of fear turned to shrieks of agony. Skin blistering and charring from the lapping flames, the trussed parents could only strain at their bonds and scream their emotional rending. The noise of the children died away as they perished and only the roar of the cleansing fire could be heard, wood popping and crackling with the heat.

"Your hearts are now ready," said the inhuman voice, "Your hatred sustains me."

He went to the female who was tied next to Malachi, and without any apparent sexual interest, pulled her clothing apart, exposing the pendulous breasts. Ignoring the swaying bosom, the figure started to press against the breastbone and ribs with his fingers, tracing a line from neck to abdomen.

"My Lord," said a soldier, kneeling at his feet in deference and holding out a serrated blade.

Taking the knife, the handle was crafted of polished bone and the bulbous knuckle provided the pommel. Heedless of her spitting and vehement cursing, he drove the knife deeply below the ribcage and started sawing upwards. Blood flowed in torrents as the sound of grinding

47

bone echoed around the village. The poor woman was barely alive by the time he had finished and every other villager observed in abject terror.

"What are you?" Malachi managed to ask the being, who looked sideways and only smiled coldly.

Returning the soaked knife to the waiting soldier, the creature delved in with both hands and displaying a strength not of this world, he pulled the ribcage apart to expose the steaming organs. People were vomiting as viscera started to spill out, but Malachi was mesmerized by the ghastly scene. Reaching inside the cavity with a reverence that was as terrifying as the previous frenzied activity, he clasped the feebly beating heart in hand. With a single yank, the organ was ripped loose in a spray of blood and torn arteries. Opening his jaws impossibly wide, the mouth within a mouth sprung forth and closed over the offering. More crimson soaked down the expensive tunic as the ravening creature withdrew and started to eat.

"Please, no," begged Malachi in a whisper.

The figure had taken the knife again and stepped in front of him. Black eyes stared, and the gaping maw expelled air which smelled of sulfur and decomposition. Fingers kneading the ridges of his chest, Malachi screamed as the knife was driven toward his tender belly.

The sudden light of the bedroom made his eyes hurt and he blinkered them while he tried to regain his composure. The feeling of the knife was still with him and he gingerly felt his flat tummy for injury. The hand came back free of blood and he sighed with relief until he saw who else was in the room. Jack was sat bolt upright and, with one of the young girls on night duty, was trying to press himself back further into the corner of the room. The small eyes were terrified, but so too were the older eyes of the carer.

"Damn, that sounded like one hell of a nightmare," Kevin commiserated.

"It wasn't just that," Malachi whispered, "The night girl quit the very next day and Jack was moved to a different home. I got to move into a single room on my own."

"So? Sounds like a great deal to me," Kevin laughed, but stopped when he saw the haunted look in Malachi's eyes.

"I overheard a few weeks later that when the girl came in the room to check why Jack was calling out, I was talking in that strange language. She said my arms were raised as I was speaking and the light turned itself off. Even worse, they said they felt the same weird feeling of suffocation, as if the air was getting thicker like a soup." Malachi was visibly shaking with recollection of the memory.

"So it carried over from your dream into the real world?" Kevin asked with wide eyes.

"I don't know what the words were, but they had a power I can't describe."

"Holy shit," Kevin whispered, drink poised by his lips but frozen in shock.

"I don't think holy had anything to do with it," Malachi replied with a shudder.

CHAPTER SIX

A burst of drunken laughter interrupted their conversation and they looked around the booth to see three men play fighting around the pool table. Over a dozen empty beer bottles lined the wall around it and they were getting louder in direct correlation to the amount of alcohol consumed.

"Hey!" Desmond called out, "Calm it down or you are out!"

"Sorry," laughed one while the other two just scowled.

"I think we might have to help Des with taking out the trash later," Kevin remarked, staring at one of the trio who was returning the glare.

"Leave it, mate," Malachi said, pulling him back into the booth, "You were supposed to be making me feel better, not get me into a fight."

"My bad," Kevin replied, clenching and unclenching his fist.

"Hey!"

Kevin had started to lean sideways to get a look at the guy again, but smiled and sat back down, "Sorry. Where were we?"

"I scared the shit out of two people," Malachi reminded him.

"Yeah, I remember now. Was there no other explanation for the light, maybe an electrical short circuit?"

"They had an electrician in and he gave it a clean bill of health, every reading was as it should be."

"Hmm," Kevin pondered, "The chanting isn't that special, everyone talks in their sleep."

"That's what they told me the first time," Malachi said cryptically.

"There were more occasions?" Kevin was dumbstruck.

"Hundreds," he admitted.

"Jesus Christ, no wonder you are frazzled. How often do you have these dreams?"

"These days it is pretty much every night."

Kevin slapped the table as he was struck by an epiphany, "That's why you always ignore women and my attempts to set you up with Laura's friends."

"The secret is out." Malachi held his hands up in surrender.

"Have you ever thought that being alone may not be helping? Just having Laura and Joey around can make my worst day so much brighter."

"It's not that simple..." Malachi tried to think of a way of explaining that wouldn't disgust his friend. There wasn't one. "Sometimes I wake up and I have wet myself, or worse. It's like I go through the same bodily reactions as the victims in my dreams."

"Fuck..." was all Kevin could add, shaking his head.

"See? I need to get my mind sorted before I can even consider romance."

The entrance door opened and a redhead walked in a few paces, looking around with confusion.

"What can I get you, sweetheart?" Desmond asked, smiling warmly.

Her face was flawless, with sultry, cupid bow lips and emerald green eyes. There was Irish blood flowing through her veins, Malachi was certain.

"My friend was meant to meet me here I think. This is the Paradise Bar, isn't it?" she inquired.

"The one and only," Desmond held his arms wide, "Let me get you a drink and you can wait for her to arrive."

"Ok, that would be nice. I'll have a vodka and Coke, please."

"Coming right up," Desmond replied and twirled away, grabbing a glass.

Noticing she was the only female in the bar, her cheeks flushed and she pretended to study her phone. The three drunks had all stopped messing around and watched her silently, like a pack of wolves ready to pounce. Neither Kevin or Malachi liked the leers they threw her way and when it became clear the two smiling guys in the booth were less of a threat, she took the drink and seated herself down behind them.

"Wow," Kevin whispered.

"I am telling Laura," Malachi joked.

"Hey, a man can window shop," Kevin grinned, "Doesn't mean he is buying the goods."

"Always the gentleman," he laughed.

Kevin's phone started to ring on the table and the name *Laura* coupled with her smiling face flashed on the screen.

"Hi, babe," Kevin said, face going through changes from smiling to concerned. "Is he ok?"

"Everything ok?" Malachi whispered and Kevin shook his head.

"Thank God," he slumped back with relief, "How the hell did he get over the top of his cot?"

More faint chatter issued from the handset that Malachi couldn't quite make out.

"Little bugger," Kevin grinned, "Yeah I'm just finishing with Mal and then I'll be straight home. Ok, love you too." He hung up.

"What happened?" Malachi asked, although he had a good idea.

"Joey fell out of his cot."

"Damn, is he alright?" Malachi asked.

"Yeah he bounced. I thought we had a few more weeks, but the little monkey is standing and pulling himself over the bars already." Kevin shook his head in bewilderment. Parenthood was a tough gig.

"It's Laura's cooking, he is trying to escape before he has to eat it."

Kevin laughed, lifted the phone up and started to redial Laura. "I'll let you tell her personally."

"Don't you fucking dare!" Malachi frantically tried to press the cancel button as Kevin moved it around to thwart him.

The phone rang and Laura answered. "Only me, babes. Malachi wanted to say something quickly."

Passing the phone over, Malachi was giving him the finger which only brought more laughter, "Hey, Laura, I just wanted to check he was ok, that's all."

"Hiya, Mal. Yeah he's fine now. I heard the thump and then the scream and I thought he had really hurt himself. A cuddle and a suck on my nipple and he was right as rain, just like my husband," Laura chuckled. She had a wicked sense of humour just like Kevin and Malachi adored them both.

"Ok, well make sure you let me know if you need anything."

"Will do, take care, Mal."

"You fucker!" Malachi threw the phone across the table and Kevin was nearly crying with laughter.

"And you say I'm whipped," he said, mimicking the cracking sound.

"You best get going, mate."

"Nah, he is a tough little blighter. I need to make sure you are fine before I go," Kevin declared.

"Honestly, you can get off. I feel a whole lot better than I did this morning and if you don't mind, we could do this again later in the week?" Malachi asked.

"Are you sure?" Kevin replied and Malachi nodded. "That sounds good to me. I'm really glad you started to open up about all the shit you've been through."

"Of course. I need to stop off and get some fish and chips for Miss Cortez anyway. She's my date tonight."

"She's a tough old girl, say hi for me."

"Will do. Love you, buddy," Malachi stood and embraced his friend who held him tight in support.

"Love you, brother."

Kevin said a quick farewell to Desmond and was gone into the night. Leaning back, the weight had been lifted a little by the bearing of his soul and Malachi smiled. The dreams were an obstacle that would need to be overcome, and Kevin probably lacked the skill to successfully psychoanalyse the hidden meanings. That he had a friend like him, who had stuck by his side loyally through all the craziness, made Malachi supremely grateful. The night didn't hold quite as much fear as it had an hour ago.

"Alright gorgeous, want some company?" slurred one of the men who was barely able to stand through inebriation.

"No, thank you. I'm waiting for a friend," she answered with a nervous smile.

"I can entertain you until she arrives," he laughed and started to dance, slowly and with much staggering.

"No, I think I would rather be alone. But thank you for the offer."

The man stood in silence, staring down at the woman with glazed eyes. Malachi was watching out of the corner of his eye and his teeth were clenched as the familiar rush of adrenaline kicked in. He wasn't a fighter by nature and only retaliated if provoked, but the trouble was brewing and his stomach knotted in apprehension of the possible conflict.

"Fucking dyke cunt," growled the man, spitting onto the table top inches from her hand.

Malachi had heard enough and was in far better shape than his adversary. Satisfied to keep the violence to a minimum, he was correct in his assumption that the other man was blind drunk. With a firm push, he went flying with arms flailing until he hit the wooden floor hard.

"You just fucked up really bad," said one of the thugs who wasn't wasted. Helping his friend up, the third man started to circle around to attack.

"I don't want any trouble; I just came out for a quiet drink. Your friend was bang out of order with how he spoke to the lady," Malachi said, trying to defuse the situation. He really didn't like to hurt people.

"I'm sure you didn't want trouble, you prick," snarled the man he had pushed as he smashed the neck of a bottle off.

"But you have found it anyway," finished his friend.

"Not so tough without your mate, are you? He was going to get it as well for staring at me, but for now you'll have to do."

"We'll have to do!" bellowed Desmond as he smashed a baseball bat onto the counter making them all flinch.

"This isn't your fight, old man."

"Old? You cheeky mother fucker." He leaped over the bar for dramatic effect, glasses smashing; the hatchway was only a few feet away.

Their alcohol bravery faltered at the solid Jamaican and his bat, Malachi smiling coldly by his side and making a *come on then* gesture.

"This place is a fucking shithole anyway!" shouted the man wielding the broken bottle. In frustration, he launched it at the wall, shattering into shards against the Jamaican flag and leaving a small rip in the fabric.

Shaking with rage, Desmond stepped forward, "You disrespected my place, and now my flag. If you come in here again, you won't be leaving." He meant it too. The Jamaican Yardie gangs were brutal and ruthless in dealing with their enemy, and Desmond was loosely affiliated by old acquaintances. He had avoided the gangster life, but there were still numbers he could call to ask a favour or two.

"You haven't heard the last of this!" sneered the trio as they left.

"I will be waiting, man." Desmond blew a kiss as they slammed the front door.

"Thanks, Des, you just saved me from getting a good hiding." Malachi shook his hand.

"It was nothing. You are my friend and brudda; I wasn't going to let that bumbaclot take a liberty," he said with passion. "Let me get you both a refill."

Desmond walked to the entrance, looked outside in both directions and was satisfied the men had left. Placing the bat within easy reach, he set to work on the drinks.

"Sir, I'm sorry but can I have a soda? I don't think my friend is coming so I will just drive home," she asked shakily.

"Are you ok?" Malachi asked the young redhead.

"I am now. Thank you for helping me," she smiled, revealing a beautiful set of even white teeth, "Please, sit down."

Heart skipping a beat at the sight, Malachi shook himself when the reality of his psychological predicament came crashing into his mind. No romantic connections, he reminded himself with regret.

"It was nothing; they were just idiots out to make trouble. I wasn't going to let him speak to you like that though." Malachi smiled back and shook her outstretched hand.

A tingle of anticipation ran up the extremity at the contact and he snatched his hand back, causing her to frown.

"Sorry, you gave me an electric shock," he lied.

Mollified by the deception, she laughed, "You help me and I end up hurting you. That's gratitude right there."

Her giggle contained such innocence and a musical timbre that Malachi found himself laughing along. It felt good after years of self-imposed isolation to make a connection with someone new, however unlikely any further development of the relationship was.

"I think I can forgive you. I'm Malachi, pleasure to meet you."

"Chloe. The pleasure is all mine," she replied, eyes wandering to his broad chest and strong shoulders.

"My eyes are up here," Malachi chided with a grin.

"Huh? Sorry." Her cheeks flushed red.

"Don't apologise, I was only teasing. Have you heard anything from your friend?" he changed the conversation to spare her feelings.

"I can't get hold of her by text or phoning," Chloe replied.

"Do you think she is ok?" Malachi asked with concern.

"Oh yes, don't worry about Gabby. She is..." Chloe wondered what to say to not insult her friend, "A bit promiscuous. I know she got chatting to the new guy at work today, I expect they are back at her place right now."

"She doesn't sound like much a friend," he proposed, then relented. "I'm sorry. It's none of my business."

"There's a lot of apologising going on today," she slapped his hand playfully, "And you are right, she isn't. But she is all I've got."

The shrug she gave and the bleak look in her eyes was familiar to Malachi. It was the same look that greeted him every time he looked in a mirror. Sensing a kinship with the pretty girl, he found himself backing off.

"Will you excuse me for a minute?"

"Of course," she said and thanked Desmond for the drink as he put them on the table.

Walking into the small, but immaculately clean toilet, Malachi leaned against the wall and took a deep breath. Like any red-blooded male he had needs, and the stunner sat in the booth only feet away was only exacerbating the desire. Hell, she was desire personified, but he was in no shape to try and kindle a love life that would end the first time she awoke in a puddle of urine. Deciding the best approach would be to shut it down and make his excuses, he pressed the hand dryer to make it appear he had used the facilities before opening the door.

"He's a good guy, trust me," Desmond whispered, but Malachi caught it.

"I thought you weren't going to come back," Chloe beamed, offering his drink.

"I have to be going, I've got work early in the morning," Malachi said and felt a twinge of pain at the look of hurt on her face.

"Oh, ok," she said quietly, looking embarrassed.

"Can I walk you to your car?" he asked, feeling like a total arse.

"No, that's fine," she picked up her purse in a hurry and nearly knocked the drink over, "Thank you for the drink and thank you for standing up for me."

She hurried through the door and out into the night, throwing one quick glance back over her shoulder.

"What the fuck is wrong with you, man?" Desmond asked, shaking his head.

"More than you could imagine, Des," he said with self-disgust.

"It's nothing that can't be overcome," he pressed. "You don't see a girl like that every day. She was into you, man. You were her knight in shining armour."

"It was only gratitude and relief, don't read too much into it."

"You pitiful bastard." Desmond scowled.

"Hey, if I wanted to get called names I would get Kev back," Malachi protested.

"You think you are alone in having problems? Everyone got problems. In my country you were just as likely to end up dead or in prison by the time you turned eighteen. I lost more friends than I can count on those streets, so don't give me that self-pitying bullshit."

"Did you ever wet yourself from horrific nightmares that you thought you wouldn't wake up from?" Malachi blurted and lowered his head in shame.

"Every day was an unending nightmare, brudda," Desmond said and reached over to squeeze his arm in sympathy. "For us it was whether we would even make it to bed safely."

"How could I explain that to her?"

"Are you getting married?" Desmond chuckled, "You have to date her first. Nothing to say you need to spend the night together until you feel ready."

"I don't know…" Malachi was caught between conflicting emotions.

"You won't have a choice if you don't get your ass moving. I haven't seen her around before and I don't think she will be coming back."

"Fuck, fuck, fuck!" Malachi's mouth was dry and his heart was pounding faster than when he had been in danger.

"*Go!*" boomed Desmond and it was just the trigger he needed.

Bursting into the night air, a mixture of dread and elation seized him in a vice. The streets were largely deserted and Chloe was nowhere to be seen. A pang of fear mixed in with the rollercoaster of feelings.

"Stupid!"

Running to the carpark which served Jim's Gym as it was the closest, all was quiet. The lights from inside cast shadows on the lot and Jim was talking to a couple of men in the reception, their shadow figures dancing on the tarmac.

"You've blown it," Malachi conceded, sighing with regret.

Only one other car park was in the vicinity, but by now she would likely have driven away. Jogging around the corner, he studied each passing car to try and see if Chloe was behind the wheel. None contained her beautiful face, and the second lot was likewise quiet and motionless. Bizarrely, Malachi started to well up and felt a yearning for the very companionship that he had been fighting for so many years. It was a moot point anyway; she had gone and he had no idea where she worked or even her second name. Her clothing had been non-descript; neither a uniform or an outfit that carried any clues to the profession. Standing on the sidewalk, the loneliness grew until it was all consuming.

Was this the extent of his remaining years? To merely exist, rather than live. Never knowing the loving touch of a wife, the laughter of his children as they grow. Suicide wasn't in his nature, but at that point he could understand the motives of the lost souls who took that final step into oblivion.

Turning to walk back to Desmond's, a muffled cry caught his attention. The source was hard to pin down with the disruption of passing cars and Malachi found himself wishing for them all to disappear. Lacking the power to displace matter, a stroke of luck caused the traffic lights to change and stop all of the passing cars. The cry was fainter now, but it came from the alley across the street. Sprinting between the idling vehicles, the darkness was nearly complete down the passageway.

"No! Please…" came a shrill, terrified yell before it was cut off.

A veil of rage descended on Malachi and, instead of calling for help, he ran into the poorly lit alley. The cars started moving again and with each passing headlight, the shadows receded for a split second, like a strobe of the unfolding attack. Chloe was stretched out sideways, pinned beneath the man who had abused her in the bar, with one friend kneeling on her arms. Her skirt and panties had been torn off and the pale buttocks of her rapist were poised between her legs. So caught up in the act, the men didn't even react to the footfalls as Malachi closed the distance.

"Mother fuckers!" he roared.

Using his weight and the momentum, he swung a kick straight into the soft midriff of the abuser. Lifting the man clear of Chloe, his small erection bounced as he rolled across the dirty ground before coming to a stop against a trash can. Gasping for air and clutching his side in agony, the second man glared and leaped to his feet.

"You're next!" Malachi pointed and it was the mirthless smile which warned him of the danger.

Hiding in the shadows of a recessed doorway, the third thug had been on lookout duty. Sneaking up behind Malachi, the blade glinted with another passing motor as he thrust it towards his back. Twisting at the last moment, the knife cut deeply into Malachi's flesh instead of burying itself into the liver which would have been fatal.

"You're a dead man," said the knife wielding thug, closing the distance with his companion.

Malachi looked for a way out, but there wasn't one. High brick walls rose on each side of the alley and the nearest window was located on the first floor to reduce the chances of burglary.

"Nowhere to go, pretty boy," laughed the one who had been holding Chloe down.

She was beyond terrified, looking around like a small girl trapped in the middle of a forest with monsters. The rapist was trying to stand up, desperate for revenge on Malachi. It looked like he would die in this dingy passageway, and Chloe would still be violated as he bled out only feet away.

"Who's first?" Malachi sneered and raised his fists, all fear disappearing. The pain from the deep gouge in his side dulled as adrenaline coursed through his body.

"I have a present for you," grinned the knifeman, the red blade dripping.

"Happy to oblige!" Malachi shouted and threw all his weight behind the punch.

Knuckles met nose and crushed it flat at the same time as the thug lunged, burying the knife into Malachi's stomach.

"Mal!" Desmond shouted from the entrance, seeing him drop to his knees.

"Let's get out of here!" called out the uninjured man, helping his friends to their feet.

"Fucking cowards!"

Desmond came charging, bat raised to take heads off. The darkness swallowed the trio of beasts, seeming to aid them in their nefarious endeavours.

"Stay with me, man," Desmond begged, holding Malachi's head. "No, don't pull it out."

The blood loss was making his head swim, but Malachi wanted to get the knife out of his body. Batting the flailing arms away so he couldn't inflict more damage to himself, Desmond was screaming at the onlookers.

"Call an ambulance, now!"

Phones were pulled out and the call was made.

"I found her," Malachi smiled, lips covered in blood.

"I know you did, brudda. You saved her from those animals," Desmond said, stroking his cold, sweaty forehead.

"Is she ok?"

Desmond could only surmise that physically she was unharmed, but mentally? That was another matter.

"She's good. You rest now, help is on the way."

"I wish I could have taken her out to dinner," Malachi whispered.

"Hey! Don't talk that way." Desmond slapped his cheeks in desperation as Malachi's eyes rolled.

"I won't miss the dreams."

Desmond's voice was dwindling, his worried face getting further and further away. As Malachi faded from the world, he felt the soft caress of other hands on his temples. Long forgotten memories of his mother and how she would soothe him with the same gentle stroking motion accompanied him into nothingness.

CHAPTER SEVEN

Pin pricks of cold tickled the consciousness of Malachi and he opened his eyes briefly to the night. The drizzle was coating his face and Desmond was doing his best to shield him from getting wet as the paramedics went to work. The face of his friend was fraught and he shouted orders at the trained medical professionals. Used to high stress situations, the female paramedic kept her cool and gently eased Desmond away.

"Sir, you have done an amazing job, but we need to help your friend now."

"He's been stabbed in the side and stomach. I made sure he didn't pull the blade out," Desmond was babbling.

"Sir, he is in good hands."

Reluctantly he ceded control of the compressive bandage which comprised a crumpled t-shirt. Seeing that Malachi had regained partial consciousness, she shouted for Desmond to come back and talk to him. The sopping red clothing was removed and in its place proper sterile pads were secured with bandage until the surgeons could treat the wound.

"Hey, buddy, we still need to visit my family in Jamaica. Do you remember how we always talk about sitting on the beach sipping Planter's Punch?" Desmond said, wiping the moisture from Malachi's face.

He wanted to reply, but being weakened by blood loss no sound would come, only a brief twitch of the lips.

Desmond's deep tones were morphing into happier, female ones. "Sweetheart, it's time to get up!" called out a voice from distant memory and Malachi closed his weary eyes.

The chill of the wet ground metamorphosed into the soft, warm cocoon of a child's bed. Opening eyes and pulling back the Thomas the Tank Engine duvet, Malachi surveyed the room of his infancy. A small television and DVD combination unit sat on a worn cabinet. Set on shelves were a collection of children's films bought for pennies from the local charity shops. A wooden toy chest that was scored and marked from years of use spoke of poverty, its lid open and the meagre toys only filling a quarter of the space.

"Breakfast's ready, champ," shouted his father.

"Coming!" replied Malachi groggily.

Throwing off the covers, he jumped out of bed and rushed to the bathroom to empty his swollen bladder. Before he could reach the bowl, the reflection stopped him dead and his eight-year-old face stared back. The freckles had faded with age and the scrawny, bony frame had been replaced by layers of muscle. Young eyes gazed back from the mirror and seemed to look at the older Malachi within. Questioningly? Or was it accusatory? The dual personality wanted to scream and warn its younger manifestation of the coming pain, but with a rub of knuckles in eye sockets and a yawn the connection was gone. After flushing the toilet, he slouched down the stairs in the way young boys do and found his parents dancing in the kitchen to Lionel Ritchie.

"We're gonna have a party, all night long!" crooned his father, waltzing the giggling figure of his mother around the cramped kitchen.

"You wish, Romeo," she answered and planted a kiss on his cheek.

"Morning, honey, how did you sleep?" asked his mother while pouring a glass of orange juice.

"I had a bad dream," answered past and future Malachi in unison, meaning wholly different nightmares from more than a decade apart. Being an unwilling stowaway through a memory, his mother only acknowledged the younger version with a sorrowful kiss.

"Oh dear, buddy. Are you ok? What happened?" asked his father, lifting him as if he weighed nothing and planting him firmly on his lap.

"I can't remember, but you and mummy were in it," Malachi answered, snuggling closer to banish the forgotten terrors.

"I know what will cheer you up," smiled his mother before planting a kiss on his forehead, *"Eggs and toast for dunking."*

"Yes please," beamed young Malachi.

"Do I get to be cheered up too?" asked his father making a pouty face. *"I had a bad dream as well."*

His mother laughed and threw a teacloth across the room, *"I know exactly what you were dreaming about, mister! Your hands were everywhere even though you were fast asleep."*

"Have some of your juice, buddy," said his father, dropping him into a chair and walking over to embrace his wife at the frying pan. *"Even in my dreams I can't resist you."*

"Smooth talker," she giggled and craned her neck for a kiss.

Malachi watched the display of affection with a child's innocence. The bond his parents shared would not become clear until he had grown up and could appreciate the boundless love he been surrounded by. Any relationship he nurtured would be judged against the example of his beloved parents. If he could make each moment shine as if it were a lifetime, to adore every breath she took and cherish every wrinkle that developed with the passage of their years together, then he would be proven worthy of the legacy.

He wrinkled his nose as their lips parted and a tongue lingered too long. *"Eww, gross!"*

"Sorry," said his mother, blushing. *"Paul, can you watch the eggs while I put the toast on?"*

"Of course, love," he replied, winking at Malachi by way of apology.

Taking a sip of the orange juice, Malachi let it drain back into the glass when the liquid soaked his taste buds.

Seeing the look of revulsion his mother came over, *"What's the matter, sweetie?"*

"It doesn't taste right. Sorry, Mummy," Malachi said quietly.

"Oh, baby. Don't be sorry." She stroked his face and sniffed at the glass, *"It must have turned since yesterday. I'll get you some water to wash the taste away."*

Raising the carton, Paul frowned, *"I can't even see the best before date."*

"It has gotten so dark all of a sudden, I think we have a storm coming," she explained, glowering at the dark grey clouds and flicking the light switch.

Above their heads, the fluorescent tube flickered and blinked on and off rapidly.

"I think it's broken," said his father, voice dwindling and kitchen fading.

The strobing white light became the familiar beacons of flashing emergency vehicles as he was rushed into the emergency room.

The corridor passed in a blur, with many vacant assessment cubicles in the initial treatment area. Being a weekday, the hustle and bustle of activity was minimal and only a lone drunk shouted from a corner about his confiscated alcohol. For a split second the trolley was aligned with the inebriated man and their eyes met. Feelings of guilt caused the bum to avert his gaze; self-loathing at his own circumstances magnified by the pitiful, bloodied stranger who had been attacked.

"We have a twenty-year-old male. He has sustained a deep laceration to the right flank and penetrating abdominal trauma," detailed the head paramedic to the emergency surgeon.

Laying prone on the gurney, Malachi felt the strangest sensation as if he was walking then realised it was only a nurse elevating his legs. The emergency team were gathered around and discussing the treatment options available, none of which mattered one bit. Malachi's only concern was to ask again about the redhead who had been assaulted but the words came out as a weak croak. An alarm started to shrill, masking the question.

"Blood pressure is dropping!"

"He must be bleeding internally. Nurse, get an eighteen-gauge cannula in and begin blood transfusion immediately."

"Yes, Doctor," she replied, hurrying to the equipment trolley.

"What is the patients name?" asked the doctor.

"Malachi."

"Malachi, I am Doctor Ballachandra," a pretty young Indian doctor introduced herself, upside down from his horizontal viewpoint.

A witty response about meeting in these circumstances only appeared as a grimace of pain. Malachi felt weaker than at any point in his short life and the soothing darkness of unconsciousness tugged at his senses. Join us, it whispered from the shadows.

"You are going to be fine." Her face betrayed the uncertainty. Before his eyes closed, the medical lamp over her head gave the illusion of a halo. The grimace of pain was replaced by a wan smile; he was going home.

"He's crashing!"

"Prep for surgery. We need to…"

Darkness was banished with the sudden illumination of the faulty kitchen bulb.

"It must be the starter; I can pick one up later. Leave it off for now," said Malachi's father, flicking the round electrical component.

"Can we afford it?"

"They are only a few pound. It's either that or wait for the landlord to fix it, which could take weeks," he shrugged.

Taking out the first slices of bread, a layer of green mould had started to grow around the edges. A faint sob escaped his mother and she replaced the rotten dough.

"I'm sorry, honey, we only have eggs. Is that ok?" she asked, wiping away the barely suppressed tears.

"That's ok, Mummy. I like them with or without," smiled Malachi, hoping to banish some of her shame.

"We can always cut the bad bits away?" suggested his father.

"It will make you both ill," she crumpled the bag and threw it away in disgust, "You're not eating rotten food."

"We can't afford to buy food until the end of the week when I get paid," muttered Malachi's father guiltily.

Malachi watched the exchange from the table, his head barely reaching above the top. The creaky wooden chairs had been claimed before finding their way into a local bonfire, but the table didn't match and sat too high for the young boy. Normally a trio of old, tattered phone books doubled as a booster seat, though his angle of view changed with each passing month. It wouldn't be long before he could get rid of the uncomfortable tomes.

"I'm sorry, love. I will have a word with Trevor and see if I can get some extra shifts." Malachi's father embraced her tightly and she turned herself away so their child would be spared the tears.

"You can't do any more than you are," she protested, "We don't get to see you enough as it is."

Being innocent of finances and the adult world, Malachi found nothing strange in being hungry most of the time. A lot of the other children in his class were skinny and the words that were being discussed in his last parent teacher meeting like emaciated, anorexic, gaunt had no meaning. His mother had cried and hugged him close through the harsh questioning. Angry and confused at the argument, Malachi had shouted at the teacher to be quiet. They had left under a pall of sorrow and fear about the threat of social services becoming involved. It had been too much to take in at the time. All he understood was that the brief rainclouds of melancholy usually evaporated when the radiance of their mutual devotion shone through. With each passing month of pennilessness, the optimism of life diminished and the clouds grew thicker and stronger.

"It's not like I have a choice, sweetheart," he explained, nuzzling the smooth neck and making her giggle.

"I will just have to keep looking for a job."

"You know there aren't any. We are lucky that I have kept mine with all the redundancies," he said, looking deep into her blue eyes.

"But you are going to work yourself into an early grave." She wasn't placated by the affection. As the months stretched into years the toll it was taking became obvious. His normally dark brown hair was surrendering to slow creep of grey commensurate to the increasing stress of the battle to keep a roof over their heads.

"At least I will leave a good looking corpse," he joked and received a punch on the shoulder.

"Don't speak that way," she begged, "Mal has only just had a bad dream about us."

Slapping his forehead in a 'what a knucklehead' gesture, Malachi's father looked over and said, "Sorry, buddy."

"That's ok, Daddy. I remember you telling me about the man on the motorbike and how he was a huge film star." Malachi responded with a grin, meaning James Dean.

What his father hadn't explained was the tragic nature of the aforementioned superstar's untimely demise. In his heart he knew that the situation was untenable in the long run, but with the global economy in recession there were people in a worse situation. For years the banks had lavished money on people without the means to repay the debt, ruthlessly exploiting the human desire for stability. The opportunity to own their own home had proven to be a temptation too far and now the houses stood empty; their abandoned contents a reflection of the hollow promises of the unscrupulous money lenders.

"We could always try and get a loan to tide us over for a while?" she offered cautiously.

"No," he dismissed the idea instantly, "We can't help ourselves by getting into debt. I know we struggle but at least we have no one chasing us for what we owe."

"You can have this." Malachi had quietly left the room and returned with his small piggy bank.

Holding it out and giving it a shake, the loose change rattled but carried no real weight. Taking the porcelain swine, his mother regarded at him with a look of purest love.

"Thank you so much, sweetie, but you earned these pennies." She handed it back, unwilling to explain that it wasn't enough to make any difference to their plight.

"You can use it to buy some bread and juice," he persisted, pulling the rubber stopper free and tipping the coins out.

"I..." his mother started crying again but Malachi didn't see, so rapt was he on piling the money into tidy piles.

"I promise I will return it all on payday, ok?" vowed his father, gently turning his sons face to look him in the eye, "Shall we take your bike and go to the grocers before I go to work?"

"Can we really?" Malachi exclaimed, hurrying away to get his going out clothes on and tumbling the lopsided metal coin towers in the process.

A lone penny rolled and his father caught it as it fell from the table.

"He is such an angel," said his mother quietly, wiping away tears of pride.

"He takes after his dad," joked Paul, surmising the table held just over four pounds. It would just about cover the fruit juice and a single loaf of cheap brand bread. The smile disappeared at the realization that he had been reduced to taking money from his eight-year-old son. He couldn't even be classed as a man any more. A real man provides for his family, no matter what.

Seeing the expression of defeat as he regarded the change in his palm, she made sure Malachi wasn't close and quickly raised her top. *"What do you think of these?"*

The pert breasts bounced and Paul burst out laughing, totally forgetting the dejection. *"How many wars could have been avoided if the women just flashed their boobs in the negotiations? Weaker sex my ass."*

"And don't you forget it!" she chuckled, nudging him with her rump.

"Ready, Daddy!" shouted Malachi front the front door.

"We will be right back," Paul kissed her, *"I love you, sweetheart."*

"Love you more."

The door was open and a draft ruffled the loose threads of the tattered carpet. Malachi was seated atop the old bike which had been repaired so many times it was a miracle the wheels still turned. It didn't make any difference though, he loved the bike and the twisted handlebars.

"Bombs away!" he cried and pushed away, letting the gradient of the access ramp carry him onto the pavement in a blur. The concrete slope had been installed for the previous tenant who had been confined to a wheelchair and the landlord refused to pay to reinstate a set of steps.

"Careful!" cried Paul.

Every time his son made the descent his heart seized in unnecessary apprehension. With the apartments being largely empty, and those that were occupied lacking money to buy a car, the deprived cul-de-sac was clear. The youngster expertly leaned into the turn and mounted the grass verge without hitting the road itself, waving back and merrily pedalling away. Paul started jogging to keep up which was part of the game.

"Get back here, you!" he called out, reaching for the giggling boy but making sure to miss with each swing.

"You're getting old, Daddy!"

"I'm going to get you, you little monster!"

A raspberry was his only response which triggered more giggling. With a screech of unoiled brakes, the bike pulled up outside the small grocery store and Paul doubled over, pretending to gasp for breath.

"How did you get so fast?" he asked through exaggerated inhalations.

"Lots of practice, Daddy." Malachi smiled, locking the bike to the wall mounted rack, "Mummy watches me while I go up and down the street."

"You are growing up so quickly," Paul said, a mixture of pride and anguish at the lost time together.

"I'm going to be big and strong, just like you!" he declared.

The sky exploded with a crashing rumble of thunder which made the shop's windows rattle in their frames. The source was directly overhead and was swiftly followed by a dazzling coruscation which bounced from cloud to cloud.

"Daddy, I'm scared," Malachi whispered.

"It's only God getting home. The thunder is Him slamming the door and the lightning is the light being turned on."

Malachi started wheezing and clutching at his throat, unable to breathe.

"It's ok, don't fight it," said a sweet female voice as he opened his eyes.

She gently pulled the breathing tube from his throat and held a tray to catch the vomit triggered by its removal. The convulsions eased off and he lay back down with a sigh of exhaustion.

"Now you can't swallow, but you can gargle the taste away and spit into this," she offered, holding out a glass and a fresh sick tray. He gratefully took a long draw to rinse away some of the bitter taste of bile and spat the contents out.

"They said you were a fighter, but goodness me," said the nurse, checking his vitals on the computer screen.

Still groggy from the anaesthetic, the room spun several times before firming up in his field of vision.

"What do you mean?" he whispered, lacking the energy for full speech.

"You only came out of surgery a couple of hours ago and with the injuries you sustained, we didn't expect you to regain consciousness for a few days at least."

"You can't keep a good man down," he smiled weakly.

"We all heard what you did for that lady. You are a hero," she gushed and planted a kiss on his cheek.

"Helping hurts," he attempted to laugh but agonising pain radiated from his abdomen.

"I'm sorry, I shouldn't have brought it up. I just wanted to thank you for women everywhere."

He had never felt so tired and, with the drugs still having an effect, found himself searching for a floating battery bar above the bed, flashing a red warning of his impending shut down.

"Lie still now," she cautioned, back into professional mode, "What are you looking for?"

"Battery," he whispered, and she nodded with false understanding. As far as drug addled conversations went, it wasn't the strangest she had ever held.

The intensive care unit consisted of four beds with accompanying equipment designed to support the patient. One bed stood empty and the other two held an elderly man and a woman who was heavily bruised around the face. Even in his debilitated state, the flames of rage ignited in his belly at the sight of the beaten lady. Accordion looking respirators rose and fell, pushing life sustaining oxygen into their unresponsive lungs. Forcing himself to look away, a mixture of scents was carried on the air; disinfectant, faint perfume from the medical staff, and the lingering acidity of the vomit on his lips. The burning sensation didn't abate and it became an increasingly painful experience. The nurse saw his discomfort and the way he doubled over, risking damage to his recently stitched wound.

"Malachi, what's wrong?"

"It hurts," he started to say until the sensation of nausea washed over him again, "Need to be sick."

"That will be the anaesthetic wearing off, hold on," she said calmly.

Before she could even offer the newly collected sick tray, a stream of blood burst from his mouth, covering her skirt and the floor. Unfazed by the sight, she reached over and hit the emergency alarm button. A nurse came running into the room as Malachi was helped onto his side to prevent choking on the unending torrent of scarlet liquid.

"What is it?"

"I think the stitches in his upper intestine may have ruptured."

The other nurse immediately picked up the phone to call the surgery team. Malachi was fading and everything went quiet, even the discomfort of blood expelling itself through his lips disappeared. In the wall to his side, a dot of gleaming light appeared at waist height. As the seconds passed and the frantic activity of the intensive care nurses bustled around him, the dot grew into a sphere eight feet in diameter. The brilliant light wasn't uncomfortable, and as his eyes grew accustomed to the glare, dark forms could be seen standing within.

"Mum, Dad," Malachi croaked, red slobber dripping into the tray.

He reached out and the pulse clamp on his finger came away, causing the already noisy machine to go into a flat line screech. A shadow reached out in response and as their fingertips touched, a sense of unconditional love washed over him. All fear fled and as the feeling of floating took hold, he closed his eyes and joyously awaited the coming reunion.

CHAPTER EIGHT

Pulling his wife close to ward off the chill, William blew out a streamer of smoke and tossed the cigarette overboard. The glowing tip fluttered away into the darkness before meeting the ocean's surface. Standing on a freshly scrubbed wooden deck with evenly spaced lamps casting spotlights over the revellers as they enjoyed the hush of the walkway, he felt relaxed for the first time in months. The tightly bound lifeboats gave off an aura of reassurance and safety, despite the captain insisting they were an eyesore. It hadn't escaped their attention that a similar sentiment doomed a voyage in the not too distant past with the loss of over a thousand souls.

"Oh, William. It has been a superb cruise, I shall hate for it to end," Margaret said, cuddling in closer to her husband.

"We still have four days until we reach Seattle, I'm sure we can make the most of it. Tomorrow we shall go for a swim and play a few games of shuffleboard before sitting down to dinner."

"I would love that," she said with delight, "You know I am not the strongest swimmer though."

"Then I will show you, my dear. There is really nothing to it," he replied.

"I will be swimming like Ann Curtis before we arrive home," she giggled.

"Don't think you get to compete in the Olympics though," William said sternly, "You need to stay home and care for our children."

"Of course, darling," she said meekly, before brightening, "When do you think we will have our first son?"

"Oh it's going to be a son, hmm?" He smiled.

"You always wanted a boy first and I shall provide you with one," she declared.

"I do need an heir to pass on the family name, father would be thrilled. I should imagine that I will be made partner within two years and then we will be secure enough to start a family."

"It seems a long way away," she complained.

"The time will vanish in the blink of an eye. You can use the opportunity to make sure the house is in order, maybe even begin to decorate the baby room in blue," William offered.

A shout carried from the corner and a member of the cruise staff came into view. Dressed in an immaculate white uniform with three stars and a stripe on the epaulettes, Chief Steward Jenkins gave them a friendly wave.

"Five minutes, sir, madam," he informed them with a curt nod, *"I suggest you retire to the ballroom to refresh your drink before the captain counts down."*

"How exciting," clapped Margaret.

"Much obliged, Jenkins. I had lost track of time," said William, slapping the mariner on the back in thanks.

"Anytime, sir. We are here to serve."

And with that he was gone, calling out to the other guests further down the breezy deck.

"You'd better take that Mae West off. It looks ridiculous and is creasing your dress," William said with a scowl.

"I just thought it was better to be safe," Margaret replied quietly, unclasping the padded life preserver. They had been nicknamed Mae Wests because of the physical endowment it appeared to give the wearer.

"Don't be so ridiculous, it's not like we are sailing on the Titanic."

Linking arms, they pushed through the outer door and entered the stunning atrium. The domed glass ceiling was *utterly black now and the illumination came from banks of golden stemmed lamps which followed the spiral staircase and crystal chandeliers placed above the thick red carpet.*

"Good evening," greeted another steward who waited at the foot of the stairs.

"It will be when I get another whiskey," joked William.

"Indeed, sir," replied the man without smiling. Peculiarly, sweat was beading on his face despite the chill of the main lobby and his eyes looked fearful.

Ignoring the unsightly perspiration as a possible illness, William pulled Margaret away and gave him a wide berth. The last thing they needed was to be coming down with the flu for the rest of the journey. Looking down as they reached the top of the stairs, the man was watching intently and begun to follow. For some unknowable reason William felt knots of apprehension as the unblinking worker took each step and hurried through the ballroom doors to be among people.

"You're hurting my arm," whined Margaret.

"Sorry, darling," he said, looking at the red imprint of his grip, "I just didn't want to miss the show."

Clicking his fingers at the waiter, they ordered a whiskey and a Singapore Sling with a crisp dollar bill promised if the drinks were brought with haste. Their table had a subdued lamp in the middle to provide extra mood lighting in addition to the high hung light fixtures above the main dance floor and stage. The place was packed with nearly every guest on-board and the cacophony of clinking glasses and laughter nearly drowned out the pianist who was playing Shostakovich while the rest of the band took a well-earned drink. The alcohol and cigarette smoke mixed with the perfumes and colognes of the revellers to provide a mixture of glorious scents and William quickly forgot about the uncomfortable encounter in the lobby.

"Your drinks, sir," said the waiter, placing the glasses on the table.

"Stanley, you are a good man." William smiled and slipped the dollar into his shirt pocket.

"My pleasure, sir," Stanley graciously excused himself.

The pianist finished the song with a flourish and everyone gave a round of applause. The dancefloor emptied as the guests retreated to collect their drinks in readiness for the captain's announcement. Stepping onto the stage, he had changed from the uniform he had been wearing all evening as he mingled with the clientele. The welcome was subdued as confusion swept through the crowd and the sporadic clapping died down quickly.

"Ladies and gentlemen, please forgive my mode of dress. I was unfortunate enough to spill a glass of red wine trying to catch a female guest who had fallen earlier." He held his arms wide in self-abasement.

Some of the guests had been convinced and congratulated him on the selfless act. Others were quietly wondering why he hadn't simply changed into a spare uniform that must have been stowed in his cabin. The black shirt he now wore had a high collar and a gold medallion swung from the neck. It contained strange glyphs and lettering that William couldn't make out from his position, but those seated closely shifted nervously.

Looking at his pocket watch, he smiled and spoke, "It is now eleven fifty-nine. If you would all like to raise your glasses, I will count down the new year."

The free alcohol served as a balm to the more cautious members and the smile of their captain was disarming. Everyone decided to go with the flow and picked up their drinks.

"Ten, nine, eight…" he counted down to zero and from the ceiling, bags of gold and silver confetti were released, twinkling in the light as the pieces fell to blanket them. The band kicked off a beautiful rendition of Auld Lang Syne and *everyone toasted each other good will and a successful year to come.*

"It was wonderful," Margaret shrieked over the din but William's attention was elsewhere.

Members of the crew appeared and lined the balcony above, though not a single one was joining in the celebration; their emotionless faces filled him with dread. Upon seeing the furtive movements of their staircase friend locking the main doors his apprehension peaked.

"Something is wrong here," he whispered to his wife who was oblivious to the unfolding events.

"What's wrong, is I am dry again," she giggled until seeing the concern written on his features.

The band stopped playing and the crowd erupted with appreciation. Thinking the performers were approaching the front of the stage to take a bow, the sight of the machine guns didn't immediately register.

"Oh my God," William gulped as every member of the cruise liner's staff raised a gun. The balcony crew was covering them from their elevated position and nervous laughs fell silent as the captain raised his own ugly looking automatic weapon.

"Ladies and gentlemen, as well as being privileged enough to take part in the inaugural voyage of the SS Freedom, you have the honour of being part of something so much greater. If you would be so kind as to wait until the rest of your fellow passengers arrive, I will explain the purpose of your detainment," the captain explained.

"I demand to know what the hell is going on!" shouted out a fat Texan, banging his meaty fist onto the table sending glasses flying.

"Please be patient, sir. All will be revealed in due course," he replied, smiling his authoritative captain smile. It was disarming most of the time, but with death in the air people weren't placated.

Standing up and increasing the volume of his protest, the man started wagging an accusing finger, *"You had better start explaining or I swear to God I will end your career. You will never set foot on a ship again!"*

The smile was gone, replaced by a contortion of barely suppressed rage, *"Sir, if you don't sit down I will kill you where you stand. Then I will kill your wife."*

"Do you know who I am?"

"No one," answered the captain and raised the gun.

Pulling the trigger, the Thomson machine gun spat fire and lead across the short distance between the men. Bullet holes punched through the white tuxedo and the slugs found their way to his pudgy face as the recoil lifted the barrel. The jaw shattered and ripped away before a final round blew out the back of his head in a welter of brain matter. Innocent victims behind the brash man were writhing on the floor and screaming from the stray bullets and his wife fell to her knees at his side.

"You killed him!" she screamed, tearing at her own hair in grief.

"One moment, madam," said the captain, snapping another magazine home.

Revellers scattered from the inevitable barrage, some trying to drag the injured away from the kill zone. Holding her head high she didn't even blink when he opened fire again, her life had already ended with the death of her beloved husband. Nearly cut in half by the assault, her body slumped to the floor and added a fresh colour to the gold trimmed rug.

"Any more questions?" asked the captain looking around the room. Apart from the faint whimpers of the dying all was quiet. *"Good."*

More patrons were pushed into the room, some with bloodied faces. They all looked terrified and the armed guards surrounding the whole room only intensified the *fear. One of the women saw the carnage at the foot of the stage and collapsed in a faint.*

"Excellent. Now that I have your undivided attention I can explain the situation," said the captain.

His friendly exterior was gone, replaced by a glowering, hate filled mask that barely looked human. Starting to pace as if gathering thoughts on how best to proceed, he swung towards them without warning and the whole room flinched.

"I think the most logical way of putting this is that you have a new captain," he started until seeing the guests searching the room, "No, you can't see him, but you can be sure he is watching. He is always watching." The last was muttered and his eyes glazed with insanity.

"William, I am scared," whispered Margaret.

"Shut up or he will shoot us too!" he hissed through pursed lips.

"Now you are probably wondering what all this has to do with you fine folk. Part of serving the new captain involves… how can I put it… a sacrifice."

The room erupted with begging and wailing. Men were falling to their knees and trying to beseech their captors for mercy but the steely eyes betrayed nothing. They would have had more luck talking to the paintings which adorned the walls.

"You have already had your damned sacrifice!" called out a woman who had missed the hail of bullets but now cradled her dead husband who had been hit in the chest.

"You misunderstand," smiled the captain, "I need half of you to die for the sacrifice to be worthy."

"What the hell do you mean half?" shrieked a man.

"You can't do this to us!" sobbed a woman.

"Of course not, my dear, we aren't barbarians," remarked the captain, nodding to unseen men, "You are going to do it for me."

As fresh dissent swept over the captives, waiters and waitresses appeared from the shadows and placed a tray on each table. The groans and sobs grew into an unceasing din as the terrified guests surveyed the proffered gifts. Brutally edged clubs, knives of varying lengths, piano wire and rope garrottes, barbed knuckle dusters, and vials of coloured liquid were a small sample of the objects on the large silver platters.

"I don't understand," whined Margaret, but William had no illusion about what was coming.

"Hush yourself," he growled and his wife started to cry even harder.

Instead of being angry at the growing tension, the captain was looking around and nodding, "I see you are beginning to understand. The choice of your demise is in your hands, quite literally. In case any of you are still confused, the liquids are some choice poisons which will cause an agonising death. How you get your loved one to drink it, I leave in your hands."

"I fought against the Nazis. You can be damned sure we will fight you too, come on boys!" yelled a young man.

Two more brave veterans joined him from adjoining tables and using the largest knives they rushed the nearest waiters. As sharp knives cut the people down, their faces showed no sign of pain or fear at death.

"Why the hell aren't they fighting back?" asked one man, cutting the throat of another waitress.

"You must know this is futile," chuckled the captain who finally gave an order to respond.

The armed guards above opened fire and the three were cut to ribbons in a hail of lead. Two more staff were killed but none took steps to move out of the way and save themselves.

"Set an example, please," asked the captain politely and the gunfire resumed.

Everyone at the surrounding tables met their fate at the blazing end of the Thompsons. When the guns fell silent more than twenty guests had been slain and tendrils of smoke rose as the red hot bullets caused tiny fires in the pockmarked threads of the carpet. Vital fluids draining from the perforated corpses quickly found the holes and extinguished the danger before it could spread.

"You needn't all perish on this fine vessel," begged the captain, "My master only demands that one of each couple should die."

Seeing how insurmountable the chances were, one older guest looked into the eyes of his wife and gave her a final kiss, "Then it shall be me."

He picked up a knife and pointed the tip at his heart.

"Stop!" screamed the captain before the gentleman could end his own life, "Maybe I am not making myself clear. One of you needs to kill the other one for the ritual to work properly. Suicide will only ensure the death of the partner."

"But why?" cried Margaret, ignoring the wishes of her husband.

"Because love is the biggest lie, my dear. By committing the ultimate sin against those you purport to adore, it will prove that it is all just a fallacy," he explained.

"I won't hurt my husband," she dismissed the notion.

"Then you are very brave, but can the same be said of your husband? Is he willing to die alongside you?"

Margaret glanced to the right to gain strength from William's stoicism; if they were going to die at least they were together for the end. Instead of affection, his eyes regarded her with fear and calculation. Forehead sweating and furrowed in deep thought, William kept glancing down at the instruments of murder.

Laughing heartily the captain mocked, "It would appear not."

"William, you can't seriously be considering his proposal?" Margaret wailed. "What about our life together, the children we were going to have?"

He wouldn't, or couldn't answer. His throat bobbed with attempts to swallow from a mouth as arid as the hottest desert. Shaking in apprehension he picked up his whiskey, ice striking the glass with a musical tinkling. Downing the liquor in one gulp, the fire burned its way into the pit of his stomach. An apt comparison to his soul which would surely be damned if he carried out the heinous act.

"William, please look at me," she begged.

"I can't." A set of knuckle dusters with sharpened points was calling to him from the polished platter. Like a secret lover, it whispered dark promises, using images of his continued existence to beguile.

"William?" Margaret could see she was losing him. His face went through changes; the fear was replaced with a smirk and he nodded to unspoken questions. Terror gripped her heart when his hand slowly reached out and picked up a bizarre implement she had never seen before. His fingers slipped into the four welcoming holes and, with a shiver of anticipation, his fist clenched around the cold metal.

"Ahh," said the captain with satisfaction, "I see my master is with you all, giving you strength. Allow him in and your doubts and fears will disappear, you will see the glory that awaits those with the vision to heed his command."

"I'm sorry, darling," William croaked, barely sounding like himself.

"You don't have to do this," Margaret pleaded, holding out her hands defensively.

"But I do," he replied, taking a step toward her, "I have too much to live for. I am the future partner of Kalladon Associates, and when father retires, I shall inherit *the whole company. You must have known you were marrying above your station when I proposed to you."*

"Well, yes," she admitted. As the daughter of a dressmaker, she wasn't part of high society but William had been smitten at first sight. He had been searching for a dress for his mother and their works were well regarded across the city.

"Then you see why it has to be you?" William said, drawing his arm back.

"Begin!" shouted the captain and all hell broke loose.

"William, no!" Margaret screamed as the weapon smashed through her feeble guard, gouging holes in her left cheek.

The second blow caught her upturned arms and the bones fractured, tearing through the pale skin. His wife rendered helpless, William had a gut-wrenching realization of what he was about to do. In spite of the self-justification and bravado, his wife was in agony and it tore him up inside. She had fallen to her knees and sat in a growing pool of blood that ran from her ravaged limbs. Her torn, bloodied face looked at him with confusion and betrayal. The anguish was nearly enough to break free of the unseen force within his mind but, like a vice, something clamped down and cast out the pity.

"I love you," William whispered, fighting through the corruption in his skull.

"Don't," she begged faintly, but it was too late.

Punch after punch was hammered into her shattered face with the spikes cratering her once beautiful features. Brain matter leaked out from the ruptures in her forehead, slopping down the expensive dress as she collapsed. A sense of malevolent satisfaction flooded his psyche and with relish he fell onto the defenceless body and commenced a frenzied attack on the remains of his betrothed.

"Good," cheered the captain with glee.

In moments the ballroom resembled a slaughter house. Screams of the dying mixed with the sounds of choking and flesh being cleaved. Thuds of metal crunching through bone echoed back from the vaulted ceiling as other victims gurgled their dissolving innards from the force fed poisons. The older man who had been ready to take his own life stood proud and tall, embracing his wife and waiting for the end. A man of morals and principles, the evil voices had found no purchase within the corridors of his consciousness. Several other couples had not succumbed and stood fearfully amongst the writhing mass of bodies tearing at each other.

"Kill them slowly!" shrieked the captain.

Members of the waiting staff stepped carefully over the carnage and pulled out razor sharp sickle knives. With swift, brutal strokes they laid open the stomachs of the uncompliant guests, disembowelling them. Struggling to hold their trailing guts in, they fell to the floor and joined the butchery. Bemoaning their grisly fate while trying to console their dying companions, the captain clapped his hands with delight.

"Most excellent," he remarked as the room gradually fell silent except for the gasps of exertion from the murderers.

"Are you satisfied?" William asked, breaking his gaze from the pile of crushed meat that was once his wife.

"You have all done well," answered the captain, "The master is most pleased."

Shadows in the room seemed to loom, reaching for the damned.

"Who is your master? The government? The Nazis?" William demanded.

"Not exactly," the captain roared with laughter, "You needn't let it concern you. If you would be so kind as to follow my colleagues, they will direct you to the lifeboats. The SS Freedom has another destination entirely."

Murmurs of concern rippled through the survivors but the guns ensured compliance and the broken men and women staggered away from their dead partners. Two hundred and eighty people had walked out of the ballroom, with any injured being put down instead of carried to their salvation. Climbing aboard the gently rocking boats, they stared without seeing. The insidious power that had promised so much was now gone, leaving the remaining guests to despair at their own hatefulness.

"Ladies and gentlemen," said the captain, "We will now be making a mayday call before we reach our end."

William wondered why he hadn't said 'port', "And what is to become of us?"

"You will be rewarded. Lower away!"

The way the captain had said the word rewarded caused William's stomach to twist in fear. It was the accompanying smirk which spoke of deception.

"Wait, take us with you," begged a blood soaked lady, dress torn from the mortal battle which had taken place minutes earlier.

The ropes creaked and the crew lowered the line of life boats in unison. William reached down for a life preserver, but upon lifting it he could see the buoyancy floats had been cut away and discarded somewhere. They were now nothing more than extra layers of heavy clothing.

"You will be joining us soon enough, my dear. Though perhaps not in the way you were hoping," said the captain over the balcony.

"You aren't going to make a mayday call, are you?" William asked.

"You are an astute fellow. We are also nowhere near any known shipping lanes so there will be no rescue, not that it was ever a possibility anyway."

As the wooden hulls reached the ocean's surface, jets of ice cold water rushed into the boats and soaked their feet.

"Oh my God, there are leaks. Pull us up!" screamed a man on a different craft.

"Well of course there are, my dear sir, how else could I ensure you all drown?" replied the captain as if he was engaging in conversation with a buffoon.

The ropes were cut and fell with a splash by each boat and the survivors yelled and clawed at the smooth metal of the topsides, desperate for a handhold on the flat surface but finding no purchase.

"Full steam ahead!" yelled the captain from further down the ship.

With an increase in pitch, the engines churned the water at the stern as the power was pushed to maximum. Some of the more knowledgeable guests knew that the wake would capsize their tiny, holed boats but any chance of survival was worth clinging to. Sliding the oars through the metal oar rings, the men started to pull with all their might. One after the other the paddles snapped and gales of laughter came from above.

"Oops, sorry!" called down one of the crew.

The rowers looked at the clean channels which had cut most of the way through the wooden handles in disbelief.

"We aren't meant to get away from the boat," William stated, utterly defeated.

Shrill moans broke the night as the high wake approached. More people discovered the life vests were now just extra weight to drag them to their watery graves. The screams turned to prayers for a God they had willingly abandoned. Waves crashed over the sides, tipping the doomed revellers into the frigid sea and those that managed to reappear coughed the salty liquid from their lungs.

"What shall we do?" asked a lady who was treading water next to William.

"There is nothing we can do," he replied.

In the distance the cruise vessel exploded, fire rising into the night from the sundered middle section. For almost a minute the area was lit up from the blazing inferno until the stern and bow gave up and slipped beneath the surface forever, plunging them into darkness.

"I'm so sorry, Margaret," William whispered.

Realising their plight was hopeless and they were all damned, he stopped kicking his legs which had lost all feeling within seconds of being submerged. As the water closed over his face and the briny deep beckoned, he tried to picture his beautiful wife for comfort. The pulverized mess melding with the carpet was the only memory which accompanied him to the depths. As his screaming lungs filled with water, he felt unseen presences grasp his limbs. They sought to take him lower than the ocean floor, to a realm where untold suffering awaited.

CHAPTER NINE

Malachi came to in the hospital ward, filled with the sense of treachery and loss that William had suffered. The empathy he felt towards imaginary people was disconcerting; they were no more real than the portrayals on stage and screen. He was willing to admit that he had cried on occasion, but it was the skill of the actor that drew a viewer in. Perhaps the dreams were his own inner movies. It was just a shame they always had to be so horrific.

"Morning, sleepy head."

"What the fuck?" Malachi spluttered in shock at his friend's voice.

"That's a lovely way to greet someone who has sat by your bedside listening to you fart and snore for three days," Kevin said with a chuckle.

"You've been here for three days?" Malachi asked, trying to sit up.

Kevin leaped up and rushed over, "Whoa, slow down, buddy. You aren't in any fit state to be throwing your weight around."

Using his armpits, Kevin managed to wrestle Malachi up and puffed the pillows behind to provide extra support. On the spur of the moment, his friend hugged him as though he were the finest china and liable to break under too much pressure. Returning the embrace, Malachi felt some of the fear dissolving like salt in water. It was still there, but diluted and manageable now.

"It doesn't really hurt," he explained, fingering the bandages on his stomach.

"It must be the morphine, you lucky bastard."

Malachi noticed the morphine bag hanging from the medical infusion stand and the slow drip of the painkiller into the tube. The dose must have been too low because he felt none of the effects of the strong opiate in his system. No itching, no feeling woozy and drowsy as the medicine numbed the damaged nerve endings.

"Have you really been sat here for three days?"

"Don't be daft, the visiting hours are only noon until eight," Kevin admitted with a grin, sitting back down.

It still meant his friend had kept him company during the most dangerous hours of his recuperation. Malachi couldn't express his gratitude through the lump that had formed in his throat and simply smiled.

Kevin had known him long enough to communicate without words, "You would have done the same for me."

"I'm not so sure," Malachi finally replied, "Your farts can curdle milk."

"What can I say? It's a gift," he agreed.

"I expect they would have already turned off your life support," Malachi said.

Kevin laughed and then got serious, "I nearly turned yours off. What the fuck do you think you are playing at going after those bastards without me?"

"I didn't plan to," Malachi protested, "I was trying to follow your advice and go after the redhead."

"And when you heard her in trouble you should have called me, I would have floored it and been back in minutes."

"By then it would have been too late." Malachi didn't need to elaborate.

"Wankers!" Kevon slammed his fist into the arm of the chair. "I knew we should have battered them all over the bar."

"You're too hot headed," Malachi said with affection.

Kevin laughed, "Says the man who took on three knife wielding rapists to save the damsel in distress. How much damage did you do before they got you?"

"Enough," Malachi replied, "Broken ribs and a mashed nose I think."

"That's a good start," he replied, scowling. Malachi knew full well what he meant.

"No!"

"Huh? What?"

"You know exactly what I am talking about. No going after them, let the police deal with it," Malachi begged but Kevin wasn't convinced.

"We will see what Des says when he arrives," Kevin glanced up at the wall clock, "He should be here any minute."

"You're a nightmare. Please don't do anything without talking to me first."

"You and your bloody 'code'," Kevin spat the words with frustration.

"Promise me."

"Yeah, ok." Kevin relaxed a little. A wide grin spread across his face, "Here comes the fit nurse I have been telling you about in your sleep."

Malachi held out a hand, "Phone."

"What?"

"Give me your phone. I'm going to tell Laura you have been perving over one of the nurses."

"Get stuffed," Kevin slapped the hand away, "Snitches get stitches."

Reaching their end of the ward, the nurse frowned disapprovingly, "If you don't keep the noise down, you will have to leave. And what was that about stitches?"

Kevin held up his hands in surrender, "Sorry. I was just happy to see my friend awake after he nearly died." It was partly the truth anyway and Malachi had to stifle a smile.

Her face softened and the lines disappeared, revealing her beauty. Hair as black as night framed a face that belonged on a Vogue magazine cover.

"Well if that is the case, I can't really blame you, but please show some concern for the other patients."

She checked the instruments to gauge his recovery while Kevin stood just out of view. Kissing his fingertips in a 'bellissima' gesture, he then proceeded to outline her curvaceous figure with his hands. Making a ring with thumb and forefinger, a final digit left no doubt about his ignoble desires.

"Would you like to explain to my colleague what it is you were doing behind her back?" a voice boomed from behind and Kevin jumped in fright.

Malachi burst out laughing after playing along while she stealthily approached with a finger raised to her lips. She was trying to maintain the scowl, but the corners of her mouth twitched in suppressed laughter.

"Er, I've got to go and make a phone call. I'll be right back." Kevin hurried off and cast one final look back at Malachi with a raised thumb and a grin. He was incorrigible.

"I apologise for my friend," Malachi said.

"I wouldn't worry, we have got used to his behaviour over the past few days," explained the playful nurse.

"He hasn't been a nuisance has he?"

"Not at all, we find him hilarious. He has been too caught up in talking to you to give us his undivided attention," she said, leaning over to check his wounds.

"Thank God for that."

Her perfume wafted under his nose and he found himself inhaling deeply. Since regaining consciousness, the realization hadn't quite hit home about how lucky he was to be alive. Though he had been ready to die, hoping to see his beloved parents again, the chance for continuation was something to be grateful for.

"Do you like it?"

"I am so sorry," he blustered. She probably thought he was a total weirdo.

"Don't be," she smiled warmly, "It's nice to get a compliment now and again."

"I was afraid you would think I was a freak, the way I sniffed at you," Malachi replied.

"It's not every day my perfume makes a man smile like that, especially a hero," she winked.

Laying back and groaning, Malachi asked, "I'm no hero. How many people know what happened?"

"Pretty much everyone," said the dark haired nurse, shining a light into each eye. Once the glare had worn off he could see their name badges, raven hair was Angela and the beautiful smelling one was called Shannon.

"The reporters have been phoning every hour day and night for progress reports," Shannon remarked.

"Fuck!"

Malachi valued his privacy and now he was under a spotlight. The monitoring equipment started to pick up on the accelerated heart rate and the nurses tried to calm him.

"It's ok," said Shannon, "We have a strict privacy policy and no information has been given out."

"Do they know my name?"

Angela hesitated which gave Malachi the answer he was dreading, "I'm afraid so."

"But you saved that lady," Shannon gushed, "You should get the recognition for being so brave."

He wasn't convinced and now his complicated life had taken on a whole new level of aggravation. The reporters would doggedly pursue him until the story broke or something else came along to satiate them. Maybe that was the answer? Just hide until it all blows over. Recovering in the hospital should take a few weeks and then he would have to ask for leave from Jim.

"I told her she is lucky to have such a handsome guardian angel," giggled Angela.

Malachi didn't immediately put the words together, "Hang on, how have you been able to tell her?"

"She visits every day too, silly."

The cardiograph lines peaked again and his mouth suddenly dried out. Only this time it wasn't from fear of invasion into his life, but anxiety about the ramifications of her seeing him unconscious. *Had he wet himself at all? Had he screamed and talked in bizarre languages?* The demeanour of the nurses gave no indication that he had caused anything out of the ordinary to occur on the ward and he dared to believe his secret was still safe.

"When your friends have to leave, she stays and sings quietly to you. It is so sweet," Shannon said.

"So anyone can just walk in off the street and see me then?" Malachi asked with more vehemence than intended. His defences were up and he was taking it out unnecessarily on the nurses.

"Not at all, you are in a secure wing with CCTV," Angela said, pointing up at the cameras.

"Kevin insisted that she be allowed to visit," explained Shannon.

"I'll bet he did, the bastard," Malachi said, cooling down. "I'm sorry, I guess I was just a little afraid the arseholes that stabbed me might come back to finish the job," he lied.

"They wouldn't get in even if they wanted to," assured Shannon, peeling tape back from his dressings.

"The police are close to making arrests anyway according to the news. Soon you won't have anything to worry about."

"Good."

Shannon had lifted the bandage and paused, a look of bewilderment passing over her face. Indicating Angela should come and look, the other nurse also frowned with confusion. Before Malachi could question them about the worrying glances they shot his way, Desmond and Kevin came back into the ward. The larger than life Jamaican was wearing a garish ensemble of vibrant colours that could have benefitted from a dimmer switch. In his hands was the biggest bunch of flowers and fruit basket that Malachi had ever seen. Disarmed by the sight, he forgot to ask the nurses about their concerns before they excused themselves.

"Behave," Shannon chastised Kevin as they passed.

"I have no idea what you are talking about," he replied innocently.

"Brudda!" Desmond put the gifts down and bear hugged Malachi, "You had me worried there."

"It will take more than death to kill me," laughed Malachi, but Desmond didn't join in.

"A man that can come back from the brink like that," he nodded knowingly, "Is destined for greatness."

"Shut up, you big lug," Kevin teased at the mystical turn in the conversation.

"You mark my words; things are in motion," Desmond insisted.

"Yeah, my bowel movements," Kevin said.

"Fuck you, man," Desmond burst out laughing and left the cosmic talk alone.

"Thanks for bringing the florist and enough fruit to satisfy the monkeys at London Zoo!" Malachi remarked.

"A man needs to eat healthy when he is recovering." Desmond offered the fruit but Malachi wasn't hungry. Kevin was starving and gratefully took a bunch of grapes and an apple.

"At least if the hospital food isn't up to scratch I can feast on all this sugary goodness."

"I'll bring you my special recipe jerk chicken with rice and peas when you feeling stronger, man," Desmond offered and the thought of the delicious food caused Malachi's previously silent stomach to growl in anticipation.

"You don't have to go to all that trouble for me, Des."

"I insist. A meal fit for a hero."

"Will you all stop calling me a bloody hero," Malachi blurted, "I got my arse handed to me three ways from Sunday. A real hero would have beaten those guys up and trussed them ready for the police to arrive. As it was, I just laid on the floor bleeding."

"I didn't say you was a superhero. A hero does what needs to be done, no matter the risk," Desmond said with conviction.

"Well, thanks for the sentiment."

Malachi was going to need to get used to the fifteen minutes of fame. He would have preferred to slip quietly into the night with little fuss but it didn't look like that was an option. Movement caught his attention and he noticed the nurses watching covertly from the doorway. He would have to ask what it was that had them so rattled when they next came within earshot. It was obviously something to do with his wounds which didn't bode well.

"Des, tell him about the search for the scumbags who did this," Kevin prompted.

"I'd forgotten about that. I have some of my boys looking for those three rapist coward mother fuckers. Word is they normally drink on the Etchingham estate, but they have been keeping a low profile. Babylon keeps doing the rounds too, but don't you worry, we will get them first."

Malachi laid back, closed his eyes and sighed wearily.

"You ok, dude?" Kevin asked.

Ignoring him, Malachi spoke directly to Desmond, "Please call them off, I don't want them killed out of revenge. Let the police and courts deal with them."

Kevin threw his hands up in anger, "See! I told you."

"Don't you think the world is fucked up enough with everything that is going on without us adding to the murders?"

Kevin huffed, but knew he was right.

"The man has forgiveness in his heart," Desmond said with respect. "You just say the word and I promise it will go no further. I have my own score to settle which demands blood, but I think a beating before an anonymous phone call to the authorities will suffice."

"They nearly killed my best friend!" Kevin welled up and Des put a supportive arm around his shoulders.

"They did kill your best friend," Desmond corrected. He had been informed of the two minutes when Malachi had flat lined, "This stubborn bastard just didn't get the memo."

"So we just do nothing?" Kevin was incredulous.

"No, man, we do what Malachi wants. He's the one who was wronged."

"Thanks, Des." Malachi turned to Kevin, "I love you, buddy. I just couldn't live with myself knowing I had been the cause of three unnecessary deaths. They will face a judgement; of that you can be sure."

Now it was Kevin and Desmond who frowned at the mystical turn in the conversation. Or was he just talking about the British court system?

"Chloe will be here soon," grinned Kevin mischievously.

"What the hell do I say to her?" Malachi was panicking.

"Does it matter?" Desmond shrugged, "If you end up offending her just blame it on the drugs."

"You won't have to worry, mate. She is a down to earth girl and worships the ground you walk on. She mentioned you protecting her dignity in the bar before it all kicked off; I think she is in love."

"Shut up, you tit. How can she love me when she doesn't even know me?" Malachi argued with a flutter in his heart.

Kevin wouldn't be dissuaded, "Love at first sight. I thought it was all bullshit until I met Laura."

"Pack in the mushy stuff, you'll make me sick," Desmond chuckled.

"I'm serious. As soon as I saw her I knew she was the one."

"If only people could see you now. So much for the hard man exterior," Malachi said, tossing a grape at Kevin who expertly snatched it out of the air.

"Good reactions," Desmond complimented.

"Damn right," Kevin nodded and ate the red grape.

A tall, cadaverous looking doctor entered the ward and made a beeline for Malachi's bed. The man would have been better suited to a funeral parlour than the NHS. Thin to the point of anorexic, the doctors gown hung loosely on his frame. The nurses had resumed their lookout from the doorway and their interest caused Malachi's worry meter to peak.

"Fuck me, are you sure you ain't dead?" Kevin whispered, "He looks like he is here to collect your body."

"Good afternoon," said the doctor, "May we have a few minutes of privacy?"

"Hey, Doc, of course. Guys, would you mind?"

Kevin and Desmond left the room and the doctor pulled across the privacy curtain. The insincere smile didn't help the overall look of the doctor and Malachi needed to know what was the matter.

"Am I in trouble? The nurses looked shocked when they had peered under the bandages. I don't mind if I need another operation, but Chloe is coming to visit soon and it would be a shame if I couldn't see her."

Malachi could hear himself rambling but lacked the power to disengage his vocal cords. Lifting the bandage, the doctor frowned in much the same way as the nurses, then looked confused. Picking up the charts, he flicked through the pages and frowned some more.

"Doc, you're killing me. What is the matter?" Malachi couldn't take it anymore.

"The chart says you were brought in just over three days ago," he mused, rubbing his chin.

"I have no idea." Malachi shrugged, and suddenly realised he really didn't know. Kevin had said three days, but it could have been weeks for all he knew.

"Peculiar."

"What's peculiar? What aren't you telling me?" Malachi was growing angry.

"I think we need to run some blood tests to be on the safe side."

Malachi's testicles seemed to shrink, "It's not HIV is it? I didn't get infected by their knife?"

"Oh no, not at all." The doctor waved the notion away, then recanted, "Well it could be, but I don't think I can remember a single stabbing where the patient contracted the disease. Any resulting contamination of blood usually comes from the fracas in which the knife was used."

"I was involved in a fight; I'm surprised you haven't heard."

"Forgive me, but I try and avoid the idle gossip of the hospital. You are lucky to be alive, in future I suggest keeping out of trouble. I will add an HIV test to the list."

Malachi ignored the disapproving tone and decided he really disliked this individual, "So what is the problem?"

"We will know what is going on in a few hours, until then just rest up and I will pop back at some point," said the doctor, walking away.

"Doctor!" Malachi shouted, "What. Is. The. Problem?"

Unused to being challenged, the man stood for a few seconds to cool his own temper before turning, "Your wounds have all the hallmarks of a stabbing," he explained.

"And…?"

"Well," the doctor cleared his throat, "I would only expect to see the level of healing you are showing after at least a month or more. Your records state three days, so something has gone awry. Don't worry, we will get to the bottom of it."

Shocked into silence, Malachi could only watch as the doctor gave instructions to the nurses who left to retrieve blood vials. Sterile tape was curled at the edges and no longer held the bandage to his skin. Curiosity got the better of him and he carefully pulled the padding away to reveal the wound. Stains of yellow and red marked the underside of the dressing, but the laceration itself was mostly just scar tissue with no scab. Picking at the stitches, they flaked away leaving a row of neat holes on his skin.

"What the fuck?" Malachi whispered to himself.

"You've seen then?" Shannon asked, startling him as she swept the curtains aside.

"I've seen something," he admitted, "Though I have no idea what it means. Could my records have been mixed up and I have been here longer than it states?"

"Nope," she said without preamble, "I was working the shift when they brought you in."

The small tubes filled with his blood as strange thoughts circulated in his mind. Did that red liquid contain an unseen horror? Malachi wasn't sure he wanted to know. His nose picked up her delightful fragrance once more and some of the worry vanished. He had come back from the brink, what did it matter if he was still ill? He vowed there and then to make each day count and live life to the full.

"I'm sure there is a simple explanation," Malachi said and Shannon smiled noncommittally, "Before I leave you have to tell me what you are wearing, it is gorgeous."

"Something by Dior, I will get the exact name when I get home and tell you tomorrow," she blushed.

Malachi reached out and took her hand, "Thank you for taking care of me."

"It's my job."

"I know, but you are still an angel," Malachi said sincerely.

Although not as svelte as Angela, her curves only accentuated her womanhood. Her sweet face would never grace the cover of any magazine, but Malachi was attracted to her regardless. She had an aura of purity and love, as if she was predestined to help people at their most vulnerable. Noticing the absence of a wedding or engagement band, he pitied a world where a genuinely good person was possibly alone.

Sure there must be a boyfriend, Malachi said, "I would love to take you and your significant other out for a meal once I get back on my feet."

The familiar shadow of loneliness passed over her, "I don't have anyone at home. Except Oliver, my cat. He keeps me company."

"I'm sorry," Malachi squeezed her hand in support, "How about I treat you to one of Desmond's famous private parties at his bar. You can bring all your friends and I shall bring mine." The list was quite small when he thought about it. Tiny in fact.

"That sounds wonderful. I'll get these to the lab and you will have the results soon."

"Thank you," Malachi said and she excused herself.

Desmond and Kevin were engaged in a hushed conversation just outside the ward. Were they talking about him to the doctor?

Before he could even tidy himself up, Kevin appeared and shouted, "See you in a bit." Then beat a hasty retreat as Angela stormed over to tell him off.

Desmond tapped his watch to say much the same thing and gave a quick hug to someone. There was no mistaking her red hair as he said his farewell and Chloe breezed into the ward. Malachi wouldn't have been surprised to hear a choir singing and doves fluttering in the background, she was that beautiful. Wearing a pair of snug white leggings and a long dress jacket, the sight took his breath away. Her hair was pulled back into a tight bun, which gave a full view of her perfectly proportioned face. The pain of the stabbing alone was worthy of the shy smile she granted him.

"Hi," she said awkwardly, unsure of what to say next.

"I might have HIV," Malachi blurted, mouth engaging before his brain.

"Oh my," Chloe replied, taking a step backwards.

CHAPTER TEN

"Maybe I should leave?" Chloe asked.

Malachi struggled to get out of bed, "No, please don't. It came out all wrong."

"Are you sure?" She didn't seem convinced.

Slumping back in defeat, he tried to smile. The miraculous healing hadn't been accompanied by boundless energy. "I was just a bit shocked to see you, that's all. Please stay."

"So do you really have HIV?" Chloe inquired.

"No, well at least the doctors don't think so. It's normal to test for it after being attacked like I was," he explained and she sighed with relief.

"Then you won't mind if I do this," she said and approached the bed. Leaning in, her lips found his until he pushed her away.

"I haven't cleaned my teeth in days," Malachi protested weakly.

"I don't care." Her soft, cherry flavoured lips caressed his own. Tasting each other, their tongues teased with promise and Malachi had to adjust position to hide his growing erection. Breaking away, she smiled knowingly at his awkward angle.

"That was amazing," he gasped, "But shouldn't you be a little traumatised after what happened?"

"I was in shock for a while," she admitted, "Then I sat with you and held your hand. All my fear washed away."

"I'm sorry for what they did to you," Malachi said, a lump forming in his throat.

"Don't you see?" Chloe stroked his cheek, "They didn't have an opportunity to do anything to me. You saved me."

"I never should have acted that way in the bar, then you wouldn't have even run into them," Malachi felt disgusted with himself.

"Kevin and Desmond have explained that you are a bit shy. I came onto you like a horny teenager, so it's no wonder you tried to let me down gently."

"I hope you don't think it was because I didn't find you attractive. You are absolutely stunning," Malachi proclaimed and she blushed at the compliment.

"Hardly," Chloe looked away, "My skin is too pale and my hair gets so frizzy. Plus, my bum is too big and my tits are too small."

"Modest too," he laughed.

"More like honest." She pushed him playfully.

"Anyone that can make my heart skip a beat and take my breath away is stunning, trust me."

"I really make you feel like that?" she asked, wrinkling her nose.

Malachi nodded, "From the second you walked into the bar."

"Wow!" She held a hand to her chest.

"Didn't you feel anything?" Malachi asked with trepidation. His own feelings were growing beyond all reason for such a short time together.

"Are you kidding me?" she giggled, "I couldn't keep my eyes off you. Then that arsehole tried it on and you came to my rescue."

"I wonder if I had handled it differently, maybe there would have been no need for all this?"

"Would we have even met if I hadn't been abused? I had decided on having one drink and then leaving, so perhaps it was fate?"

Malachi thought about that for a moment. Was someone, somewhere, just moving pieces around a board for their own amusement. Of all the bars in the city, what were the chances Chloe and her friend would pick that exact one? Add the thugs and their unwanted advances which Malachi felt duty bound to intervene in, and it left many unanswered questions.

"When you put it that way, I'm glad I was stabbed," Malachi grinned.

"Don't say that!" Chloe was mortified, "I could have lost you before I had a chance to properly repay you."

"You don't owe me anything, I was just doing what any man would do."

"Now who's being modest? You're my guardian angel," she declared and kissed him again.

Each touch set his nerves tingling with desire and separation drew a twinge of disappointment. His penis throbbed and he had to ruffle the covers to conceal his embarrassment. She wasn't blind and smiled with mischief at his writhing attempt to hide the bulge. Christ, it was like being a pubescent teenager again.

"I'm sorry."

"We need to stop saying sorry," she stroked the hair from his forehead, "It just proves how attractive you find me."

"Or it's the morphine?" he offered.

She raised an eyebrow questioningly, challenging him to repeat the words.

"Ok, it's you. I don't know what has gotten into me, the last thing you need to see after being attacked is my little fella bobbing around all merry."

"He's not that little," she observed with a wry smile.

"Don't encourage him!" Malachi laughed, "Let's talk about something else. I just realised I don't even know who you are, apart from a gorgeous redhead called Chloe."

Sitting down, crossing her legs she pretended to straighten an imaginary skirt to look prim and proper, "Ask away, what do you want to know?"

"Everything," Malachi answered, "What do you like to eat, to drink? Favourite colour? What do you do for a living? What are you parents' names? Favourite music?"

"You really did mean everything. Ok, from the top. My favourite food is Chinese, specifically noodles and Szechuan chicken. Favourite drink is anything with alcohol in it." Chloe looked horrified, "Oh goodness, please don't think I am a lush."

"Don't panic, we all enjoy a tipple," Malachi assured her.

"My favourite colour is purple and I work as an administrator for a small accountancy firm. It's not too glamourous but I am working to achieve my degree in economics through the Open University."

Malachi looked confused. He hadn't heard of it, "Where is the campus? Is it local?"

"No, it's online, silly. I wouldn't stand a chance of paying my bills if I needed to attend a real university. My parents' names are Valerie and Gordon; they are both accountants too."

"Why don't you work for them?" Malachi asked.

"I wanted to make my own way in the world. Does that make sense?" Chloe said, frowning.

"Of course. I guess it wouldn't feel as well earned if your folks had a hand in it."

"Exactly!" She beamed. Others had asked the same question and thought she was crazy. She could've been earning two or three times what she did as an admin assistant.

"Will you ever go and work with them?"

"Once I have made a career of it dad said that I could join them. They would both like me to start tomorrow but they respect my wishes," she explained.

"They sound great." Malachi felt a pang of jealousy.

"They are," she continued, "As for music I have to admit that I am a pop princess. I love anything cheesy from the charts that I can get on the dance floor and just let go to. Please don't hold that against me."

Pulling a stern glare, Malachi looked at her for a few moments and then burst out laughing, "I like pretty much all types of music. I have no problem with a bit of cheese."

"Now how about you?" Chloe sat forward with interest.

"There's not much to tell really," Malachi said.

"Don't be bashful, someone who puts themselves in danger to help others must have led quite a colourful life."

"Not really," Malachi shrugged, "I try and keep myself to myself."

"You could have fooled me," she teased, "Ok, answer the questions you asked me."

She waited patiently, the first woman to actually be interested in his existence apart from his mother and Miss Cortez. Seeing that she was getting worried, he began, "Favourite food is Jamaican. I have Des to thank for that, the spices and flavours are out of this world. Drink would have to be plain old, no frills beer."

"Didn't I see you nursing a cocktail when you were sat at the table?" she mocked light heartedly.

"Hey, even a man can be tempted by something sweet now and again."

"And do I tempt you?" Chloe purred.

"More than you will ever know," Malachi admitted.

"I interrupted you, sorry. Please continue."

"My favourite colour is turquoise," he said and she snickered. "A man can like turquoise!" he protested.

"Not black, or red, or blue. No favourite football team colour?" she giggled at his bluster.

"What can I say? I am in touch with my feminine side."

"That is very noble." Her laughter was increasing in volume and she had to stifle it behind a fist.

"Thank you," Malachi made an attempt to bow from his position, "I work as a personal trainer and nutritionist at Jim's Gym."

"The one with the bendy weightlifting bar on the sign!"

"That's it. It's just around the corner from Desmond's place. The pay is awful which is a shame as I love the work."

"It shows," Chloe whispered quietly, admiring the ripple of his muscles.

"Erm, excuse me. I remember telling you before my eyes are up here," Malachi joked.

"You did, didn't you?" She slapped him playfully again, then let her fingers linger, "I can't help it if you are pleasing to the eye."

"I will have to start stuffing my face with burgers and pizza."

"Don't you dare!" Chloe looked horrified. "Oh God, that sounded really controlling. You can eat whatever you want, it's none of my business."

"I was only joking. I know how much crap is in that processed stuff. I prefer to cook from scratch without chemical additives." Malachi rubbed the top of her hand.

"Amazing body and you can cook too. Marry me?" She nudged him, only half joking.

Ignoring the proposal, Malachi coughed and tried to change the subject, "If I were forced to listen to any type of music, I think it would have to be trance. I just love the laid back beats and vocals; they seem to calm me."

"Do you need calming then?"

"I do at the moment, yes," Malachi said honestly. If his erection didn't go away the next visit by a nurse or doctor was going to be an awkward examination.

"You missed one of the questions," Chloe told him. It was the most difficult question of all.

"My parents died in an accident many years ago. I was raised in orphanages, which is why I suppose I keep to myself mostly," Malachi said, a tear running down his cheek. The recent near death experience had brought all the old feelings back, just when he was finally starting to come to terms with being alone.

"I'm so sorry." Chloe wrapped her arms around him and held him tight. It was a gesture of love with no sexual motives and the painful memories combined to quell his rampant urges.

"Thank you," Malachi said and she stayed perched on the bed.

"You don't mind, do you?" she asked, meaning her position.

"No of course not," he replied. In truth, a few moments earlier she would have felt an incessant prodding, but thankfully he had reined in the lust.

"I won't ask you about them again, ok?" she said, rubbing his chest, "You can talk to me when you feel ready."

"Don't take it personally, I haven't even really spoken to Kevin about them and I've known him for over ten years."

"I can't imagine how hard it must have been. Maybe I take some of the pain away though?" she said hopefully.

Malachi was falling for the girl and the thought of being a part of her life did provide a respite from the pain. She reminded him of his mother; quick to smile and laugh, with a heart as deep as an ocean should any man be lucky enough to claim it. As Malachi lay there gently rubbing her leg, she seemed to give off an inexplicable energy. His fingers tingled with a sensation similar to static electricity, only milder and more soothing. Removing his fingertips broke the contact but he could feel it radiating from her. Was it an aura? Or were the drugs creating phantom responses to his growing affections.

"I could stare at you all day," Chloe whispered, stroking his face.

"But how would I be able to marry a hotshot accountant and live a life of luxury if you don't keep up the studies?"

Making a mock shocked face, she asked, "You're not marrying me just for my money are you?"

"Of course not," Malachi declared, aghast at the accusation against his character, "I'm marrying you for your parent's money too."

"You're awful!" she giggled.

Keeping a straight face, Malachi said, "I'm serious. As soon as I put a ring on your finger I expect to be taken care of. I don't want to work in a gym for the rest of my life."

"Really?" A flicker of doubt entered her voice until Malachi couldn't hold it back and burst out laughing. "You really had me going! Don't do that!"

"I couldn't resist," he took her hand, "But no, I don't want you for your money. I wouldn't care if you were penniless. More to the point, what on earth do you see in me? I earn minimum wage and smell of sweat most of the time."

"Other than the fact you probably saved my life you mean?"

"If Keanu Reeves taught me anything in Speed, relationships based upon extreme circumstances never work out," Malachi said, equal parts joking and serious. It was in the back of his mind that she could be attributing strong feelings to him because of the trauma, but only time would tell.

"Then we have to base it on sex," she fired back in her best Sandra Bullock voice. It was terrible, but the kiss that followed made up for the butchery of the American accent.

The mention of sexual liaisons to come filled him with fresh concerns and Chloe sensed the tension. As she drew back Malachi clutched at his abdomen and winced in pain, a subterfuge to prevent more embarrassing lines of questioning.

"Did I hurt you?" Chloe gasped.

"No, I think the morphine may be wearing off," he replied and felt foolish when she looked at the half full drip bag.

The innocent deception had worked and Chloe poked at the tube. Lacking any understanding of medical treatment, she said, "Let me go and get the nurse, I'll be right back."

"No, please stay," Malachi was keenly aware of the clock ticking down to eight PM. Every moment was valuable and he would be heartsick when she finally left for the evening.

"Well I do charge by the hour, are you sure you can afford me?"

"Hang on, I thought you said you worked in admin?" Malachi nearly choked with laughter as her expression changed to horror.

"Oh my God I sounded like a prostitute!"

"I'd pay you," Malachi grinned.

Playing along, she stood up and opened her jacket, then put on the voice of a Victorian streetwalker, "Do you like what you see guv'nor?"

"You would make a sexy lady of the night," Malachi whistled his approval, then clicked his fingers as he was struck by an epiphany.

"What is it?"

"I don't want you to think I am going insane, but have you got your phone on you? Have you got internet?" Malachi asked breathlessly. The next few seconds, despite his caution to Chloe, could truly mark him as a fruitloop and he had second thoughts.

"It's right here," she said, taking it from a pocket, "Do you want my number?"

113

"No," Malachi said and inwardly berated himself as her face dropped in disappointment, "I mean of course I want your number, but there is something I would like first."

"Ok…" Chloe looked unsure.

"Can you do a search for a cruise liner. It would have been in the nineteen fifties and called the SS Freedom."

Without judging the strange request, she opened the browser and the familiar tippity tap of the keypad rang out. Malachi's stomach was clenching with apprehension as her face studied the results without revealing any success. Just when he was about to slump back and accept the inevitable descent into psychosis, Chloe jumped in her seat.

"Got it!" she came to the bed excitedly and pointed, "There. It was a luxury cruise liner that served the best and brightest of high society. Only the richest could afford the prestigious journey."

The story bore a photograph of the newspaper headline at the time, yellowed from its time in storage. The date read 9th April, 1951 and the headline read 'Another Titanic? Disappearance of popular cruise ship leaves families distraught'. Malachi couldn't breathe properly and with each brush of his fingers, the accompanying picture was brought into closer focus. Taken from the dock, it was a landscape image of the port side of the vessel. Immaculately dressed people lined the railing, smiling proudly. Nearly every face staring out were those he recognised from the nightmare. Whether it was just his perception or the knowledge of what these evil murderers had done, their eyes looked devoid of life. Except for the wrinkles of the older crew, the tell-tale laughter lines of genuine humour were absent. Their lips smiled but their eyes glared. It was like looking at a row of well-dressed sharks who had learned to mimic human expressions.

"Why the interest?" Chloe asked, frowning. She hadn't missed how his breathing had become little more than shallow gasps as the rest of the story was read.

"Erm," Malachi had to think quickly under the scrutiny of the psychotic captain on the screen, "I just remembered it from a television program I watched and didn't know if the name was correct."

"It has you really rattled, are you sure that's all it is?"

"I had a bad dream about it while I was…" he couldn't exactly say asleep, "Unconscious. It brought the memories back."

It was the truth. Almost.

"Oh, baby," she rubbed his arm, "I assumed if you were sedated you wouldn't be able to dream."

"I wish."

Malachi had to force his eyes away from the hypnotic gaze of the dead captain. What the hell? Looking back, he could have sworn he saw the man sneer but it must have been a trick of his mind. The story begun by honouring a list of important military retirees that had been lost with the ship. Speculation was rife about what had transpired on the doomed voyage. Engine failure, a navigational error, even a hijacking at sea were mentioned. No wreckage was ever found by the search craft which had been dispatched. They couldn't have known of the deviation in course which had been made from the original passage plan and their search grid was off by two hundred miles. The rest of the article comprised mechanical information and the capacity of the lifeboats, none of which were ever recovered. Nothing came close to the true horror of what had taken the nine hundred and sixty-two souls on that fateful day.

"Malachi are you ok? You look like you've seen a ghost."

Chloe was oblivious to how close she was to the truth.

"It's nothing. I was just thinking about all those poor people."

"I know. It must have been terrifying," she whispered.

Shannon returned and said quietly, "Visiting time is up. I'll give you a couple more minutes, though."

"Thank you," Malachi smiled warmly.

"Anything for my favourite patient," she winked and left them alone.

"I think she has a crush on you," Chloe teased.

"Well I am a fine specimen." Malachi flexed his biceps and Chloe squeezed them appreciatively.

"You're *my* fine specimen. At least I'd like you to be?" she asked.

"I don't know," Malachi shook his head, "I think I need to keep my options open. Today I have struck lucky with an accountant and a nurse, tomorrow I could meet a princess and marry into the royal family."

"Knowing your luck you would kiss her and she would turn into a frog," Chloe laughed.

"I thought that was a prince?"

"Who cares, just kiss me," she leaned in closer, "I won't ever turn into anything. Except maybe a naturist."

The kiss contained a yearning for more and by the time their lips parted both were breathing heavily. Neither wanted the night to come to an end but it was unfair on the other patients who needed peace to heal. Fluttering a hand by her face, Chloe tried to calm down.

"Before you go I have a gift," Malachi said, leaning over to the massive floral arrangement to pull a single red rose out.

"Aww," she held it close, "I love it. No one has ever given me a rose."

"I hope you don't mind I had to steal it from Desmond. My salary barely keeps a roof over my head."

"I will cherish it forever," she said honestly and kissed him goodbye, "I'll see you straight after work tomorrow."

Watching her go was one of the hardest things Malachi had ever experienced. Turning the corner, she glanced back and blew another kiss. Irrationally he wondered if it would be the last time they would see each other. Orphaned by circumstances out of his control, he was keenly aware of how delicate life could be. Giving himself a mental shake, he dared to imagine for the first time that he may be able to share his life with someone amazing. If love was truly on the cards, he would need to seek out psychiatric help to expel the inner demons.

"You aren't really meant to have anything solid yet, but I can get you some yoghurt?" Shannon offered.

"That would be great, thanks."

"Be back in a jiffy," she hurried off to collect the treat.

CHAPTER ELEVEN

As the spoon scraped the last morsels of strawberry yoghurt from the plastic bowl, Malachi found himself wondering about the dream of the boat. His lie to Chloe about remembering the story from a television program had a ring of plausibility about it. Had he seen a Discovery Channel documentary in the past when it had been mentioned? Remembering a show about a salvage mission via remote submarine to the Titanic caused him to frown in concentration.

"Were other missing boats mentioned?" he asked himself.

Nothing immediately sprung to mind which left only bizarre theories of why he had dreamed of the deaths, real or imagined. The ocean held no real attraction to Malachi, he had surfed a few times but never felt the siren song of the high seas. Even if he had received a vision of their grisly end, it didn't explain the hundreds of other nightmares he had suffered with human looking people in alien lands. His mind swirled with contradictions until he gave up trying to piece it together. Exhaustion was asserting itself again and as his eyelids became heavier, the mental picture of Chloe beckoned him to follow.

The growing vibration in the concrete floor caused murmurs of disturbance around the pitch black room. Someone shouted angrily from one corner about the coming aliens, before falling back into their vivid dreams of invasion. Cardboard rustled as people adjusted position, and Taren reached down to reassure herself that Zulma was still there. Fingers found the warm skin of her shoulder and an invisible hand reached out in response, stroking her.

"Go back to sleep," Zulma whispered groggily, still half asleep.

"You know I can't sleep through these things," Taren replied, moving her body closer under the blanket.

Zulma sighed and rolled back the sheet before leaning in expertly for a kiss. They were so used to darkness that, even blind, each could read the others movements without knocking heads. With a final stroke of the cheek, Taren broke the contact and sat up.

"I really need to use the toilet."

"Do you want me to come with you?" Zulma asked, rubbing her back.

"Would you mind?"

"Of course not, baby. We may lose our spot though."

"I don't mind," Taren replied, "I prefer having you watch out for me."

Faint light started to illuminate the wide tunnel, rolling back the shadows in the room. Eighteen people were crammed in the filthy space, laid under whatever could be scavenged from the overworld. The previous week, Zulma and Taren had managed to bring back a set of boxes which had been stripped down by Raiden. He had then made up small pods to provide some privacy, but they were strictly first come, first serve. Someone would take the opportunity to claim the bed space while the two women answered natures call.

"Did you want to wait until it's passed?"

"No, I like watching them. I try and imagine what it would be like if we had a life still. Our old home, food to eat," Taren said and started to weep quietly.

"At least we are safe," Zulma replied, hugging her lover close.

They had been deemed CWONS, or citizens without necessary skills, when the technological revolution had started. Teachers of infant children in their old life, they had fled underground when the government started forced

119

retraining programs. Only three professions remained; manufacturing weapons, soldier, or material reclamation; both metals and organic substances. The last role involved collecting body parts and munitions from the battlefield, usually under heavy fire. Recycling had gone beyond plastics and the scorched meat was converted into energy bars. The announcement had been met with an outpouring of horror which was swiftly silenced.

Taren shuddered at the memory, "At least we get to choose what we eat, too."

"Yeah, when we can catch a rat or two," Zulma grinned, nudging her in the emaciated ribs.

Standing in the doorway, the tunnel stretched for over one hundred feet in diameter. The labyrinthine system spanned every mile of the occupied territory and each victory required more tunnels. A slave army had been amassed during the revolution and they were worked until they dropped dead. Spaced along the tunnel itself were thick, magnetic steel plates which switched angle dependant on the direction the vessel was travelling. Surrounded by magnetic fields, terrible headaches were an everyday occurrence. Anyone with fillings had taken the opportunity to have them removed by a dentist who had been moving eastward. An end to the agony was a price worth paying for the lack of anaesthetic.

"Here it comes," Taren whispered.

"Stand back a little, I hate it when you get so close."

"Sorry," she replied, stepping back into the room.

It was always a strange sensation when the transport raced past. First the air pressure would build and make their ears pop, then it would create a vacuum which could suck a person straight into the tunnel. It had happened to a young man several weeks ago and the force had thrown him clear across the chamber. With leg broken and the bone piercing the skin, there was nothing they could do and he died from infection within a week. His body had been carried half a mile away, but Taren was sure she could smell the decay at times, wafting to them on the changing air currents. At least the poor man had ensured the longevity of his old friends by being a convenient food source for the rats.

"The aliens are trying to suck our brains out!" screamed the disturbed man, punching himself in the head. They had long ago stopped expecting him to understand that it was a mixture of headache and pressure.

"Go back to sleep, it will be gone in a few second," shouted Zulma loudly enough to be heard over the growing roar, with no better result than the previous hundred times.

Writhing on the floor, the hysterical man tore at his face, drawing blood from recently scabbed wounds. The light intensified and the bullet shaped craft raced past, comprising over twenty sections of dull grey metal.

"That was big," said Taren sadly, "They must be really pushing on the northern front now."

"With any luck they will all kill each other and we can try and rebuild the world without all the hatred," replied Zulma through gritted teeth.

As the gale diminished the two women hurried out into the tunnel to make use of the dying light. Their toilet comprised a small chute which carried the constantly flowing water which penetrated the thick walls. It tasted bitter which they all said was due to the poisonous world it came from. The truth was it was probably untold chemical pollutants, gradually destroying their vital organs. At least two of the group had started urinating blood, and those were only the ones willing to admit to the ailment. If it hadn't been partially filtered by the ground it passed through, they would likely all be dead by now.

As Taren squatted, positioning herself as best she could over the hole, she asked, "Do you ever regret running away?"

"Never," Zulma smiled warmly, kissing her on the hand, "They would have separated us for one."

"I couldn't stand being away from you," Taren replied, fresh tears threatening to flow.

"Hey, I won't ever let that happen, I promise."

Taren finished and used some of the cleaner water to wash herself. It was a choice between a mild skin rash or being totally unhygienic and she just wouldn't allow herself to become one of the 'stenchers'. A name unkindly given to those travelling the tunnels on foot who hadn't washed for months.

"Let's get back, we have a busy day tomorrow going topside. It would be great if we could find some discarded food in one of the bins," Zulma said, pulling Taren to her feet.

In years past she would have ignored people begging for change to buy food and even mock those who rifled through other people's waste. Now the thought made her mouth water and stomach grumble in anticipation. She shook her head, feeling guilty for how she had judged the unfortunate homeless.

"What's up?"

"Oh, nothing," Taren sighed, "I was just thinking about how far we have fallen. We are reduced to living in squalor without light and eating rotten food or rats."

"It will get better, it has to," declared Zulma hopefully. The signs weren't promising and the war machines that vied for control showed no sign of slowing down.

They were nearly at the shelter when a fresh glow bloomed around the bend over half a mile away.

"Another transport?" Taren questioned, brow furrowed.

"Impossible, it's coming from the opposite direction."

Understanding shattered their confusion.

"It's the exterminators!" Taren shrieked until a hand silenced her fearful cry.

"Quiet," cautioned Zulma, "We need to wake the others and get out of here, quickly."

Sleep was blown off in an instant at the mention of the exterminators. The overworld rulers didn't appreciate anyone who tried to shy away from their duty and sent the most sadistic killers into the tunnel systems to hunt and butcher anyone they could find. Disbelief paralyzed some in the group as they had never come this way before. An old baseball bat was produced, but it would be useless against the weapons of their pursuers. It had only been used once before on a pair of thugs who had tried to take some of the meagre bedding.

"Which way shall we go?" Taren asked. She was terrified and rightly so, stories travelled with people who swear they were left alive to spread word of the butchery they witnessed.

"We head west, away from the bastards and then split at the intersection. From there we keep splitting into smaller groups which will make it harder for them to track us all."

Taren ran into the tunnel and skidded to a stop. There was light from the western tunnel, but could have sworn it had been coming from the east. Turning slowly, she could see light coming from both directions and the temptation to lay down and curl into a ball was overwhelming.

"Shit, we are trapped. Which way can we go?" Zulma asked, more to herself than the others.

"Nowhere," replied alien guy, lucid for the first time, "The nearest access hatch to lower tunnels is more than a mile away."

Some fell to the ground and started wailing, while others stood tall and accepted what was coming. The beams in the distance quickly found their target and started bobbing wildly as the killers started running toward their prey. As the men and women from each direction neared, they slowed their pace and aimed the composite material guns at the group. A woman stepped forward and introduced herself.

"My name is Major Davion," she smiled at the cowering people, "I head up the third quadrant tunnel intervention force."

"You mean you are a murdering bitch!" snarled one of the newer members. Weakened by starvation, his bravery disappeared and he looked at the floor, waiting for the shot that would end his life.

"You really shouldn't listen to the ramblings of crazy people," she continued affably, "We don't do anything like that. We are merely here to take you topside and put you to better use."

"And if we don't want to go topside?" Zulma said, glaring at Davion.

"Then I guess you escape from the training schools and we have to come and find you again," she laughed, "You would be keeping me in a job, so I should be thanking you."

"What if we tried to escape right now?" she pressed, defiance in her eyes.

"Oh, you would be shot," explained Davion, "Come on, you can't blame us. We have targets to meet."

"Rounding up starving men, women, and children. You can go and fuck your targets!" Zulma hissed and spat on the Major's pristine uniform.

Taren cowered even more, whimpering in fear for her lover's life. A flash of hatred passed over the woman's features, but was quickly replaced by the disarming smile.

"There is really no need for that," she chastised, before reaching for her radio and pressing the transmit button, "Send the prisoner transport."

"We will never be a part of your evil regime."

Grinning at Zulma, she replied, "I think you will find you will be helping more than you ever thought possible."

"We will see," muttered Zulma.

The team faced them all against the rough wall and patted them down, reaching into their loose clothes for a grope. Their intimate delving wasn't challenged by their superior who watched with amusement. After the bat was taken, they were all handcuffed and had their feet bound with velcro straps. The familiar vibration started again and soon a single section craft rounded the corner, though at a much lower speed than the military transport. As it approached, the magnetic plates adjusted to pin it in place and the squat, ugly craft hovered two feet from the floor.

"All aboard!" cried the major and her team burst into hysterics, far in excess of what the quip deserved. They knew how important it was to massage her ego.

With a hiss, a seal released and a door slid into the main body of the vessel. Inside were more uniformed soldiers and they lowered a set of steps for the prisoners. One by one the ankle restraints were removed and the man or woman reluctantly climbed aboard. Everyone in the group had been astonished by the sudden silence of the alien guy but as soon as he was hefted to his feet all hell broke loose. Lunging forward, he bit deeply into the face of his guard. Worrying the nose like a dog, he ripped it free and the man screamed in pain. Laughing like a madman, with blood oozing from his mouth, alien guy made a break for it.

"I told you that you would never get my brain!" he whooped.

"Shall we open fire?" asked one of the guards.

Before Major Davion could answer, alien guy lost his footing. The awkward gait and his handcuffed arms ended up tripping him on an overlooked bolt and he went sprawling. His head smashed into the corner of a magnetic plate without hands to break the fall and the sickening

125

crunch echoed up the tunnel. Over the short distance it was impossible to miss the spreading blood and the twitching legs.

"He's a goner," Major Davion muttered, "Go and grab his body, we can still use it."

Taren was next and Zulma thrashed against the restraining hands, "You're all monsters."

"Perhaps." Major Davion nodded, stepping to the side to avoid the body as it kicked and bucked from the catastrophic brain injury.

Taren stepped up into the waiting arms of the transport guards and their leers filled her with fear. Only the knowledge that she and Zulma would be together prevented her from fainting. Drawing strength from her girlfriend, she smiled once more and was swallowed by the massive, cylindrical machine.

"Ok, pack it up, we are out of here," Davion ordered and the remaining guards stepped into the craft.

"Wait, what about me?" Zulma cried out, struggling to stand.

Major Davion climbed aboard and pulled the steps up, before throwing a set of keys as far down the tunnel as she could.

"We don't need you," Davion explained.

"I don't understand, please let me aboard with Taren and I will do whatever shitty job you want me to do," Zulma begged.

"You silly, naive woman, she isn't going for any training. With all the conflict, food is running low so we are collecting as many as we can. By this time next week she will be nothing more than a box of energy bars for our brave soldiers."

"Please, no!" shrieked Zulma. Her heart was tearing into pieces and her limbs wouldn't obey her commands to stand up.

"An army can't march on an empty stomach," replied Major Davion.

"Then take me too, you evil whore. If I'm going to die then at least it will be with the woman I love," she glowered, hatred dulling the fear.

"I have another plan for you," Davion smirked, "You see, I know that there are hundreds, if not thousands of you down here hiding. You won't take the easy way out, you're a fighter. I can see it in your eyes. So when you find some likeminded people and decide to try and save your beloved wife, we will be waiting."

"And if I don't rise to the bait?" she tried to bluff.

"As with the rest, she will be dropped alive into the boiling machine to make the flesh easier to remove. A just end to a traitor!" Davion declared with a sneer.

"I will kill you if you harm a hair on her head!" Zulma snarled.

"I'm counting on it," clapped Davion excitedly, "Good luck and I'm sure we will be meeting again soon."

With a pneumatic hiss, the door closed and the heavy plates shifted position on the wall, pushing the craft along the tunnel. In seconds the magnetic field had propelled it out of sight around the bend. The darkness grew, leaving her totally alone except for the drying blood of alien guy and the small set of keys.

Overcome with grief, she screamed into the emptiness, "Taaaarrrrrreeeennnn!"

Malachi awoke with a strangled choke of terror. The walls seemed closer and as he finally took in his surroundings, the change of venue was apparent. He was in a private room with a single door, which was closed. The only light came from the small, square of window which was set at head height. Trying to rub his face of the cloying sweat from the nightmare, his wrist stopped dead before it got close. The thick, leather strap which held his arm firmly was repeated on each limb and he thrashed around wildly, desperate to be free of the bonds.

A face appeared at the glass and Malachi nearly passed out in relief. Shannon smiled back at him, but with a reticence that hadn't been there before. It was as if she were afraid of him.

CHAPTER TWELVE

"Please level with me, why on earth am I trussed up like a Christmas turkey?" Malachi asked as Shannon finished her checks.

She hesitated for a moment before heading towards the doorway, unwilling to engage in conversation. The dramatic change in her demeanour scared Malachi more than the restraints. Something he had done had caused her to withdraw and erect the professional barriers which all medical staff were trained in. Considering yesterday he had been her hero and she was gushing over him, the transformation in her attitude was inexplicable. All he had done was suffer from a nightmare for Christ sake!

"Shannon, I'm sorry for whatever I did to you," Malachi whispered, slumping back on the pillow in defeat.

As she prepared to close and lock the door, she hesitated again and turned.

"I have a few more checks to make, and then I will pop back, ok?"

Her face had softened a little and he could see her turmoil.

"Thank you," Malachi smiled wearily.

The door closed and the lock was engaged which told him that he was considered a danger to others as well as himself. What the hell had he done during the dream to warrant such precautions? A million possibilities poured though his mind, none of them good. Praying that he hadn't struck out and hurt someone in the throes of the horrific fantasy, he flexed his whole body one part at a time. Nothing felt bruised or sore, not even the knife wounds. Realizing the possibilities were endless and trying to narrow them down a waste of energy, he watched the door instead, willing Shannon to hurry on her rounds. Minutes stretched out and the longer he stared, the worse a growing tension headache became. When the stabbing pain became almost too much to bear, the noise of a key turning brought some relief. Shannon entered with visible reluctance and the pain was gradually replaced by gnawing fear. Judging by the apprehension on her face, wetting himself or vomiting everywhere was the least of his worries.

"I don't really know where to begin," Shannon explained, sitting as far away as possible in a corner of the room.

"Please tell me what I did for starters. The last thing I remember was eating yoghurt last night," Malachi said with exasperation. He would have thrown his arms up if they hadn't been tied to the bedframe.

"That wasn't last night," she said quietly.

"Huh?" Malachi was even more confused.

"You ate the yoghurt three nights ago," she stated and Malachi's mouth fell open, "We thought you had fallen back into a coma when you couldn't be roused."

"Three days?" Malachi repeated.

It just didn't make sense; the vision had lasted in real terms about half an hour, no more. With most studies agreeing that the average duration of a dream was in the region of an hour depending on the individual, it left over seventy hours unaccounted for.

"After the first day the doctors simply advised we let you sleep, or whatever it was you were doing," Shannon continued. Why had she placed such emphasis of the last part of the sentence?

"What I was doing?" Malachi met her gaze.

"Nothing," she begun, "At first." Her eyes gave away her fear.

"Did I wet myself again? I do that sometimes during my nightmares," Malachi admitted his embarrassing affliction, hoping to see a look of understanding on her face.

It didn't appear, but he could see she desperately wished it were that simple. "The first thing happened when you were talking in your sleep. The curtains started to flutter and we assumed a window had been left open during visiting hours. Every single one was locked up tight but the curtains still danced around on their hooks like they were being blown about."

"Could it have been the air conditioning?" Malachi offered, but she shook her head.

"ICU doesn't have air conditioning, only the windows which are meant to be kept shut at all times. The strangest thing was that there wasn't even a breeze making them move, the air was totally still," Shannon explained.

"Is that all? An unexplained moving curtain?" Malachi blurted out and immediately regretted it when he saw her face.

"That was the start of it," she replied, "The talking continued, but it was all gibberish. At least that's what it sounded like. Angela was sure you were chanting or something, it reminded her of a vacation she had taken to Tibet. The monks there have a throat chant that they use to meditate and relax. You didn't look relaxed."

"I was having a bad dream," Malachi said, unwilling to admit that it had involved sacrificing his wife and non-existent child to a creature not of this earth.

"It must have been a doozy," she sympathized and continued, "The next thing that happened wasn't during my shift so I only have hearsay to go on."

When the silence threatened to drag on, Malachi prompted her, "Go on, what happened next."

"We had a lot of electrical disturbances which our engineers couldn't figure out. We almost lost a patient when his oxygen machine was turned off and the warning buzzer didn't respond."

"Wait," Malachi cried out, "You don't think I did it, do you?"

"Of course not, you were unconscious the whole time," she replied, less than convincingly.

"Shannon, please be honest with me. Do you think I could have got out of bed and fiddled with his machine's power supply?" Malachi was dreading the possibility he could hurt people during a sleepwalking episode. It wasn't something he had done before but with the ever worsening state of his mental health, it may be a new affliction.

"No, you were totally out of it. There is no way you could have turned it off... physically."

"Why did you say it like that?" Malachi asked.

Shannon chewed on a fingernail, a habit which she had beaten over a decade ago. It gave her a few moments to gather her thoughts for what she was about to explain, "I think you could have done it with your mind, without even consciously knowing what you were doing."

"You have got to be kidding me," Malachi groaned.

"No, hear me out," she persisted, mistaking his protest, "I love watching shows about the paranormal on TV. They call it UTE, or unconscious telekinetic energy. There have been reports of people moving objects around while in a sleep state."

Her excitement had momentarily overcome her unease, but upon realizing she had pulled the chair closer, she quickly shuffled back.

"You probably think I'm nuts," Shannon laughed sardonically.

"Not at all, you mistook my meaning. Things have happened to me before and your explanation is probably the closest I have ever come to an answer that makes any sense."

"That wasn't the end of it," she said, but much quieter. Excitement at the paranormal possibilities couldn't erase the horrified accounts of Ben, her friend who worked in the mortuary.

"Go on," Malachi urged, needing to know but dreading what was to come.

"It was the third day and I was working. Just after lunchtime you started to become more agitated, hitting yourself in the face and screaming the name Taren over and over again. It became so bad we had to restrain you before you caused more damage to yourself and move you away from the other patients," she explained.

"But my face feels fine?" Malachi said, scrunching his nose, moving his eyebrows and stretching his jaw.

"You looked a lot worse yesterday," she replied, "You had bruising around your eye and a small split to your lip."

Feeling with his tongue, the skin felt unbroken. The healing he had experienced in the dream! Was he able to use the power of his mind to regenerate his own tissue? This was fast becoming even more surreal and it raised even more questions.

"And me beating myself up is what has you so afraid?"

"No," Shannon answered and shook visibly, "It was what happened downstairs that has me freaked. Not that Ben has told anyone else, he knew they would think he was crazy and fire him."

"Who's Ben?" Malachi asked, becoming frustrated by the ambiguous answers.

"He is my friend and he works as a porter for the hospital. One of his duties is he transports the bodies of anyone who passes away in the hospital or is brought in after an accident and didn't make it."

Malachi waited for her to continue even though he was screaming inside.

"During the worst of your... seizure, he was moving a lady into the freezer."

Shannon was tempted to change the subject and make up something else that wasn't so otherworldly, but she had come to like Malachi a great deal.

"And?" Malachi was on tenterhooks.

She opted for the whole truth as Ben had recounted it, "The woman sat up on the pull out shelf and reached for him."

Malachi could barely draw breath, but managed to ask, "Could it have been a nerve thing? Or maybe they had made a mistake in declaring her dead."

Shannon merely shook her head, "She died during surgery. She had been involved in a car crash and was in a bad way, there was little the surgeons could do with all the internal bleeding. Besides, she wasn't the only one to… animate."

"What do you mean?" Malachi was beginning to think he was still in a dream within a dream. None of this could possibly happen in the real world.

"Well the other compartments had deceased people in them too, and Ben said it sounded like they were all trying to hammer their way out," Shannon had gone as white as a ghost, an apt phrase with all the paranormal explanations.

"Are you serious?" Malachi asked with a grin, "I bet Kevin and Des put you up to this."

Her face remained unchanged; nobody was that good an actor, "I wish they had."

"So you're saying I summoned fucking zombies?" Malachi laughed derisively.

"No, not zombies. Ben said the woman looked frightened and reached for him for support. After about five seconds the… how can I say it, life went out of her and the other drawers fell silent too."

"This is a nightmare, it has to be," Malachi said and pinched his side. Pain, but no awakening. Shit!

Shannon ignored the comment, "After a couple of minutes Ben gathered his wits and placed her back into the drawer. He told me how he watched her face to see if there was any more activity, but she was at peace again."

"So you are saying I brought the dead back to life?"

"Not necessarily," Shannon replied earnestly, "What is the human body but a biological machine? Maybe your telekinesis can affect the motor within a person who has passed away?"

Malachi wasn't buying it, "But didn't you say she looked scared? Can my power create emotions too?"

"Probably not," she admitted, "And when he went and checked the other bodies, their faces all looked terrified. Ben explained their fingernails were torn off as if they had been trying to claw their way out of confinement."

"I'm a fucking monster," Malachi whispered to himself.

Shannon ignored her own instincts and went to him, taking his hand in hers and gently stroking it, "Not at all, I think you are just gifted."

"All of this is just speculation anyway," Malachi said defensively, "There could be any one of a number of explanations for the things that happened."

Shannon smiled warmly, "Absolutely."

"But you don't think so?" he asked.

She shook her head, "The timings were all around your most violent outbursts."

"Have you told anyone else about this?"

"We have all taken a vow of silence," Shannon giggled, turning an invisible lock by her lips, "You have earned yourself some major brownie points with the staff here and can trust us."

"You're an amazing person," Malachi sighed in gratitude, turning his hand and interlocking his fingers with her own.

"I try my best," she blushed, "Oh, I almost forgot!"

"Not more stuff?" he groaned.

"No, good this time," she beamed, "Your blood tests all came back clear."

For the first time since waking he was a little more at ease, some good news was just the treatment he needed.

"No HIV either?" he asked hopefully.

"Sorry," her face dropped a little, "We have to wait a few more weeks for the results to come back. They need to see if your body creates an antibody response."

"Oh," Malachi replied.

"If it helps, the doctors don't think it is likely based upon the story you told. The chances of blood mixing between a broken nose and a stab wound with how quickly the fight ended is practically zero."

"That's something I suppose," Malachi said without enthusiasm.

Shannon glanced at her watch and put the chair back into position, "I have to go now, but I will come and check on you in a while. Your chart has been updated to sedate if you exhibit any more violent spasms, so at least you can rest peacefully. After the 'morgue incident' you were given lorazepam and it calmed you immediately."

"Thank you, sweetheart. I don't know what I would have done if you weren't working today," Malachi said gratefully.

"Probably just lay there tied up," she fired back with a grin.

Malachi burst out laughing, "You're so mean, but right."

"I'm bad to the bone, baby. I'll be back in a while; the doctor will be along shortly to sign off on removing the restraints. As it wasn't a conscious assault he will more than likely take them off and monitor you more closely this evening."

"One second!" Malachi called out, "Am I in a psych ward?"

Shannon leaned back through the door, "No silly, you have just been moved to a private room down the hallway so you can't disturb our more well behaved guests." She winked and was gone.

Alone once more, Malachi's mind began to wander. The first image that popped into his head was Carrie, covered in blood and massacring everyone trapped within the school building. Could he really be capable of doing something similar? The world was full of assholes, but it didn't necessitate roasting them in an inferno of revenge. His life hadn't been marred by a psychotic religious parent either so it was unlikely he would herald a worldwide douche barbecue.

"X-men," he whispered with excitement.

If he was a good guy, then naturally he would be more suited to the team under Professor Xavier. He already had the body for spandex, he just needed a superhero name...

"The Human Pincushion."

Accurate, but lacking that certain pizazz.

"Captain Normal."

He didn't feel like someone with powers. Nothing had ever manifest while he was awake to make him feel anything but unremarkable.

"The Dream Lord," he whispered. It sounded badass, except he wasn't the lord of his dreams. A real lord wouldn't wake up crying and wetting themselves from pretend nightmares.

"Sleep Freak."

That fit far better and the momentary excitement had worn off. He slumped back down and looked around the small room. A small television was mounted on a retractable bracket on the clean, white walls, ready to provide entertainment but at present dark and watchful. The windows looked out on an adjacent hospital building, though from his angle he couldn't make out what purpose it served. Heads bobbed to and fro on some unseen errands and Malachi wished he could move around freely. Where the hell was the doctor?

"I wonder," Malachi pondered, looking at the power button on the TV.

If he could perform telekinesis, then the simple act of pressing a button should be child's play. Staring intently at the small, black knob, he projected a force towards it and concentrated. Seconds passed and the tension headache started to return with a vengeance. You can do it! He thought to himself. If you can resurrect the dead, you should be more than capable of pushing a small spring loaded mechanism.

"Shit," he muttered and gave up. So much for being a mighty superhero.

Tilting his head back he could see the casing which housed the oxygen, medical air, electricity, and emergency button. It seemed a bit dangerous to have the button out of reach and Malachi would be having stern words with Nurse Shannon upon her return. What if he had needed to scratch his nose?

"You had to think it, didn't you?" Malachi asked himself as the tip of his nose started to tingle.

Within seconds it was intolerable, the proverbial itch that can't be scratched. He tried reaching his shoulder but the restraints held them just far enough away to make it torturous. Twisting in the bed, he tried to ruffle the pillow with his head and rub the nose into the fabric. The cheap sponge filling would not be moulded into anything which would help and he slammed his head back into the pillow in frustration.

"I'm not interrupting anything, am I?" asked the mortician looking doctor. The lanyard was visible this time and the name Dr. Franken was printed alongside a smiling picture of the physician. The name and grimacing attempt at a smile only added to his dislike of the man.

Malachi's mood soured instantly and the sensation on his nose was forgotten, "Not at all, I just had an itch on my nose that I couldn't reach. Plus, I couldn't reach the emergency button."

The gaunt doctor ignored the jibe and reached down between the mattress and the bedframe, withdrawing a button attached to a wire. The wire curled and led to a port within the electronics on the wall.

"You mean this button?" chuckled the doctor, placing it in his hand like a child.

Malachi felt like a moron and was going to fire back, but decided to play it calmly to ensure the restraints were removed, "Sorry, Doc, I didn't look around properly."

"That's quite alright," he replied and proceeded to explain about the variety of tests that the laboratory had carried out on his blood.

"So I am fit and well?" Malachi was placated by some of the good news.

"I'm afraid I cannot confirm the HIV results until the second round of tests in three months. But if I was a betting man, I would hazard a guess that we will find nothing untoward."

"That's a relief," Malachi said. It wasn't that he didn't trust Shannon's judgement, it was just better hearing the prognosis from someone more senior. Feeling guilty at the thought, he vowed to make it up to her later.

"Now we come onto the more serious matter," Dr. Franken said.

"You've heard about the last three days then?" Malachi asked, feeling betrayed by Shannon.

"What? No. I have been away at a conference. All I can see are some night terrors necessitating isolation," he shook his head after looking at the chart, "I was talking about the wounds you suffered and their inexplicable timeline."

Malachi felt even worse. Something about the drugs and the surroundings was throwing him off and now he really needed to make it up to the loving nurse.

"So there is something wrong with me?"

"Quite the opposite actually," smiled the doctor, and the gesture was warmer than before, "The dates were accurate, which means that your rate of tissue regeneration is quite remarkable."

The usually morose doctor was bubbling with excitement and it transformed him. Maybe Malachi had been too quick to judge.

"Is there a name for what I have?"

"No, I'm afraid not. There have only ever been two cases which even come close. One was in what is now North Korea. In the late nineteenth century a farm boy of eleven years old was rumoured to have suffered a shattered leg when his beast of burden was startled by something. An injury that grievous, at that point in time, would have often meant amputation or death, especially with the added internal trauma of bone fragments." The doctor was nearly clapping with joy as he recounted the tale until he saw Malachi's frown.

"Sorry, please bear with me. The records are sketchy at best and will undoubtedly have been embellished over time. It would appear that after only a week, the limb that had been little more than jellied meat, was strong enough to bear weight. A further week and he was back out ploughing the fields as if nothing had happened."

"And there is no way the story could have been made up?" Malachi asked and the doctor paused.

"Well, of course. But the second occurrence was more recent and documented fully as well as being corroborated with pictures. It's amazing what you can find on the internet," Dr. Franken beamed.

"You can't always believe what you read on the web," Malachi cautioned.

"Indeed," he agreed, "Which is why I managed to track down the doctor who had carried out the treatment of the man. He is very old now, but never forgot that particular patient."

"Where was it?"

"New York, USA. It was September, 1965 and his name was Clarence Voight. He and his family were asleep when it is alleged a group of Mafioso took his wife and daughters, before torching their house. Revenge for a botched business deal or so they say. Mr. Voight suffered third degree burns to over seventy percent of his body."

"Third degree is the worst, right?" Malachi asked, trying to remember the hospital programs he had watched.

"Yes, it is very deep and with that amount of damage, normally fatal. The doctor said it was a miracle he survived the first night, but they put it down to a fighting spirit and his desire to see his wife and children again."

"And did he?"

"Did he what, survive?" Dr. Franken looked confused, "Of course, hence me telling the tale here today."

"I meant did he ever get to see his family again?"

"Oh, I see. No, they were never found, but I'm getting off track. You have to understand that for this type of injury, it is usually measured in months or years of treatment and painful skin grafts. After only three days, the burnt flesh had started to peel, revealing healthy tissue beneath."

"Wow." Malachi was intrigued.

"My thoughts exactly," grinned the doctor, "Now comes the strangest part. After a week, Clarence just ups and disappears from the ward and was never seen again. The investigation by the police department revealed some accelerant in the home which was not typical of previous Mafia arson cases. They would strive to make examples of people and a genuine victim would never be able to escape. Some officers even harboured the notion that he had self-immolated with guilt and was the cause of the three missing persons. The case was never closed."

Malachi couldn't reply and just laid there in shock.

"Well I think I have seen enough to judge you are not a danger," said the doctor cheerfully, undoing each bond.

Malachi groaned with pleasure as he sat up and stretched the knotted limbs, "Thanks, Doc."

"I have booked a visit with Dr. Llyod later today. He is our resident psychologist and can start to get to the root of the night terrors you have been experiencing."

"I'll be fine," Malachi started to argue until a glance from the doctor stilled the protest.

"Nonsense, in this day and age there is no reason a hero should suffer from such ailments. In a lot of cases, simply talking through past traumas can uncover a root cause which can then be dealt with," he explained.

"You called me hero," Malachi pointed out.

"Yes, well I did say I ignore idle gossip. I didn't, however, say I ignore the evening news. My apologies for being so gruff with you when we first met, it was wrong of me," said the doctor sincerely, offering a hand.

Expecting it to be freezing cold, Malachi was taken aback by the warmth and strength in the firm grip, "Not at all. Thanks for all you have done for me."

"My pleasure." He went to leave, then abruptly turned, "I almost forgot to mention, I would like to see you on a non-clinical basis after you have been discharged. I think if we can try and find the source of your exceptional gift, we could advance modern medicine by a century at least. I have also called in a few colleagues who would love to see your progress as well, would you mind?"

"I'm sure I can manage that," Malachi agreed.

"Tremendous!"

As the doctor nearly skipped out of the room with childish exuberance, Malachi allowed himself a moment to process the new information. Although practically unique, the fact that others had displayed similar biological traits eased his anxiety. It could be a leap in natural evolution which would eventually bear the human race to a higher plane where disease and pain could be eradicated. Or he could be one of the first mutants and he would soon develop amphibian skin and a taste for insects. It was becoming clear the truth wouldn't easily be uncovered, so he turned the TV on. With a remote this time, which actually worked, unlike his mind. An old episode of Columbo was playing and Malachi would have given anything to have the intrepid, fictional detective on his side.

"You'd find the truth, wouldn't you?" Malachi asked the screen.

The dishevelled homicide detective turned to face the culprit, and uttered the infamous words which had doomed countless killers, "There's just one more thing."

Malachi smiled to himself and felt more at ease than he had for many months.

CHAPTER THIRTEEN

"You do know I'm perfectly able to walk," Malachi said over his shoulder.

"I know that, I just wanted to take you for a ride," Shannon giggled as she gained speed down the empty corridor.

He laughed at the double entendre and held his arms wide, imitating flying, "It's like a reversal of Kate and Leo in Titanic."

"You can paint me naked with a million-dollar necklace anytime," she replied, half serious.

"What would Oliver have to say about that?"

"He would probably try and claw your eyes out," Shannon admitted, slowing down at the disapproving glare of a duty doctor.

"He's a protective little beast then?"

"A bit too much sometimes, besides, I would be the one with my eyes clawed out if Chloe could hear me flirting with you."

"I'm sure she would understand, after all, I'm irresistible," Malachi joked, pulling a model pose with a hand holding his chin in quiet contemplation.

"You're into her though, aren't you?" Shannon asked hesitantly.

Malachi didn't want to hurt her feelings but leading her on would be just as spiteful, "Yeah, I really like her."

"She's a lucky girl to find her Prince Charming. I don't think I will ever be so lucky," she replied despondently.

"Hey, yes you will. Someone as great as you has an amazing guy waiting out there, I promise," Malachi reached back and patted her hand.

"Maybe," she sighed, coming to a stop outside a door with Dr K. Lloyd MRCPsych embossed on the frosted glass, "Here we are."

"What, no plush reception with calming pictures and a harmonious Feng shui?" Malachi teased.

"This is the NHS, just be happy we even have a spare room for you," she laughed, shaking off some of the depression.

"I'll walk back once I am finished."

"I won't hear of it!" Shannon declared, "I will be back after my break."

"Isn't this a job for a hospital porter like your friend, Ben?"

She looked away and blushed, "Well, yes. But I wanted to do it so just shut up and enjoy the five-star transportation."

"Thank you." Malachi gave her a quick hug, "I'll see you soon."

She smiled and walked away, leaving the wheelchair in a storage alcove further down the corridor. Seeing he was still watching she called out, "Saves me pushing it all the way back again."

With a final wave, Malachi knocked on the door and a friendly voice called out from within.

"Come on in!"

Pushing through, the room was typically hospital and bore no semblance to any of the elegant offices he had seen on TV. A single desk with a computer sat in the corner, the screen dark. An attempt had been made to brighten the walls with cheap, store bought pictures of winding rivers and countryside. To Malachi they just stuck out like a sore thumb and looked ridiculous. In place of leather sofas were two chairs which had been stolen from a nearby ward. Seeing the bemused look, Dr. Llyod stepped forward and held a hand out.

"You will have to forgive the surroundings; the director of the hospital doesn't deem it necessary to provide much budget for 'psychological issues'," Dr. Llyod emphasised the last words with finger speech marks.

"It's just not what I expected," Malachi replied.

"Well at least you're off to a good start." The doctor indicated he should sit.

"Pardon me?" Malachi asked.

"You obviously have awareness of your surroundings and how pitiful they are, if you hadn't paid attention I would be a little more concerned. Nobody truly sane would enjoy divulging their secrets in here."

"I see," Malachi smiled and sat down.

"So you are..." he checked a few hastily scribbled notes on a pad, "Malachi. And I am Dr. Llyod, but please, call me Kenny."

Malachi couldn't get comfortable in the high backed leather chair, which was as much to do with the firm padding as the purpose of the meeting. He was fidgeting terribly and the knowing smile of the psychiatrist wasn't helping.

"How do we do this then, Doc? Sorry, Kenny." Malachi wanted to get right to it.

"This is just an initial evaluation, so don't panic. We will just discuss a few details about your life and experiences, and from there I will formulate a treatment plan. Every case is different, so I can't promise an immediate improvement, but what I will guarantee is that I am here to help." Kenny smiled and Malachi felt more at ease.

Settling back and taking a deep breath, Malachi replied, "I hope you can, because I am close to breaking point."

"Let's start with some basic information, shall we?" Kenny turned to his jotter, "Dr. Franken has referred you to me for violent night terrors, is that correct?"

"Yes, but the physical side has only been the past few days, before that it was just…" Malachi paused. He had already shared his embarrassment to more people in the past week than his whole life, one more wouldn't make a difference.

"It was just what?" the doctor pressed.

Letting out a pent up sigh, Malachi finished, "Wetting myself and vomiting."

"Please, don't be embarrassed. Nothing you share with me will ever leave the room, I can assure you of that. It is imperative that I know as much as possible about the physical symptoms as well as the dreams themselves. Now, the seizures have only happened recently?"

Malachi thought for a moment, "Actually I'm not quite sure. I live alone and sometimes wake to find my bed a warzone, perhaps it has happened before but this is the first time it has been observed."

"It could well be. Can you remember the first time that you awoke to the bed being in disarray?"

Memories of the orphanage and his scared roommate flashed through his mind, "It may have been when I was twelve. Some occasions are better than others."

"So it is intermittent?" Kenny wondered.

"Yes, so is the peeing and being sick. It doesn't happen every time I dream."

"Interesting," he smiled, "Well I think it will help you to know you are not alone. Studies show that about eight percent of the adult population suffer from night terrors, or chronic nightmares as they are sometimes called, at some point in their life."

"So I'm not alone?" Malachi daren't believe it.

"Not at all. There are thousands of people in a similar situation, and we are able to help in most cases."

"And in those you can't?" Malachi asked, praying he wasn't one of the 'other' cases.

Kenny coughed and sat forward, "I don't think it will be an issue with you. The majority of those cases involve a severely damaged mind, often as a result of years of psychological trauma or PTSD from service personnel. You aren't in the armed forces are you?"

"No."

"Good, I can cross that off the list, we will get to other possibilities in a moment. Before that, where do *you* think the dreams come from?"

"I don't know. I assumed it was my hormones from puberty, but when it carried on into adulthood I just hid them away and tried to get on with my life."

"And there was nothing else that might have triggered them?"

"Well my parents died in a car accident when I was eleven, and I was placed in an orphanage," Malachi said quietly. Tears welled and threatened to overflow, a response so common that the doctor didn't even acknowledge the show of weakness. Malachi was grateful for that and quickly composed himself with a rub of his eyes.

"Well that certainly constitutes an early trauma. Did you receive grief counselling?" Kenny was scribbling notes.

"No."

Shaking his head, Kenny replied, "It's disgusting how people are failed by the system in this country."

"It wasn't so bad, the staff were fantastic to me," he conceded.

"But they can't replace parents. Didn't you have any relatives to take you in?"

"Unfortunately not."

"I think this horrible event may have been a key trigger to the dreams that followed. Normally a bereavement will run its own course in time. The dreams can be a way of the mind coming to terms with situations that are too painful to face in the waking world."

"Maybe," Malachi countenanced, although the nightmares didn't involve his parents in any way. He would bring that up when it seemed appropriate.

"I'm afraid I need to ask you some personal questions now, and they won't be pleasant. I need absolute honesty if we are to be successful, do you understand?"

"You want to ask about sexual stuff?"

Kenny nodded.

"Ok," Malachi prepared himself, "Shoot."

"Did either of your parents ever touch you inappropriately? It doesn't necessarily have to be your genitals; it could be a lingering hand or a kiss at bedtime which seemed wrong."

"Never, we were a really happy family," Malachi declared.

"You said there were no relatives around after your parents passed. Were any on the scene during your formative years who may have had the opportunity to be alone with you?"

"No, we were totally on our own."

"Hmm," Kenny wrote down some more details, "Ok, now we get to the orphanage. Did any member of staff or other child approach you sexually, male or female?"

"No," he shrugged, "If I'm honest the carers were fantastic. It wasn't like the film Oliver where we were mistreated and fed gruel. Even the other kids were supportive as we all had some bad shit in common."

"Were they all orphans too?"

"In a manner of speaking. Some had been taken from parents who were so high and drunk all the time it was as if they didn't exist. Most were like myself, both parents gone and no living relatives. Or relatives that were willing to take them in anyway."

"Curious," he jotted down a couple of bullet points. "Ok, that leads me onto the next line of questioning. Were you victimised at school? As an orphan you would have been a prime target for the less understanding pupil."

"I had a bit of trouble but I dealt with it early. After that, school was just school, sitting still and learning."

"You mean you fought back?"

Malachi nodded.

"Good for you," Kenny replied with a grin.

"I didn't feel too good about it, I still don't. I have always tried to avoid confrontations if I can."

"That's noble of you, a lot of people enjoy inflicting pain," Kenny replied with a faint smirk.

"Not this guy."

"I can see you are going to give me trouble," Kenny pointed accusingly, "Whatever is going on will need a lot more digging to uncover. Tell me about the dreams, does it always involve the death of your parents?"

"None of my nightmares have been about my parents," Malachi said.

"Excuse me?" Kenny said with surprise, turning to his notes, "Apologies, I just assumed. What are the dreams about? It may give a clue to the underlying issue."

This was it. A time to unload all of the fear and distress that followed Malachi into the depths of his sleeping imagination. A decade of dread every time the pillow moulded to the contours of his head and eyelids closed, delivering him to the realm of untold horrors. If anyone could help it was surely this affable psychiatrist. A man who had dedicated his life to exploring the vast abyss that was the human mind.

"I see death, blood, and suffering. I dream of evil," Malachi whispered.

"Go on." Kenny had sat up straight and was more intent on the conversation. Malachi didn't notice as a thousand nightmares converged into a show reel of genocide.

"I watch villages put to the torch, with men, women, and children butchered in the hundreds. I watch creatures that can't exist tearing worlds apart, the people unable to die, only suffer in agony forever," Malachi was pouring the terror out, laughing and crying at the same time, "And do you know the latest? I have seen things that I couldn't possibly see, witnessed massacres from the past committed by people that actually existed! How can I see these things and be sane?"

The doctor's eyes were wide with astonishment and he was writing so fast the words were illegible. As Malachi finally slumped backwards and waited for Kenny to section him, the doctor merely sat back himself and smiled knowingly. Chewing on the pen tip, he stared for long moments until Malachi felt increasingly uncomfortable. The cheerful shrink had taken on the look of a predator, surveying the meal on offer.

"Are you ok?" Malachi asked warily.

Shaking himself, the look was gone and the smile returned, "Of course, I was just processing what you told me."

"Do you think I am insane?" Malachi had to know.

"Not at all, you are one of the sanest people I have ever seen."

Sighing with relief, a weight lifted from his shoulders; the road to recovery could now begin.

"That being said," Kenny continued, the sting in the tail now coming, "I think we need to see each other a great deal more. We can help you come to terms with this affliction."

"We?"

"I mean the NHS," Kenny recovered quickly, "I will prescribe you a course of Prazosin to begin tonight. It was originally found to be a good way of treating high blood pressure. One of the side effects has been to drastically reduce the impact of nightmares in those who take it."

"I'm not keen on drugs."

"It's only a stopgap until I find a better alternative. We can then try image reversal therapy when I have more time with you. It's a way of controlling the dreams instead of letting them control you."

Malachi submitted to the expert opinion, "I will give them a chance, ok? I am happy to try anything right now."

"Good man." Kenny smiled, before writing on the green pad, "The dosage is noted down too."

Pointing to the amount to take, he ripped the prescription off and handed it over.

"I can't believe I may be able to get past this and have my life back. Thank you so much, Kenny."

"It's my pleasure," he said, shaking Malachi's hand again. "Soon this will all feel like a distant memory."

With a spring in his step, he left the room to find Shannon wasn't back yet. The doctor gave a final wave and closed the door firmly and locked it. Reaching into his trouser pocket he withdrew a phone and flicked it open before dialling a memorised number. After exactly four rings, a connection was made and a female voice spoke.

"How may I direct your call?"

"Can I speak with Mr. Creighton?" Kenny asked nervously.

"I'm sorry, there is no one here by that name," she replied, but kept the line open.

"Vie kulas sephiras," Kenny replied with the phrase he was given at the start of his ascension.

"Thank you, I will connect you immediately," she replied without emotion and the line changed.

A deep voice answered, "Yes?"

"Sir, it's Dr. Llyod," Kenny said respectfully, his stomach fluttering in fear. No matter how many times he spoke to the man he was always terrified. Mr. Creighton liked that.

"What is it?" he asked abruptly.

"I have a seer, sir."

"Are you sure?"

"One hundred percent, sir." Kenny knew that mistakes were dealt with swiftly and severely.

"Good. If you can arrange the removal of his eyes and tongue, I will send a team to deliver him to the Clerics of Kylous."

"That won't be a problem, sir. I will arrange to see him in two days and he will be prepared by the weekend."

"Excellent. Call me when it is done, my team will be on standby," he said and hung up.

With a shuddering breath, Kenny closed the phone and sat down before he collapsed. Although never doubting his decision, the path laid out before him was fraught with uncertainty. Once he had proven himself he would be untouchable, but until that time it wasn't only his life that could be forfeit.

CHAPTER FOURTEEN

"As you can see, the wound has now totally healed," Dr. Franken explained, turning Malachi onto his side to observe the flank injury too.

"This is incredible," remarked a doctor with a French accent.

The physicians huddled around and talked amongst themselves while Malachi looked on. Dr. Franken seated himself by the bed and patted him on the leg, "I told you how unique you were."

"When you said colleagues, I assumed you meant from inside the hospital, not from across Europe," Malachi whispered. The tiny, private bubble that was his life had gone continental and he found his heart palpitating with anxiety.

The doctor could see his concern and spoke quietly, "Don't worry. These are doctors who I trust not to make rash judgements. They have asked permission to follow our sessions together but it will not be publicised without your express consent. We are all somewhat quirky in the eyes of our peers as we don't take it as inviolable that medicine itself has all the answers."

"So I won't be front page of any medical journals if I don't want to be?"

"Not at all," Dr. Franken declared, "We can keep your anonymity intact from the first session; I will formulate a non-disclosure contract which we will all sign. The information we glean from you will be kept on my own encrypted server at home."

"Thanks, Doc," Malachi breathed a sigh of relief.

"That being said, if at some point we find what is locked within your genes which allows you to regenerate, I would like your permission to share it with the world. A suitably apportioned research laboratory could synthesize any genetic anomalies and use them to help people."

"And I suppose the profit would be split equally between us?" Malachi asked, meeting the doctor's gaze.

"Well I suppose so, yes," Dr. Franken backed off a little with distaste, "I wasn't so much thinking about money, more being able to help millions of people to live a full and active life. If we can unlock your regenerative ability, we could eradicate Alzheimer's disease overnight. No more watching our loved ones become strangers to us, prisoners within their own mind. Heart disease and cancer would be things of the past."

Malachi was satisfied with the response and smiled, "That was the answer I wanted. If we can create something wonderful I want it used for good, not for the profit of a select few who then decide who lives and dies."

"You have my word," declared the doctor, placing a hand over his heart.

"So what happens now?"

"First thing that happens is I sign your discharge papers and you go back home. We keep this as low key as possible to ensure nobody gets wind of what we are doing. You resume your old life and I see you on a weekly basis, possibly more frequently if we have a breakthrough."

"I like the sound of getting back to normality, I am already behind with my rent because of the hospital stay. I'm going to need to pull a lot of overtime to get back on my feet," Malachi replied.

"It could have been worse if you needed to stay in for many weeks like normal people," winked the doctor.

Malachi laughed, "At least my superpowers have stopped me from being evicted."

"I wouldn't worry too much, your housing has already been paid for a year or more," replied Dr. Franken.

"What do you mean?"

"There was a party at your friend's bar in your honour. They collected enough to tide you over for several months on top of the rent payments," explained the doctor.

"I don't like taking charity," Malachi said, a mixture of gratitude and irritation, "People worked hard for that money and I don't deserve it."

"Nonsense, lad. In today's society, what you did was amazing. Most people would have walked on by and minded their own business, but you ran headlong into the fray."

"You make it sound like I stormed the beaches on D-day," Malachi huffed.

"Very trite," admonished Dr. Franken.

"Sorry, Doc. I am just tired of people saying I'm a hero for running into an alley and getting stabbed. It wasn't brave, I was scared to death."

"Without fear, there can be no courage!" proclaimed the doctor.

"Gandhi? Martin Luther King?"

"No, it was on a Facebook meme," he said and they both laughed.

Chloe's smiling face appeared at the small window and the group of experts excused themselves. As she walked in, Dr. Franken peered around the doorway.

"I've left my personal details on a piece of paper. If you have any questions, then please don't hesitate to call. I will be in touch in the next few days when I have made all the necessary arrangements. Ok?"

"Sounds fine. Thanks again, Doc."

"It was my pleasure," he nodded to Chloe, "Take care of that one, he is more special than you could ever know."

And with that he was gone. Chloe cupped both cheeks and kissed Malachi passionately.

"At least you cleaned your teeth this time," she joked.

"I had the doctors coming to see me, I had to scrub up a bit," Malachi replied.

"You're lucky you are still a patient or I would punish you," Chloe replied.

"I'm not sure that is such a bad thing," he chuckled and climbed out of bed.

"Keep misbehaving and I will have to put on my leather suit and break out the whip," she winked.

A tingle of anticipation threatened to cause an awkward protrusion, so he turned away to get changed. Seeing Chloe was staying put, he said, "Are you going to watch me the whole time?"

"Damned right I am," she grinned.

"Pervert," he chuckled and started to strip.

Ordinarily, this level of intimacy would have caused more apprehension, but he felt so at ease in her presence that it didn't matter. She spent most of the time making sounds of approval or whistling and Malachi was laughing so hard by the end she had to turn away and let him finish.

"I thought it was only men who were meant to wolf whistle?"

"I'm all for equality between the sexes," Chloe giggled and embraced him tightly, hands caressing Malachi's firm buttocks.

"I'll get you done for sexual harassment," he said, pretending to fight off her amorous advances.

"You wait and see what I do to you later," she whispered, biting her lower lip.

The old nerves returned and Malachi wasn't sure he could go through with it. What if she wanted him to stay? What if she wanted to stay at his place? The pill that Dr. Llyod had prescribed seemed to do the trick with the nightmares, or it could have just been a coincidence that last night was one of the dreamless sleeps. He prayed it was the former.

"I can't wait to be out of this place," Malachi said, changing the subject.

"I don't like them either. The smell is just awful," Chloe replied.

"You said that you had a surprise for me when we spoke last night?"

"I do, but you will have to wait and see when we get there," she answered mysteriously.

"So what is it?" he begged. "I hate surprises."

"You won't hate this one," Chloe confirmed.

"It's not…"

"Oh no," she laughed, "You know we are going to spend the night together, that's not a surprise."

Butterflies fluttered into life in his stomach at the thought. But what would be would be, he had already explained his nightmares and they didn't seem to faze Chloe. Whether the same could be said of the more rambunctious aspects of his dreams would be another matter. The last thing he wanted to do was scare or hurt her while suffering from a nightmare. He would suggest they stay in different rooms, that should prevent some of the issues. In the longer term… Malachi was at a loss. It all relied on Dr. Llyod and his methods.

"Am I going straight home?"

"Maybe, maybe not. Stop asking questions and let's get going," she said, lifting the bag with his belongings.

"Here, let me," Malachi asked, holding out a hand.

"How very chivalrous," she bumped her hip against him, "But I've got it."

At the reception desk, Shannon was just putting the finishing touches to his release forms. Normally accompanied by a physio regime or a course of medicine, Malachi's was simply a see you later. The muscle had no signs of weakness and with the wounds bearing only faint scars now, antibiotics were deemed unnecessary. Angela wasn't working this particular shift but had left a message for Malachi to pass on to Kevin saying that if he was ever single, to give her a call.

"I don't believe that guy," Malachi said, shaking his head.

"Angela loves a bad boy, but it doesn't stretch to messing around with married men," Shannon replied.

"He's devoted to Laura anyway. He might make a few noises but he loves her and the kids to the moon and back."

"We got that impression too," Shannon smiled and handed over the form, "Just a quick squiggle there and we are all done."

Signing the form felt like he was being released from captivity and he handed it back gladly. Taking a copy and giving it to Malachi, the nurse filed the rest of the papers into the medical documents and put it in the tray to return to storage.

"Thank you for all you've done, and that doesn't just mean the treatment." Malachi looked to Chloe.

"Just cuddle her already!" she laughed.

"You're welcome," Shannon replied, muffled by his sweatshirt.

"My turn," Chloe added and embraced her too, "I will be forever grateful for what you did for him."

"It was nothing, just make sure you treat him right," Shannon said, her tone hard.

"You have my word," Chloe answered and they linked arms and pushed through the electronic exit doors which Shannon had opened remotely.

"Sorry about that, I think she gets a bit protective."

"Not at all, I would be exactly the same," she replied, pulling him closer.

They left the hospital and Malachi closed his eyes, breathing deeply. Instead of fresh clean air, it was tainted by the scents of the city. Car exhausts mingled with food outlets and stacked garbage ready for collection. It was a smell he knew and loved.

"I'm parked in the multi-storey carpark," Chloe explained.

159

They explored each other in greater detail, discussing politics, religion, and other topics. Surprisingly they had an awful lot in common which only went to prove to Malachi that she really was the one. Their most contentious issue was whether bankers should be locked up for a long time, or for a longer time due to their greed. Chloe was in the longer camp.

"Here she is," Chloe said proudly as they reached her little Peugeot.

"Why am I not surprised you are driving a 207?" Malachi teased. The small coupe was a firm favourite among the female population of England and he was certain at least ninety-two percent of young women drove them.

"Shut up," Chloe laughed, "It's a great little runner and unless you want to catch the bus, get that fine ass in the passenger seat."

CHAPTER FIFTEEN

Darkness ruled the room, only broken by the projector and its images which flickered against the pull down screen. The older technology was favoured to prevent any link to a hackable source. Tips of cigars and cigarettes occasionally glowed into life before dulling, momentarily granting faces a vague, orange glow. Security shutters were fixed firmly in the closed position to ensure privacy for the meeting. The atmosphere was charged with nervous energy and several of the newer members fidgeted with excitement. Acceptance into the group had come at great personal cost, but the benefits couldn't be over exaggerated. As the last slide rolled, a graph showed a steady increase over the coming years which brought murmurs of approval from around the table.

"So as you can see, ladies and gentlemen, the projected growth of our assets is more than double that of our nearest competitor. Some would call it shrewd business, but when you control the board it is easy to minimise exposure," said a gloating, male voice from the head of the table.

"Can we not speed up the acquisition of the businesses I identified earlier?" asked a snooty female. She was highly ambitious and this irritated some of the other board members who feared their own positions.

"All in good time," replied the man, "Until we have control over all of the key financial regulators, the scrutiny we would place ourselves under would be unacceptable."

"But I think we should at least consider the proposals," she continued and groans of disapproval echoed around the smoky room, "We could advance our cause by at least three years."

"Lights," commanded the chairperson.

In seconds the projector was turned off and the shutters started their ascent. A member of the security team disabled the signal jamming software now that the key aspects of the meeting had passed. The table itself was marble with leather inserted in the centre to provide audio and visual connections which would be brought back into service after the meeting. Thirteen executive chairs surrounded it, six to each side with the director at the head of the table. For each member of the committee, a pair of armed guards stood quietly at the sides. Protection of the highest level drawn from the most elite units of the world's fighting forces. Their salaries would have made bankers blush, but no expense was spared in ensuring the longevity of their charges.

"Thank you."

Drake Creighton surveyed the representatives before him with cold calculation. Each of them were invaluable, though ultimately replaceable in the grand scheme of things. Looking at each in turn, he finally settled on the eager woman and stared for a few seconds, cowing her. Satisfied she had reigned in her outbursts, he stood up and started to explain.

"I appreciate your drive, believe me," he nodded to her, "Three years is nothing when the bigger picture is taken into account. Our ultimate goal is centuries in the making, so thirty-six months is but a drop in the ocean."

"I understand, sir. Please accept my apologies," she grovelled. The sycophancy was greeted by more groans from the seasoned associates and she glared venom around the table.

"Just remember that this is an endeavour where we all must work in unison. I will not allow any conflict of personalities to jeopardise what we are so close to achieving, is that understood?" Drake asked the room and they all concurred.

A gentle rapping on the door caught their attention and one of the guards looked to Mr. Creighton for permission before allowing entry. His personal secretary hurried over and whispered in his ear, "I'm sorry, sir. I know interruptions aren't allowed but I think you need to take this call."

Not known for flights of fancy, her face left no doubt about the importance of the communication.

He took the handset, "Thank you, Jo. If you could all please excuse me, we will meet again in a fortnight's time."

The bodyguards ushered each of the twelve out to the waiting limousines and further guards. Anyone watching would have been mistaken for thinking they were seeing a meeting of heads of state, rather than a secretive group of business associates.

"What is it?" Drake asked without preamble.

"Mr. Creighton, I have some information which you may find helpful," smarmed the French voice.

"And what might that be? I don't have time for games so get to it."

"I was thinking this may help with my application for the French circle?" the voice persisted dangerously.

"If you don't get to the point in the next five seconds, you will not only be removed from the list, you will disappear forever along with your family!" Drake hissed into the phone. He was tiring of the boldness of underlings, perhaps it was time for a display to get them back in line.

"I'm sorry, sir," gulped the French doctor audibly, "I was told at my initiation that one of the things I must be observant for is any abnormalities in patients I come into contact with."

"And?" Drake sighed with frustration.

"There is a patient who has exhibited healing far in excess of any normal human," he started to explain and Drake sat bolt upright in his chair, "He was brought in with multiple stab wounds and nearly died. This was about a week ago."

"Continue," Drake said breathlessly. News like this was momentous and he pressed a concealed button under the desk.

"I have joined a small circle of surgeons who are interested in this abstract field. Up until a week ago, the only other documented case was an American national."

This wasn't news to Drake and he waited for more information.

"The severity of the wounds was such that it would normally take many weeks, if not months of treatment. However, in this case, he was completely healed after seven days."

A huge man entered the meeting room, summoned by the button. Heavily scarred from countless suicidal missions from his time as a mercenary for hire, he waited patiently by the door for further instruction. Drake held up a hand to say 'one moment' and he nodded in reply.

"Where is this man now? I can call the French office and have a team ready within an hour."

"He isn't in France, Mr. Creighton, he is in the UK," explained the doctor.

"I don't follow," Drake said with irritation.

"Dr. Franken called us and asked if we would be interested in taking part in a unique research project..."

"Did you say Franken?" Drake shouted.

"Yes, sir. I'm sorry, have I done something wrong?" asked the doctor fearfully.

"No, you have done well, Mathis. Stay by the phone, I may need to speak to you shortly," Drake said and hung up.

The gigantic beast of a man stepped forward, muscles straining in the Armani suit. He wasn't overly garrulous and communicated with grunts much of the time. Drake liked that about him but on this occasion he was too furious to show it. Reaching for the water decanter, he flung it across the room and it shattered against the wall. As the liquid streamed down the walls Drake dialled a number, basically smashing at the keypad. When the angry thrusts led to the wrong number being entered, he was ready to kill someone.

"Krauss, tell me about the last person you murdered," Drake was shaking with rage. But it was nothing new to the guard.

"Politicians family. Cut them to bits," he replied.

Drake remembered and smiled, calming down a fraction. The man in question had stood in the way of certain business interests and had to be removed. A burglary gone wrong was arranged, and installed in his place was a man far more open to mutually beneficial arrangements.

Dialling the number again, it started to ring and he nodded to Krauss in gratitude. On the second ring it was answered, "Dr. Llyod. You have made a mistake, and you know how much I hate mistakes," he growled through clenched teeth.

CHAPTER SIXTEEN

"If you look right there, we can see that the cartilage has deteriorated further," Dr. Franken showed the elderly woman who squinted before putting on a set of glasses.

"Does that mean I need surgery?"

"I'm afraid so," replied the doctor, sympathetically, "It's the only way that we can reduce the pain and get you active again."

"It would be nice to get out in the garden," she said cheerfully.

"I expect your gladioli would be grateful for your magic touch."

"How do you know about my flowers?" gasped the woman.

"You told me about them during our last consultation, Mrs. Pearson," Dr. Franken smiled.

She was taken aback, "I can't believe you remember that."

"A good doctor listens," he explained, "I pride myself on trying to give my patients the personal touch."

"And we appreciate it, dearie."

"Now, the way this will work is we invite you in for a pre-op assessment. This will involve some questions followed by checking your height, weight, pulse, blood pressure, and taking a swab for MRSA. We will also need a urine sample," he outlined the first stage.

"And if everything is ok?"

"Depending on the questions we may need to do an electrocardiograph. It's merely a precaution and someone as young as you will fly through it, I'm sure. I know it is impolite to ask a lady her age but how old are you?" he flicked through the notes, "Fifty-five, sixty?"

"You are such a charmer. I'm seventy-six." She beamed at the good natured banter.

"Are you sure?" he feigned shock, then broke into his own smile. "Well I just pray I look as young as you if I reach that age. Somehow I doubt it."

"Will I be bedbound? I can always get Burt to move our bedroom downstairs for a while."

"We try and get you mobile as soon…"

The door burst open and the panting form of Dr. Llyod rushed in, startling Mrs. Pearson. His eyes were wide with terror and she shrunk back, fearing an attack.

"Now what on earth is going on?" Dr. Franken stood up, furious.

"Why didn't you tell me about his other history? Do you know what you have done?" shouted the psychiatrist.

"What? Who the hell are you talking about? You're making no sense, man." He helped Mrs. Pearson to her feet and ushered her out of the door.

"Malachi, the stabbing victim. Why didn't you tell me about his healing abilities?" Dr. Llyod was beside himself, pacing then sitting before standing again.

"I'm at a loss, why would his physiological traits impact your psychological assessment. I thought it was just a preliminary induction?"

"That's not the point!" Dr. Llyod slammed a fist onto the table, scattering notes. "I should have been told."

"What is going on here?" Dr. Franken confronted the shrink and stood a whole head taller.

"I need to find him." Dr. Llyod nodded to confirm his own idea, "Yes, that's it. What ward is he being kept on?"

If he could keep him occupied until the collection crew arrived, it might be enough to mitigate some of Mr. Creighton's disciplinary measures. Specifically, the one that involved the butchery of his whole family before he was flayed living.

"He has been discharged," Dr. Franken explained, oblivious of the ramifications to the animated psychiatrist. "This is most irregular; I will be speaking to the board about your behaviour."

"No, no, no that can't be!" shrieked Dr. Llyod who then crashed out of the room just as abruptly as he had entered.

"What on earth?" mumbled the surgeon to the slowly closing door.

****

Got to hold it together. Got to hold it together. What are those nurses looking at? Are they laughing at me? Fucking whores! They have no idea what is going on, he thought to himself. The whole world seemed to be shrinking, walls threatening to squeeze the life out of him, ceiling descending in his fevered mind. The crazed doctor actually ducked to avoid the imaginary obstacle and the nurses giggled again.

"Fuck off!" he cried out, wiping frantically at his streaming eyes. This only brought more laughter and disapproving tuts from the duty doctors at his unprofessionalism.

Time seemed to speed up, hurtling towards the inevitable reckoning with Creighton's psychopathic henchmen. The big man himself would do the final wet work, he always did with a subordinate who fucked up. And there were no other words for what he had done.

"Dr. Llyod, can I arrange a meeting with you this afternoon?" asked a smiling, young doctor, blocking his path.

"Not now," he tried to reply, but the words were choked and unintelligible.

"Are you ok?" he asked, still smiling, "Please, it won't take long."

"Stop fucking smiling!" screamed Dr. Llyod and punched him; a blow given extra power by terror and adrenaline.

Flailing backwards, nose shattered and pouring blood, the doctor fell against a tea trolley. Without thinking, his reactions had been to clutch at the steel side. His angle of fall and the momentum of his body pulled the whole lot over, covering his body in boiling liquid. The facial injury was instantly forgotten as every nerve screamed in protest at the scalding agony. People came rushing to help, giving Dr. Llyod a wide berth as blisters sprouted on the young physician's face and forearms.

"Oh my God, why did you do that?" asked one of the previously giggling nurses, but he didn't acknowledge the question.

"Someone call security," came another fading voice.

As he stumbled down the never ending corridors, the only thoughts in his mind were for his loved ones. He needed to get control before he saw the duty nurses on the intensive care station or they would know something was amiss. Leaning against the wall, he took ragged breaths until his galloping heart slowed to a canter and stepped to the locked doors. Swiping his access card across the reader, a green light blinked on and he pressed through, wiping as much of the free flowing perspiration away as possible. The desk was unmanned and a childlike whine escaped his lips as he looked around desperately for a member of staff.

"The notes!" he said to himself and started to rifle through the paperwork.

"Hi, Dr. Llyod. Is there something I can help you with?" asked Shannon cheerfully until he turned to face her. His eyes were wide and red, as if he had recently been crying. The incoherent mumbling pouring from his mouth didn't help his façade either.

Coughing to buy a second to compose himself, he tried to smile and asked, "The young man I saw, Malachi I think his name was. I am trying to find his medical notes."

Something wasn't right with the man, that much was obvious from his pacing and sweating. Thinking quickly, she replied, "They have been taken back down to storage. I'm sure you can catch up with Craig if you hurry, he just picked them up on his rounds."

"No, that won't do!" he screamed and flung the contents of one desk onto the floor.

"Then I don't know what to suggest," Shannon replied bravely, although she was terrified the maniacal doctor would turn his attention to her.

"The computer, that will have his address!" he laughed madly and sat down, tapping away at the keyboard.

Shannon looked under the desk and saw that Malachi's notes hadn't yet been collected and if Dr. Llyod was more focused he too would have seen it. Moving around the counter, she surreptitiously nudged the plastic container deeper into the gloom. Whatever reason he wanted to find Malachi for, she was certain it didn't bode well for the young man.

"Where is it?" shrieked Dr. Llyod, "It has to be here!"

Shannon had made up her mind to disconnect the electricity supply to the computer if he managed to pull up Malachi's patient details, but the records were empty. Frowning in confusion, she looked again as the computer flashed with 'Patient not recognised. Please try again'.

"Fucking computer!" shouted the doctor, slamming his fist into the keyboard, "Work, damn you!"

A growing audience was gathering to see what the disturbance was about, keeping a respectable distance to minimise their danger. Once again, 'Patient not recognised. Please try again' came up on the screen and Shannon was dumbfounded. She had watched him carefully input his correct name, but for some reason all trace of Malachi was gone from the main NHS database.

"Please, no. No, no, no," muttered Dr. Llyod, tearing at his hair.

"Security are on their way," called out a doctor from the end of the corridor.

Leaping to his feet, he grabbed Shannon by the throat, "You said Craig took the notes! Which way did he go?" Specks of spittle covered her face.

"I don't know, he didn't say," she lied, trying to pry his hands loose.

"You're all in on this aren't you?" he accused, letting her go and wagging a finger at everyone. "You want me dead."

With flailing arms and a banshee wail he sprinted out of the intensive care unit and was gone.

"Are you ok?" asked Penelope, a trainee nurse.

"Yes, I'm fine," Shannon replied, shaking from the encounter.

"You're not fine, sit down." Penelope ushered her to a chair. "Let me get some antiseptic wipes for the scratches."

Shannon felt at her throat and the fingertips came away with traces of blood. They weren't deep and a simple plaster would suffice. All around her, calls were being made and people gossiped in hushed tones. The only thing on Shannon's mind was the box in the shadows and the information it contained.

****

"Sir, we are here. How do you want us to proceed?" asked the police officer.

"Find that fucking doctor and ensure he gets what we need. After you have found the target, bring him and the doctor to the asylum where I will deal with them," Drake replied.

"As you wish."

Climbing out of the car, the two men looked to any casual observer members of the local constabulary. No one knew that their uniforms were fake and had been collected from a nearby safe house as well as the police car itself. Concealed beneath their fluorescent coats were silenced pistols but they were under strict instructions to maintain the cover at all costs. Questions could prove problematic and would necessitate some high level phone calls which, at present, were not necessarily going to end in a positive outcome.

"Where do we start?" asked Minford.

"The security office is just inside the accident and emergency department. We check in with them so it doesn't look suspicious," replied Carter.

The automatic doors hissed and parted for the two men who looked around the waiting room. Only a few people were sat in the chairs, varying levels of pain etched on their faces as they waited to be seen by the doctor. Carter nodded to the receptionist who smiled warmly before returning to her phone call. As they approached the glass window of the security office, it was apparent the doctor had been causing quite a scene. Radios chirped with updates and the chief gave a thumbs up to the officers.

"Come on in!" he called out, pressing a door release button.

"What seems to be the trouble? We had a call saying there was an altercation?"

The call in question had involved eavesdropping on the police frequencies and picking up the assault. Most of the local force was occupied after a pile up on the local motorway and would be unable to attend for at least twenty minutes, which meant they had to work fast.

"One of the doctors has gone crazy, hitting members of staff and making a right scene. He is currently down in records smashing the place up. I've pulled my guys and told them to lock him in, we don't get paid enough to take on a nutter," said the chief unapologetically.

"We're here now so you can rest easy. We'll deal with him."

"I'll show you down to the basement where they archive all the notes, it's about two minutes' walk."

This left just under eighteen minutes to achieve the desired outcome. The stairwell was in disarray, with paper strewn everywhere; images of procedures and doctor's letters had been tossed around like confetti. Craig the porter was nursing an abraded cheek and an injured arm after being pushed down the stairs.

"Tell the officers what happened, Craig," directed the security guard.

"I have no fucking idea," he snapped, "I was just bringing the notes back and this idiot starts to have a go at me. He looked through the files I had and then went mental when he couldn't find something. Before I knew what was happening, he had pushed me and I fell over the cart down the stairs. I'm going to knock him out when I get hold of him."

"It's not worth losing your job over, let the authorities deal with him."

Craig just scowled in response; his pride had taken as much of a battering as his body.

"Keys?" asked Carter, holding out a hand.

One of the security team handed the bunch over with the correct key already selected. The two burly men descended to the cacophony of cursing and objects being broken. Twisting the key, the lock disengaged and they pushed through the accumulated paperwork which had gathered by the door.

"Dr. Llyod?" called out Minford.

A face appeared around the nearest filing racks and glared at the men, "Fuck off, I need to find his address. I know it's here somewhere."

"Sir, we are here to help. Mr. Creighton sent us," explained Carter and the doctor fell silent.

Peering around the shelves again, he couldn't have looked more scared or pitiful but it meant nothing to the fake police officers, "No, you can't take me. I have nearly found it."

"We don't have the time for this. Why didn't you check on the hospital system?"

"Don't you think I've tried, you moron? He has vanished!" shouted Dr. Llyod before going back to his rampage.

"Even if his notes were here, you will never find them amongst all this, you fool," Minford snarled. He had lost patience and grabbed for the doctor, backhanding him hard enough to bring the destruction to an end.

"Now think. Where else could the information be kept? Do you remember his last name? Anything we could use to find him on the web? Think, Doctor!"

"I'm trying," he wept. His mind was so addled by fear that he couldn't picture his notes and the surname of the young man. By now it wouldn't be safe to return to his office as security would be checking for narcotics or other cause of the mental break.

"Sixteen minutes," Carter said to his partner.

"Wait!" Dr. Llyod gasped, "I don't know where any other records are kept but there are two people who will know his name. Dr. Franken and Shannon, one of the ICU nurses."

"Good, let's go. We have to cuff you so it looks genuine, you will then point them out to us," Minford explained.

Dr. Llyod shrunk back but Carter was waiting and wrestled him into submission. After being secured they left the records room and met the security team.

"The doctor has provided us with a worrying tip off that there is a group of people within the hospital who are creating a synthetic drug from morphine and distributing via fake patients. He feared for his safety which is why he struck out at people. We need to get to a couple of people before they have a chance to destroy evidence, do you understand?" Carter lied to the chief.

"Bloody hell! What do you need us to do?"

"Two of the suspects are Dr. Franken and nurse Shannon Walker. I need to ensure they don't leave, so if you could man the exits for us until backup arrives?"

"You can count on us," nodded the chief and started barking orders. This was the most excitement they had ever experienced within the hospital and as the two henchmen guessed, they were loving every minute and eager to help.

While the security team dispersed to watch for signs of their quarry, Dr. Llyod was frogmarched to Dr. Franken's office. The door was locked and on closer inspection through a break in the blinds, the room was deserted.

"Looks like we are relying on the nurse," said Minford.

"Twelve minutes," Carter remarked.

"Take my card, swipe it there," the doctor instructed and the trio converged on the reception desk. The mess was still being tidied and the nurses scowled at him. Looking around behind the counter, the records box was open with the lid laying on the floor. Bitch!

"Where is Miss Walker?" asked Minford to one of the women.

"I don't know, probably gone home after being traumatised by that prick," she snapped, pointing at Dr. Llyod.

"I think I saw her heading to the changing rooms. She said she wanted to clean up," said another member of staff.

Leaving the reception, they rushed towards the female facilities and barged through. The room was empty, but the faint smell of smoke hung in the air. Tracing the source to one of the private shower rooms, Carter drove a hefty boot at the door and shattered the lock. Shannon leaped in fright and dropped the smouldering notes out of the window. She had managed to destroy most of the file, including all references to his address and name before being caught. Her fear was replaced by resolve and she stood up proudly.

"I'll mind the door," said Minford.

"You fucking whore, you have no idea what you've done to me!" snarled Dr. Llyod.

"Miss Walker, I need to ask you a few questions." Carter grinned, pulling a knife and stepping through the cloud of smoke which billowed from the room.

As the alarm started to shrill, it concealed the tortured screams from within.

CHAPTER SEVENTEEN

"Surprise!"

The whole bar erupted with spontaneous cheers and hollering. Malachi tried to shrink back out of the door but Chloe gently pushed him forward.

"I'm sorry, but they insisted," she whispered loud enough to be heard over the din.

"Get your butt in here, man!" yelled Desmond, pouring a pint of lager.

Around the bar were cheap banners saying congratulations and get well soon. Desmond saw the look of amusement on Malachi's face and shrugged.

"It was all I could find," he said and roared with laughter.

Kevin and Laura walked over and hugged them both, "It's great to have you back, buddy. Next time you wait for me though!"

"There won't be a next time," Chloe said disapprovingly.

Laura nodded, then turned to Kevin, "And there won't be a first time for you!"

"I was merely going to help my friend up if he fell over and laid on the ground again," Kevin feigned a look of betrayal, "You know I hate violence."

"Yeah right," Malachi replied and they all laughed.

"Come on, let's get a drink in you." Kevin dragged him to the bar through a huddle of back patting and good wishes. Some of the people he knew, some he didn't.

The cold beer was delicious and he sighed as the frothy liquid saturated his taste buds. Desmond raised a glass and the whole bar followed his lead.

"For the conquering hero!"

Three cheers rung out and his cheeks flushed. Being the centre of attention wasn't something he was ever going to get used to. Chloe could see his growing discomfort and suggested they sit down. Tables had been lined up with finger food and the four picked a few morsels before slaloming between the other guests to the only free booth in the bar.

"I know you don't like this sort of thing, mate. We will give it an hour and then sneak you out the back door, ok?" Kevin patted him on the shoulder.

"I just get overwhelmed by all the attention," Malachi replied honestly.

"It was either here or we held it at your place. Although it would have been cooler to jump out at you in the dark, you would have probably keeled over," Kevin joked.

"That would have been much worse," Malachi was grateful, "There would have been nowhere to run except out the front door and that would have been a dick move."

"That's why Des and I decided to throw this bash and get it out of the way. After today you will be forgotten and just another bum working at a job they hate."

"I sure do like the sound of that," Malachi grinned.

"The only difference is you now have a beautiful companion to share your life with," Laura added.

"Aww, thank you." Chloe blushed.

"They've only known each other a week, don't go buying a new wedding hat just yet," Kevin chuckled.

Laura looked horrified, "Kevin, don't say things like that!"

"I was only joking. I give it at least three months."

Malachi nearly spat his drink out and Laura slapped him on the arm, "You're awful. How long did you give us?"

"As soon as I hit forty I'm trading you in for a younger model."

"What makes you think I won't trade you in before I'm forty?" Laura countered.

"You know you're punching above your weight with me," Kevin laughed and leaned away to avoid the coming slap.

"I'd say it was the other way around," remarked Chloe with a grin.

"Thank you," Laura said.

"Fuck me, if I knew you finding a girlfriend was going to cause me this much aggravation I would have told her you were gay," Kevin scolded.

"I would have believed you too," admitted Chloe, "Someone as good looking as Malachi could definitely pull it off."

"Thanks... I think," Malachi replied.

"It was a compliment, silly."

"Have any of the papers managed to pin you down and get the story yet?" Kevin asked.

"No, and I won't be doing any interviews either. Like you said, eventually they will lose interest and it will all blow over. Then the only thing I have to worry about is stopping Mr. Darlington beating up the other customers," Malachi replied with a chuckle.

"Mr. Darlington?" Chloe inquired.

"I'll tell you about him another day. He is a legend, not to mention a true gentleman too."

"He is," Laura confirmed.

Desmond approached through the crowd, twisting and turning to avoid a collision, four cocktails perched atop a tray overhead. It was a feat no less impressive than an Olympic floor routine and he finally reached the booth without spilling a single drop. Malachi clapped his respect and Des smiled.

"Here you go folks. A special treat for my special friends."

"Thanks, Des, but you really must stop giving us free drinks. At this rate you will be bankrupt within a fortnight," Malachi replied. He hated taking twenty pounds' worth of free drinks, let alone the thousands that had been collected for him. If it was possible, he would try and find a way of giving the money to charity. The local children's hospice was always deserving of donations to help the poor kids.

"It's nothing," Desmond dismissed it and left them to answer the ringing phone behind the bar.

"So you two, what have you got planned for the future?" Laura asked.

"We are just going to take things slowly," Malachi said, missing the look of hurt on Chloe's face, "With my life being such a cluster fuck at the moment, I don't want to take Chloe down with me."

"Hey!" Chloe pushed him, "We are in this together, remember? If I didn't want to help you then I wouldn't be here."

"Help with what?" Laura looked confused.

Kevin glanced at Malachi who nodded his permission, "Mal has been having some really bad dreams. Like *scare the living shit out of you, I can't ever sleep again* type dreams."

"Oh my goodness, why didn't you say anything?" Laura reached out and held his hand.

"Too embarrassed," Malachi admitted.

"But he has told us now, and we are going to help him get past the nightmares," Kevin declared.

"Yes we are," Chloe added.

"Especially after the last one you had. Three fucking days of being totally out of it, tearing the room apart in fear until they had to sedate you."

"I was so scared," Chloe whispered, "They wouldn't let me see you and I thought maybe you had taken a turn for the worse."

Laura took it all in with astonishment. She had heard of night terrors but the awful experiences of Malachi were on a whole other level. "Do you want to come and stay with us for a while? Both of you. We can swap the boys around to give you a room to share."

"No!" Malachi responded aggressively. Laura flinched at the reply and Malachi quickly finished, "I wouldn't want to impose on you. The dreams can be horrific and I don't want to scare you or the kids."

"I understand," she said, "But the offer is always open."

"Hang on a minute, if Malachi moves in how will I be able to walk around stark bollock naked?" Kevin was outraged.

"You will just have to put underwear on. It's bad enough when you answer the door to my mother in your mankini," Laura replied.

The bright green mankini was well known to everyone in their circle and after enough beers, Kevin would disappear and come back looking like Borat. The joke never failed to raise a laugh at parties, but his mother in law felt a bit more awkward at the inappropriate attention.

"My house, my rules!" Kevin stated defiantly and they all laughed.

"Seriously, though. We are here for you in whatever way you need us, ok?" Laura said sincerely.

"Thank you all so much. A week ago I thought this shit would never end. After seeing Dr. Llyod and sharing with you guys, I finally believe there may be some hope for me."

"Of course there is, you have a friend like me!" Kevin leaned over and punched his shoulder.

"Kevin!" Laura was aghast, "Don't hit him. He only had surgery a few days ago."

"And now look at him, he's fit as a fiddle. Mal, show Laura the scar."

Malachi surveyed the room for eavesdroppers, but everyone was lost in their own conversations. Turning away from the bar, he stood as far as the booth would allow and lifted his t-shirt. The two wounds were practically gone, with only a faint discoloration remaining that didn't even resemble a scar.

"Wow, how is that possible?" Laura asked, her mouth open wide in amazement.

"I have no idea. I was tested in the hospital with no success. Dr. Franken is going to see me once a week to try and get to the bottom of it. He says it may be possible to cure all sorts of diseases if they can unlock the secret."

"That's incredible," Laura said.

"And it will make you filthy rich," Kevin added with a wink.

"I don't want to be rich. I just hope I can help people to get better."

"Yeah, but a couple of hundred million isn't considered rich these days," Kevin announced. "You can always lend me fifty mill then I can buy a yacht and hold wild parties with loads of models."

"You come back smelling of skank and I will John Bobbitt you while you sleep," Laura threatened.

"I love it when you get all kinky," Kevin teased and kissed her.

"I'm serious about the money though. I will be doing it for other people, not to make money. I think I may be able to take a few pounds out so I can buy us all a nice house each, that way we won't have to worry about mortgages."

"There's a lovely nine bed house going down the road at the moment for a cool two million," Kevin joked.

"Keep this up and I'll buy you a leaky caravan," Malachi fired back with a grin.

"You know I'm only kidding. I just want to see my best mate better," Kevin said and they grasped hands.

"With you all by my side, I know I can do it."

Desmond waved across the bar to catch Malachi's attention. He pointed to the toilets and Malachi nodded in agreement.

"Everything ok?" Chloe asked.

"I'm sure it's nothing. I'll be right back," Malachi assured her and excused himself.

Moving through the crowd led to several more delays as people congratulated him. One woman even propositioned him until he explained he was taken. Pushing through the door, he was greeted with the scent of bleach and pine urinal cakes. Desmond was pacing nervously in the small bathroom area and locked the door swiftly.

"What's got you so worked up, Des?" Malachi inquired.

"The phone call was from my boy Legacy; they found where those three bumboclots were hiding," Desmond explained.

Malachi sighed with frustration, "Des, I told you that I didn't want anything bad to happen to them."

"I know that, man. But honour demands they understand what you could have done to them. Who knows, it may even straighten them out."

"You and your bloody honour," Malachi groaned, "And I'm pretty certain that if they are willing to rape a girl and stab me, then they are too far gone anyway."

"You never know; a near death experience can focus the mind." Desmond tapped his head, "It will take half an hour, tops. I promise."

"Shit, Des, you are putting me in a really awkward situation here. What do I say to Chloe?"

"Just tell her I need a hand collecting some more alcohol."

"That's pretty weak, Des.

"Fuck, man. Tell her the truth then, that you need to get some closure on the shit that happened," Desmond replied with agitation.

"I don't need closure, though. I have already moved on," Malachi replied, "But I can see you need it, so I will go with you to make sure you don't do anything foolish."

Relief washed over Desmond's face and he embraced his friend. "Thank you, Mal. The car will be waiting out front, I'll meet you there."

After Desmond had left the room, Malachi rinsed his face with cold water. What the fuck are you doing? he thought to himself. You wanted a quiet life and now you are about to get into a car with ruthless gangsters to save the lives of three men who left you for dead. If the roles were reversed, Malachi was certain he would have received no mercy from the trio. They were feral, a blight on society, but that didn't give him the right to act as judge, jury, and executioner. Did this make him a coward? Possibly. At least he would be able to live with himself, though.

The door slammed open and a man stumbled in that Malachi didn't know. Seeing the drunken stranger was going to start a conversation, he quickly excused himself and made his way back to the booth. Chloe smiled warmly and his heart melted at the sight. Their love was only just beginning, but Malachi knew it would burn as brightly as his parents had all those years ago.

"I have to pop out and help Des for half hour. I will be back as soon as I can," Malachi leaned over and kissed Chloe.

"I don't understand," she said with suspicion, "This is your party, why can't he get someone else to help?"

Deciding that he would always be honest with her, he came clean, "Des has the three guys that attacked us. I know you think I'm crazy, but I want to make sure they don't get killed."

"You're a better man than I am, Mal. I would pull the trigger myself," Kevin grumbled.

"And you would leave me and the boys on our own," Laura scolded, "I think he is doing the right thing."

"Me too," Chloe said quietly. It was clear the memory of that night would haunt her for some time.

"I won't be long."

"Mal?" Chloe stopped him.

"Yeah?"

"Be safe," she replied.

Acting on impulse, Malachi mouthed the words *I love you* and Chloe smiled, before mouthing them back and blowing a kiss. The buzz of the silent exchange diminished with each pace he took towards the entrance. Stepping into the fading afternoon light, the waiting car filled him with apprehension. Desmond was talking to one of the gang members and beckoned Malachi over.

"Mal, this is my brudda, Legacy," Desmond introduced the dangerous looking individual and they shook hands.

"Des tells me good 'tings about you," Legacy replied, appraising the young man.

"Des hasn't told me anything about you," Malachi said with a shrug.

"I'm glad to hear that," he laughed, "Safer for everyone. Let's go."

As the door opened and a stench of cannabis enshrouded the pair, Malachi couldn't help feeling like he was about to make a deal with the Devil. Desmond never got involved in the drug trade or other illegal activities of the wider Yardie gang and it was for this reason alone that Malachi didn't turn tail and run back into the bar. Drum and bass blared from the speakers, making the windows rattle.

"Can we turn it down a little?" Malachi asked and the others burst out laughing.

"Of course," Legacy smiled, twisting the control knob, "Now let's go and see our three friends."

The laughter sounded maniacal and Malachi looked out of the window, seeing Chloe chatting to Kevin and

Laura. He prayed he was doing the right thing as the BMW raced away from the bar, leaving her outline on his vision.

CHAPTER EIGHTEEN

Malachi was silent for the entire journey. Desmond tried to engage him in trivial conversation about work and football, but he didn't respond. With each passing mile in the drug purchased luxury motor, the feeling of dread grew. Civilization was left behind and habitation gave way to open fields and an old industrial park. The factories had long ago ceased manufacturing their various goods and the hulking machines stood silent, victims of the drive for globalization and cheap imports. It provided a haven for prostitution and drug dealing, with the plethora of dark alleys and tunnels a boon for making an escape from law enforcement.

"Nearly there," Legacy informed them.

Faces peered from the darkness, their eyes glinting with the passing light of the vehicle. Some calculated, unaware of the occupants. Others shied away, recognising the car and the menace it brought. They rounded a corner and pulled up alongside another two high end saloon cars, each with a steely eyed minder. As they all climbed out, Desmond gave a reassuring nod to Malachi. The two guards embraced the newcomers and eyed the young, white man warily.

"We tying him up?" asked one of the men.

"No, he's with Desmond," Legacy explained, "He's here for retribution too."

Mal glanced at Des and he shook his head in apology, he would clear up the misunderstanding once inside. The Yardies gave him a cautious nod and showed them through the side door before returning to their watch. A filthy hallway led them deeper into the building. The plaster ceiling had collapsed and paint was peeling from the walls like a snake shedding skin. Yellowed light flickered under the door they were approaching, casting dancing shadows. Echoing laughter carried through but it was without mirth. It was more akin to the cackling of hyenas as they tore at a stricken beast.

"Welcome," grinned one of Legacy's crew, holding his arm out to invite them inside.

The room itself was partially stripped of machinery. Crane topped gantries and a few smaller machines had survived the decommission when the business had transferred production to a more tax friendly country. The emptiness was eerie, a bleak contrast to the harsh discord which would have been abound during the more successful years. In the midst of the desolate floor space were three chairs, and in each one sat one of Malachi's attackers. Candles had been set in a wide circle, their lazily drifting flames giving an occult feel to the proceedings.

"What the fuck is this all about?" shouted out one of the men. It was the one who had stabbed Malachi. Twice. The nose was still crooked with a makeshift patch below his two black eyes.

The gangsters all turned in unison at the arrival of their Don. Legacy greeted them all and Malachi took up position behind the captives until he knew what would transpire. One of the dreadlocked members was sharpening a knife while staring at the thugs, the metallic rasp carrying around the room. Another placed a skull at their feet and started to daub a thick red liquid on the floor, drawing a circular pattern around them.

"Des, what the hell is going on?" Malachi whispered.

"It's all for show, man," Desmond explained, stifling a laugh, "It's meant to be old Obeah voodoo but they haven't got a clue about the vevés so they are just drawing a pentagram."

"I don't like this," Malachi replied. His initial hunch to steer clear was proving to be the right choice, except it was now too late. He was surrounded by a gang of murderers who were taking the spectacle to the extreme.

"Chill, Mal. Considering what could have happened to them, this is nothing," Desmond assured his friend.

Malachi wanted to leave. The impulse to run screaming for the door was close to taking hold, but for some strange reason he felt a sense of responsibility for the three pathetic creatures. Their utter confusion at what was unfolding kept him rooted to the spot and as their terror grew, so did Malachi's. He would need to ride this out, and not just to protect Desmond's honour. By sticking around, he was fairly sure their friendship would ensure the potential rapists all walked away to face a proper trial and justice, instead of winding up in a hole in pieces.

"It is ready," declared the fake priest.

Stepping forward, Legacy stared evilly at each of the prisoners for a few seconds, appraising them. "You wonder why you been brought here, what you could have done that requires a payment in blood."

"What are you talking about, we don't even know you guys," pleaded the one who had lain atop Chloe.

Malachi started to grind his teeth in anger, the sheer animalism of the ritual speaking to him on a primal level. He had to picture Chloe's smiling face to drive out the darkness which was settling in his heart.

"You may not know us," Legacy snarled an inch from the man's face, "But we know you."

"Please, tell us what we have done. We will make it right, I promise," begged the third man between sobs.

"Only your souls will suffice," declared Legacy, cutting their clothing and exposing their bare chests.

"What the fuck do you mean our souls? There's no such thing!"

Legacy leaned in close, looking around as his associates all laughed with secret knowledge, "We will see."

189

Taking the pot of blood, he painted crosses on their chest where the heart was located. They tried thrashing around to avoid the liquid, but machete's appeared at their throats, stilling the dissent.

"Des, this has to stop!" Malachi hissed.

"Soon, man," Desmond said dazedly. He was caught up in the same reverie as Malachi, only it was more powerful. This was the religion of his ancestors, believed to have origins in the Ashanti tribes of Northern Africa. The slaves had used it to gain strength for their ordeal and work evil against their brutal masters. Malachi had been through far too much recently to make light of the ritual, irrespective of the flaws in its delivery.

"First we cut out your hearts while you still breathing," Legacy explained, "Then we eat dem hearts."

"No, please."

"Oh God, I have children."

The Don went back to chanting in a Jamaican patois, swaying and rolling his eyes for dramatic effect. All three men had reached a peak of fear, their bodily functions giving in. As the smell of urine and faeces reached Malachi, the gang members laughed at their discomfort. It was difficult for Malachi to process the link between his colourful friend, and the sadistic monsters around the room. Their upbringing had been tough, but he couldn't understand the continued association and loyalty. England allowed people to thrive on their own merits, which Desmond had used to great effect. Their tangled relationship was beyond his understanding, so he returned his attention to the psychological torture.

"It's time," Legacy nodded to Desmond. The three men mistook his intent and started screaming in terror, fighting unsuccessfully against their bonds. This only brought more cheer to the cold blooded killers around the room.

"Shut your fucking mouths!" Desmond shouted, stepping into view.

"You!" gasped the knifeman.

"I told you I would see you real soon," he smiled and turned to Legacy, "What are their fucking names?"

"Patrick Olech," he read the driver's license and pointed at the rapist, "Chad Trimble," the knifeman, "And Stanley Rothmuer."

"Now we get to deliver vengeance for your insults," Desmond stared at the men.

"All this for a shitty flag?" demanded Patrick.

The whole room took a menacing pace forward, guns and machetes raised. The brash man shrivelled, blabbering apologies for the unintended slight.

"Des, I know what you told us, but this one is a special case," Legacy growled, "I want him."

"No," Desmond placed a restraining hand on his friend's chest, "With respect, brudda, this goes down as I want."

"You're lucky I love this man," Legacy told Patrick, before throwing a punch that rocked his head back.

Spitting teeth from a ruined mouth, he tried to apologise again. "I'b thowwy," was all he could manage.

"Mal, come forward," Desmond said.

Malachi joined him in front of the attackers, trying to remain stoical. They were beyond pitiful and the stench was growing with each passing second. Watching him with growing apprehension, they waited fearfully for the order that would end their lives. They had tried to kill this man and rape his girlfriend; it was no less than they would expect.

"I see you know my friend too," Desmond smiled, taking the knife from Legacy. He turned the blade over and over, seemingly hypnotized by the razor sharp edge.

"Oh fuck. Look, we didn't mean anything by it, we were just drunk and acting out."

"*Acting out?*" Desmond screamed, slashing the knife inches from his face.

"Ok, ok!" Stanley wailed, "They always get carried away and hurt someone. I try and keep them in line."

Malachi had heard enough. Pushing Desmond to one side, he leaned in close, "I seem to remember you holding her down while that bastard tried to rape her."

"They made me!"

"It looked like it," Malachi whispered, remembering Stanley's face poised above Chloe as he had raced down the alleyway. The way he licked his lips in anticipation of what was to come.

Desmond could see the change in Malachi and pulled him back, "Are we having a change of heart? My boys are ready to go all the way if you want, just say the word."

Malachi had shut out the room and didn't hear the offer. It was only himself and the three who had wronged him now. Deep inside his heart a black void opened, pulling him through into a maelstrom of rage. Out of the darkness rose a single thought; revenge. Unseen presences whispered and cajoled, seeking to set him free of the burdens of morality. Seething and bubbling with a convincing malevolence, his mind felt assaulted by the pernicious mutterings. The men didn't appear as pathetic anymore, their twisted visages resembled those from the night Malachi was attacked. They sneered and laughed at his weakness, mocking him for being too weak to act as a real man. For some unknown reason they were now free of their bonds, pointing at Malachi and rubbing at their penis's through urine saturated trousers.

"Do you want to die that badly?" he asked the men who clutched at their sides and roared with hilarity.

"You don't have it in you," sneered Patrick, "I'm going to fucking destroy Chloe when I get my hands on her. I'll give it to her far better than you ever could, you faggot!"

"And I'm going to piss all over her battered face," Stanley giggled, revealing his own warped sexual proclivities.

"I'm not going to stop until you bleed out in the gutter next time," Chad declared, "Then I'm going to cut your bitch open and watch her try and hold her guts in. Maybe there will be a baby, that's always a plus."

They thought he was weak, that he wouldn't protect those he loved. All it would take was one word and they would be butchered and gone from this world, never to threaten another innocent again. He wanted to do it. Positively ached with the need which spread through every fibre of his being like a malignant cancer. It tried to crush his sensibilities, dull his predilection for mercy and understanding. The corruption pulsed in time with his heart, flowing around his body like lava in his veins. The heat settled in his right hand, and looking down he could see the knife which Desmond had been holding.

"Do it," Stanley begged.

"Cut my throat," pleaded Patrick, "It would be so easy."

"Just imagine how it would feel," coaxed Chad, "The power of life and death. The giver of divine judgement and retribution against the forces of evil."

"It doesn't feel divine," Malachi said to the trio and their faces twisted in hatred and malice that wasn't in any way human.

The grasp on his consciousness was slipping and Malachi could finally sense the external force that was invading his psyche. Creeping in the darkest crevices of his mind, it tried to play on memories long forgotten, twisting them to its own ends. The entity could feel its grip loosening and with one final, desperate surge it tried to bury itself. Malachi focused on his parents and Chloe, the purest people he had ever known, drawing on their love to break the shackles.

"NOOOOOOOOOO!" Malachi screamed, tearing at his own head.

With an inhuman howl the force was driven from his mind, retreating into the abyss from which it spawned. The room lightened and Malachi felt the burning sensation on his scalp for the first time. In his anguish he had torn the skin and his fingers came away bloody.

"What the fuck was that?" Desmond asked, startling Malachi.

The three men were being lifted from the floor. Their eyes betrayed a new level of terror that hadn't been present at the mere thought of death.

"What happened?" Malachi asked, noticing the Yardies also regarded him with fear and respect.

"You was mumbling, then you seemed to go into a trance," Desmond explained.

Legacy walked over, bowed slightly in deference and finished the tale, "Things started to happen in the room. Noises and wailing. It was as if the gods answered your call."

It certainly wasn't a god, or a benevolent deity anyway.

"It was like something was getting ready to blow, and then you screamed and it was like being hit by a truck. It wasn't just them fools who got knocked on their asses."

"He has the power," whispered one of the crew to Legacy with wonderment.

"He does," agreed the Don.

Everyone watched Malachi, as if waiting for instructions from him despite the fact he was just an outsider. He couldn't explain the bizarre manifestation which had caused a shockwave from his subconscious. The psychic usurper, had it been imaginary or a real being seeking to turn him against himself? It had felt so real. His mind felt violated, and like a common snail Malachi could sense the oozing trail it had left as it was driven out. This would be a question for Dr. Llyod. Or a priest!

"What do you want from me?" Malachi blurted, still reeling.

"They think you are a shaman," Desmond whispered and still they stared.

"You don't believe in all that stuff, do you?" he asked.

"I've seen things in my time, but nothing like that. You have magic in you, man," he replied.

Malachi could see Desmond regarded him differently after the inexplicable psychic eruption. The last thing he wanted was to alienate one of the only friends he had ever had.

"Des, it's me. You don't have to be worried," he said, reaching out a hand.

"I'm not worried, brudda," Desmond replied, pulling him in for a reassuring embrace.

"I don't know what's happening to me," Malachi said, lost and bewildered.

Desmond pointed to the captives and said, "Make a decision about them. Then we go and get you all the help you need."

Malachi looked around at the Yardies. He hadn't even wanted to come here, and now he had a gang of heavily armed psychopaths treating him as if he were their messiah. On top of all that he had the fate of three scumbags in his hands. Fuck! Sensing the growing darkness, Malachi could feel the tentative probes of *the other*. It was the only name that seemed to fit at the moment. Tired of the whole thing, the anger subsided and he made a point of mocking his inner enemy with pictures of mercy.

"Tie them up and leave them somewhere, then make an anonymous call for the police to collect them."

Legacy approached the men, pointing a newly drawn pistol at each of them, "If it were my choice, I would carve you up. You owe that man your life. Every breath you take from today is because of his forgiveness."

They all sobbed with relief, thanking Malachi for his decision. The vision of them mocking his ability to protect his loved ones was still raw so he glared at them all.

"If I hear you fight the case in court to get off lightly. If I hear that once you get out of prison you go back to your old ways. If I hear anything at all about the three of you, ever. My friends will finish this and it will be like you never existed," Malachi explained, trying to sound as menacing as possible.

It was an empty threat because he would never willingly order the execution of anyone, no matter how bad they may be. The pulse of energy and the uncertainty of what they were in the presence of ensured it would be heeded, irrespective of the falsity.

"Des, you still want me to fuck them up before dumping them?" Legacy asked.

He thought about it for a few moments, then decided against it, "I think they know what we could have done to them. Tie them, drop them, and then come to the bar. Drinks on me."

A murmur of approval went around the group and Malachi nodded his thanks. Desmond smiled back, but it had a guarded quality that wasn't there before.

"We are still friends, aren't we?" Malachi asked, fearing the answer.

"Of course, man. I just never seen something like that and it scared the shit out of me," he replied.

"You don't think I'm... bad, do you?"

"Fuck no!" Desmond said with a firm shake of the head. "You are the most forgiving person I know. There is nothing but good inside your heart."

Malachi smiled and decided against explaining the events leading up to the psychic explosion. How he had battled the darkness within and very nearly lost. Hopefully

Dr. Llyod would be available soon; he needed to talk it through with someone who might understand it.

CHAPTER NINETEEN

Cannabis smoke wafted into the back of the car from the driver and Legacy reached forward, slapping him around the back of his head, causing the cigarette to fall in the footwell.

"Ave some fucking respect, man," he growled as his drivers frantically tried to retrieve it while still navigating the road safely. It hadn't been an issue on the first journey, but now the don was especially concerned with Malachi's comfort.

"Honestly, it's fine," he said, trying to defuse the situation, "I can open a window."

"You want to save the whole world," Legacy burst out laughing.

"It will take more than me to sort this planet out," Malachi chuckled.

Legacy's smiled died, "That's noble, man, but this bumbaclot should have asked first. He has no clue who he's in the presence of."

"I don't really know what I am," Malachi said quietly.

"You is a shaman, you 'ave the power."

"Fuck me, will you stop saying that," he blurted. Fearing a violent response, he apologised.

"No worries, man. There are strange times coming, I can feel it. If you ever need me and my bredren you call, ok?" Legacy said with conviction.

"Thank you," Malachi replied. He wasn't quite sure how he felt about having a whole gang of murderous gangsters on his side.

Pulling up outside Desmond's bar, Malachi was heartened to see Chloe still happily chatting with Kevin and Laura. Inexplicably he had expected her to be gone; psychically sensing the dark ritual he had been a part of and running for her life. Maybe she would be safer away from him until he could unravel the bizarre occurrences. For once his unbreakable principles bent a little; he just didn't want to be away from this beautiful girl for a minute. Justification boiled down to the fact that in Chloe he had an anchor, a reason to try and fathom the dreams and his burgeoning telekinesis.

"Thank you, I think," Malachi said, shaking hands with Legacy.

"It's nothing, man," Legacy nodded, "Des, I'll be back when the fuckers are locked away."

"Thanks, brudda." Des hugged the man and waved as the BMW raced off into the night.

Malachi held Des back before he could open the door and pulled him to one side, "You can't ever tell anyone about what you saw. I have to find a way to figure this shit out before I really hurt someone."

Des looked hurt, "What do you take me for, Mal. It will go with me to the grave, I promise."

"I'm sorry, mate. All this shit has got me so twisted I don't know whether I am coming or going." Malachi ran a hand down his face, sighing.

"Listen," Des placed a supportive hand on his shoulder, "I know an Obeah priestess that might have some answers. Now I'm not saying that you are a shaman or voodoo witchdoctor, but she may be able to help. All religions have aspects that are taken from core beliefs; miracles, magic, good and evil."

"You think my power might be evil?" Malachi still felt the dark taint.

"It's all relative, man. Power is power. If you use it to do ill, then it becomes evil. If you use it to protect people, then it is good. The choice is in your hands," Des explained.

"I guess that makes sense," Malachi replied. If he had ultimate control over the forces rather than the forces controlling him like a puppet, he could help people.

"What are you grinning at? A minute ago you had a face as miserable as sin."

"Sorry, Des. Just imagining that I may be able to use this for good like you suggested. If I can ever figure it out."

"Tomorrow I make the call. Come and see me in the afternoon and I will take you to see my friend."

"Thanks, mate. I don't know what I'd do without you," Malachi said, hugging the huge, dreadlocked Jamaican.

"Don't thank me. If you have powers I'm going to use you as security for the bar," he laughed, "I'd never have any trouble again."

They entered the bar to another round of applause and more back patting. The only difference was the food was gone and the congratulations were a great deal more slurred than earlier. Chloe jumped from the booth and kissed him, softly at first but quickly developing into a more passionate clinch.

"Get a room you two," Kevin made a gagging sound.

Chloe laughed straight into Malachi's mouth, ending the contact in fits of drink fuelled giggles.

"You're just jealous," Malachi teased, reaching down to plant a sloppy kiss on Kevin's lips.

"Eww, get off you wrong'un," Kevin spluttered, pushing him away.

"Don't even act like you didn't enjoy it," Laura teased.

"He could have had a shave first," Kevin complained with a grin, "I'm going to get stubble rash now."

"It won't be the worst rash you have ever had, you dirtbag!" Malachi laughed.

"I was young and single. There's no law says I wasn't allowed to have some fun."

"There is now, *my* law," Laura said sternly.

"Sweetie, you know I only have eyes for you," Kevin declared.

"Yeah, right. That's why you've been eyeing up that blonde at the bar for the past half hour," she fired back.

Kevin pulled a shocked face, "I can't help it if she is in me eye line, can I?"

"Your eye line is that way," Laura pointed at the opposite side of the booth, "You have to crane your neck to even see her!"

"You know I get a stiff neck if I don't exercise it. I was just making sure I didn't seize up so I can drive you home safely with a full range of movement," Kevin explained with a straight face.

"You are so full of shit," Laura giggled, pushing him in the shoulder.

"You know I'd never cheat on you, babes," said Kevin, leaning over for a kiss.

"Get a room you two!" Malachi shouted out, much to the amusement of the other partygoers.

"So, what are your plans tonight, my little lovebirds?" Kevin inquired.

"He will be coming home with me where we will get to know each other more intimately," Chloe said, stroking his leg under the table

"Be gentle with him, he's only just come out of hospital," Kevin chuckled.

Malachi's mouth was dry and he could only grin stupidly. If he had tried to talk it would have come out as a croak.

"I can't make any promises," Chloe giggled.

The front door crashed against the wall where someone slammed it open. Everyone turned to scowl at the noisy intrusion as seven men poured in.

"Hey, be careful. What the fuck is this all about?" Des shouted, coming from behind the bar to see what was going on.

Dr. Llyod looked around the room, flanked by four burly men in white hospital uniforms and with two police officers to the rear. Seeing Malachi, recognition and relief pinched his features.

"That's him, that's the one!" he ordered and the four orderlies pushed through the crowd.

"What's this all about?" Chloe asked.

Malachi was dumbfounded, "I have no idea, but that's Dr. Llyod. He's the psychiatrist I am seeing to help me get over my dreams."

"It doesn't look like he is here to help now," Kevin growled and put himself between the four men and his friend.

"Get out of the way, sir. This doesn't concern you," grunted the biggest of them.

"I think it does. What the fuck do you want with my friend?"

"Your friend has to come with us right now or there will be trouble," he threatened.

"I don't think so," Kevin said, squaring up to the man.

Malachi stood and called to Dr. Llyod, "What's this all about, Kenny? I thought we had arranged a visit for next week?"

His manic eyes and sweat drenched brow did not belong on any rational professional and what had earlier seemed a friendly face was now something to be feared. Something was very wrong here. The nurses, for that's what their identification badges showed them to be, were losing patience. Every time they would try and reach for Malachi, Kevin would block their arm.

"You have to come with us, you are a danger to all these people and yourself," Dr. Llyod ranted.

The crowd started to jostle the men, reminding him that Malachi was a hero.

"Where's the paperwork then?" Desmond demanded, confronting the doctor. "You can't just grab people off the street like soviet Russia."

"As a trained psychiatrist, I assure you I am correct in my diagnosis. That man has a history of violence and shows psychotic tendencies. His terrible dreams are a manifestation of his desire to maim and kill," Dr. Llyod babbled.

"That was meant to be confidential!" Malachi shouted furiously.

"See," the doctor remarked to the crowd, "Prone to uncontrollable anger."

"Go fuck yourself, I'm not going anywhere with you," Malachi replied.

"Oh I think you are," growled the head nurse, trying to push Kevin to one side.

The atmosphere was already charged but at the contact all hell broke loose. Kevin ducked away from the meaty hand, rolling underneath it before throwing an uppercut. The crack carried throughout the whole bar and the big man fell back, his broken jaw lolling. The two policemen were wrestling with Desmond, and Malachi used his body to shield Chloe and Laura from the danger. The nurses had underestimated Kevin and each time one would try and take him down, another punch opened up their faces. Four more nurses barged through the entrance, making eight beefy men for a single man. Malachi's mind was suddenly clear and he knew what had also confused him. The nurses had far more in common with a group of mercenaries he had seen on a documentary. Scarred and tattooed with dead eyes from the horror they had witnessed or perpetrated.

"You're not medical staff, who the fuck are these people?" Malachi shouted at the doctor.

Kevin had finally been taken down and thrashed on the floor. Laura screamed her rage and threw herself into the fray, raining kicks and punches on the dazed nurses.

203

"You have to come with us, Malachi," pleaded the doctor, "Please don't let anyone else get hurt." The implied threat was enough.

"Ok, call off your dogs and I will come with you. Let my friends go. Now!"

"Malachi, you can't," Chloe whispered fearfully.

"I have to," he replied, reaching down and squeezing her hand, "It will all get sorted, I promise."

"Ok," agreed Dr. Llyod and the men carefully released Desmond and Kevin.

The four new arrivals took hold of Malachi and guided him towards the door. Kevin was still facing down the other group and the head nurse stepped forward.

Words garbled by the sagging jaw, he said, "I'll see you again."

"Come and find me when you can take a punch," Kevin laughed dismissively and his men dragged him away before he could be hurt further.

Desmond was already dialling on the phone and called out, "Don't worry, Mal. I won't let the bastards get away with this, you're all going to lose your jobs!"

"Thank you for your cooperation," said one of the policemen as they exited.

"Fuck your cooperation," shouted Chloe, pushing towards the bar.

Everyone gathered around to hear the one-sided conversation.

"Police... Yeah, I want to speak to whoever is in charge... I don't care if this is a call centre, put me through to my local station... You can't help, just put me through... Thanks..." he cupped the receiver, "They are just putting me through to the Metropolitan Police.

Chloe was sobbing and Laura did her best to console her, "Don't panic, we will have him back in a jiffy, sweetheart."

Desmond held a hand to quieten the crowd, "Yes, I want to report two of your officers and find out why the hell they assaulted me to facilitate the kidnap of one of my dear friends... My name is Desmond DeCosta... As I explained, two of your officers, badge numbers 3226 and 6701 came into my bar and assaulted me... Why? Because I wouldn't allow them to kidnap my friend without showing me any paperwork... His name is Malachi Alderton... No, they were accompanied by eight men dressed in hospital whites, and a Dr. Llyod who is a psychiatrist... They claimed that Malachi was a danger and he needed to accompany the doctor. Now I know bullshit when I hear it and the amount of muscle they brought with them was totally over the top... No, as I said before, they showed me no paperwork, just started to rough myself and my customers up until he went with them willingly... No that's not the end of it, he only went with them willingly so that no one else got hurt. I want to know where he has been taken so I can contact my solicitor... Yes, I'll hold."

"What's going on?" Chloe asked.

"The sergeant is just checking the database to see what facility he is being taken to. As soon as I mentioned the solicitor he was a bit more helpful."

"Yes, hello... Of course I am sure about the badge numbers, they were an inch from my face when they were trying to wrestle me to the floor," Desmond explained. His face changed from angry to bewildered before the conversation continued, "But that's just not possible, these guys were in their thirties at most. Shaved heads, thick set from working out... Ok, I'll wait by the phone, but for fuck sake, please hurry."

A hush of apprehension fell over the bar as he slowly replaced the phone.

"What's wrong?" Chloe tried to ask while chewing on her knuckle in dread.

Desmond took a few moments to compose himself before speaking, "The badge numbers are obsolete; the officers they belonged to retired last year and were both in their late fifties. There is also no record of an operation involving a Dr. Llyod from the mental health service."

"What does it mean?" Kevin asked.

"It means they weren't real police, and they have no idea where Malachi is being taken," Desmond replied vacantly, mind reeling.

Chloe broke down completely and fell to the floor.

"What are the police going to do?" Kevin demanded.

"They are coming to take statements and will send a car to Dr. Llyods address. Did anyone see the vehicles they left in?" Desmond asked the crowd.

"There was one police car and two private ambulances. Not like the ones which attend emergencies, more like patient transports," explained a young woman who had been stood by the front window.

"How will they find him?" asked Laura, cradling Chloe as she wept.

"I have no idea. I think we may need some help," he admitted, taking out his mobile phone and dialling. "Legacy, we need you and your boys, Malachi has been taken. I'll explain it all when you get here, but make sure you come locked and loaded, whoever they are, they mean business."

Desmond ended the call and stared at the wall phone, willing it to ring with good news. The green plastic mocked him with its silence.

CHAPTER TWENTY

The drummer finished with a flourish and an audience of ghosts cheered their appreciation. Gordon Franken smiled and leaned back in the leather recliner, basking in the glory years of jazz. A saxophonist blew the first chords of Moment's Notice, the next song on a John Coltrane album that he adored. Music was infinitely more enjoyable back in the fifties and sixties than the awful modern hullabaloo. Closing his eyes, he imagined himself sat at a table in the front row of Manhattan's Jazz Gallery Club. The hazy atmosphere of cigarette smoke giving the world famous quartet on the stage a spectral quality. Gordon was totally lost in the moment until the shrill din of the smoke alarm ripped him from the bygone era.

"Oh, my goodness!"

Rushing into the kitchen, the bloated silver foil of the popcorn dish had ruptured and the kernels were ablaze on the stove. Twisting the lever on the tap, cold water flowed into the sink, and using a cloth, he quickly tossed the fiery contents into it with a clatter and a hiss. Steam carried the stench of charred corn and Gordon shook his head with amusement. This was the second time it had happened this month.

"No more jazz during popcorn preparation," he told himself while wafting another cloth across the tripped detector.

In a few seconds the clamour of the alarm stopped and he opened the window to air out the stinking room. Once the pan had cooled he wrapped and binned the blackened popcorn packet and wiped it dry. Igniting the burner again, he set another portion of buttered popcorn to heat through. For a moment he considered returning to listen to another song.

"Don't be a fool. That's what got you into this predicament in the first place," he warned himself.

Giving the pan a final shake, the last kernels popped and he carefully poured the contents into a glass dish. Taking a bottle of popcorn butter, he looked around guiltily and drizzled the yellow liquid over the steaming treat. Life was far too short to worry about cholesterol, he thought with a grin. He patted his thin stomach and thanked his fast metabolism for hiding the evidence of his overindulgences. God forbid his colleagues or patients finding out about the naughty habit with all the lectures he gave on the subject of obesity.

"Nothing wrong with a little hypocrisy, Gordon," he chuckled as he sat back down at the desk.

His hand hovered by the small stereo on the right, before turning it off completely. The distraction would be too great and he wanted to fully focus on the rough draft of his examination plan for Malachi. Saying goodnight to John Coltrane, he pulled down his tattered note pad. Years of scribbles and cut out articles were spread throughout the leather bound jotter. It was beyond priceless to him and had been a gift on his first wedding anniversary to Marjorie. She had passed eight years ago and this played no small part in his melancholy demeanour. A part of him had died in that hospital room that night.

"That's quite enough of that," he said with a firm nod. Memories could be dangerous and if he gave them free reign, inevitably the brandy bottle would be taken down which would end any meaningful research.

Twin screens glowed in the low light of the office. Apart from those and a small desk light, all was shadow which is the way Gordon preferred it. A spreadsheet lay open on the left screen which he had started to populate with dates and times. Each would be used for a different set of examinations and tests, some with the aid of the colleagues he had presented to Malachi earlier. Their fields were varied which ensured the greatest chance of unlocking the gifts he possessed. On the other was a browser tab with a dozen pages open. Looking at the subject matter it was varied, and in some cases, downright bizarre. Religious healing and folk medicine, alongside medical studies and science fiction. Gordon was a firm believer that as humanity developed, science fiction would ultimately become science fact. Clubs and rocks had been replaced by nuclear armaments in the space of a few thousand years. This raised the obvious possibility that humanity was far better at creating ways to kill each other than ways to heal each other.

"If we blow the planet up, all of this will have been for nothing."

There was that morbidity again. Shaking himself, he opened the emails and clicked on one of the messages. He had read it over fifty times and it still sent shivers down his spine. It was dated two days ago and carried the name: Dr Lance Olsen. Gordon read it again.

Dear Gordon,

Thank you for your email, it is always nice to hear from a physician that is as deeply committed to furthering our understanding of medicine as I once was. Sadly, time hasn't been kind to me and with my failing eyesight I can only work in a limited capacity as a verbal consultant.

I spoke to Jenny, with whom you inquired about myself, and she assures me you are well respected in Britain. I apologise for the need to do some background research on you, but that case has always haunted me and I wanted to be sure you weren't affiliated with THEM. The threats I received toward my family have always troubled me, but as I near the end of my life I can only assume I have been long forgotten.

Mr. Voight, or Clarence, was brought in on a stormy night with ferocious lightning the likes of which I had never seen. The clothing was fused to his body from the fire, and as the attending physician on duty, I put his chances of survival at lower than one percent. We stabilised him and called in the burn specialist who agreed with my initial prognosis. He was in surgery for many hours to remove the charred clothing and clean the wounds. I have to be honest and admit that I was shocked upon arrival for my next shift that he had not succumbed in the night. Fluids were being administered intravenously and his condition was critical but stable. After a few more hours the surgeon who had saved his life even had begun the process of planning skin grafts. It was remarkable.

My initial wonderment was as nothing compared to what I felt after just three days. Suppuration of the wounds had stopped which was unheard of for such a short space of time. One of the nurses came running to find me during a routine dressing change and what I found was incredible. The burnt tissue had started to peel like a common sunburn and underneath was smooth, undamaged skin. Morphine was being administered at a high enough dose to ensure any normal person would remain unconscious to facilitate the healing process. I say this so that you can fully appreciate the profound confusion I felt at seeing his eyes open and, for the most part, alert.

I will remember the few moments of unguarded conversation for as long as I live. The drugs were still having an effect and his eyes were glazed when he spoke these words to me.

"My dreams didn't lie, all that they have promised is flowing through my veins."

I insisted he was delirious and to lay still, but he continued.

"I doubted I could do it at first, I thought my love made me weak. In the end it proved to be exactly what they desired, you see. By giving of my own flesh I was reborn."

I was, by then, aware of his story and called for the detective who had been stationed outside the door. He had gone for a cigarette break and I sent a nurse to retrieve him with utmost haste. He only uttered a single further sentence before the effects of the opiate wore off and he was fully in control of his faculties once more.

"This world will now fall into darkness. No one can stop us."

After this final uttering his defences were up and he played the part of a dutiful husband and father to a tee when the detective returned. The police were unable to use my testimony of his words as they couldn't be relied on in court. Any lawyer worth his crust would have the judge rule it as inadmissible; simply the drugged ramblings of a distraught patient. I knew that he regretted talking to me because I would often find him glaring while I was in the room. On the fifth day my wife received a visit from two police officers. They suggested if I wanted to ensure the safety of my family I should forget the name Clarence Voight. On the sixth day the same officers were stationed at the door of Mr. Voight and on the seventh he was gone. The inscrutable men claimed they hadn't seen anything and he couldn't possibly have got past them, which I knew was a lie. We were on the fourth floor for goodness sake. After making some subtle inquiries with the police station I returned from work to find my home broken into. A picture of my family had been removed from its frame and lay on my pillow, defaced and ruined. After that I did as instructed and forgot the name for over fifty years.

You can imagine my surprise when after all this time, you came onto the scene with your questions. It would seem the cases are related in some aspects, but polar opposite in others. I found Clarence to be an extremely unpleasant individual, whereas in your experience, Malachi seems to be a reluctant hero. My patient displayed arrogance while your showed modesty. It's all rather peculiar and I would be delighted to stay in contact over the course of your trials with any advice I can provide. I'm just sorry that I am too frail to make the journey and assist in person.

Please don't hesitate to call me with any more queries.
Yours faithfully,
Lance.

Gordon rubbed a hand over his face and sighed with amusement when he left a smear of butter juice. He had been so rapt on the words that he had finished the savoury treat without even realising it. Taking a small handkerchief from his breast pocket he wiped most of it clean and would take care of the rest in the bath later. What was he to make of it all? The spreadsheet held little interest at this point and he found himself doing further searches on Clarence Voight and the mystery surrounding the whole episode. Another hour passed in the blink of an eye until he was interrupted by a ping indicating he had a new email. Bringing up the page, the sender box was blank, which was bizarre enough. Moving to delete it as junk he was shocked to see the mouse pointer ignore his movements, and instead, opened the message.

GET OUT NOW. THEY ARE COMING.

"What is this nonsense?" he asked the empty room, although now it didn't feel like he was alone. He could feel eyes on him, but from where he had no idea.

Someone had managed to sneak a virus past his protection. He would write a strongly worded email to the company in the morning to express his displeasure. Without warning the mouse pointer moved again and highlighted the text, before circling around the warning in a blur.

"You're not getting my details, whoever you are," Gordon grumbled and turned the power off. The removal of the monitor light plunged him into deeper shadows and he quickly turned on the overhead light to fend off the growing apprehension. In the back of his mind he was going over Dr Olsen's email. Could it all be connected? If he was truly in danger, then so was his new friend in the states. Frantically trying to calculate the time difference, he decided it was irrelevant; he needed to be warned. Lifting the receiver, he placed it to his ear and flicked the pages in his contact list. It didn't immediately sink in that there was no dial tone and with growing frustration he pressed the cradle. Nothing. Where was his mobile?

"At work," he sighed, "You old fool."

He hated the contraption and often left it in his drawer, preferring the bulky handsets of old. Now he wished he could magically summon the infernal device. A heavy rapping on the door startled him and he nearly fainted when he saw the face pressed to the office window. A cheerful smile appeared on the lips and he shouted through the glass.

"Sorry, Dr. Franken, it's the police, sir. We need to ask you a few questions."

"At this time of night?" he asked the officer.

"If you could let us in, we will be out of your hair in no time."

"Fine, I'll meet you at the front door," he pretended to sigh.

"Many thanks, sir."

When he entered the hallway, he turned left and rushed for the kitchen. Retrieving his key and wallet he figured it would only be a minute at most before the policemen would grow frustrated and search around the perimeter. They may be what they said they were, but Dr Olsen's message and the inexplicable warning on his computer couldn't be ignored. He could contact the authorities later to clear up any confusion if it was all above board. Looking back as the knocking increased in frequency, he barged straight into the man waiting outside the back door.

"That's funny, Doctor. I could have sworn you said you would meet us at the front door. Are we in a hurry?" Carter smiled coldly, pushing Gordon back into the room.

"What is the meaning of this?" Gordon demanded.

"Don't worry, this won't take long," Carter replied, reaching inside his jacket and pulling out a hypodermic needle.

CHAPTER TWENTY ONE

Walking out into the chilly night air he could see the worried expressions of Chloe and his friends through the window. With a wave he made his way around the vehicle and disappeared from sight. The ambulance doors were opened and his minders helped him inside.

"Please, lay down," Dr. Llyod asked, the earlier madness now gone. He was back to the friendly and supportive smile, but Malachi now knew what it concealed. It was a convenient mask to allow him to move among normal people undetected.

"And if I don't want to?" Malachi challenged, preparing for a fight.

"They will hurt us both, and our friends and family," he answered quietly and Malachi could see it was the truth. He was no less scared than Malachi in the presence of the brutes who moved to climb aboard and he felt a twinge of pity.

"Ok, fine."

Laying down on the trolley, he stared up into Kenny's face as he tied the restraints. The doctor could see he was tensing, and attempted to calm Malachi before he tried to tear free, hurting himself and the doctor.

"This is really the best way for everyone," he whispered, "All you have to do is hear them out."

"Hear who out?" Malachi asked. He hated the secrecy, but hoped that perhaps *they* had some answers for him which could explain the recent events.

"All in good time," replied Kenny, tying off the last of the bonds.

"Where are you taking me?"

"Somewhere quiet," he said.

"An asylum?" Malachi pressed.

"Yes and no," replied the doctor enigmatically.

"When will I get a phone call or see my friends? They will want to know I'm ok."

"That depends on your answers and the decision you make."

"Will you stop talking in fucking riddles!" Malachi shouted.

"I promise that all your questions will be answered soon enough," said the doctor calmly, reaching into his trouser pocket and retrieving a phone. After dialling he held the phone to his ear, "Mr. Creighton, we have him. We are in transit towards the destination."

"Is that who ordered this?" Malachi demanded.

The two nurses which accompanied them responded to a subtle nod from the doctor and held Malachi down firmly, using a hand to stifle the protests.

"Yes, sir, I understand. I will see you in a few hours. Thank you, Mr. Creighton."

Pulling out a tray, the doctor picked up an item and at the sight of the hypodermic needle Malachi started to thrash and fight for all he was worth.

Leaning in close, Kenny said, "Malachi, this isn't to hurt you. They need you to go to sleep for what comes next, that's all."

Seeing his position was hopeless, Malachi opted to ride it out and wait for an opportunity to present itself. Offering his arm, the doctor swabbed the crook of his elbow and slid the needle into the skin with a sting. Malachi's arm felt cold and heavy as the anaesthetic coursed in his bloodstream.

"Don't fight it," Dr. Llyod said, leaning in closely.

Vision blurring, Malachi's eyelids slowly closed and he fell into a deep well of unconsciousness.

"How was the meal sweetheart?" asked Malachi.

"It was exquisite. I just can't resist their Duck à l'orange," Chloe replied, thanking the waiter.

"Shall I bring the dessert trolley, sir?"

"Can we have five minutes?" Malachi said and the waiter was gone, resuming his position to watch the tables. He was nothing if not attentive with the merest nod bringing him running.

"Who would have imagined when we met ten years ago that we would be sitting in the Ritz, drinking bottle of Cristal like film stars?" Chloe was buzzing with excitement.

The restaurant was one of the finest in England. Marble pillars held aloft the opulent ceiling. An oval segment was inset like a jewel and bordered by engraved brass flowers. Blue sky with puffs of cloud had been painted in the center to give a feeling of space and tranquility. Jeweled chandeliers twinkled as they lent gentle lighting to the diners below.

"It's all down to our hard work. I always knew we were going to be successful," Malachi said.

"Ever since you secured those government contracts, it's as if we have been blessed," she gushed.

A couple of gentlemen in Saville row suits patted him on the back as they passed and congratulated him on the newest deal. Each of the impeccably tailored garments was worth more than the value of their first cars.

"Who was that?" Chloe whispered.

"Sir Alistair and Sir Mizen. They work for the government behind the scenes, I suppose you could call them fixers. If you need access to certain members of parliament, they can arrange it."

"So they're powerful men?"

"Very."

"Wow," Chloe said with awe. They had looked like her grandfather, only with a much better fashion sense.

"Don't be intimidated, they are teddy bears once you get to know them. As long as you stay on their good side," Malachi said with a mischievous grin.

"And we are on their good side?"

"Of course. I can give them something no one else can," Malachi explained with a callous looking smirk.

"You mean we can?" Chloe didn't like the tone he had used.

Just as quickly, the look was gone, "Of course, sweetheart. Our business is going to do great things in the next few years, mark my words."

Their waiter politely coughed to get their attention and placed two glasses down on the table.

"Courtesy of the gentlemen at the bar," explained the waiter, nodding towards the two knights of the realm who had just walked past, *"A Sidecar for the lady, and a Dalmore 62 for the gentleman."*

Malachi raised his glass of scotch whiskey in toast and the men at the bar raised their own, before swallowing the contents and disappearing through an archway to the side of the bar.

"That was really kind of them," Chloe smiled while sipping the cocktail.

"I should say so, the drinks are about two thousand pounds each," Malachi replied, tasting the exquisite liquor.

Chloe nearly choked with surprise and spat the drink over the table, but etiquette prevailed and she swallowed forcefully, "Why on earth would they buy us such expensive drinks?"

"Because today is a special day," Malachi said with the same smirk.

"My goodness, we really are moving up in the world. Do you remember when we first met and we were happy to drink supermarket wine?" Chloe giggled.

"A lot's changed since then."

"I know," she replied, starting to feel the effects of the drink, *"It seems like a wonderful dream."*

"Indeed," Malachi whispered as he watched her eyes glaze over.

Clicking his fingers another figure hurried over from the archway and helped him to get Chloe to her feet. Making apologies about her overindulgence and excitement the other diners smiled their understanding before gossiping amongst themselves.

"I think I has drunk a bit much," Chloe slurred between their supporting arms and neither man acknowledged her.

Moving through the arch, the waiter pulled a thick curtain across the entrance in their wake before returning to his duties. The corridor was similar to much of the hotel except for the evenly spaced CCTV cameras which tracked their progress. The sumptuously carpeted floor wound away to the left on a downward gradient and between every three cameras were recesses. Fierce looking men and women stood inside the alcoves cradling suppressed Uzi's, with holsters visible between their jackets carrying side arms. Every one of the hidden figures bowed their head in respect as the trio made their way lower and lower down the spiral walkway. After five minutes the temperature had dropped significantly and their breath fogged slightly with each exhalation.

"Are you taking me to bed?" Chloe asked dully, "I don't think I should have had the cocktail."

Both Malachi and his companion looked at each other with secret knowledge.

"How many guards are there?" Malachi asked as they reached what seemed to be a dead end.

"Including the ones you can't see, sir? About two hundred in the building itself. In the surrounding area we would be talking close to five hundred more."

"Good," Malachi responded, satisfied.

"An event like this is treated with the utmost care and planning. Every one of the men and women would lay down their life to protect yours."

"And you?" Malachi questioned.

"Without hesitation," the man stated with certainty.

Before more could be said a faint hiss accompanied the solid brickwork sliding to the right via hidden mechanisms. Beyond the entrance electricity was absent and the walls were made of aged stone instead of brickwork. Black candles were mounted on iron holders, flames fluttering at the intrusion of the fresh air. As the door quietly slid closed behind them it looked like they had stepped into a medieval castle.

"How much further?" Malachi enquired.

"Not far now, sir. Another minute and we will be there."

Malachi noticed the streaks of minerals coating the moist stone and started to feel a sense of claustrophobia. The air itself smelled oppressive, as if it didn't want to give the life sustaining oxygen it contained. Considering what was about to occur, the anxiety was the stuff of childhood and beneath a man of his power.

"We are here," whispered his companion who would not, indeed could not enter the next chamber. It was forbidden.

"Appreciate the help," Malachi stated, taking Chloe's full weight on one arm and shaking the man's hand.

"It was an honor to assist you, sir," he replied and turned away.

"Just a few more steps," Malachi told his wife as they parted more thick drapes and entered a small antechamber.

The room was no more than ten feet wide and fifteen feet long, lined with age worn tables covered in powders and poultices. The tops were arrayed with a greater number of candles, giving more light to the dank space. The yellowed brightness of the flames gave prominence to the carved etchings in the stonework around the room. Glyphs and words in a language that were totally alien to Malachi spoke of darkness and evil. He could feel the power radiating from the inscriptions and knew he would soon understand their purpose.

"We will prepare her," came a voice from one hooded figure out of three that had joined him.

The two shrouded people pulled Chloe through the next archway as she fought weakly and called back to Malachi. The drug she had swallowed was designed to void itself quickly after ingestion and leave the person with no side effects.

"You must put this on," said the third person; a woman judging by her voice and delicate fingers. The robe was also black, with gold stitching bearing more of the images and lettering from the walls. Solid gold clasps held it in place as he lowered it over his head, letting it sit heavily against him. The garment seemed to caress Malachi, with hidden hands inside the fabric rubbing and stroking his shoulders and back. All tension dissipated and the covered woman beckoned him to enter the next room.

As he ducked below the curved stone, the room was awe inspiring. Circular, with a high, domed ceiling and nearly fifty feet in diameter. The walls were made of polished black obsidian, but the amount of time and effort that would have been required to create the underground chamber was incalculable. A dozen wooden doors led from the main chamber to unknown destinations and in the center of the high dome, a thin chute drizzled a thick liquid into a font below. The light was weaker in the room and it wasn't immediately clear what rippled within the bowl.

"This way," urged the woman in a whisper.

Opposite the archway stood a grand mirror ten feet tall. Set in a frame of solid gold filigree, the polished surface reflected Malachi's form and that of his son and wife who were knelt facing it. Both of his kin looked terrified and it triggered a pang of momentary doubt. The cloak itself seemed to pull tighter and the imaginary hands massaged the hesitation away.

"Malachi, what is going on? I'm scared," whimpered Chloe.

Ignoring her, Malachi turned to the woman for instruction.

"First you must drink," she intimated, pointing to a small chalice which sat on the edge of the font.

Stepping close to the basin, the meagre light revealed the blood within and Malachi felt a surge of revulsion. With each drop from above, the thick liquid gave off ripples which lapped at the lip of the bowl.

"I don't know if I can," Malachi protested.

"You must, it is the only way to open the correct conduit," she insisted and scooped up a small amount, "By drinking the blood of innocents, they will be able to hear your plea."

He had come too far to let a little sensibility ruin the plan, so with a deep breath he tipped the cup back and drank the offering. The coppery taste wasn't unpleasant and a shiver of anticipation vibrated through his body.

"Malachi, what are you doing?" Chloe looked at her husband who was now smiling while blood dripped from his chin.

"Daddy, I don't like this place. Please can we go home?" begged his young son.

"We are home," Malachi replied vacantly.

The unholy blood was in his body now, being absorbed and mixed with his own. The woman smiled in the shadow of her hood and rejoined the circle of thirteen acolytes which stood in a crescent behind Malachi's bound family. Closing her eyes, she started to utter the blasphemous words of a long forgotten language.

"Pae youlon gath ip nyk'zor sertool."

Malachi swayed with the mesmerizing voice and looked on in wonder as the mirror started to ripple in the same way as the blood had moments ago.

"Koz'dhar mer nutro cael'quo."

All members lowered their heads in reverence except the female who knelt before Malachi and held out a small knife made of bone. The blade itself was carefully filed into a sharp edge and the size of the weapon indicated that it could only have belonged to a small child.

"Please help us, sweetheart. We love you so much," Chloe begged but the effects of the corrupted blood had removed all empathy from Malachi.

"Daddy, you're scaring me," sobbed his little boy.

He looked down upon his family as if they were no more than discarded meat. They had been bound at feet, knee, waist, and chest to stop any movement and further held in place by loops of rope tied to steel rings in the floor. Moving behind them, he cut deeply into his own wrist, severing the tendon. Blood pulsed from the wound and he held it above each of their heads, soaking them in his life essence.

"Oh, God. What are you doing?" screamed Chloe.

The wound was raw and Malachi smiled to himself. In a matter of seconds, the two edges of severed skin and vein drew themselves together and healed, staunching the flow.

As if the mirror was made of liquid mercury, a face pushed out from the surface to look at them all. The silver visage was nearly as big as the mirror itself and was surrounded by protrusions that could only be horns. It took in each servant of darkness, before finally settling on Malachi and his family with it's huge, saucer eyes.

"Who has summoned me? Make haste or I shall devour you all!" shouted the voice of nightmare.

"It is I, Malachi, who has summoned you. I bring you an offering to seal the pact that has been agreed!" Malachi shouted back, undaunted by the monstrous countenance.

"What do you mean by offering?" screamed Chloe, terror compressing her chest. Their son had already fainted and lay prone on the cold stone floor.

"SILENCE!" screamed the voice as the face pushed even further from the mirror toward her.

"Malachi, please," pleaded his wife, shrinking back. He looked at her with disdain and returned his attention to the mirror.

"I have heard your name, mortal," acknowledged the face with a slow nod, "And it would seem we would both benefit from this arrangement."

Malachi laughed, "Don't play me for a fool. You know that I have far more to offer in this accord than you."

The huge head mulled this for a few moments, "If the prophesies are true, then you may well be correct. Do you enter into this covenant of your own free will?"

"I do," Malachi declared.

"And you give your oath that for all time you will serve as His champion?"

"For eternity!" Malachi proclaimed.

"Very well, your offering will suffice," gurgled the hellish voice and pulled back into the mirror, stilling the surface for a few moments until a massive, clawed hand reached through and plucked Malachi's son from the floor. Before Chloe could react, he was pulled through the looking glass and gone forever.

"Jack!" she screamed so loudly her vocal chords ruptured. Unable to make any words, she spat on Malachi and regarded him with a look of purest hatred.

The empty hand reached through once more and Chloe was ripped from the rope floor binding and drawn into the mirror kicking and struggling. When she disappeared through the vertical surface, the awful face reappeared.

"It is done; you are now immortal. Go forth and bring death and suffering to the masses in readiness for Him."

"It shall be done," Malachi said and bowed, the first sign of respect he had shown the entity.

As it retreated within the mirror, the surface rippled one more time and fell still. Malachi approached it and laid his hand on the glass, expecting it to sink into the impossible, upright liquid which had been there seconds earlier. It was solid again and his palm only created a misted outline in the cold chamber. Just as Malachi went to turn away, a pair of small hands pressed to the opposing side of the glass, creating their own impressions. Before he could react, they were snatched away and the condensation faded as if they had never existed.

"You have done well, the world is yours for the taking," cackled the cloaked woman madly.

Coming to in a strange room, Malachi was filled with a feeling of utter barrenness. In the dream he had gladly sacrificed his own family to fulfil a contract with something evil. Was he capable of committing such an abhorrent act?

"Please, God. What is wrong with me?" Malachi beseeched. When no answer came he closed his eyes and wept.

A small inspection window opened with a squeal of age and Dr. Llyod's face peered in.

CHAPTER TWENTY TWO

"Sir, you need to calm down," ordered PC Vardy as Desmond harangued him.

"I'll calm down when you tell me what the fuck is going on and why there are people pretending to be police officers!"

"We've already told you, there is a BOLO on all three vehicles," continued Vardy.

"What's a BOLO?" Chloe asked, her face a mask of tear streaked makeup.

Vardy looked at her in annoyance, "Be on the lookout for."

"You can drop that fucking attitude, man. She is beside herself with worry about her boyfriend," Desmond growled.

"I'm sorry, miss. This is just a delicate situation because we have criminals impersonating officers out there. It could be terrorist related, we just don't know," Vardy explained.

"Malachi isn't mixed up with anything like that," Desmond declared.

"I didn't say he was," replied Vardy, "My gut says it's something entirely different, I just don't know what and that bothers me."

"What can we do to help?" Kevin asked. He had been going out of his mind ever since his friend was taken and the lacklustre police response wasn't helping.

"At present, sir? Nothing. The city is quite a big place…"

Kevin leaped forward and Laura had to hold him back, "I know it's a big place, you smart assed prick."

Holding up his hands in a gesture of placation, Vardy was used to high stress situations and continued, "I was going to finish that it's a big place, but we have all available resources out scouring as much of the surrounding area as possible. I should have chosen my words more carefully."

Kevin let out a pent up breath, "I'm sorry, officer. I feel so useless just standing here."

"That's totally understandable, sir. If you should choose to go and look for him as well, all I would ask is that you don't do anything except call us immediately if you find them. Any group that is able to steal three emergency vehicles and go to such elaborate lengths aren't your average kidnappers. This has all the signs of a professional outfit."

"If that's the case, what are our chances of getting him back?" Chloe asked reluctantly.

"It depends on the motives, miss. If it's a ransom, the chances are good. We have a solid negotiating team behind us. If it's something else though, I can't say. Sorry," Vardy replied.

"Will you keep us informed?" Desmond asked as the officers made for the exit.

"Of course, sir. We have your number and will let you know of any developments the second we have them," Vardy said, turning back towards the entrance. Like a dog seeing a threat, his disposition changed instantly as Legacy stepped through the door, followed by nearly twenty of his 'associates'.

"Evenin', officer," Legacy grinned as the policeman glared and pushed by.

"Fuck, man. You couldn't have waited two minutes for them to leave?" Desmond groaned.

Legacy smiled even more, "Nah, brudda. Me and Vardy go way back, he has a real hard on to put me away. For life this time."

"Maybe it would be best if you didn't antagonise him then?" Desmond said, hugging his friend. "Thank you for coming."

"After what we saw, Mal is a blood brudda now."

Desmond made a face and shook his head, warning him to be careful with his words.

Legacy rolled his eyes, "Shit, sorry, man."

"It's ok," Chloe stepped forward and unexpectedly hugged the gang leader, "We know Mal can do... things. It's probably why he has been taken. I can't express how grateful I am for your help."

Legacy smiled and his crew chuckled at his blushes; he hadn't been the source of anything good for a long time.

"Do you have the guns on you? If the police call in backup and raid us you could be going to prison faster than you think," Desmond cautioned.

"We gangsters, but we ain't stupid, brudda. The weapons are kept in separate vehicles so only one man is at risk."

"What do you have?" Kevin asked.

"Don't you even bloody think about it, you'll end up blowing your dick off!" Laura shouted and the Yardies all started laughing at the dressing down.

"I was just interested," he replied, humiliated.

Laura came over and held him close, "You love Mal and so do I. But he wouldn't want you putting yourself in danger, especially with the kids at home."

"She is right, man," Legacy patted him on the back, "Des has told me you a brave mudda fucka, but leave the wet work to us. Once you go through that door, there's no way back."

"What can I get you all, drinks are on the house," Desmond told the room.

"Only soda for my boys, we need to stay frosty," Legacy ordered and saw the confused look on Kevin's face,

"What? Did you think we would get fucked up first? Some of us were JDF before moving here."

Laura turned to Desmond, "JDF?"

"Jamaica Defence Force. It's our armed forces back home," he explained.

"Where did everyone go, man?" Legacy asked, seating himself at the bar.

"I shut the party down when it all kicked off," Desmond explained, "I figured we would need some privacy."

"Good call. What's the plan?"

"I have no idea; did you make the calls?"

Legacy nodded, "All my runners and road men are looking out for them too."

"And I've spoken to every mental health ward in the city, none of them have admitted Malachi. So where the fuck did he go?" Desmond grumbled in frustration.

As the room erupted in spontaneous discussion, the front door open and two men stepped stealthily inside. Dressed in loose fitting grey tracksuits, they could have been boxers out for a training run. The lack of sweat put paid to that theory. Desmond reached for his bat under the counter and tapped gently on the bar with his other hand to get Legacy's attention over the din. Nodding toward the door, he turned and slowly the room fell into silence as people noticed the newcomers.

"We're closed," Desmond told the pair and when they remained standing at the entrance, Legacy's men surrounded them, ready to attack.

"We don't want any trouble," said one in a gentle voice that didn't suit his rough look, "We are here to help your friend."

"What da fuck you know about it?" snarled Legacy, going nose to nose. His men crowded in, concealed blades held in readiness for any order to use them.

"We know he was taken earlier tonight and for that I apologize," he continued, unfazed by the danger.

"So it was you!" Desmond pulled the bat from under the bar and raced around, barging through the group.

"No, my apology was because we couldn't get here sooner and get him to safety," replied the man.

"Who the fuck are you people?" Kevin demanded, adding to the press of flesh surrounding the pair.

"I am Michael, this is Jacob. If you would all sit down, we can explain all that we are permitted to," Michael offered.

Legacy looked at Des and nodded, "Let them through."

Several of the gang stood by the door, just in case they made a break for it, but the two men casually seated themselves at the bar as if this was nothing out of the ordinary. They looked at the expectant faces and begun.

"The people who took your friend are our... 'competitors', you could say."

"You make it sound like a business," Laura remarked.

"In a very loose sense it is," Michael nodded, "They are trying to recruit him to their cause. From our research into Malachi, we don't think he will be open to their proposals and, I'm afraid to say, that puts him in mortal danger."

"No!" cried Chloe, holding her face in her hands.

"And what if you had found him first, would you have tried to recruit him? What if he had said no to you, would that have endangered his life?" Desmond asked.

"Not at all. We believe in free will." Michael seemed genuinely insulted. "He would be a boon to our cause, of course, but not at the expense of forcing him to comply. We don't work like that."

"Who is *we*?" asked Legacy.

"I can't divulge that information."

"Then why should we trust you? You could be working for *them*." Legacy pulled a knife and waved it in front of Michaels face. "Maybe we should ask you more persuasively."

"I can assure you, it wouldn't make any difference no matter how much you tortured us. If we worked for the others, we wouldn't be about to tell you exactly where he is being held, would we?" Michael explained.

"Ok, man," Legacy put the blade away, "Two questions. Where is my brudda, and why waste time talking to us if you know? I know ex-military when I see it, and you have seen a lot of action. It's in the eyes."

Michael smiled. He had misjudged the man as a simple thug, but there was more than meets the eye with the dreadlocked gangster, "Question one. He is being held in Springfield Sanatorium…"

Desmond scowled and interrupted, "Why the fuck have they taken him to an abandoned asylum?" The old place was a favoured haunt for ghost hunters and urban explorers.

"It has… significance," Michael replied, "I can't say more than that, so please don't ask. As for the second question, my Jamaican friend, we are here because we need your help."

"What sort of help?" Chloe asked.

"I won't sugar coat it, we need guns and men who can use them. We have done some quick research and I know some of you were infantry in the old country."

"Something I don't get," Legacy said, "You are mercenaries, and the other men are also mercenaries by Desmond's reckoning. Where is the rest of your team?"

Michael stared for a few moments, then decided honesty was the best policy, "They are on the way, but won't make it in time to help save your friend. We used to be soldiers of fortune, that is true enough, but now we fight for something greater."

Legacy nodded sagely, "I know what you mean, man. Mal has da power, doesn't he?"

The conversation wasn't going quite the way Michael thought it would and the people knew a lot more than was expected, "In a manner of speaking, yes. That is what they want from him. If they can't get it, they will kill him before dawn."

Laura consoled Chloe who was sobbing uncontrollably. Her hands covered her ears like a child who didn't want to hear the grisly end of a scary story.

"You can count on us," Legacy clasped the man's hand, "Da man has a good soul. If I need to give my life to save his, perhaps The Lord will forgive my sins."

"I can understand that sentiment," Jacob agreed, the first words he had spoken. Their deeds were unknown, but their haunted eyes spoke of cruelties beyond imagining.

"Tell us what you need," Desmond said, ready to do whatever was necessary.

"We have a small cache of weapons, but not enough for all of you," Michael replied apologetically.

"Don't sweat it, man. We got pistols, AK's, a handful of grenades, and a couple of Russian PK's." Legacy grinned at Desmond's open mouth. "Fall of communism, brudda. There is nothing you can't get from Eastern Europe if you have the money and the contacts."

"Won't all that gunfire warn them you are coming?" Kevin challenged, "What's to stop them killing him the second you open fire?"

"Don't worry, we have that covered, trust me." Michael stood up and patted his back.

"Easy for you to say, he isn't your best friend," Kevin huffed.

"He could very well be the best friend to all of us if things work out," Michael replied cryptically.

"What the fuck are we meant to do while you go all Rambo?" Kevin grumbled, hugging Chloe and Laura. The thought of being left out tore at him, but he knew his ability to fight was limited to fists, not guns.

Jacob walked over and spoke to the three, "Go home, pick up your kid from the babysitter, and wait. We will send someone to fetch you as soon as we are able to."

Laura pulled him back as he turned away, "What do you mean fetch us?"

"For safety, just in case. Their reach is vast and we need to keep you out of harm's way," Jacob replied and would not be coerced into giving any more information.

"We need to move out now," Michael informed everyone, "If you follow us there is a public carpark near to the facility. From there we go on foot through the surrounding woodland to get right on top of the place."

"Sounds like a plan," Desmond and Legacy agreed in unison and the bar started to empty.

As the sports cars started to follow the strangers in convoy, Desmond leaned out of Legacy's car to talk to Kevin, Laura, and Chloe who were feeling useless.

"As soon as we get him I will call you," he smiled, trying to ease their fear, "We got the baddest mother fuckers this side of the Caribbean on our side. They don't stand a chance."

They couldn't find any words and just nodded. With wheels spinning, the car shot off into the night, leaving them alone.

"Let's go home," Kevin said morosely.

CHAPTER TWENTY THREE

Malachi worked at the aged leather straps, rubbing them against the corroded bedframe. Moonlight penetrated weakly through the broken windows, casting a luminous square onto the dust covered floor. Sections of the ceiling had collapsed and joined the wind-blown debris. The padded walls, once white, were now mouldy and torn at floor level; probably the work of rats seeking comfortable nesting material. Dark patches on the square foam could have been general grime, but the resemblance to hand drawn smears spoke of the likely cause being blood or excrement. A new noise caught his attention and he cocked an ear quizzically. Muffled vibrations carried through the jagged window and it could only be a helicopter landing somewhere within the grounds.

"Come on, come on," Malachi said through gritted teeth.

It had been several minutes since Dr. Llyod had last peered in. His manic excitement and constant need to assure Malachi of his safety was more terrifying than if he had pointed a gun through the inspection hole. The lengths they had gone to, assured him that he was anything but safe, and the silenced pistols carried by the police officers only confirmed his fears. Any official armed response unit had a very unique mode of tactical dress, certainly not common beat uniforms. Flickering light bounced around on the wall outside the room which he could see from his prone position. They were using candles which seemed an unreliable source of illumination when battery operated lanterns were so cheap.

"Malachi, there is really no need for that," chastised Dr. Llyod and he flinched in surprise. The doctor must have returned stealthily to the door after apparently walking off earlier.

"Funnily enough your words don't fill me with a lot of confidence. I'm already in a locked room with bars on the windows so where am I supposed to go if I could get free?" Malachi sneered.

"The door doesn't lock," Dr. Llyod informed him, opening and closing it a few times to prove it, "The mechanisms are rusted."

"So why keep me bound to this rotting bed?"

"For our safety," Dr. Llyod said without a hint of irony.

Malachi laughed derisively, "Your safety? Who the hell do you think I am?"

"Mr. Creighton will be here any moment and he will explain everything."

"Who the fuck is Mr. Creighton?" Malachi demanded.

A look of fear twisted the man's face, "He's the boss and the one man on this planet you need to convince."

"Convince? Of what?"

"I can't say," murmured the doctor.

"I'm sick of all this bullshit," Malachi sighed to himself.

Dr. Llyod's face changed and he beamed through the hatch, "You will be so excited when you find out the truth."

Malachi ignored the ramblings of the lackey. If the one who was behind all this was on the way, he may as well lay back and compose himself. He had to stay strong and hide the gnawing dread which threatened to rob his strength. Maybe he could brazen it out, convince them he was the wrong man or wasn't a threat to whatever they had going on. All he wanted was to go back to his quiet life and try to build something with Chloe. Instinct told him it wasn't going to be that simple.

"Here he comes," gasped Dr. Llyod at the sound of approaching footsteps.

Malachi could identify two separate approaching footfalls, one clumping and heavy on the floor, the other graceful, like a cat. It could have been his overactive imagination, but after all he had witnessed in his dreams, he wouldn't have been shocked if a feline visage appeared, surveying him hungrily like prey. The reality was almost as shocking and he couldn't stifle the gasp. A horrifically scarred mask stared in, square jawed and utterly without emotion. It was only a nervous tic that caused his left eye to squint a little which told Malachi this was a real face and not some ghastly Halloween prop.

"Krauss, get out of the way. You will frighten the poor boy," came a soft voice.

"Good," grunted the monster and his face rose out of view to show his broad chest. He had actually been crouched to look through the spy hole which put his real height at over six and a half feet. Mouth going dry, Malachi could only watch in apprehension as a new face appeared. The differences were stark; beast had been replaced by beauty. It was the only word that Malachi could think to describe the grinning face that peered in. His proportions were perfect and the brilliant, white teeth actually twinkled like a toothpaste commercial from the moonlight. Brown eyes and carefully shaped eyebrows were topped with hair which wouldn't look out of place on a movie star. Unbeknownst to Malachi was the fact that the man paid for a famous stylist to fly from the states to carry out the cut on a weekly basis.

Opening the door, he stepped in and shook Malachi's bound hand, "Hey, buddy. It's great to finally meet you in person. I'm Drake Creighton."

Unable to avoid the grip, Malachi instead wiped imaginary filth from his palm onto his trousers. The massive, scarred guard scowled and took a menacing step in the room.

"Hurt him?"

236

Drake looked shocked, "Goodness me, no! Malachi has had a trying few days and our rude collection of him can have only exacerbated the problem."

"A little?" begged the brute.

"Krauss, go and stand in the corridor, your presence is scaring our friend." Drake waved him away and he left slowly, all the while staring at the bound man.

"If I'm a friend, why the fuck did you kidnap me and hurt my friends?" Malachi demanded and he could hear the hulk growling just outside the door. He clearly didn't like his employer being spoken to in this fashion.

"You have my sincere apologies for the manner in which we approached you, but if my men are speaking the truth, then it was your friends who instigated the altercation," Drake replied, holding his hands together and begging forgiveness. Malachi couldn't argue the facts of his statement, but the nature of his kidnap was another matter.

"When you say your men, you mean the fake police and medical personnel?"

"Well, yes," Drake shrugged, "I had to improvise quickly and it seemed the easiest way to ensure compliance. I could have arranged some of our legitimate contacts to collect you but that would have taken time and left a paper trail."

With his hunch confirmed, Malachi knew his situation was far more dangerous than before. The desire to have no official records didn't bode well for his chances of survival if the meeting was unsatisfactory to his captors. Steeling himself, Malachi decided that if he was going to die, at least he would go to his grave with some answers.

"So what is it you want from me?"

Drake stood perfectly still and appraised the youngster for a few seconds, the turned his head and asked for a chair. Staring again in silence, Malachi became increasingly uneasy at the gaze. After a minute, a sweating Dr. Llyod returned with a rusty chair and placed it by the bed.

"There you go, sir."

"Aren't you forgetting something?" Drake asked impatiently.

Dr. Llyod looked around the room mortified, until he followed his boss's eyes to the filthy seat covering.

"Oh, yes, of course," he gasped, hastily removing his jacket to place on the stained upholstery.

"Thank you, now get out." Drake glared at the man as he retreated and then turned his attention back to Malachi.

"That's a good way to upset your workforce," Malachi chided, "I can see why Mr. Krauss is so upset too."

"A shepherd must tend his flock, my friend. Sometimes that requires being less than civil and I am afraid Dr. Llyod has made some mistakes which could've had catastrophic consequences for myself and our organisation," Drake explained.

Dr. Llyod leaned around the doorway to defend himself but Krauss's massive hand closed over his mouth and pulled him back out of sight.

"I'm sure physical abuse is also grounds for a grievance procedure," Malachi said.

Drake smiled and called out, "Do you wish to make a complaint Dr. Llyod?"

The answer was muffled through the meaty fingers of Krauss, "No, sir."

Drake turned back to Malachi once again and smiled with satisfaction, "There, see, no harm done. My employees understand they are all small parts in a very big wheel. Parts which can be replaced with relative ease."

"Jesus Christ, you talk as much incoherent bollocks as the bloody shrink," Malachi slumped down on the bed in anger.

"I'm sorry. Having the company of Mr. Krauss leaves me little conversation so I tend to waffle on a bit when I meet someone of importance."

"Happy to disappoint you," Malachi laughed, "I'm just a gym bum. I fold towels and help people get in shape; I'm as far from important as you are likely to find."

Drake wagged a finger, "That is what you *do*, not what you *are*."

"And what is it you think I am?" Malachi asked with baited breath.

Instead of answering immediately, Drake stood up and leaned in towards Malachi's stomach, "May I?"

"I normally expect a meal and a movie first, but if you insist."

Lifting the shirt, he pressed at the muscles in an effort to find a sign of the stab wound. Finding nothing, he pursed his lips and let out a whistle of appreciation.

"Amazing."

"Look, if you aren't going to blow me, then at least give me some answers," Malachi pleaded.

"I can't tell you everything," Drake said apologetically, "But before you complain, it's not because I don't want to. I am simply not permitted to."

"I'm sure your bosses wouldn't mind," Malachi coaxed.

"It is they who will explain everything… if you can be persuaded to join our cause and commit your talents to them without question."

"My talents?" Malachi asked.

"Your visions, your healing powers, your growing telekinetic gift, plus any others which may not have manifested yet," Drake replied with the same excitement which Dr. Llyod had displayed earlier.

"You know what is happening to me then?"

"Yes. After being told of your dreams we initially thought you were simply a *seer*. By your age, most people who have observed the things you have would be totally insane. The fact that you are still a fully functional member of society shows a remarkable resilience. You have my respect." Drake bowed a little on the chair.

"There are others like me?" Malachi asked in a whisper, "People that can see all the horror and death?"

"Yes, of course," Drake smiled reassuringly, "Many are born every year, but often commit suicide before we can save them." He left out the eye and tongue removal from the explanation.

"How do they live with it? It has destroyed me, and my life."

"This will come as a shock, but they are easy to control if you know how," Drake shrugged.

"You've got to be shitting me." Malachi could only shake his head in disbelief, "I've tried to stop them all my fucking life and here you are telling me it's easy?"

"Please, forgive my nonchalant reply, I have never been afflicted, so I can't relate. If you had approached one of my clinicians sooner, we could already have you shutting them out and getting on with your life." He smiled down at Malachi like a father calming a child after a bad dream. Only Malachi's nightmare had lasted for over a decade.

"How long would it take?" Malachi needed to know.

Smile broadening, Drake could see that he had the young man hooked, now all he needed to do was reel him in, "It can take anything up to a week to condition the mind properly. In your case, though, I would estimate about two to three days."

"Holy shit," Malachi could hardly believe it, "That quickly?"

Drake nodded enthusiastically and Malachi nearly fainted with relief. Finally, some respite from the vileness which pervaded his slumber.

"What about my healing? Am I some kind of freak?"

"Not at all, the healing is part of what you are. In time, like a butterfly emerging from a chrysalis, your ability will be greatly enhanced. To the point that short of a brain or heart injury you will be able to withstand any amount of punishment."

"Shut up!"

"Honestly," Drake beamed, "It is an amazing gift you have and we can nurture it to its full potential."

"That leaves my random acts of telekinesis. I am told I can make curtains move and affect lights and other electrical appliances, plus..." Malachi paused, fearful of revealing the horror of what nurse Shannon had told him.

Drake could see there was more and leaned forward, "You can tell me, I won't judge."

The words felt sacrilegious as they left his mouth, "I made the dead move."

If Drake had leaned any closer, he would have either fallen off the chair or been close enough to kiss. "So your telekinesis was strong enough to lift a body? Your stronger than I thought."

"No... I mean I think they actually moved. On their own. And I made it happen," Malachi replied and felt the bile rising.

"You have necromantic powers too?" Drake gasped and sat back, rubbing his chin thoughtfully, "And you have had no tutelage?" A note of suspicion had entered his voice as he regarded the youth.

"Tutelage? I did at school." Malachi frowned, ignorant of the real meaning of the question.

Drake considered this for a moment and his face relaxed a little, "We have people who know the old ways. They could help you to harness this gift."

"Gift? More like a curse," he spat.

The scowl was back and Malachi could sense they were getting to the life or death negotiations. Drake was more intent and thoughtful as he asked, "So that kind of ability doesn't appeal to you?"

"It sickens me," Malachi wouldn't sugar coat the answer just to please him.

"Really?" Drake's million-dollar smile was gone now and he looked more like the individual Dr. Llyod was terrified of. The man beneath the warm smile and immaculate hair was finally revealed.

"Really." Malachi met the stare and nodded firmly.

"That's a real shame," Drake sighed, "But we can work without it. Who knows what your opinions will be after a few years?"

"The same."

"Fine, be contrary," Drake replied, "The rest of your talents would be invaluable to our organisation. Think very carefully before you answer my next question, my young friend, I want you to be totally honest, ok?"

Malachi nodded. He was already certain the meeting wasn't going to go well with the disappointment that was apparent when he spoke of his revulsion at waking the dead.

"The vision that my employers sent to you in your dream while you were brought here, what did you feel?" Drake asked slowly, studying Malachi's face.

Unable to suppress the shudder of horror, Malachi replied, "They made me see that? How is it possible?"

"My employers have tremendous powers too," Drake nodded and leaned forward again, eager for an answer, "Now how did you feel?"

"I felt like an abomination. Giving my own family over to that fucking monster? I'd sooner put a gun to my head and pull the trigger."

Drake looked confused and angry, "And the promise of limitless power and immortality doesn't sway your opinion?"

"Even if it were possible, what is eternity without love?"

Drake leaped to his feet, pointing and snarling, "You bloody fool! You could have had it all and instead you choose a made up concept designed to weaken us. Love? Ridiculous."

Malachi knew that it was all over, but he wouldn't lie just to save himself. Instead he tried to reach out a hand, "I pity you."

Drake needlessly slapped the hand which couldn't reach his, "Save your pity for yourself. What is love compared to wealth and power anyway?"

"Everything," Malachi smiled and Drake went berserk.

Smashing the chair into the wall until the frame split, he looked around desperately for more items to smash. Krauss had rushed into the room to see what the disturbance was and glowered at Malachi for upsetting his boss.

"Hurt him now?"

"No," Drake held up a hand, panting from the exertion, "But break Dr. Llyods arms and legs. I will deal with him later."

"No!" shrieked the psychiatrist who tried to bolt for the door.

Krauss moved with an impossible speed for someone of his bulk and grabbed the collar of the doctor. Dragging him back into the room he threw him against the padded walls with enough force to stun him. Falling to the floor in a daze, he didn't immediately feel the huge boot as it stamped down on one forearm, crushing the bone. A split second of shock preceded the ear piercing screams as Krauss repeated the attack on the other arm. Both limbs flopped uselessly with fragments of the break protruding through the flesh, blood mixing with the plaster dust into a gory paste.

"Stop it, please," Malachi begged.

Both Krauss and Drake looked at him in amusement.

"You ask us to spare this man, even though he has doomed you, your friends, and family to a violent death?"

"We all make mistakes," Malachi replied, and even through his agony, the young doctor smiled. "And if you touch my friends I will make sure you pay for it in the most painful way. Do what you will to me, just leave them out of it."

"I'm afraid I can't," Drake said, holding up a phone, "The order has already been given."

"If anything happens to them, I swear to God I will end you all," Malachi growled, straining at the straps.

"Enough bluster," Drake dismissed him and returned his attention to the broken doctor, "Now his legs."

Krauss tried to smile and the rictus was awful. His damaged face contorted itself into a mask of disjointed nerve endings and twitching muscle.

"Don't move," grunted the hulk as he repositioned the doctor's legs.

Two more cruel stamps and both legs were broken. Dr. Llyod lay still, eyes fluttering in unconsciousness, the pain finally too much to bear. Drake was clapping his enjoyment and prodded at the floppy limbs with his foot.

"Finish him?"

"No, I will come back after we have dealt with our esteemed guest," Drake replied and then fell silent, looking around in surprise. Vibrations shook the room, causing streamers of dust to cascade down upon their heads. On the bed Malachi was glaring at the men, shaking with fury.

"My, you are a strong one. It's a shame that you couldn't see the bigger picture and the glorious future that was in your grasp." Drake nodded to Krauss.

"Heed my warning well..." Malachi started until the boulder like fist of Krauss connected with his head, knocking him out cold.

"Such a shame," Drake sighed, shaking his head, "Prepare the ritual room."

CHAPTER TWENTY FOUR

Michael stood by the rear doors of the Ford Transit van as Legacy passed out weapons to his men. He was amazed at the amount of firepower that the gang had stowed away and they had been reliably informed this vehicle was only one out of four. The others were all kept under lock and key and moved frequently to avoid detection. Although every rule said that these men were on opposing sides of law and order, the Yardies had seen some of what Malachi was capable of. Coming from a culture that held deep seated beliefs in religion and the supernatural, they had accepted the events with no question or doubt. Redemption came in many forms and, maybe tonight, these killers and hoodlums could claim back part of their stained soul.

"Do ya want the PK's?" Legacy asked, interrupting his thoughts.

Michael thought about it for a moment and declined, "We will need to be light on our feet. I don't think we will have a standing battle with them when it all happens, they will cover each other and retreat so the light machine guns will just slow us down."

"Ok, man."

All the vehicles had been parked under an outcrop of huge branches to try and maintain as much cover as possible. With luck, no one would use the woodland trail this late at night and they could be in and out with minimal exposure. The isolated nature of the abandoned asylum meant that the sound of gunfire would be difficult to pinpoint, if indeed anyone reported it at all. Shrouded in shadows, Michael and Jacob stood before the men to explain the finer points of the mission.

"Thank you all for doing this," Michael begun, "I won't lie to you, it will be dangerous. The men we are

246

going against are some of the most skilled mercenaries on the planet and they work for an organisation that allows no failure. Their belief is absolute and they will fight accordingly, so watch your asses. As I mentioned to Legacy, their primary concern will be the safe extraction of their employers who will have arrived for the coming ceremony. They are not our target today, but if you happen to get a clear shot, then take it."

Jacob stepped forward, filled with admiration for the troops who hadn't made a murmur of protest when told they faced such a deadly foe, "Our only concern today, is the retrieval of Malachi. I know you have seen some of what he can do, but I can only add that it is the tip of the iceberg. His value to us, and the human race as a whole, cannot be overstated. If he should perish here, then we may very well be on the brink of Armageddon."

"You're shitting us, man," Legacy replied, sure they were exaggerating.

"Not at all," Michael assured him, "There are things in motion that have taken centuries of planning. Do you think the wars, hatred, and evils in the world are purely coincidental? Everything has been manufactured for one outcome, and only that young man has a chance to stop it."

"Guess he's not," Desmond said to Legacy with a slap on the back, "How we doin' this?"

"We approach slowly through the woods and wait on the signal."

"How will we know the signal?" Desmond wondered.

"When all hell breaks loose, that will be the signal," Jacob replied, "We have scouted the building thoroughly a year ago after a tipoff the opposition were using it. Despite it being abandoned, the fence is brand new and there will undoubtedly be foot patrols. Two man teams with a sixty second call in if previous encounters are anything to go by."

"This ain't gonna be a stealth incursion then?" Legacy asked.

"No, our job is to create a diversion and keep them pinned down as much as possible."

"Ok, let's get this done."

"Myself and Jacob will be using the night vision to scout the forest ahead. We move slow and careful; any loose items should be stowed away. Our target is a small drainage culvert that overlooks the main gate around half a mile north east as the crow flies. Any questions?"

None came and the glasses were slipped onto their heads, banishing the darkness. The luminous green images gave a perfect day bright view and in two columns they moved out in silence.

Owls hooted and took flight as they passed, seeking tender mice or voles to feed their young. Each man stepped carefully in an attempt to avoid the revealing sound of breaking twigs. After every twenty meters, the two point men came to a stop and scanned the surroundings until they were satisfied they were alone. The speed of the events of the past few hours meant it was unlikely they could have amassed a force large enough to patrol the grounds as well as the surrounding countryside, but it was better to be cautious with the stakes so high. Above, the moon moved between clouds, providing meagre light for their passage before snatching it away once again.

Michael knew that if they hadn't been able to enlist the aid of the drug gang the mission would have been impossible. It was such a paradox; that to do good, they needed to enlist men who might otherwise be deemed evil. God truly moved in mysterious ways, he thought with a wry smile.

After half an hour of careful navigation the trees thinned out and the goggles were no longer necessary. The grouping of clouds had moved on and left the moon exposed which gave them enough light to work with. A short run of thirty feet separated their cover from that of the ditch and it would need to be timed perfectly to avoid detection.

"What do you see?" Legacy asked in a whisper.

Taking out a thermal imager, he looked out on the scene from behind the tree. Four guards were at the gate; two more pairs of guards were moving away around the perimeter.

"Eight guards on foot," Michael whispered, scanning the face of the building.

Inside the main doors was a concentrated heat source which could have been anything from four to ten more guards. These were more than likely the elite bodyguards of the upper circle, and the most fearsome of their enemy.

"More inside the entrance."

"Say when," Legacy whispered.

With a final scan, Michael removed the imager and paused. Sure he had seen something else, he put them back to his eyes and looked at the upper floors. A faint yellow glow came from one of the windows and he ducked down.

"Sniper on the third floor, eighth window from the left, get behind cover," he hissed and the men quietly scattered into their surroundings.

"Has he seen us?" Legacy asked breathlessly.

None of the guards showed any urgency or change of habit. The patrol patrolled and the M4 carbine cradling guards at the gate scanned the road for signs of movement.

"I don't think so, but I can't see how," Michael was waiting for the first crack of gunfire, "There is no way a competent sniper wouldn't have seen us."

"Luck?" Desmond asked from another trunk.

"It must be, we have to move back, but try and keep the trees between you and the scope," he ordered and the men melted back into deeper cover.

"What is going on?" Michael asked himself in the darkness. A series of chittering crickets was his only answer.

CHAPTER TWENTY FIVE

Scrambled images coursed through Malachi's mind following the blow. His parents reaching imploringly, screaming silently of their fear. People he had interacted with briefly in his life waved as he passed, looks of sorrow creasing their features. Chloe, reclining in a high backed chair, nursing a new born infant who, impossibly, stared directly at him and smiled. Drake, his smile stretching ever wider until the flesh tore and an indescribable horror tore itself free from within his trunk and through the ravaged orifice. Then he was falling towards a frozen lake, his face impacting the thin, frigid surface and plunging him into icy depths.

"Wakey, wakey, rise and shine," chuckled Drake.

Malachi looked around in shock, cold water running down his face and chest. He was upright, but unable to move his body in any way. Staring down, he could see he was on some kind of upright wheelchair, strapped tightly. He had seen this device before in a movie a couple of years ago. What was it? He pondered, coming out of the daze. *Silence of the Lambs*!

"I will eat your liver with some fava beans and a nice Chianti." Malachi laughed to himself and sucked air through his teeth.

"Very good Dr. Lecter," smiled Drake.

"Is this really necessary?"

"Unfortunately, yes. We can't have you running off before the sacrifice, can we?" Drake replied, leaning in to dab at his drenched face with a silk handkerchief.

Bravado disappearing, a fine sweat broke out on Malachi's brow and he was unable to talk through the terror which gripped his heart. The thought of dying shouldn't have been the cause of such anxiety, after all he had died once only a few days ago. It was the sure knowledge that a sacrifice didn't employ an anaesthetic to dull the pain before execution.

"Dead man," grunted Krauss with a throaty chuckle.

"There is no need for such mocking," Drake sighed at the ugly hulk, "We are above gloating over the vanquished."

"I'm sure we can come to an agreement," Malachi blabbered in panic, "I won't ever do anything to go against you."

"No, I'm afraid not my friend. You are far too powerful to be left alive," Drake said sombrely.

Krauss laughed, "Not threatening now."

Drake sighed again, "Indeed he isn't because he knows he has lost. We must be magnanimous in victory."

Krauss pulled a face and scratched his head.

"He's full of shit and tries to sound more intelligent than he really is, don't worry about it," Malachi said to Krauss, voice trembling in spite of his attempts to rein in the fear.

"It won't work," Drake replied, ignoring the insult.

"What won't?"

"Trying to rile me so I order my friend Mr. Krauss to kill you," Drake replied, shaking his head in disappointment. It was such an obvious ruse that Malachi felt foolish for even trying.

"Sorry."

"The pain of your death will be fleeting," Drake explained, "It is what comes after that will be more unpleasant."

"Yeah, after," laughed Krauss.

"What do you mean, after?" Malachi demanded, straining uselessly against the rigid bonds.

"You will see for yourself soon enough," Drake whispered in his ear.

The patter of many footsteps echoed down the grimy corridor and Drake smiled in satisfaction.

"Ah, the guests of honour have arrived."

Six hooded figures gathered around and looked at the prisoner. Ages and genders varied wildly but they all had a look of contempt on their faces, except one young woman.

"I thought there had to be thirteen of you?" Malachi asked and they looked at one another in surprise.

"He has seen some of our rites in his visions," Drake explained, "It's nothing to be concerned about."

"Bring him," ordered the oldest woman.

"I know you!" Malachi exclaimed, recognising the voice. She had been the one to promise him the world in return for his family.

"All you will know is the taste of my steel as it cuts out your heart, scum," she scowled.

"What a charmer you are, you poisonous old whore."

"Gag him," Drake shouted.

Krauss pulled a roll of duct tape from his jacket and Malachi couldn't help himself as he teased, "What else you got in there, Frankenstein?"

"Knife. Gun."

"I don't suppose I can convince you to shoot the wicked witch? How the fuck she is still alive at one hundred and twenty is beyond me," Malachi mocked. Krauss stretched the tape across his lips and leaned in hard, mashing his cheeks painfully.

"I'm sorry, Mother, he shouldn't have spoken to you like that."

"Don't worry about my sensibilities, child. A butcher doesn't concern itself with the bleating of a sheep, does he? I would love to see how much he laughs when our master welcomes him to his new home."

What did that mean? Malachi tried to prise the tape away with his tongue but the stuff was resilient and held fast. Mother smiled at his discomfort and it was the most hideous expression he had ever seen. Without further discussion they moved off, gurney wheels crackling on the lifted floor tiles. A low chanting started among the hooded priests and priestesses, accompanying them as they proceeded.

Room after room they passed down the long hallway, and the chanting seemed to draw power from the building itself, creating the same oppressive pall that Malachi had experienced before. Screams and wails of bygone times sprung from thin air, the emotion of the unspeakable cruelties trapped within the walls of the asylum. At times he could see the faint outlines of people in his peripheral vision, tearing at their hair or thrashing wildly. Turning his head to look directly at them banished the apparitions, but their suffering permeated through his soul. Like a sponge, he absorbed the anguish and despaired.

"You can feel them, can't you, boy?" croaked the old hag, peeling the tape loose to feed on his fear.

"There are so many," Malachi whispered in horror.

"Indeed." She smiled the dreadful smile again, "We built this facility two hundred years ago to care for the mentally infirm. Or at least that was what we told the public. More innocent blood has been spilled within these walls than on any battlefield in the history of man. Their torment provides a conduit."

"A conduit to where?"

Mother would only tap a knowing finger to her hawkish nose.

Reaching the stairs, Krauss carefully manoeuvred the gurney down one step at a time. The wooden treads were old and riddled with mould from the open roof and Malachi cringed with each creak and groan of the worn timber. Combined with his metallic transport, they must have weighed over three hundred pounds, and how they made it down in one piece was a miracle. Krauss grinned at

Malachi without so much as a bead of sweat or slightly laboured breathing. What was he, a machine?

"Report," demanded the old woman.

"All teams report," barked the most senior soldier.

The radio crackled into life, "Team One clear, Team Two clear," on it went through eight teams and then the sniper responded, "Sniper team. I had a malfunctioning scope for a few minutes, but the picture has come back so it may just have been an electrical glitch. Apart from some wildlife, the perimeter is clear."

Drake looked at Malachi and tutted, "Did you mess with my sniper's scope when we were disciplining Dr. Llyod?"

"I have no idea, I fucking hope so," Malachi said, spitting in his face. He had been quietly gathering as much phlegm as possible and the thick, green mucus ran down his face. If words couldn't make a quick end of it, perhaps this disgusting act might.

"Krauss, hurt him badly," squealed Drake, wiping at the clotted drool.

"Don't you dare," hissed Mother and Krauss shrank away in fear.

"But, Mother!"

"But nothing," she snarled, "if you are fool enough to keep taunting him, then you deserve it. Stupid child."

"Someone has mummy issues," laughed Malachi which only served to turn Drakes skin a deeper shade of red.

Krauss replaced the tape and Mother pushed a section of rotten plaster which sunk back into the wall. To their left, a door swung inwards on freshly oiled hinges which signified this place was used regularly. To what end would be revealed when they reached their final destination. A passageway stretched out before them and the familiar glyphs were drawn in dried blood on the walls and arched ceiling.

"Soon our advantage will be insurmountable and it will simply be a matter of time before this world falls," explained Mother to the group.

"It will be glorious," Drake replied.

They arrived at the antechamber and Malachi had a feeling of déjà vu. The proportions were different to his dream, but that was probably due to the differing location. Krauss released the straps and before Malachi could struggle free, grabbed him in a bear hug. Carrying him through to the sacrificial chamber, Krauss's grip tightened further. Unable to draw breath through his compressed chest, his vision blurred and unconsciousness beckoned. Taking advantage of Malachi's weakened state, Krauss laid him on the sacrificial altar and secured the chains across his body.

"You wait here," Mother ordered Drake in the outer chamber.

"But, I…"

"Here, I said!" she shrieked and he conceded with a childish snort.

Stepping into the room, the six spread out around the stone monument with Mother at Malachi's head. She thanked Krauss for his service and he smiled and bowed before leaving the chamber. A smaller, but no less impressive mirror similar to the one from his dream leaned against a wall and Malachi was filled with gut wrenching dread.

"Spit on me, boy, and I will cut off your lips and tear your tongue out, do you understand?" Mother said, staring down.

Malachi nodded slowly, trying to control the violent tremors of fear and she peeled away the tape.

"What is this place?"

"I think you know," Mother stroked his face with a leathery hand, "You have been shown a similar room. In here we talk to those who listen."

"It's the mirror, isn't it?"

"Yes. It once belonged to one of our earlier supporters; Countess Elizabeth Báthory. You may have called her 'The Blood Countess'. She was a visionary who was imprisoned unjustly by cowards who couldn't comprehend her noble aims. What difference do the lives of a few hundred commoners make when compared to the possibility of immortality?"

"As long as there are people like me, you will always face resistance to your evil," Malachi declared.

"With your death, there will be no more *people like you*," she informed the young man, "Your existence is only made possible by the culmination of a series of unique events. The chances of it happening again are infinitesimal."

"You're out of your fucking mind," Malachi sighed and lay still, resigned to his fate. His life had been filled with heartache and perpetual dread every time his head lay on the pillow. He was beyond exhausted with it all.

Reaching in to her robe, she pulled a sickle shaped blade out and closed her eyes, "My masters, it is I, Ursula Creighton. I implore you to answer me."

Nothing happened at first, so she continued.

"Xazuxal, Mordreth Jord, mighty generals of the underworld, I beseech you. We bring you an offering; a mortal with the blood of the divine flowing in his veins!"

The candle flames wavered, stirred by an unseen presence. The unblemished surface of the mirror rippled and a malevolent voice rebounded in the chamber.

"Why do you disturb me?" It gurgled, undulations playing on the reflective glass.

"I offer you the life of this man, Malachi. He is a shroud walker and sworn enemy to all that we stand for!"

"Truly?" It asked, and a face peered out, but different to the one in Malachi's dreams. Long snouted, with rows of

nightmarish fangs snapping hungrily, it studied the young man on the altar.

"Yes, my lord. We offer him to you to further show our loyalty."

"He is familiar to me, this whelp. Ahhh," It sighed in recognition, *"Berumozun sent him the vision to test his compassion."*

"Yes, my lord. He failed the test and now pays the price."

"I can smell the goodness in him," It snarled, *"Finish it quickly, I want to taste his soul!"*

"As you wish, my lord," Ursula nodded and raised the knife overhead.

"No!" cried the young priestess, shucking off the robe to reveal twin fully automatic Glock 17 pistols in her hands and a vest filled with blocks of C4 plastic explosive.

The crazed woman, shot a withering glare her way and the knife plunged down in slow motion. Raising the guns, she let off short bursts of fire and the bullets tore through the old woman's arms, practically severing them except for some tendons and ligaments.

"Kill him!" ordered the being furiously.

Swinging one arm to her left, she squeezed the trigger and a network of holes appeared in the surface. The glass shattered into a thousand pieces, sending the entity back to its own dark realm with a howl of denial.

"Mother!" cried out Drake, rushing into the room and a hail of gunfire.

Chips of stone pelted his face and he ducked back into the antechamber out of danger. The stranger swept the room with one arm, firing the last bullets and ignoring the risk of ricochets. With her free hand she released the chains and pulled Malachi to cover behind the solid stone altar. Landing awkwardly, he winded himself and lay writhing as his shocked lungs tried to draw in oxygen.

"Stay down," she shouted, reloading.

Malachi wanted to reply that he wasn't able to stand but the words were locked inside his paralysed diaphragm.

Now that he was safe, she managed to pick off two of the council before they bolted through the door. The lead tore through their robes and bodies, coating the walls in fresh blood.

"Kill them?" grunted Krauss.

"Yes, kill them both now!" Drake shrieked, "I need to get mother to safety."

"You take one step inside this fucking room and I press the button on my vest. I will bring this whole building down on your heads!" she called out.

Sounds of frantic escape from the other council members carried through as well as the deep bass of Krauss as he spoke to his boss. Her ears rung from the confined gunfire, but she knew they would be discussing pulling back and taking them in the main lobby. She smiled down at Malachi as the heavy boots ran away.

"You're nearly safe, backup is coming."

CHAPTER TWENTY SIX

The serenity of the night was shattered by the shouts of the guards as the faint sound of gunfire reached Michael from inside the asylum. Half of the patrolling guards ran back into the building and the ones that remained took cover by the stolen emergency vehicles parked at the entrance.

Taking advantage of the confusion, Michael called out, "Now!"

They all knew their role and half of the group laid down suppressing fire on the sniper's window and crouched guards. Legacy and three of his men broke cover and ran full pelt for the ditch. One of the four was stopped dead in his tracks and pitched backwards as a hole punched cleanly through his chest, swatting him to the floor.

"Shit! Stay down!" Jacob shouted. The sniper was taking a risk by not seeking cover, but knowing the fanaticism of the opposition it wasn't surprising. With the angle of fire, they would need a lucky shot to have a chance at taking him down.

Michael watched as a man fell screaming to the ground, thick slivers of wood piercing his chest from the bullet which had drilled straight through the trunk he had sheltered behind.

"Spread out and stay mobile or he will pick us off one by one," Michael yelled and they started to scatter, diving into any small depressions they could find. During a lull in the shooting, he jumped up and ran to the ditch, landing beside Legacy.

"Do you have any flashbangs?"

"Two and one frag."

"On my mark, light up the night. It'll mess with his scope for a few seconds and may give us a window to get to the side of the building."

Dirt kicked up from the automatic fire which raked the muddy bank, pinning them down. Another loud crack preceded a gurgled scream which faded away as the victim died.

Michael shouted into the night, "Jacob, take four men and flank the east wing. Go in via the fire escape if you can and flush him out."

"You got it!" came his reply.

Legacy nodded to his men; all three twisted the pin on their respective armament and lobbed them. The two flashbangs arced towards the open grounds and the fragmentation grenade landed amongst the guards sheltering by the vehicles. A dull crump went off a split second before the twin cracks of the flashbangs banished the darkness with brilliant light. Flames climbed into the sky from a ruptured fuel tank and the police car flipped over before landing on one of the soldiers, crushing his upper body and head. The remaining guards bolted for the entrance, unsure if the group possessed any more explosives. Muzzles flashed from the ground floor windows, the soldiers inside covering their retreating brothers in arms.

"They made it!" Desmond shouted after seeing Jacob and his team disappear inside the building.

From the western wing, a low whine gained in pitch as an engine increased power. It was the unmistakable drone of a helicopter powering up.

"They are on the run!" Michael allowed himself a sliver of hope that they may succeed. With each escaping aircraft the enemy force would be weaker; the security detail minding each council member leaving with them.

Desmond and another man started to strafe the sniper position with gunfire, then ducked out of sight while Michael and Legacy's position did the same. No return fire came from the upper window; only those on the ground floor still resisted while their bosses escaped. A piercing whistle caught his attention and Jacob waved from the third floor, running a hand across his throat to show they had neutralised the target.

"Sniper down, prepare to move up!" Michael called.

The heavy pressure of rotor blades disturbed the air as the first helicopter made off, beacons flashing. It was quickly joined by another and the men who had moved west opened fire on the flying transports. Sparks jumped from the fuselage and the pilots made evasive manoeuvres, dropping away and using the western woodland as cover.

"Leave them, we need to keep the ones inside occupied!" Michael shouted.

****

"How many mags do you have left?" Jacob asked Zeeks, the only man standing after the shootout with the sniper.

"Two, you?"

"Half. Shit!" Jacob replied, slapping the magazine home.

"Da rifle?"

"He sabotaged it before we killed him," Jacob sighed, "All that's left is his sidearm."

"What da plan, man?"

"We push down and flank the men on the ground floor, try and flush them out of the western wing," Jacob explained, pocketing the three spare magazines of pistol ammo.

Stepping out into the hallway, bullets ricocheted from the floor and walls. A round took Jacob in the left shoulder and he fell to the floor. Zeeks dragged him with one hand while unleashing a whole magazine down the wing to cover their retreat. None of the bullets found their mark, but the enemy ducked into the rooms on either side of the corridor out of sight.

"I guess dey da ones doin' the flushin'" shouted the Jamaican, "How bad?"

Jacob felt inside and the blood was spurting from the wound, soaking his hand. Zeeks loosed off a few rounds around the doorframe to keep the approaching men on their guard.

"They hit the artery."

"Fuck, we need to get you out of here, man." Zeeks tried to lift Jacob by his good arm until he pushed it away.

"No, there's too much at stake and I won't make it anyway." Jacob chambered a fresh round into the pistol, grimacing in agony, "I'll cover you while you get down the fire escape."

"Don't be a fucking wiseass."

"You've done enough, my friend. You have given us all a chance," Jacob said solemnly, "Now go!"

The suddenness of the counterattack took the three guards by surprise as they cautiously moved between doorways, closing the distance. Jacob was firing before he left the room and the puncture wounds blew soft padding from the walls. The next bullet took the closest man in the face, blowing a hole out of the side of his head. Zeeks didn't need any urging and he bolted for the staircase.

"You won't win, you bastards!" Jacob shouted, running down the corridor and firing indiscriminately.

A chunk of plaster caused his foot to skid and he went down hard, sliding along the filthy tiled floor. The second man was aiming at chest height and his finger instinctively pulled the trigger, but the bullets cut through the air two feet above the intended target. Jacob fired four rounds in quick succession and they entered his groin and abdomen before erupting from the upper back and coating the ceiling red. Jacob cried out as the gun was shot from his hand, shattering several fingers.

"Don't fucking move!" snarled the third mercenary, alternating the sight between the injured man and the open stairwell.

"I know you are only following orders," Jacob said to the mercenary, "I need you to know, I forgive you."

"Shove your fucking forgiveness up your ass. You murdered my friends, and as soon as I'm done with you I'm going to find your pussy mate and bleed him."

"I'm ready," Jacob smiled, closing his eyes, "Do it."

"You think it's going to be that easy? I'm going to shoot your balls off, then your dick, and finally your..." was all he managed.

Zeeks ran down the hallway, firing off single shots that tore the man's internal organs to shreds. With one final cough of blood, his finger went into spasm on the trigger. The bullet punched into Jacobs chest below the ribcage and rebounded from the solid floor, back into his body.

"Brudda!"

Jacob couldn't reply. His lungs were quickly filling with blood from the catastrophic damage and he could only reach out a warm, thankful hand to the gangster. By coming back into the fray, he had spared his new friend the indignity of being brutally executed by the evil soldier. Grasping the hand, Zeeks cradled Jacob's head as the darkness settled over him.

"Sleep now, soldier," Zeeks whispered, holding Jacob tight.

Radios crackled into life from the bodies of the men as he faded away, "Sniper team, report... Sniper recon team, report... Fuck!"

****

"Got to go," said Krauss, shielding his boss from the gunfire.

"But mother," Drake sobbed, throwing the radio and kneeling by her side.

"Gone."

Her face was harsh, even in death. Instead of the muscles relaxing, her face contorted in a malicious scowl but the vacant eyes confirmed her passing. She would be taking her rightful place alongside everyone who had the courage to dedicate themselves to the cause. Drake stood up and tried to shake Krauss in his anguish, but he was like a tree trunk, solid and immovable.

"I want Malachi dead! I want that fucking whore who shot mother dead! I want anyone they have ever talked to dead!" Drake stamped his feet like a petulant child.

"Five men left. Not today," said the big man, shaking his misshapen head slowly.

"Sir, all other parties are at a safe distance, recommend you evac too. They are moving on our position."

A stray bullet shattered a glass lamp within inches of Drake's head and he ducked down with a squeal. Krauss nodded to the guard and hauled the body of Ursula onto his massive shoulder. Pushing Drake ahead, they quickly distanced themselves from the main lobby. The ragged stumps of her arms left a wet trail in their wake and the rear guard stepped carefully as they followed, treating the blood as if it were sacred. Reaching the exit to the open grounds at the rear, Krauss held Drake back while two of the remaining soldiers checked ahead.

"How the fuck did she infiltrate the inner circle?" Drake lifted his mother's head and shouted at the dead face, "How could you not sense what she was?"

"Dead."

"I know she's dead, you moron!" Drake screamed at his bodyguard.

"Sorry, sir," Krauss said, lowering his head in shame.

Drake sighed and patted the man on the rock solid back. His earlier outpouring of grief was more to do with the insufferable delay to their plans than compassion for the dead woman who had given birth to him.

"No, I'm the one in the wrong. You have always been loyal to me and it will be rewarded, I promise."

One of the soldiers came running back, "Sir, we are clear. They have entered the main lobby and aren't making any attempt to engage us from the western corner."

"Of course not, they have what they want," Drake said, grinding his teeth, "Him."

"Come," said Krauss, guiding him into the turbulence of the helicopter blades.

Climbing into the Bell Huey luxury transport, Drake dialled a familiar number and closed his eyes. "It's me... No, I'll explain later... Proceed and call me as soon as it's done. If we can't kill him yet, at least we can kill his spirit."

The chopper dipped its nose and sped away, leaving the decaying asylum behind for the last time. It was compromised now, and all the malevolent power they had spent centuries attaining would bleed from the walls like a wounded beast. Within months it would be just another crumbling relic of bygone times. What a waste.

****

"Is that a real bomb vest?" Malachi asked the fearsome looking brunette.

"Yes," she replied, pistols still aiming at the antechamber.

The sounds of battle had been going on for nearly half an hour; the chatter of machine guns and at least once, the vibration of an explosive detonation. For the past five minutes the exchanges had diminished to the point of silence and she finally lowered the guns.

"Would you have blown yourself up?"

"Yes," she replied without hesitation.

Malachi felt sick inside, but at least it would have been better than the alternative, "Thank you for saving my life. I'm Malachi."

"I know," she said sternly, looking down at him.

"And you are?"

"Amaris."

"Who are these people?" Malachi asked, chancing a look around the altar and seeing the two sprawled bodies.

"I can't tell you. The people I work for will explain everything if we get out of here in one piece."

"Fuck me," Malachi said, exasperated, "They can't tell me, you can't tell me. How do I know you aren't just as bad as they are?"

"Don't sulk, you sound like a child," Amaris replied, face softening, "And we aren't as evil as these bastards. They are the bad guys; we are the good guys. That's all you need to know right now."

"You said if we got out of here in one piece? It sounds like the fighting has stopped, so who came to our rescue."

"Some friends."

"And why are you still so nervous?" Malachi was confused.

"Because if we lost, in a few moments their most fanatical troops will come pouring down that hallway to take us out. If they need to die in the explosion, they will gladly pay that price."

"Shit," Malachi whispered, peeking out again.

Amaris pulled him back and crouched low, listening to the sound of running footsteps. Sighting the shadowy doorway, she started to take the tension of the trigger in readiness.

"Amaris, it's Michael. Are you down here?" shouted a voice from the dark passage.

Visibly relaxing, Amaris released the trigger and holstered the pistols. "We are in here, Michael. I have someone you may want to meet." Holding a hand out she helped Malachi to his feet and smiled.

Michael hurried through into the room, surveying the carnage and the unholy glyphs on the walls. Coming to a stop directly in front of Malachi, he quickly looked him up and down before hugging him tightly.

"It's an absolute honour to meet you, Malachi."

"Er, yeah, you too," Malachi replied awkwardly, hugging the stranger.

"Told you we had your back, brudda," said Legacy, entering the room with Desmond.

"Des! Legacy! You did this?" Malachi yelled and ran to the pair. Hugging Desmond tight, he turned to Legacy. What was the etiquette for a gangland kingpin? The fearsome Jamaican grinned and embraced him, settling the quandary.

"Ma boys did me proud," Legacy said quietly, mourning his fallen.

"But why? I only met you tonight," Malachi couldn't make sense of the motives.

"There is something about you, man, we can all feel it in our blood," Legacy explained, "All the shit we do on the street ends today. If Michael will have us, we be joining his crew."

Michael and Amaris joined them and she explained, "There is a process, but after what Michael has told me about how your men handled themselves tonight I know we need warriors like yourselves at our back."

"Dis place is full of dark magic," Legacy whispered, ignoring the compliment and glancing around the room.

"Bad things happened here for a long time," Michael said, "I'll explain everything once we are safe."

Legacy was still swaying in a trance, "I can hear the screams. So many people."

"We need to go now," Amaris insisted and Desmond gently shook his friend.

It took a few moments for the haunted expression to fade and Legacy still glanced around warily as they ran from the evil heart of the asylum up into the lobby. The remaining Yardies had looted the bodies and replaced their empty AK's with the dropped weaponry.

Legacy's second in command whispered in his ear and he frowned, deep in thought, "We got company coming. You gotta get outta here."

"We all need to go, you included," Michael urged.

"Nah, man. I'll stay here with 'alf my men and take the heat."

Amaris could see the bond between the two disparate men had grown strong, so she pulled Michael to one side.

"If they find all these bodies with no gunmen they will start a massive manhunt and potentially catch us all before we can get clear. The police securing Legacy and his men will buy us a small window to get out of the area. If Malachi is taken into custody he won't survive the night, you know how far they have infiltrated."

"Damnit," Michael kicked at some broken glass, sending it shattering down the hallway, "But what about them?" He pointed at Legacy.

"One man dying while restrained is far easier to explain than a whole gang. We will get the best lawyers on the case as soon as we are safe," Amaris explained.

"She's right, man," Legacy nodded, "We be out on bail in a day."

The sounds of sirens were faint but closing fast. With a few brotherly embraces and goodbyes Amaris, Michael, Malachi, and four of the surviving gang members jumped across the ditch and set off through the woodland to their vehicles. He had a million questions, but they needed to stay focussed on the task of navigating the pitch black woodland safely. Their night vision goggles had been lost in the gun battle and a torch beam may have alerted any passing police response team of their location. They made good time despite their disadvantage and the wail of sirens continued through the whole journey. Malachi gave up counting after the twelfth emergency vehicle. Nothing was stirring as they looked out on the carpark from the concealment of the trees.

"Clear," Michael whispered after scanning the carpark until he was satisfied.

"Amaris, you take Malachi in the car. I will go in the van in case we run into anything that needs a battering ram to move. If the rest of you wouldn't mind following behind in the BMW?"

Desmond and the gangsters nodded their agreement.

"Where are you taking me?" Malachi asked.

"A safe house until we can move you to one of the facilities we own," Amaris replied.

"Wait just a minute," Malachi blustered, "When will I be able to go back to my old life? The nice easy life where no one was trying to fucking sacrifice me!"

Michael looked at Amaris and then back at Malachi, "Now they know you exist. Never. They will hunt you from this day forward until either they are all dead, or you are."

"Well that's fucking marvellous!" Malachi shouted, starting to feel claustrophobic. The world was closing in, smothering him with a blanket of fear.

"It will be ok, man. We all got your back," Desmond tried to console him but the laboured breathing became gasps of panic.

"I know it's bullshit, Malachi, but it is the only way to keep you safe," Amaris said, holding his face to try and calm him.

Her eyes told a tale of their own loss, and gradually his breathing returned to a safer pace. "What about my friends? Can Des go home?"

"No, I'm afraid you will have to come with us too. Teams are on the way to collect Chloe, Kevin, and their family right now. Until we can end their schemes, they will use anything they can to weaken you," Michael added.

"Just who are these people?" Malachi said, feeling very small in the face of their power.

"I promise the people we are taking you to will give you all the answers, but we need to hurry."

"Ok, I'll go, on one condition. I want to return home and collect the picture of my parents," he replied softly, "It's the only one I have of them."

"They could be watching your home. It simply isn't safe," Michael dismissed the idea out of hand.

"You said yourself that you took them by surprise and they are now on the run. If I was so important do you think they would have posted guards on my home when they already had me?"

Amaris thought for a few moments, "Ok. But you tell me where it is and I get it. You will stay in the car for your own protection. I don't want to take any chances."

Michael pulled her to one side and started to whisper angrily, "With all that's at stake you want to risk it for a picture? Are you crazy?"

Throwing off his hand she snarled back, careful that Malachi couldn't hear, "If we want him to fight these people, what incentive does he have if we can't even collect a picture of his parents for him? You know we may not make it in time to save his other friends, so if this picture can be his light in the darkness, then I will die to get it."

Michael pondered the risks. He knew the horror that awaited the young man on the path laid out before him. If he didn't go insane when it was explained to him, the picture might prove to be the only talisman capable of warding off the encroaching evil.

"Ok, we do this as quickly as possible before they can regroup," Michael relented and they climbed into the vehicles. Turning out onto the road in the bulky van, another ambulance blared by, lights flashing red and blue. *You're too late*, thought Michael to himself as they made off into the night.

CHAPTER TWENTY SEVEN

"You think this is a fool's errand don't you?" asked Malachi, miserably.

Amaris took her eyes from the road for a moment and looked at him. The passing traffic caused his face to bloom into focus and then disappear back into the shadows on a loop. In the past few days his whole life had changed; his friends were gone and he had the added burden of knowing it was all because of his supposed 'gifts'. The toll it was taking on his mental health would have to be watched closely in the coming weeks.

"Yes and no," Amaris replied, "I know you are in a world of hurt, so if this picture can help you then it's worth the journey."

"Why did this happen to me?" Malachi asked, more to himself than Amaris. "Because of some fucked up healing power and my fucking dreams, all my friends are in danger!"

"I can't really answer that question. The people I work for deal with the prophesies and when we get you to safety, they will tell you all you need to know."

"Can't you at least tell me why they wanted me dead so badly? No one goes through all that organisation without a damned good reason."

Amaris sighed, he deserved at least the rudimentary facts she had been shown, the rest would come from the Archbishop. "All I know is that you are a warrior, ordained by God."

"Stop the car," Malachi ordered, "You're just as nuts as they are."

"Listen to me," she said with as much sincerity as possible, "I know this will be a lot to take in but your healing abilities are only the start of it. I have the same gift only on a much smaller scale and my visions are just snippets, not a full manifestation of the occurrences like yours."

"What do you mean occurrences?" Malachi stared at her.

"They will answer those questions. In its most simple terms, you are part of a battle between Good and Evil that has raged for millennia."

"You expect me to buy this bullshit?" Malachi huffed.

"When you see what they have to show you, you will know the truth," she replied. Communication of the cause had never been her strongest asset and she decided to leave it to those who could explain it with more articulation.

"If this is true, why didn't they just shoot me in the head as soon as they found out what I was?" Malachi questioned the inconsistency in the tale.

"If they had managed to recruit you in the asylum, it is not an exaggeration to say this world would have been utterly lost. It is believed that they have their own individual with your skills. The two of you together would have been unstoppable," Amaris said and shivered at the mere thought.

"So I say again, why not just put a bullet in my head when I refused?" Malachi wasn't convinced with all this religious mumbo-jumbo.

"If you are what we think you are, by sacrificing you it would have increased their power exponentially. You were far too valuable for a simple murder."

"You all keep talking like this. What is it you think I am? A freak of some kind?" Malachi was getting angry.

"You could be a shroud walker," she said quietly, respectful of the title.

"What the fuck is a shroud walker?" he laughed sarcastically.

Amaris glared at him, "You shouldn't mock it. If it is true, you would have the ability to pierce the barriers between realms. You would have powers beyond imagining."

"The psychos at the asylum said the same shit," Malachi sighed and turned to look out of the window.

Realising it would take more than her declarations for the truth to sink in, Amaris fell quiet too. As their convoy rolled through the empty streets, she could only pray that he would accept his destiny and fight for all that was good in the world. Time would tell.

"We are nearly there, it's just around this corner," Malachi remarked, but it wasn't necessary.

The lead vehicle knew exactly where to go and pulled into the dingy side road; several of the streetlights were broken and had been for many months. A deprived area like this was often at the back of the queue for allocation of repairs. The patches of gloom were sundered by the headlights of the passing vehicles before being swallowed by darkness once again.

"That one," Malachi pointed.

The convoy was slowing down, finally coming to a full stop in the middle of the road about forty feet from his building. The lack of brake lights didn't seem remarkable to Malachi until he turned to face Amaris.

"It's further down," he explained and frowned at the dull quality of his voice.

She was looking directly ahead with eyes half shuttered. Her face was masked in shadow so there was nowhere near enough light to provoke a squint.

"Are you ok?"

The words were lifeless and didn't sound right. Inside the confines of a car, speech would normally rebound with a particular audibility, but it felt like he was talking underwater. The air itself seemed to be muffling the acoustics. Amaris hadn't moved an inch, not even a faint twitch or flicker of the eyelid.

What the hell was going on? He reached out and touched her face gently, stroking the skin which was still warm and firm. Still no response, not even a murmur of protest. Malachi pressed a little harder and the cheek dimpled at the contact, then remained sunken as if it were made of playdough.

"I'm dreaming," Malachi laughed, "I'm still in a coma and all this is just a bad dream."

Although it didn't feel like any of the dreams he had experienced so far. Squeezing his eyes tightly shut and concentrating with every fibre of his mind, he willed the vision to disappear. Opening one eye, he was still seated in the car with a waxwork imitation of the woman who had recently saved his life.

"I've finally fucking snapped," Malachi whispered.

Was he bound in a padded room again? High on a cocktail of anti-psychotics and dribbling onto his pillow. Could he even escape from this new reality? Fear knotted his guts at the thought of being trapped in this frozen dimension forever. Reaching tentatively for the door handle, it clicked and opened without issue. Stepping onto the pavement, Malachi breathed in deeply. The air smelled of his street, though feeling thicker as it was drawn into his lungs. The communal rubbish bins were all in their normal position, garbage overflowing and laying on the ground ready for the rats which frequented the concealing shadows.

Glancing up, one of the working lamps illuminated a bat poised in mid-swoop about to pluck a moth from the air. Inches separated the omnivore and its prey with the inevitable feast being postponed by the inexplicable pause in time. Fear grew into frustration and Malachi kicked out at an empty beer can. Instead of clattering down the street, it flew a short distance from the kicks' momentum and then hung at head height, unaffected by the strictures of gravity. It brought back memories of watching bullets being fired in water; the density of the liquid working against the fast moving projectile. In those cases, the lead slug had then sunk, which only confused Malachi further. Pushing at the suspended can, it moved forward by a few inches and then stopped again. To his right, the exhaust of the lead vehicle was belching fumes which hung in the air like a cloud.

"Can I wake up now please?" he screamed into the night.

When the request went unanswered, Malachi tried to apply logic to his predicament. They had all slowed and then stopped, which indicated a gradual cessation of time itself. As utterly impossible as it was, that was the basic premise of the dream. What was this 'vision' supposed to represent? In all other nightmares he had witnessed unimaginable horrors, but this one was absent of literally everything. Mind going around in convoluted circles, he was tempted to lay down on the ground until the vision passed or his brain finally gave up. It was only when he turned to his block of flats that he noticed the aberration.

"What the hell?" he gasped at the sight before him.

The ten storey block of cramped apartments was encapsulated in a purple hued sphere. The shell crackled with flickering energy and it appeared liquescent, with shifting, nebulous patterns playing across the surface. Malachi hadn't noticed the faint hum which emanated from the orb in his confused state until now. Whatever this thing was, it was obviously the key to the dream itself so he left his frozen companions and approached. The pitch of the vibration didn't increase with proximity and standing before the shell itself, he reached out a finger and touched the surface. A chill shot up his arm, akin to electricity but without the accompanying danger. Instead of the surface being solid, it was incorporeal and provided no resistance to his probing hand.

"Whoa," Malachi whispered in awe as his hand disappeared up to the elbow.

What else is there to do? He thought to himself and stepped through the flickering skin. The sensation was similar to the irrepressible shudder which accompanied the phrase 'someone walked over my grave'. Inside the bubble, the motionlessness of the outer world was gone. Music carried through from a ground floor flat and on the eighth floor a window opened, creaking loudly on unoiled hinges.

"Ok, what now?" Malachi asked, trying to divine a purpose in the bizarre scene.

Taking a step backwards replaced the building with the purple barrier and with another forward step he was back at the foot of the building.

"At least I can go and have a lie down," he conceded with a smile.

Could someone sleep within a dream? He was about to find out and the thought of his soft bed and gloriously cold pillow was enough to get him rushing up the concrete steps to the entrance door. The code released the lock with a loud buzz and he pushed through into the foyer. Numbered letterboxes lined one wall, with a counter on the other. The desk served as a place for people to talk to the building supervisor, except he mostly hid away these days. With requests for general maintenance routinely refused by the landlord, he had put up a noticeboard for people to pin their issues on. When these too were ignored, the tenants started to use more colourful language and now it represented nothing more than a means of venting their dissatisfaction. The curse words were in a range of languages; Mataeusz, a young guy from Poland, had explained some of the phrases and it never failed to make Malachi chuckle.

The hallway was covered with graffiti from the friends of a previous occupant. They had taken offense at his eviction and returned in the dead of night before the codes could be changed. Lettering six-foot-tall warned of their gang affiliation and the building had been placed under police protection for a week. The storm had died down and nothing more happened, least of all a meaningful effort to remove the spray paint. As well as the building supervisor, five more apartments lay on the ground floor with a basement below. At the end of the corridor was a lift, but it hadn't worked in months.

"I wonder?" Malachi said, pondering whether the faulty elevator would work in the dream.

Nothing happened when he pressed the button and the red LED's showed it was staying on the third floor where it had ground to a halt many week ago. Obviously lacklustre management carried over into the realms of fantasy too. The stairwell was dimly lit; a cost saving measure that didn't take into account the elderly tenants and the hazard it posed to them. Sighing at the greed which seemed to be infesting the human psyche over the past few years, he thought about Miss Cortez and her failing health. If he ever woke up, he was going to tear the landlord a new one in the local newspapers. Nothing concentrated the thinking of a cockroach like a light being shone upon them.

"Hi," said a voice from the next floor and Malachi looked up to see Claire smiling down through the railings.

"Hi, Claire. How's your mummy and daddy?" he asked, studying her closely. She was exactly as she looked in real life, with pigtails and her trademark odd socks swinging from thin legs through the steel rails.

"They are fighting again, that's why I am hiding in here," she sighed.

"Sorry to hear that, honey. If you get cold or lonely, come and knock my door, ok?" Malachi said to the dream child.

"Thanks, Mal," she waved as he entered the fifth floor.

One of the hallway lights was on the fritz and fizzed and flickered from the faulty connection. All the place needed was a bloody fire! Reaching up, he removed the glass covering and twisted the bulb loose. Hissing as the hot surface burned his palm, he pulled a sleeve down to hold it with. In spite of his normal placid nature, Malachi was going to tear the landlord a new asshole tomorrow. Or whenever the drugs wore off. Could he even complain about defects in a dream?

"Jesus Christ, you've really cracked," Malachi shook his head at the jumbled thoughts. What he needed was a pillow and the back of his eyelids, then this whole mess could go to hell.

CHAPTER TWENTY EIGHT

The door to his flat was ajar, and he hesitated at the threshold. All the lights were on, but he couldn't see an intruder from his limited angle. Pushing the door wide the hinges creaked, announcing his arrival. Fucking building! No one rushed at him with a weapon so he stepped inside and could hear the faint hiss of static coming from the bedsitting room. Peeking around the wall, a balding head was sat on the sofa facing the madly dancing screen. Maybe this was the point of the dream. The face would turn and it would be an older Malachi, still alone after all these years. Mocking his attempt at happiness with Chloe.

Opting for a bold approach, Malachi shouted, "What the fuck are you doing in my flat?"

Showing no signs of being startled, the head turned slowly until it revealed itself. The face wasn't Malachi's; either in the future or at any point in time. The eyes were too small and beady, with a bottom lip that drooped a little as he regarded the newcomer.

Recognition was followed by a small nod, "I knew you would come here. They told me to just get it done, but I knew," said the man in an American accent.

"Who are you?" Malachi asked, although he was certain he knew.

"Who I am doesn't matter, what I am here for is of much greater concern to you," replied the man.

A burst of understanding flooded Malachi's head as he thought back to the news pictures Dr. Franken had shown alongside the tales of miracle healing, "You're Clarence Voight!"

The man's eyes narrowed coldly, "Clever little bastard, aren't you?"

Malachi threw his head back and started laughing madly, "Not really. I work in a gym."

Clarence was confused by the reaction and even more perplexed when Malachi proceeded to drop a bulb in the waste bin and then fill the kettle up. Taking a cup down, he added a teabag and one sugar, "Do you want a cuppa? It will have to be black though, I'm out of milk."

"Not really," answered Clarence.

Malachi opened the refrigerator and found a fresh pint of milk on the shelf, which only brought more laughter.

"If I didn't think I was dreaming before, I know I am now," Malachi smiled at the intruder, holding aloft the bottle, "I binned my last bit of milk on the day I was stabbed."

Unblinking, Clarence watched as he made the brew and then held a hand out to indicate Malachi should seat himself. Sipping at the sweet flavour, the young man then held up the cup in toast at the dream apparition.

"Do you understand what is going on here?" Clarence asked slowly, to make sure the words sunk in to the unhinged boy.

"Of course," Malachi nodded, "I'm tied to a bed, high as a kite on drugs in the hospital."

"Not quite," Clarence replied, "Your situation is far worse than that."

"Look, I know you killed your family. I know you were a bad man mixed up with Mafia shit. But really? This is the most disappointing nightmare yet," Malachi said derisively.

Clarence frowned. He was starting to lose patience with this brash little upstart, "You aren't dreaming."

"Of course not," Malachi chuckled, "I'm trapped in a bubble of purple energy like Barney the fucking Dinosaur's ball sack. Time has stopped outside and inside the teste I am sat drinking tea with a man who should be in his nineties, but looks forty. Give it a rest, I'm going to my make believe bed."

Clarence hadn't been prepared for this. He felt insulted by the dismissive tone of the youth and the way he rinsed out his half-finished mug of tea as if nothing was happening, "Come and sit down."

"Fuck off," Malachi gave him the finger.

"I SAID SIT DOWN!" Clarence's voice boomed and he thrust out a hand.

Malachi felt a compressive force wrap itself around him as he was dragged backwards into the chair. The back of the seat hit the wall as it skidded across the floor and smashed a hole straight into the plaster.

"That's a neat trick," Malachi clapped enthusiastically when the force withdrew, "Who taught you? Darth Vader?"

"Very good," Clarence conceded with his own chuckle, "Your humour may make it easier when my friends are tearing you apart."

"Typical Darth Vader, getting your lackeys to do your dirty work," Malachi tutted.

Clarence sighed with disappointment, "I came here expecting a worthy adversary. You are nothing but a piffling child."

"Ouch, I'm hurt." Malachi rubbed at pretend tears.

"You will be soon enough, trust…"

"Malachi?" called Miss Cortez's frail voice from the hallway, interrupting him.

"Ahh, you have a guest," Clarence grinned evilly.

"Are you there, dearie?" she asked, entering the flat.

"Now you will have to decide if you are dreaming or not," Clarence whispered.

"Mal? I hope you don't mind, but I got you some milk. I didn't know you were going away."

Doubts crept into Malachi's consciousness. As Miss Cortez stepped into view, Malachi tried to cry a warning but with another flick of the wrist his mouth snapped shut painfully and his arms were pinned against the rests. The fantasy was so convincing that it might just be real; the feel of the leather on his forearms from the chair, the slightly bitter aftertaste of the tea.

"We are in here," Clarence called out cheerfully.

"Oh there you are," she smiled at the pair, "I thought I heard a commotion."

"It was more a difference of opinion," Clarence explained, "But now you are here we can see who was right."

Ignoring the stranger, Miss Cortez looked at Malachi where he seemed to be struggling against invisible bonds, "Mal, what's going on?"

"Go and put the kettle on," Clarence said quietly, staring at Malachi.

"I don't think…" She was stopped midsentence by an inexplicable force.

Clarence waved at her and she was forced into the kitchen, step by painful step. The tension on her hips caused her to cry out in agony as she pressed the power button. The kettle rumbled into life, taking only seconds to reheat after Malachi's earlier drink. The spout spewed steam with the promise of what was to come. Malachi knew it too and struggled even harder.

"Leave her alone," Malachi growled.

Clarence raised his eyebrows, "I'm impressed. You have some fight in you, boy. It's a real shame, I would have enjoyed having an apprentice."

"Go fuck yourself!"

"Manners maketh the man," chastised Clarence.

"Mal, I'm afraid," cried the sweet old lady.

The emotional reaction was too realistic and Malachi started to consider this insanity may be actually happening.

With a nod, she was made to reach out and pick up the kettle. Her bony frame was illustrated starkly by the thin nightgown and she held a delicate arm out. Malachi screamed and strained against the pressure, managing to lean forward in protest.

"So much wasted power." Clarence shook his head.

With a final glance, Miss Cortez poured the contents of the vessel up and down her arm, adding to the screaming in the room. The boiling water ran from her blistering flesh and splashed from the floor onto her exposed legs. Malachi was sobbing with guilt at the punishment his friend was receiving. All to make a point about a reality that couldn't possibly exist in a sane mind.

"You're a fucking dead man," Malachi snarled and stood up.

A momentary flash of uncertainty passed over Clarence's face and he let Miss Cortez drop to the floor, using all his power to restrain Malachi. Forcing him against the wall, Clarence lifted his arm and his prisoner thrashed against the psychic shackles, feet rising from the floor.

"How the hell do you exist? You should be an old man," Malachi seethed, staring down at the average looking, non-descript monster.

"The gifts I possess have been bestowed on me by a power as old as the universe itself. You could have had them too, but you were too short sighted. Hasn't this taught you anything?" Clarence asked, indicating the carnage.

"You're immortal," gasped Malachi, "That's why your family disappeared. You gave them as an offering."

"My choices have been made!" he screamed, "I don't answer to you, boy."

"You'd better kill me now, because if I ever get loose I am going to beat you to death with my bare hands," Malachi roared with righteous fury. His soul yearned for retribution against the evil creature below and it felt... good.

"You mistake my intent. My job here is to make it look like you went berserk and killed everyone," Clarence explained.

"You don't know me at all, any of you!" Malachi shouted, "I would never hurt an innocent person."

"Of course not, that's why I am bringing some friends. Once they are finished with you all, this building will resemble a slaughterhouse and the evidence I've hidden will point to an obsession with mass murder and links to a cult. A group of psychos finally lose it and act out their fantasies." Clarence mulled over his own story, then nodded. It was a believable narrative.

"And what if I kill all your friends? Then wait for the authorities to find us?"

"This doesn't work that way, I'm afraid. My friends are legion," he declared proudly.

Malachi exploded with laughter, "A pathetic prick like you only has two friends, and they are used to masturbate with."

Clarence shook with rage, but held it in, "Laugh. Cry. It makes no difference. This realm sits outside of time; you should have noticed on the way in."

"Neat trick," Malachi replied.

"Indeed. It also means that for as long as life exists within this plane, this building will never be free. Everyone will die, it is only a matter of... time," Clarence grinned at his own pun.

"And your friends will die too, do they know that this is a suicide mission?" Malachi taunted, "You're a filthy, family murdering, friend killing, degenerate."

"Sticks and stones," laughed Clarence, "And you needn't worry about my friends. They aren't what you would call... alive, but they certainly exist and are hungry. Always."

"I'll be sure to cook them some bacon and eggs," Malachi retorted.

"I tire of this inane exchange," Clarence said, turning away, "Gan vordis palox mer."

The air seemed to change and the lights dimmed for a few brief moments. Malachi tried to think of a witty insult but something had changed and he was also terrified for Miss Cortez who had fallen completely silent.

"The ritual is complete. They are coming."

"Before you disappear in a puff of smoke like a comic book villain, answer me this. If this isn't a dream and you can really stop time, why not just use that to take over the world?"

"I was going to use the front door actually," Clarence shrugged, "And not that it will do you any good, but there are rules which we must all abide by in this game. We mustn't go upsetting the head honchos!"

"A game?" Malachi shook his head, "You really are a fucking lunatic."

"Goodbye, Malachi," Clarence said, before disappearing out of the flat.

With every pace that his new nemesis took, the strength of his power diminished until it vanished completely and Malachi fell to the floor. He was on his feet in an instant, rushing to the unconscious form of Miss Cortez in the kitchen area. Anguish tore at his heart and he forgot about the soaked linoleum. In almost comedy style his feet flew out from underneath him and he skidded across the floor on his bottom, nearly sideswiping his friend. Cursing his stupidity, he quickly recovered and kneeled by her side.

"Shit! Miss Cortez, can you hear me?" he asked, patting her cheek.

There was no response and the most pressing concern was to try and protect her blistered arm and lower legs. Think! What did they always say in first aid training? Call the emergency services. Hoping against hope, Malachi removed his mobile phone but there was no signal and no internet coverage.

"Water!"

Opening the cold tap, the liquid flowed into the bowl, ready to soothe the scald. All he needed was cloths to soak. The joy of living in such a small space was that within a few paces he was at the small linen cupboard pulling a pile of towels all over the floor. Taking the plushest, he plunged them into the frigid liquid until they were saturated. Lifting them out of the bowl, he froze for a moment at the possibility the sudden plunge in temperature could cause her to get hypothermia. At this point it was the lesser of the problems so he carefully wrapped the limbs with the moist cloth.

"What is going on in here? I've had people knocking my door with reports of screaming," said a gruff voice. It was Paul Fontell, the building supervisor. Thank goodness he chose now to come out of hiding.

"Paul, get in here. Miss Cortez has been badly burned," Malachi called out.

Running into the kitchen, Paul nearly slipped on the kettle water and looked around with suspicion at the scene, "What have you done to her?"

"Nothing! We were attacked and I don't know what to do." Malachi was frantic with worry.

"Call 999, it's not rocket science," Paul mocked.

"Don't you think I haven't thought of that? There is no signal, we are cut off from the outside world."

"Yeah, right," he sneered, his face changing from smug to perplexed as his phone confirmed it.

"If you aren't going to help, then fuck off!" Malachi shouted, "Scurry back to your flat and hide like you always do."

"There's no need for that," Paul replied, hurt by the truth in his words.

Malachi blanked out his sulk and felt at the neck of his kindly neighbour. No blood surged through the artery so Malachi leaned down to her open mouth to check if he had been mistaken. No air passed her lips.

"Get over here, we need to start CPR!"

Paul joined Malachi and for once he felt useful. As the younger man compressed her heart muscle, he gave two breaths and waited again. Malachi was crying though the whole procedure but he wouldn't quit. Even after several minutes of unsuccessful resuscitation he kept going until Paul gently eased him away.

"She's gone, mate. You did all you could."

"This is all my fault!" Malachi shouted, punching the nearest cabinet door.

Splinters of wood exploded across the room from the impact and Paul pushed himself backwards in shock. At most it should have dented the finish, but instead it looked like a small bomb had gone off, shattering all the crockery inside too.

"I thought you said you didn't do this to her?" Paul asked nervously.

Malachi ignored him and looked at his hand with puzzlement. The rage that had built up was released with the strike, adding his own mental hatred to the physical attack. He would explore this later, if there ever was a later.

"I didn't do this. It was some American guy who left just before you came in," Malachi explained.

Paul was on his feet and making for the exit, stopping in his tracks when realization dawned. He had seen the guy! "Was he about five- eight, mid-forties with thinning hair?"

"Yeah, that was him. Clarence Voight," Malachi growled, the anger rising again.

"I passed him in the hallway," Paul gasped, "He seemed so cheerful and friendly."

"He just made Miss Cortez pour a kettle of boiling water over herself. I'll bet he was feeling pretty happy, the sadistic bastard!"

"Shall I try and stop him?" Paul asked, until the words sank in, "Wait, did you say he made her pour it over herself? You mean he held her arm while she tipped it."

"No, I mean I watched as he somehow controlled my friend with his mind. He made her walk over, boil it, and then scald herself."

"But that's just not possible," Paul whispered, fearing he was being taken for a ride in some elaborate ruse.

"A month ago I would have agreed with you," Malachi said, thinking back to the extraordinary events he had witnessed, "Now I'm not so sure."

"You're nuts. I am going to find a way to contact the police, they will get to the bottom of this."

"Listen, Paul. I understand how crazy this all sounds, but humour me for a moment and look out of the window. Tell me what you see," aske Malachi.

The supervisor hesitated, certain this was a trick to corner him inside the tiny apartment. The look of grief on Malachi's face was impossible to fake, so against his better judgement he approached the glass and threw back the drapes.

"See," Malachi said quietly.

There was no mistaking the faint purple glow on Paul's skin, the way it danced and flickered in reflection of the sphere. He opened the window, leaned out and looked in every direction before slowly closing it. Doing a great impersonation of a statue for a few seconds, he turned to Malachi in disbelief.

"What the hell is it?"

"You will think I'm even more nuts," Malachi answered, gently lifting the body of his beloved neighbour.

"Try me," Paul urged. The shimmering surface left little in the way of doubt.

Malachi refused to speak as he carried Miss Cortez through into his small bedroom. With hot tears coursing down his face, he lay her head onto his soft pillow and covered her with the duvet in respect. Before he pulled it over her face, he kissed her on the forehead and brushed a loose strand of hair away. Feeling the anger growing like a pressure cooker, he turned to Paul.

"If you believe that murdering bastard, and I have no reason not to after what I have just seen, we are trapped in this... bubble. I need to try something because I was able to come and go at will. Maybe he has sealed it now, or I'm stuck because of the time spent inside. Would you mind coming with me?"

"This has to be a nightmare," Paul muttered, shaking his head.

"Careful," Malachi cautioned, "I thought exactly the same thing and it got Miss Cortez killed."

"Ok, let's go."

Malachi paused by the entrance and carefully removed the picture of his beloved parents from the frame, before leaving his apartment. They ran to the stairwell and Claire was still hiding from the violent argument her parents were engaged in. Instead of beating on each other, they chose to smash and throw things. It was just as traumatic for the poor girl nonetheless.

"Honey, do you think you could go and fetch your mum and dad for me. Tell them to knock on every door and gather all the residents, then meet us downstairs. We have a bit of an emergency," Malachi explained.

"Ok, Mal," she answered without hesitation, jumping up and heading to her own home.

"She's a great kid," Malachi said to Paul who just grunted.

Malachi would have gone into a rant about the joy to be found in actually taking an interest in the building's occupants, but time was running short. He could feel something in his bones, like the vibrations on a track as a locomotive thundered towards you. It was out of sight at present, but when it hit things were going to get really bad.

They hurried through the foyer towards the entrance until a door slammed open behind them.

"What the fuck is going on?" slurred a female voice. It was Zelda, the resident hippie alcoholic and she could barely stand up without the aid of the wall.

"Just get back inside," Paul tried to take charge, "We have a situation which we are trying to deal with."

"Don't you try and tell me what to do!" she shrieked, wagging a finger at whichever of the several Pauls had spoken.

"Zelda, we don't have time to argue with you. If you don't go back indoors, I will bill you for the vomit I had to have cleaned out of the carpet," Paul shouted back.

Realising she would be sacrificing cash that could buy more cheap wine, she relented, "Ok, no need to be so grouchy."

"Thank you," Paul replied, "We will collect you shortly so leave your door on the latch."

They left her fumbling with the mechanism which, judging by her condition, would keep her occupied for at least five minutes. Pushing through the entrance, the view of the orb was breath-taking. It rose and curved over the roof by at least thirty feet so they wouldn't be able to reach the top in any way.

Malachi hesitated by the crackling surface. If they were trapped it would mean a confrontation with whatever was coming, and there was no way on earth it would be pleasant. If his dreams were linked to this, then the monstrosities he had seen rise would devour them all screaming.

"Here goes nothing," he whispered, poking a finger out. The digit sunk straight through with no resistance and he whooped with joy. Stepping through, the night outside was still frozen like a photograph. He could just make out Amaris in the driver's seat of the vehicle from the streetlight. With a quick fist pump, he jumped back into the sphere.

"Fuck you, Clarence!" Malachi shouted, wishing the degenerate could see as he ferried everyone out of the building to safety.

"That's great, now my turn," Paul beamed, eager to be away from this insanity. He reached out with both hands, confident he would meld through the surface. He would have had greater luck trying to push through solid concrete.

"I don't get it," Malachi whispered, pushing his whole arm through.

"We're trapped," Paul said, trying one more time.

"Wait a second, hold on to me while I go through. It may work if we are linked."

They clasped hands and Malachi hopped through. He could still feel the warm, clammy grip on Paul and tried to draw him through. As soon as the other man's skin made contact with the energy, it stopped dead. He tried to adjust his grip and pulled again, but it wouldn't penetrate the surface. He could feel Paul frantically tugging, desperate not to lose contact with the only person with knowledge of what was going on.

"Think!"

How could anyone be expected to fathom the madness that was taking place? The feeling of responsibility became a crushing weight and a familiar enemy probed his resolve. You could just let go, get back in the car with Amaris and wait for whatever was coming to do what it desired. You wouldn't even need to listen to the carnage; it will all be over in less than an hour. You could even have a quick nap.

"Go fuck yourself!" Malachi shouted into the night, silencing the whispers.

He knew they were evil. What he wasn't too sure of was whether it was his own dark nature, or that of the other being who wanted to control him again. The power was wasting its time trying to convert Malachi, his parents had instilled a virtuous nature incomprehensible to the evil entity. Clarence had been human once, and understood his quarry on a deeper level though. He knew that Malachi wouldn't leave innocent people to suffer. With one final scream into the nothingness to vent some of the bubbling hatred, he re-joined the trapped people.

Paul let out a shuddering breath with relief, "I thought you were going to leave us."

"Never," said Malachi, "I was trying to think of a way out of this thing."

"And?"

Malachi didn't need to spell it out and shook his head instead.

"Shit!" Paul shouted, punching the sphere. His knuckles came away bloody, confirming its solidity.

Malachi slapped his forehead, a new idea coming to him, "If we can't go up or sideways, maybe we go down."

Searching the ground, they settled on a recently tended flowerbed. The disturbed soil gave way under their frenzied digging and with their posture they resembled two dogs trying to bury a bone. At a depth of eighteen inches they sat on their heels, gasping with exertion. The orb curved away underneath them too.

"Maybe if we go deeper?" Paul asked, standing up and wiping the mud from his hands, "I can see if we have a shovel in the maintenance room."

Malachi knew in his heart it would be fruitless, "There's no point. I have a feeling this goes all the way under us."

"How can you be sure?" Paul cried, grabbing Malachi by his t-shirt.

"I just am," Malachi gently eased the terrified hands away, "We need to get everyone together and get ready for what's coming."

"What do you mean, coming?"

"We have been sealed in here for a purpose," Malachi explained, then paused. How could he tell Paul that all life would need to end before the energy would disappear?

"Why are you looking at me like that? There's more to it, isn't there?" Paul asked.

"You want the truth? Clarence said that everybody would need to die or we are trapped in here forever."

"Are you shitting me?" Paul laughed morbidly, "If we are trapped we die from starvation anyway."

It was a good point, except dehydration would do for them long before the hunger could end their existence. Malachi thought about the inconsistencies and outright insanity of their predicament. It wasn't beyond Clarence's cruelty to inflict a slow, agonising death on them. He certainly had the power. Was it the time the murderer would need to spend in a world of suspended animation? He was immortal, so it was unlikely impatience would be an issue.

"What am I missing?" Malachi pondered.

"Whatever it is, you better figure it out."

"No shit, Sherlock," Malachi replied, "I'm trying to save your lives, so cut me some slack."

"Ok, I'm sorry," said Paul, "Let's get inside and we can put our heads together."

Out of the seventy occupants of the building, only twenty were waiting in the lobby. Claire was stood with her mother and father, guilt etched on their faces from the stares they received for the latest commotion. Most of the others were unknown to Malachi and he felt a pang of sadness that they had all lived so close together, but shared nothing. Except death, perhaps.

"Why have you called us all down here?" demanded Claire's father, Anton.

"There is a problem," begun Paul, trying to choose the right words, "For some reason we are trapped in the building."

"Are the locks broken?" asked another young woman, "Just call a locksmith for God's sake. I now have to try and get my baby back to sleep, thanks a lot."

"It's not that simple."

"Get out of the way," Anton barrelled through the group. Taking hold of the handle, he wrenched it and fell flat on his ass when it offered no resistance.

"Honey!" Claire's mother shrieked and ran forward.

"Fuck off!" he shouted as he stood back up, pushing her away and marching towards Paul, "I thought you said the door was broken!"

Malachi stepped in the way and stared him down. Throwing objects was totally different to a physical altercation, especially against someone in shape. Anton himself was unkempt and overweight, which only served to illustrate his deficiencies.

"Please, calm down and take a look outside. That's what Paul meant when he said we were trapped," Malachi said calmly. He pitied the whole family and certainly didn't want to get involved in a scuffle in front of Claire.

The group moved off through the door and Malachi followed. The oohs and aahs wouldn't have been out of place at a firework display as the tenants surveyed the purple wall. An older lady reached out a hand, but the others hissed and warned her off.

"It's harmless," Malachi explained, "Just impenetrable."

"What do you mean?" Anton sneered, fear and hurt pride triggering his false bravado.

"Try it," Malachi urged, "You can't get through and we need to work together to figure a way out of here."

Anton huffed, then looked at the others. They all thought he was a waste of space and he knew it; the way they would scowl as he passed and whisper when he was out of earshot. Opting to put on a show and prove it was all bullshit he walked forward, until his face mashed flat and sent him reeling. The shock wore off and he flew at the barricade, punching and kicking.

"Daddy, please stop," sobbed Claire, hugging her mother.

"Anton, come on," Malachi placed an arm across his shoulders, trying to be supportive, "Let's get back inside."

"Get your fucking hands off me!" Anton snarled, throwing his arm off. "I don't take advice from a psycho who screams all day and night."

"There's no need to be like that, Anton!" Paul shouted.

"You can fuck off too. We haven't had a working toilet for weeks," Anton marched toward the supervisor, "We have had to use a bucket. Yeah, a fucking bucket!"

Murmurs of support were forthcoming from several in the group and Paul lowered his head with embarrassment. "I'm sorry. They don't give me anywhere near enough money to look after the place."

Anton wouldn't let up and started prodding him painfully in the chest, "I bet your place is like a palace though, and you don't even pay rent."

"I pay exactly the same as the rest of you, I volunteered to take on the role as I wanted to help others," Paul replied quietly, massaging the tender spots, "I don't even have a working boiler. I have to shower in cold water."

All of the righteous anger fled Anton and he took on the same pose; eyes down to avoid the recriminating stares. His wife went to his side but Claire wouldn't, the alienation was already forming in their relationship.

"Can we go under it?" slurred Zelda. She had miraculously joined them without breaking her neck navigating the steps and stood swigging from a half empty wine bottle.

Impressed by her lucidity in the drunken state, Malachi replied, "Already tried over there. It goes under as well as over."

"Well you can't have dug deep enough!" she declared in the absolute certainty that only alcohol could provide.

She reached out carefully, trying to stand the bottle on the low brick wall which surrounded the building. Missing completely, it dropped inches wide of the edge and shattered on the ground. Her mind was made up and she dropped to her knees, burying her fingers into the soil and throwing it over her shoulder. The loose clods rained down on the group and they stepped back out of range.

"Should we stop her?" Paul asked.

Malachi didn't answer. In fact, he couldn't answer. The locomotive loomed in his vision, the light blazing and growing in intensity. The darkness rejoiced and finally the truth of why they wouldn't be left to starve was revealed. Like everything else which had haunted Malachi's sleeping, and waking world, they were to be sacrifices. They must be made to suffer excruciating agony in their final moments to please a being not of this world. Satan? Lucifer? The Devil? Impossible. They were all titles used to control the gullible, to trigger the imagination with fear of eternal souls and damnation. But all the pieces fit. The imaginary train hit Malachi, hurtling through like an apparition in his mind.

"They're here," Malachi whispered.

"Who're here?" asked Paul, looking around and seeing nothing out of the ordinary.

"I don't know, but whatever they are, I know that they are utterly evil. We need to get inside and fortify the place. Now!" Malachi started to hustle people to the precarious safety of the building and Paul attempted to pull Zelda away from her task.

"Leave me alone," she snarled, pushing him away, "I said you hadn't gone deep enough. Just look, the soil is moving now so I must be close."

The alcohol had numbed any common sense, otherwise the sight of the rising mound of earth would have rung alarm bells in her mind. Paul was backing away, riveted on the sight as Malachi rushed over to see what was causing the delay. He could only point at Zelda who was clapping with glee until the surface broke. From the hole poured a stream of vileness which made Malachi's blood run cold. A mixture of insect, arachnid, and multi segmented creatures scurried over one another. The resemblance to earth's critters stopped there as they were all the size of a small dog, their sleek, black carapaces reflecting the orb light. Catching a glimpse of something, Malachi nearly vomited with revulsion. Each and every one of the things had the head of a baby or small infant. Now free of the ground, they gave vent to their screeching wails and it sounded like a nursery from darkest nightmare. Claws and pincers snapped at each other in their desperation to reach the tender flesh of the drunken woman.

"Oh my God!" screamed Paul, turning to run for the door.

Malachi wanted to help, but they moved with incredible speed and in seconds Zelda was buried under their weight. Their razor sharp mandibles went to work, severing through joints and bone, dismembering the woman in a welter of blood. Her agonised shrieks were cut short as an abomination resembling a scorpion took her head, raising it high on the stinger in triumph. Momentarily satiated, the horrors started to feast on their bloody meal, feeding it into hideous, fanged maws.

"I'm sorry," Malachi whispered to her ravaged head until it was lowered and the pincers started to crush through the skull to reach the soft, grey meat inside.

"We have to go!" Paul squealed, pulling on his sleeve.

More monstrosities were rising from the hole, scurrying to reach the two men. They bolted and raced for the door which was the source of a wrestling match between Anton and two of the other tenants.

"We have to fucking close it you idiots!" he shouted, trying to prise their fingers away.

"Wait, they are nearly back!"

"We can't take that chance!" Anton cried, pushing for all he was worth.

Hitting the door hard, Malachi drove him back and he fell to the floor again. Resisting the urge to kick the coward, he flung the door closed and turned to the terrified group. Anton hugged his daughter tightly and Malachi felt some of the animosity melting away; he was only trying to protect the young girl.

"What are those awful things?" Claire asked, pressing herself against her father.

"I don't know what they are, honey, but we need something to block this doorway. The glass won't hold for long!"

"I have a table in my flat. It's heavy and if we can prop it up it may hold," offered Paul.

"Paul, wait," Malachi called out, "Do you have a set of keys for this whole place?"

Skidding to a halt, he replied, "Yeah, did you want me to get them."

"Yes. We need to be able to get in the other downstairs flats and try and block their windows up too."

"What are we going to do?" screamed an elderly lady, making them all cringe.

"I know you are scared, but if we all work together I'm sure we can get through this," Malachi said, trying to calm the situation.

"You're on your own, we are going to the roof to get away from those things!" shouted another man and half of the group hurried after him, including the old woman.

"But we need your help!" Malachi shouted as they retreated.

"Forget them," Anton snarled, "Let's help Paul get that table."

The change in demeanour was remarkable, but his parental instincts had finally kicked in and he was going to do all he could to protect his family. Paul was already at the door with another man, trying to force it through, but the legs were preventing it going through.

"Anton, help break the legs off," Malachi ordered," I'm going to try and shift the counter."

The unit itself was very sturdy, with rows of shelves topped with various pamphlets and paperwork. The weight would buy them some time, and with the table top pressed to the glass the monsters would have to tear their way through. It was securely bolted to the floor and wall, and Malachi could feel how difficult it was going to be to move. Gritting his teeth, he let out a growl and wrestled with the desk. Out of the corner of his eye he could see the swarm slowly surround the building, but they weren't making a headlong dash to get inside. Why? He thought to himself. *To savour your fear*, gurgled the dark entity with an evil chuckle.

"Nearly done, Mal," huffed Anton. The legs were proving to be a bit more difficult to pull off, which was encouraging from a strength point of view. They were just lucky their dinner guests didn't seem to be in any great rush to breach the building.

"Great work," Malachi replied, getting a firmer grip on the counter, "Now if I could just move this fucking thing!"

Summoning all the hatred and terror, Malachi used it the way he had in the flat. The energy pulsed through his veins and with a rending crash, the fixings broke away, leaving large lumps of brick and plaster all over the floor.

"Jesus Christ, I knew you were strong, but that was amazing," Anton gasped, twisting the table top into place against the glass.

"Help me move this against it!" Malachi ordered.

With more grunting and swearing, they wedged the heavy desk against the wooden top. It was a passable barrier, but wouldn't last long against the weight and viciousness of their enemy's claws. He had seen the ease in which they had hacked through poor Zelda and knew they were as sharp as any axe.

"What now?" Anton asked. His transformation was welcome and Malachi patted him on the shoulder, a gesture which wasn't met with anger this time.

"We seal up each room one by one. The only good thing about living here is there are only two windows in each flat."

They all made for Pauls apartment, and blocked the openings with whatever came to hand. A bedframe, reinforced by a wardrobe and then stacked with the contents of his kitchen sealed one, while the other just had a leather sofa leaned against it. Malachi knew it wasn't good enough, and so did the rest of the group.

"It isn't going to hold, Mal," Paul said, shoulders slumping in defeat.

"What else can we do?" Anton argued.

"Why aren't they doing anything?" Claire asked quietly.

Malachi looked over at her, despairing at the impossible task. He wouldn't explain that they were simply enjoying the hunt; it would leech even more of their scant hope to know that such things could think on such a malicious level.

"I don't know, sweetheart. I think they might be scared of us, just like all those normal creepy crawlies," Malachi lied.

"Do we carry on blocking the other flats?" Paul was desperate for an order and Malachi felt renewed pressure at being cast in the role of leader.

"I don't fucking know, Paul. Stuff like this doesn't happen to me every day," Malachi shouted.

It was Anton's turn to offer support and he squeezed Malachi's shoulder, "We know, mate. But we have no idea what is going on and need your guidance."

Sighing, Malachi closed his eyes and thought, "We have two choices. Either we go down into the basement which will be easier to defend, or we go up as high as possible and try and hold them off."

"We could end up trapping ourselves in the basement," Paul replied, entirely missing the fact that they were trapped anyway. The added claustrophobia could be their undoing, though.

"We go upstairs then. Gather whatever weapons you can find, knives and stuff."

"What about the table legs?" Anton asked, hefting one and swinging it in an arc.

"Good idea, they should crush a few bugs," Malachi replied.

His stomach fluttered at the prospect of fighting the scuttling beasts, the way their twisted child faces would shatter under the blows. He was driven to near paralysis by the thought, and none of the others had really seen what they faced, except for Paul. When the time came to do battle, there was no way the rest of the tenants would be able to put up an effective resistance, but what other choice did they have? After collecting anything which could be useful, they gathered by the broken lift.

"Do you think Zelda might have some flammable spirits?" Anton asked, staring at the open doorway.

The stench of neglect wafted out and up the stairs on the currents of air. The carpet was rank and the walls were smeared with unspeakable stains which only filled Malachi with more desolation. The woman had nothing in life, and died a death so awful it was beyond description. The universe was just one big cosmic fuckup, he thought.

"Nothing with alcohol would survive in that place," Paul answered, "Besides, we would probably just end up setting the building on fire with us on top of the bloody thing like a Guy Fawkes doll."

"Good point," Anton conceded.

"Should we block the fire escape, just in case?" asked a young man in a tracksuit. He was one of the sources of constant loud music, but it wasn't the time to pick him up on the antisocial behaviour.

"I think it is pretty solid," Paul replied, banging a hand against the heavy wood.

In reply, a terrible rending came from the other side. The sound of splintering wood was accompanied by a bulge in the door from the pressure which was being brought to bear. A hole appeared, punched through by the tip of a claw which then clamped down, trying to make the opening bigger. With a yell of fear and disgust, Anton slammed the table leg down and the black chitin was shattered. An oozing yellow ichor dribbled down the inside of the door and with a childlike shriek of pain, the injured claw was pulled back. An eye appeared at the gouged wood, staring at them all with hatred.

"Holy Mary, mother of God," whispered an old man before crossing himself.

"We have to go," Malachi ordered, pushing them clear and up the stairs.

"What was that thing?" Anton asked.

"I have no idea," he answered, stopping at the first landing, "I'm going to knock them all and tell them we need to head up to the roof."

"I'll come with you," Paul offered.

"No, get them to safety. I will join you as soon as I can."

"They are demons, here to take me to Hell for what I have done," sobbed the old man, falling to his knees. Everyone looked on with bemusement as he started to pray.

"What the fuck are you talking about?" growled Anton, dragging him to his feet, "We don't have time for this."

"I couldn't help myself. I have a sickness that made me hurt those children!" he shouted at Anton, trying to justify his actions.

"What the fuck did you say?"

The man fell to his knees again and started praying with more urgency, the words pouring out, "God, if you see fit to spare me, I will show the authorities where they are buried and take my punishment. I deserve it."

"You vile bastard!" Anton snarled and kicked out.

The prostrate man was sent flying down the concrete stairs, bones breaking in the tumble. At the bottom he landed awkwardly, his neck twisting with an awful crunch. The bloodied face stared up at the group, a mixture of pain and the terrifying recognition of where his soul was going.

"Why did you do that, daddy?" whimpered Claire, hiding behind her mother.

"I... I... I... didn't mean to," he stuttered, "I was just filled with rage when he said about the poor children."

"What's done is done," Malachi finished, ignoring the gloating whisper. It was thriving on the fear and hatred, like a psychic vampire.

"He's right. Let's go." Paul took charge and led them upwards.

Malachi went door to door without success. People were either fortunate to be out, or they were scared and ignoring the knocks. He shouted through the letterboxes just in case and moved floor to floor doing the same. By the time he reached the roof access, only six more had joined him.

"No one else?" Paul enquired with disappointment.

"No."

"Hopefully they aren't home."

"Some were out," Malachi replied, "But others I could hear moving around. I think they are just scared."

"I don't fucking blame them," said Anton.

"Shall I go and open their doors? We could talk them into joining us," Paul offered.

"No, you could get hurt if they think you are a threat. We have to worry about everyone up here first."

Dozens of eyes stared, looking for leadership and salvation. The burden was heavy and Malachi would have given anything to go back to his old, simpler existence. He had to think of a plan, an angle which he hadn't seen which could spare all their lives. The mocking laughter on the periphery of his mind didn't help, and he drove it away.

"What shall we do?"

The roof was square, with a low parapet wall surrounding it. Three structures sat atop it; the small access door for the staircase, a larger building which housed the communal water cisterns, and finally the lift machinery housing. Walking to the edge, he leaned over and shivered. The creatures were hundreds strong, with a small group working at the entrance doorway. They thrust and worried, tearing at the timber barricade and tossing the pieces aside. Hurrying across the flat roof, the fire exit to the rear had already been breached and the monsters were slowly entering. They didn't need to rush as there was nowhere for the potential victims to go.

"We are going to die, aren't we?" Paul asked, leaning against the wall to look over.

"Be careful!" Malachi yelled, grabbing and pulling him back just as the deteriorating brickwork fell away.

"Holy shit, thank you," Paul gasped. The next few hours would judge if Malachi had been right to save him from a quick plunge and the painless oblivion it promised.

The rubble tumbled end over end, bricks and coping stones coming apart as the cement crumbled. Crashing to the ground the debris crushed nearly twenty of the insectoid abominations, their yellow blood spraying the walls. Inhuman cries of pain pealed from the horrors and Malachi allowed himself a wry smile. How'd you like that, you rancid bastard? He asked the darkness. It laughed darkly, *my friends are legion, for every one you kill a thousand wait to take their place.*

"Let's put that to the test," Malachi answered.

"Put what to the test?" Paul asked.

"Half of you, start hitting and kicking the walls. As much as you can safely break loose to squash these bloody things!" Malachi growled, "The rest of you, if you would please pile as much stuff as you can find by the staircase. We won't block it until we are sure no one else is coming."

There was such finality in those words, but he couldn't bring himself to say 'when everyone below is dead'. He had heard children and it tore at his conscience. Thankfully they were all grateful for the distraction and spread out around the perimeter, beating against the weak surface or collecting flower pots and other discarded junk. Chunks of the wall broke free piece by piece and rained down, scoring dozens of kills on the hellish monsters. The gatherers proved industrious, tearing up any loose slabs that had been laid on the roof. In minutes a sizeable pile waited to block the staircase and the edge of the roof was too dangerous to approach.

"What now?" Anton asked, red faced and sweating.

Malachi didn't know; they had done everything they possibly could within the constraints of the spherical prison. He walked over to the shattered wall and knelt, before crawling forward slowly and peering over the edge. Thousands of eyes stared up, twinkling with malevolence. The bodies of their fallen were being dragged back towards the hole, showing a kinship that baffled him. No, wait. This was the wrong side of the building which meant that they had risen from more than one tunnel. How was any of this possible when the orb surrounded them?

307

"Because they come from somewhere else," Malachi answered himself. He could sense the entities slow nod. They dwelled in the underworld, where nightmares didn't just exist in the realms of slumber.

Screams resounded up from below, shaking him from the unearthly thoughts. They couldn't see what was happening, only judge the fate of the victims by their madly dancing shadows on the wall. The fighting was short lived and soon replaced by the wet sounds of flesh being ripped from bones.

"Those poor people," whispered Claire.

"Shall we try and reach the others again?" Paul asked in desperation.

Malachi thought for a second. He wanted to protect those on the roof, but couldn't ignore the plight of the other occupants any longer.

"You all wait here, I can get down and back faster if I don't have anyone to worry about," he stated and started to descend.

"Malachi!" Anton called, stopping him, "Look."

The noises had obviously confirmed the insane ramblings which had poured through the letter boxes. Men, women and children were filing up the stairs, shielding their children from the sights below. Malachi did a quick calculation of the doors he had knocked which he suspected still had people inside. The numbers tallied, minus the two lowest floors which had already been overrun. He said a silent prayer and smiled with relief at each terrified face that passed.

"Paul, Anton, I think we should block it now. What do you think?" Malachi asked.

The two men were hesitant to make a decision which could cost lives. In the circumstances, the chance to shut off at least one avenue for the skittering beasts seemed a good call and they both nodded. More activity commenced as everything which could be lifted was thrown down into the concrete staircase. In less than two minutes it was choked with debris, but there were still voids and small passages where it was thrown haphazardly instead of placed properly.

"They will still be able to get through!" Anton shouted, looking around for anything to plug the gaps.

"It's hopeless," said Paul, sitting on the cold roof, head in hands.

"Maybe not. Would everyone mind standing back?" Malachi asked.

The brick structure was around eight-foot square, topped with a flat concrete slab acting as a roof. Looking at his filthy hands, he wiggled the fingers and felt the strange tingle emanating from them. It was similar to pins and needles, just without the discomfort. Using the tip of his forefinger he traced a line across the cement joint and it didn't feel different, the nerve impulses were exactly the same. Clenching a fist, he pulled his arm back and punched the supporting wall.

"Shit, that hurt," he hissed, cradling the bloody knuckles. Now he knew how Anton felt.

"What are you doing, you bloody fool?" A voice from the crowd asked.

"Shut up and let him do his thing," Paul barked. He knew what Malachi was trying to replicate and didn't want any interruptions.

What am I doing wrong? He asked himself, clenching and unclenching the painful fist. The power was there, waiting to be released, but for now it was like a gun with no trigger. The kitchen played through his mind, mixed with guilt at being unable to save her. And he had forgotten her body!

"Fuck!" Malachi screamed into the purple night, startling the onlookers.

Even now the monsters would be feasting on her meagre flesh. Dirty, filthy, fucking bastards. The rage flared brightly, like a blacksmith's forge being driven by powerful bellows. Using the blind hatred, he drove another punch at the wall and it exploded inwards, taking a sizeable amount of brickwork with it.

"What on earth?" gasped an elderly lady.

"Everyone, get back," Malachi shouted, his teeth bared in a snarl.

Driving more and more punches around the wall, the brickwork crumbled and with one final blow the roof collapsed into the void. The added weight compressed the rubble and debris to provide an impenetrable barrier.

"Way to go," Paul patted him on the back. The rest of the crowd were either watching cautiously or backing away, regretting they had sealed themselves on a roof with this freak.

"I think it's only delaying the inevitable," Malachi whispered sullenly, feeling the same sense of hopelessness which Paul had recently displayed.

"I don't know what the heck is going on, but you can use the power to protect us all," Paul said, nodding eagerly as if he had just solved the whole crisis.

"Paul, I can't punch them all to death," Malachi threw his hands up in frustration, "There are hundreds, maybe thousands now."

"There has to be a way," Paul replied meekly.

There isn't, whispered the voice. There was a subtle change in the tone, though. The boundless confidence was gone, Malachi could feel the first stirrings of anxiety, or even fear in the being. A wave of visceral hostility washed over Malachi from the entity. *It's time to finish this, you impudent whelp*, it sneered.

"Holy shit, they are coming!"

"Get your weapons ready, we are going to send these sons of whores back to hell," shouted Anton, readying himself by the ledge with his trusty table leg.

Most of the group gathered any weapon they could and formed up. The older members looked resolute, standing tall in what could prove to be their final moments. The younger generation drew strength from their elders and stood side by side, ready for whatever was coming. Malachi crawled forward and his testicles shrivelled, a sensation he had imagined existed only in fiction. The sight was incredible and horrifying at the same time; a dark blanket of reflective carapaces which rose to cover every inch of wall. Thousands of legs clicked against the wall like hailstones on a tin roof as they climbed ever higher. The question of how they were able to support their weight during the ascent was answered with the flaking brickwork and cement. They had enough power to drive the tips into the wall itself.

"Oh my God," whispered Malachi, seeing the futility of their efforts.

They can't help you now. No one can, gloated his nemesis.

Malachi was grateful for the hated mutterings as they fuelled his anger. Holding out a hand, he felt foolish, but it was worth a shot. Sending out his consciousness, he channelled all of his fear and hate into an invisible slab of energy. Slapping his open palm against the broken wall, the bugs below were crushed flat, sending a rain of black shell and yellow gore onto those below. For the briefest moment they paused in shock at the slaughter, mewling like scared infants.

"What happened?" asked Paul, risking his neck by looking over the edge.

Before Malachi could answer, the creatures shrieked and scurried up the wall with a renewed vigour. Malachi could sense their desire for revenge and jumped back just in time to miss the first grasping legs. A face rose above the edge and the group cried out their horror as it inspected them all. The visage would have been cherubic if it hadn't

311

been comprised of obsidian black skin with evilly glowing red eyes. The younger fighters started to back away, breaking the line as the fear sapped at their will.

"No, we have to stand together or they will overrun us in seconds," he cried, trying to rally the deserters.

"We can't fight that," sobbed Claire's mother.

"We don't have a fucking choice!" Anton shouted, then let loose a resounding war cry.

"Malachi will use his powers, but we have to help him!" Paul added, hefting the table leg ready to swing.

The timing corresponded with the rising monsters and any that were able, or willing, ran forward to strike. Knives clashed with chitin armour, driving through the shell into the soft flesh. Table legs and lengths of pipe whistled through the air, given more power by the terrified hands which wielded them. Malachi focused his mind, forming the crushing energy and slamming it down like an invisible hammer on an anvil. Minutes passed and the confidence in the group grew with each wave they successfully repelled.

"If we can keep this up we may have a chance!" Paul shouted.

Malachi didn't reply. He wouldn't tell them of the voice and the way it was laughing inside his mind. The entity was holding the swarm back, tiring the humans and preparing to break them both mentally and physically. Where could they go? If they withdrew and formed a circle the creatures would have a chance to mass on the roof itself. The pipework for the water cisterns travelled down a wide access void to each property, but it would only trap them in the basement. This applied to the lift as well which was awaiting a new motor; that was if they could get past the stranded cab.

Malachi was ready to throw in the towel and the unseen enemy rejoiced. A yearning carried through the gloating and he could sense that his soul was the ultimate prize. They hadn't managed to claim it at the asylum, but now its minions would succeed where Dr. Lloyd and the evil bastards had failed. *I can't wait to meet you,* it crowed, imposing images of the torture and cruelty it would inflict upon him.

"Hold them back for me!" Malachi shouted between the crunching and screeching.

Picking up an abandoned torch, he rushed into the much larger structure that housed the tanks. Thousands of litres of water sat in two individual cisterns with the pipework running from points in their base. The iron tubes twisted to the rear of the room before dropping out of sight. He only knew the void existed after a rare visit by a plumber to sort out a split pipe behind the wall itself. Insects and spiders also lived in the space, but they were the common species of earth, not creatures from another dimension. It was an eighty foot climb down into the basement itself and the thick pipes would make an adequate ladder. They had a means of retreat at least; escaping would be another matter.

A gurgling scream broke his thoughts and he ran back onto the roof. One of the sides of the building was about to fall to the monsters; two people were thrashing against the slavering jaws, and losing. Arteries were torn and blood spurted across the rooftop, covering their fellow defenders. An arachnid horror turned and sprayed a thick web around two more people and they fell to the floor. Moving with lightning speed it raced over their bodies and drove a huge stinger into each of the victims. Screams of agony fell silent as the virulent poison worked its way through their system. Any that went to their aid were hamstrung and swiftly devoured by the mass of beasts.

"Oh God, it's melting them," groaned Anton who vomited, adding his dinner to the spreading pool of blood.

Sure enough the two cocooned victims were racked with spasms as the immobilising venom started to corrode through their bodies. Skin peeled and flesh liquefied as they watched. The sounds of slurping as the spider consumed the poor people triggered another bout of sickness.

"Retreat, get back to the water tanks!" Malachi shouted to the remaining survivors.

"What's the plan?" Paul gasped, trying to catch his breath. He was covered in the slimy yellow liquid and it dripped from his weapon like mucus.

"We can't stay up here and the only way down is through there," Malachi indicated the maintenance shaft.

"Then we will have no way out," Paul replied fearfully.

"Up here we're totally exposed. I didn't think they would be able to haul that bulk up the outside of the building," Malachi said, cursing himself for the mistake.

"I won't make it down there anyway, son," said an elderly man, holding his wife close, "These old hands are past taking my weight."

He reached out and everyone could see the twisted bones from the creeping arthritis, like a gnarled tree branch. His wife reached out her own hand and stroked Malachi's cheek fondly.

"Thank you for fighting so bravely, we will try and hold them off so the rest of you can get to safety. At least we will die together," she smiled, all fear flown.

"No, we can help you down!" Malachi's declared. Heart breaking at their ageless love, he could easily imagine his parents showing such devotion had they not perished so young.

"It's ok, son. You gave us a chance, now it's our turn to do the same," he replied with a shake of his head. "I'd have preferred to choose my own way, like a step from the edge in the arms of the woman I love. They will have to work hard for it if they want another meal!"

Malachi's admiration for the couple was limitless and he tried to get them to reconsider, but it was pointless.

"What about the lift shaft?" Paul whispered in Malachi's ear. He was trying to help the brave souls to commit suicide, but the short fall could prove non-lethal. Malachi wouldn't countenance the idea of leaving them writhing in pain atop the roof of the lift, bones shattered and protruding from their frail flesh.

Three more older tenants gathered around, taking the heaviest weapons they could carry into battle. The creatures had finished feeding on the fallen and their bones were scattered far and wide. Turning their myriad eyes on the huddled mass, they started keening like excited babies.

"No," Malachi said, holding the people back.

"You don't have much time," explained the old man.

"I can't get you all down, but I may be able to give you a clean death?" Malachi declared, meeting his gaze. Every fibre of his being was repulsed by the idea of being the architect of five deaths, but compared to the alternative it would be a merciful act.

"Please, son. I don't want to die by their hands," replied the man, tears brimming.

"Get around the sides of the tank housing!"

Everyone complied instantly and Malachi stood facing the doorway and the wall it was set in. Instead of conjuring the hatred, he fed from the love of the couple and the memory of Chloe and his beloved parents. Holding out his hands, he imagined two handles set into the brickwork. With a roar he wrenched backwards and the whole wall crumbled at his feet, including the door.

The massive water containers were exposed and he warned everyone, "Hold on tight, it will try and carry you away!"

Using one hand to root his feet to the concrete floor, the other was thrust at the steel tanks and then torn aside. The steel sides squealed in protest as they were peeled back like a sardine can, and the released water poured forth like dual tidal waves. Even with his energy the water pushed at him, threatening to drag him away and the others held on for dear life as it spread across the rest of the roof. Sweeping his arms, he directed the water around the whole roof in a powerful wave. Caught unawares by the cleansing water, the abominations shrieked their denial as they were carried over the brim to their deaths. The roar of water diminished to a trickle as the last few litres poured from the sundered vessels.

"That was incredible!" Paul yelled.

"No time for celebrations, they will be coming. Get everyone moving. Now!" Malachi shouted, pointing at the dark shaft, "The pipes will be wet so be extra careful with your grip and footing."

Malachi averted his gaze when the five elders approached. He had just created a window for suicide which left a stain on his soul that might never be erased. The wife of the brave man hugged him tightly, and the rest followed suit, embracing him with their love and gratitude.

"I know you think this is a bad thing you have done, but you have saved us from an awful death," started the man, sensing the conflicting emotions in the youngster, "Now we can be at peace. We will tell your parents what a hero you are."

"What?" Malachi didn't think he had heard the words correctly.

"We were good friends with Miss Cortez," explained his wife, aware that time was running down, "She always used to talk about you and how much she cared for you. We know you lost your parents at a very young age, but they would be so proud to see what you have become."

Malachi couldn't speak through the lump in his throat and watched in silence as the five approached the roofline. Turning their backs to the drop and the waiting horrors, they linked hands and smiled. With a final nod, they leaned back and let gravity take them. No shouts of fear or remorse carried up before the sickly thuds, and Malachi consoled himself with the knowledge they were now in a better place without pain or the slow creep of decrepitude.

"What you did was a kindness," Anton stated, startling Malachi, "Never forget that, mate."

"It sure doesn't feel that way," relied Malachi miserably. "How is it going?"

"The shaft is awkward and you can only fit one person atop the other, not side by side. It's slow going but if we can hold them at the roof they should all make it."

Malachi pushed through the remaining people to glance down. Claire was aiming the torch down the narrow tunnel to help people find good places to hold on. Seeing her friend, she smiled and offered the light.

"No thanks, sweetheart. You are doing a great job," he said, turning back to Paul and Anton.

"What is the plan for when we get down there?" Paul asked.

"Honestly? I have no idea," he shrugged his shoulders, "We barricade it and hold out for as long as we can. I intend to take as many of those bastards with me as possible."

"Mal?" called Claire.

"What's up?"

"Something is happening down there," she replied, playing the beam around the shaft.

Malachi looked out to the roof, though none of the things had appeared yet. Leaning over he could see what she meant, the wall was starting to bulge in places. Streamers of plaster fell from the creaking laths and the descending people started to cough and panic.

"No."

Yes, replied the voice, unleashing hell.

The walls burst inwards under the weight of the miscreations who had lain in wait. The trap was sprung and the ambushed people were plucked like tender morsels from their perches to be devoured by the waiting hordes on the lower floors. The screams echoed up the narrow confines of the shaft briefly and Malachi leaned against the side of the cistern and slumped to the floor. Burdened by the increasing losses his mind was in danger of shutting down. Though in no way culpable, his nature wouldn't allow him to shuck off the responsibility.

And then there were eight, chuckled the evil voice.

"Fucking hell, now is not the time to wallow in guilt!" Anton shouted, leaning down to shake him.

Malachi was paralyzed with indecision and stared fixedly on a patch of rust on the opposing steel cistern. Fractured memories played in his mind of happier times and places; the first ice cream he had eaten on Bognor Regis sea front, a cold Christmas morning with the open fire crackling and the sound of tearing paper on his only present. Then the image of Chloe as he had first seen her; stunning but innocent and vulnerable as she glanced around the bar.

"Mal, please help us," Claire asked softly, "We need you."

An inner battle raged in his head. The promise of blissful ignorance which withdrawal from the real world would bring, or the hope, however slim, of finding a way out of the horror. Catatonia teased, offering him the soft hospital bed and the first kiss with Chloe. You could have that moment forever, it whispered.

"They are coming and I am scared," whimpered Claire pitifully.

Anton pulled her and his wife in close to await the inevitable. The sound of chitin on pipe was getting louder as the creatures climbed up the empty ductwork. A long forgotten memory flashed into being, causing Malachi to flinch. It was the feeling of falling, followed by the sound of impact as the car hit water. He remembered the slow bob as the weight of the engine pitched the vehicle ass up in the river before sinking like a stone. And the smiling face at the window, the current causing the man's hair to float eerily in the murky light of the riverbed. I won't leave you, the serene mask promised as it drove the tire iron towards the glass.

"I won't leave you!" Malachi snarled, using the memory to break free of the malaise.

"Thank you, Mal," Claire said, flying into his arms.

"You ok?" Anton asked warily.

"No," Malachi replied honestly, "But we are going to try and do as much damage as possible. Get to the lift housing."

Shadows danced at the lip of the shaft and Malachi ushered everyone to safety. He didn't have time to destroy the larger brick structure and instead stared at the thick steel pipework. With deafening twangs, he tore each one from the base of the tanks, twisting them into life like brown flecked snakes. A monster resembling a millipede scurried over the edge, its rows of legs propelling it forward at Malachi. With a flick of the wrist the tube stabbed through, pinning it like an insect on an entomologist's display board. Forcing the tube back it dragged the screeching beast toward the hole where even more of its companions were struggling to push through. Using the impossibly flexible metal, Malachi wove it together like a cage, ripping through the mass of black armour and sealing the hole.

"Try getting through that!" Malachi shouted and picked up the discarded torch. The beam flickered for a moment and with a firm shake, the connections were remade and it burst into life.

The shaft was filled with all manner of loathsomeness and the bottom of the duct gave them full access to the basement. Gritting his teeth, he glared at the descending pipework and tore it free of each apartment with his mind, before twisting it together in an impassable latticework of steel. The seething horde shrieked their frustration and thrashed futilely at the prison.

"Mal, hurry up," Paul urged, mouth gaping at the tangled mess of pipes and the dying, squirming things crushed within it.

They ran over the drenched rubble of the wall Malachi had torn down and met the others in the motor room. Thick steel cables ran up and over the drum before disappearing through an aperture in the floor to hold the elevator aloft. A steel trapdoor was open and he dared a peek down before he had to look away.

"You ok?" Paul asked.

"Just a bit of vertigo," Malachi explained, "I'll be fine."

"Shall I lock the door?"

"The roof is not safe," Malachi replied, swinging the heavy door shut, "It will buy us a few minutes at least. Do it."

With a quick rattle they were sealed within the building and they could all feel the final confrontation fast approaching. Malachi pondered whether he would be better going first or forming the rear guard. Kicking the door, it returned a dull thud which indicated it was sturdy enough to offer some resistance to the monsters.

"Follow me down, I will clear the way of anything lying in wait."

"Do you think they will spring through the walls or doors again?" Claire asked, a haunted look in her eyes.

"No, sweetheart. The lift shaft is concrete lined and the doors themselves are metal. We would hear them long before they could get to us," Malachi assured her, praying his assumption would prove accurate as he descended.

"I'll follow from behind," offered Anton.

"Thanks, mate," Malachi nodded, "Let's get this done."

Don't look down! Don't look down! Don't look down!
Malachi chanted in his head as he moved through the
trapdoor, then looked straight down. The stranded elevator
loomed up at him and he felt dizzy for a few seconds.
Holding on tight to the rungs of the maintenance ladder, he
took a deep breath and concentrated on the wall inches
from his face. Fat lot of good he would be if there was
breach on the way down and he needed to fight.

"Get a hold of yourself," he whispered angrily to
himself.

"Did you say something, Mal?" Claire asked from
above.

"No, honey," he replied, slightly envious of her calm
demeanour.

Scraping and tapping echoed up the vertical passage
from the steel doors. Every floor was the same and Malachi
knew they were being herded towards a dead end. He had
reached the empty cab when the first hammer blow
reverberated down from the roof door. Everyone let out a
cry of surprise, and they redoubled their efforts.

"They are nearly through," Anton shouted down.

"Daddy, please hurry," Claire called up.

"Mal?" Anton called.

"Save your breath and get moving!" Malachi shouted
in reply.

"I'm going to hold them here," he called back.

"Daddy, no!" cried Claire, trying to go back up the
ladder.

"I have to baby or they will be able to get you," Anton
explained, looking down at them, his voice tempered with
love, "Mal you do whatever it takes to keep them safe, do
you understand me?"

"I will," Malachi replied.

"I'm sorry for everything I've done, I love you both so
much," Anton called, blowing a kiss to his wife and child.

Hot tears ran down everyone's cheeks as he gave a final wave and slammed shut the steel hatch. The padlock being engaged was such an awful sound of finality that Malachi would have covered his ears if he hadn't been clinging to the ladder. Reaching up, he tried to rub Claire's thin leg to show how sorry he was, but she was still determined to climb past her mother.

"Claire, you can't get to him," sobbed her mother, no less distraught.

"I need you to help me, Claire," Malachi cooed, "I can't do this without you."

Reluctantly, one foot stepped down, followed by the other until they reached the basement doors. Pressing the manual release, he pulled them apart and helped everyone to step through. Grunts of exertion and the crashes of battle accompanied them all the way to the basement. As their intensity grew to a crescendo, Malachi puled Claire in tight and held his hand over her free ear.

"She shouldn't hear this," he husked, barely able to speak, "Come here."

Claire's mother joined the embrace and used her body to replace Malachi's hand, shielding her child from the heart breaking sounds. Anton finally succumbed and the agonised screams cut right through the survivors. Paul was on his knees, trying to hold it together through the tears. The silence that followed was as stark as the screams and Claire's mother collapsed in a faint. Thankfully, two of the other three survivors had seen the life go out of her eyes and gently eased her to the ground.

Are we having fun yet? Chuckled the voice.

Knowing he would appear insane, Malachi couldn't fight it anymore and addressed the being directly, "I don't know who you are, but I have a feeling I know what you are."

Then you know that I will always win against a mere mortal.

"That may have been true until now, but I know I have powers and that you fear them, which means you can be harmed. So no matter what it takes, I am going to find you and destroy you," Malachi growled.

"Who are you talking to?" Paul looked around the empty basement.

Impossible.

"Then why do I sense doubt in your voice?" Malachi mocked, enjoying the role reversal.

I don't trade insults with cattle. Enjoy your last moments, because we will be putting your bravado to the test very soon.

"Save the threats for your minions," Malachi spat vehemently, "I will repay every ounce of pain you have caused here today, now begone!"

Using his energy, Malachi drove the entity out before it could reply.

"You were talking to Clarence?" Paul asked, misunderstanding the one-sided conversation.

"No," Malachi shook his head, "The being that he serves." It sounded crazy.

"Oh, ok."

"You believe me?"

Paul shrugged, "With all that's happened I have no reason to doubt you."

Malachi patted him on the back; their survival to this point was in no small part down to the previously hated supervisor. Surveying the basement, it became apparent they were at the end of the line. The high set windows were purposely narrow to deny access to thieves. It left only three ways out; the lift shaft, the main stairs up to the apartment building itself and the emergency access. There were no surprises waiting for them behind the doors, they knew their assailants were waiting. Fresh screeches came from the pipe duct but the steel was thick enough to fend off the snapping claws.

"What do we do now?" Paul asked.

"I don't know."

The others had all seated themselves on a set of abandoned dining chairs and stared vacantly. It was the same feeling of hopelessness which had nearly crushed Malachi and he couldn't blame them. Claire's mum had regained consciousness and stroked at her daughter's hair. The room comprised rows of cages which came with each flat for storage. Thick pillars were set at eight feet to spread the weight of the upper floors. A redundant furnace with a madly spreading ductwork system sat in one corner. It had been the source of heat to the whole building for several decades until spare parts were made obsolete. It was cheaper to fit small heating boilers to each property rather than replace the iron monolith. The mains electricity was brought in via a massive fuse board, set within another lockable cage. An insane idea formed in Malachi's mind and Paul caught the frown.

"What is it?"

"Can you remember science class at school?" Malachi asked mysteriously.

"I'm nearly fifty, I can't remember last month let alone thirty years ago."

"We covered electricity and my teacher had a rhyme he used to use," Malachi racked his brain, "It went something like 'the volts jolt, but the mills kill'."

"Great, but what does it mean?"

"If I remember correctly, a normal home will have a two hundred and thirty-volt supply. The mills refer to milliamps which is the bit that kills you."

"I don't see what the fuck this has to do with our current situation," Paul said, shaking his head in confusion.

"Bear with me," Malachi pleaded, "I was told, and this is word for word, that as long as life exists within this plane, this building will never be free."

"And?"

"We need to make it so there is no more life in this building."

"Mal, we don't have time for this shit. They will be in here at any moment," Paul sighed.

How could he possibly sell the idea to the group who were all staring at him?

"Electric shock can stop the heart. No heartbeat means no life. No life means this all ends," Malachi said slowly, unsurprised at the horrified reaction.

"You want to kill us all?" Claire sobbed, hiding behind her mother.

"I have friends in the street who can help once we get rid of all the monsters, sweetheart," Malachi tried to reach for her but she shrank away.

"Mummy don't let him hurt me."

Claire's mother studied Malachi's eyes. After the events they had endured she trusted his judgement and knew Anton didn't give his life for them to ignore their only chance.

"Will it work?"

"I don't know," he replied honestly.

"How would we go about it?"

One of the men jumped out of his chair, "Are you out of your mind? You can count me out of that bullshit!"

"Then we all die down here," Malachi said, slumping into one of the chairs.

Claire's mother grabbed the man and shook him violently, "You will not be the cause of my daughter dying, do you fucking hear me?"

"It's a simple choice," Paul said, calmly separating the pair, "Either we try the electricity and the worst case scenario is we die. Or we wait for them to get in here, tear us to pieces and then eat us. I know which choice I'm taking."

"Shit!"

"Look, I know this is totally fucked, but I can't think of any other way to save you all," Malachi explained.

The man paced back and forth, mind reeling at the impossible choice. With a deep sigh, he stopped walking and faced the rest of the group. "What do we have to do?"

"The time window will be narrow. If I can't get you medical attention within a few minutes you won't wake up."

"Jesus Christ," said the man nervously.

"I will need you to all do it in quick succession for it to work. If all goes well I can step out of the sphere and end this thing," Malachi explained, reaching out with his mind and tearing the cover from the fuse board, exposing the wires.

"There are so many things that could go wrong!"

Paul sighed with frustration, "It's a chance versus no chance."

"I'm afraid so," Malachi commiserated.

The incoming mains would be of a much higher ampere than the building side of the fuse so he pulled one of the domestic live conductors free in a shower of sparks. A frenzy of scratching and screeching commenced at the doors as the creatures tried to gain entry.

"They know what we are trying to do!" Paul shouted.

"No, it's the one controlling them who knows. It's now or never," Malachi looked at each of them in turn.

"Tell us what to do," said the man with resignation.

"I don't know enough to be sure of the best way. All I can remember is the electricity will need to pass through your heart to stop it. Don't touch the wire with an open palm as the shock could cause your muscles to contract and you would end up clutching the cable and frying."

"Fucking marvellous."

"Use the back of your hand on the wire and put the other on the cage," Malachi said with urgency, "Stand on this wooden box to act as an insulator for your feet."

"Claire, I need you to do what Malachi has said," her mother said with a brave face.

The inhuman din was growing and the doors were starting to fracture. The child held out a hand and Malachi squeezed it supportively.

"Ok, Mummy," she said quietly.

Standing on the box, she placed one hand against the cold metal of the protective cage and poised the other an inch from the wire. Malachi moved everyone back to protect them and nodded at the young girl. The basement erupted with a flash and a loud crack, throwing Claire free of the fuse board.

"Get her away from here, Mal. We will do what's needed," Paul declared.

Picking up the limp body, Malachi checked for a pulse, but there was nothing. Her hands had small scorch marks from the contact and her mother gave her a tender kiss on the forehead.

"I'll see you soon, baby."

"Go!" Paul shouted, pushing him for the exit.

Malachi raced for the crumbling emergency access door and screamed his hatred at the vile monsters who were nearly through. An explosion of energy sent the remaining door and obliterated creatures in all directions, clearing a path across the short distance to the orb's shell. Hoping against hope, Malachi tried to walk through with the body, but it just compressed against the surface. Repositioning her body and freeing an arm, he extended his hand and it passed through without resistance.

"Fuck!"

It's not going to work, he thought as the next flash came from the basement doorway. Then another. And another. The insectoids were swarming towards him and the open basement door, eager to finish the sacrifice. Placing Claire gently on the ground, the hatred was all consuming.

"Go back to Hell, you filth!" screamed Malachi, waving his arms like a composer.

Waves of hellish beasts were crushed or tossed aside violently as he protected the basement and himself. Shrieks of anger came from the roof and Malachi looked skyward just in time to see the suicidal dives. They were attempting to crush him under their weight and he had to divert his attention to form a shield above his head. With sickly crunches they impacted, exploding in yellow bursts of gore. One final flash and a crack echoed in the basement which signalled the last survivor had touched the cable. It was now or never. Either the attack would cease or the bodies would be consumed. At least they wouldn't feel the pain.

"You failed," Malachi taunted the entity.

What? How is it possible? I will feast upon your soul for all eternity! It was beyond furious at losing its quarry.

"I will come for you, whatever your name is; Berumozun, Xaxuzal, Mordreth Jord." Malachi promised, unsure if he could actually fulfil the threat.

Before it could reply, he stepped backwards out of the sphere and the effect was instantaneous. A howling wind burst into life and the surface turned translucent, fading gradually as the energy dissipated. An invisible vortex dragged the hideous abominations back into the pits from which they had spawned, screaming their frustration and hatred of the living. The scattered remains of the fallen steamed away, their black armour vaporising as easily as the pools of yellow gore. In seconds, no trace remained of the otherworldly foe, but the bodies of the elderly still lay undisturbed. Although broken and bloodied, their faces were serene which assuaged a little of the guilt in Malachi's heart.

"Come on!" Malachi was losing patience as every second counted in the resuscitation.

The purple orb faded more and more until all that was left was a thin spider web of crackling power. Like a lightning strike, the energy raced to the ground with a loud snap and everything came back to life. Engines rumbled and a can rattled down the street. With a screech of brakes, his minders leaped from the vehicles in shock. Amaris came sprinting, her guns drawn and scanning for targets.

"Where did you go? One second you were next to me and the next you are stood outside the building looking like you've seen a ghost?"

Her eyes took in the bodies and realization dawned of what had happened. The briefings didn't prepare her for coming face to face with the true power which they fought against.

"Shut up and help me!" Malachi shouted, breathing air into the young girl in front of him, "There are more people in the basement who need you. Be careful of the electricity, now go!"

Without asking questions, Desmond, Michael, and the Yardies holstered their weapons and hurried through the destroyed doorway. Amaris covered them, guarding Malachi as he frantically compressed the girl's chest. Tears coursed down his cheeks, the true magnitude of what he had been through hitting him like a hammer blow.

"Come on, baby!" Malachi sobbed.

"Malachi, we need to go," Amaris urged, trying to pull him away from the body.

"Get the fuck off me!" he cried, "It's because of people like you that she is here in the first place."

"That's not fair, I'm not that different to you," she replied with a pained expression.

"Ok, then the people you work for," Malachi hissed, "The fucking elites and their games that always end up with the innocent suffering while they hide in their ivory towers. I'm sick of it!" Shouting the final words, Claire started to cough, drawing in precious oxygen.

"Bring her and lay her on the back seats. We can keep her safe too."

Michael appeared at the doorway and he showed little hope, "Get out of here! We will do all we can for them but you must go!"

"She has been electrocuted and needs medical treatment," Malachi said, rolling her into the recovery position while she coughed and gagged.

"We have some of the most gifted medical professionals on the planet, I promise she will receive the best care money can buy."

Malachi sighed with exasperation and picked Claire up. They hurried to the car and he laid her gently inside.

"Where's my mummy?" she croaked.

Malachi looked at Amaris for support, "She's coming in the other car, sweetie. Malachi will keep you company until she arrives, ok?"

"Are all the monsters gone, Mal?"

"Yes, honey. Your brave daddy scared them all away to keep you safe," he said, fresh tears flowing at the self-sacrifice.

"Is he dead?"

"I'm afraid so, sweetheart. But he will always love you, never forget that."

As Amaris drove away, the two distraught passengers consoled each other as best they could. Malachi knew the crushing weight of grief the poor girl would be placed under if her mother succumbed to the injury and he hugged her even tighter. In the darkness of a side alley, a man watched them pass by. The side of his face was lit up by the screen of his phone.

"Drake, he got away," he said and hung up before the barrage of questions could begin.

Finally, he had a worthy adversary after decades of boredom and indiscriminate slaughter. Clarence smiled.

EPILOGUE

Malachi watched as Claire was ushered away into the side chapel under the care of two priests. Amaris urged him to continue and each footstep on the stone floor of the nave echoed around the empty cathedral. Candles fluttered in the aisles, disturbed by the hurried entrance and subsequent slamming and bolting of the doors. At the altar a man stood looking up at the image of Jesus on his cross, head pierced by a crown of thorns and a trail of blood running from the spear wound on his flank. Malachi could attest to the pain and looked away, feeling a puzzling guilt that he had survived where the Son of God hadn't. In a way, his incredible resurrection had striking parallels to the tale of Christ, only without the cave. *I'm going to Hell;* Malachi shook his head at the blasphemy. Why was it that places of worship always set his nerves on edge and jumbled his thoughts?

"Are you ok?" whispered Amaris.

"Fine," Malachi replied, "I am just frazzled after what has happened."

She smiled and held out a hand. Malachi was even more perturbed when he took the offered hand and carried on walking towards the transept which sat before the ornately carved marble altar. A man in black robes with a red skullcap and a red sash turned to the pair, appraising them as only men of the cloth are able. Cheeks burning with unnecessary shame, Malachi looked away. The imposing stare left him feeling naked, his tainted soul exposed and judged.

"I am Cardinal Beauchamp, and you must be Malachi?" His accent was East End London and it completely threw Malachi.

"I... er... I'm..." he mumbled.

"Please forgive my accent. I was a son of the East End before I became a son of God. I like to stay true to my roots, plus it makes for interesting meetings in the Vatican."

"I'm sure," Malachi found his voice and shook the firm hand.

"Shall we go?" asked Beauchamp, indicating a side door.

"Go where?"

"Somewhere safe."

"And here's not safe? What about Claire? I'm not leaving her if this place is in danger," Malachi pulled the man to a stop.

"You *are* the danger, my son. We need to take you to a place they will never find you, and Claire will be kept here until her mother arrives. Once reunited they will both be taken into hiding where the others will never be able to find them. Not even the Pope will be able to access the information."

Malachi was pulling on his arm like a small infant with excitement, "You mean she made it?"

"Three of the survivors of the attack pulled through thanks to Michael and your friends, Claire's mother being one of them," explained Beauchamp with a smile.

"Oh thank God!" Malachi nearly collapsed with relief.

"Oh no, my son. This was all your doing. Never could I have imagined that you would make it out of there in one piece, let alone formulating a plan to save the poor souls within. Incredible."

"I couldn't save all of them," Malachi replied with sorrow.

"Listen, Malachi," Beauchamp stopped him outside of the wooden door, "In the past there hasn't been a single case of anyone making it out. Today you made that four, plus yourself. It is nothing short of a miracle."

"You're telling me there have been more of those spheres?" Malachi was aghast.

"Many, but that can be for another day," said Beauchamp, "I'm sure you want to know what is happening to you and what transpired today?"

"Yes," Malachi could barely draw breath.

The cardinal placed a key in the lock, twisting it this way and that until Malachi was about to offer his help. It was only when the seemingly wooden door hissed from unseen pneumatics and slid into the floor that the truth was revealed. This was no ordinary chapel, and inside was a steel staircase which led down in a spiral. Descending the steps, Malachi was awed to finally come out in a larger room deep below the floor of the cathedral itself.

"Is that what I think it is?" Malachi whispered.

Beauchamp laughed and patted him on the back, "Indeed it is. You thought only Bond villains could afford underground tunnels and transports?"

A cylindrical passageway ran off into darkness and the small vehicle was mounted on twin rails. It resembled an old carriage from Victorian times with velvet seats and mahogany siding. The only thing that gave away the futuristic nature was the bank of small electronic screens and controls set within the far side of the cab.

"I was expecting a tube to zip me away at two hundred miles an hour," Malachi joked

"We have more modern pods, but I wanted to have a comfortable ride with you. The best we can hope for is about fifteen miles an hour I'm afraid."

"Will this take us all the way to the place you were talking about?"

"Heavens no," laughed Beauchamp, "It's only about four miles long and that alone cost a fortune. This was designed as an escape route if the need ever arose to get someone to safety and there are many more across the country. You are officially the first actual fugitive to use it. Climb aboard!"

"Thank you."

Beauchamp pressed a button and a series of light bloomed in the tunnel. After a few hundred feet the tunnel curved and disappeared into gloom, and with a whine the electric motor propelled them away from Claire and the cathedral. A pang of sadness at the separation twisted him up inside and a tear rolled down his cheek. He didn't want to ask, but needed the answer.

"Did you manage to get Chloe, Kevin, and their family to safety?"

"No, I'm sorry. They were gone when we got there, which could mean they just went to ground as a precaution. We will keep looking and I promise if I get any news I will tell you immediately."

Long seconds passed as Malachi held his head in his hands, mourning all those that had, or may have, fallen to the evil forces that were trying to kill him. With a deep breath, he looked up into the patient eyes of the cardinal.

"Let's have it then."

"As ridiculous as all this may sound, please bear with me as I tell the story," cautioned Beauchamp, "It is the unvarnished truth and I hope some of what you have experienced will make it easier to believe."

"Ok."

"There is a Heaven and a Hell, but not as it is explained in the Bible. The same misinformation applies to the universe and it is all inextricably linked with the awful events you have been involved with," Beauchamp started and Malachi didn't argue which was encouraging. If he could be made to understand, he may be convinced to fight.

"I suppose the easiest way to explain it is as a cosmic game, played out between two beings who are unfathomable and infinitely powerful. God, or whatever her true name is, is benevolent. Satan, Lucifer, whatever name he carries between worlds, is purest evil. The universe was created by these two entities to play host to their eternal struggle for dominance with us as their pawns. We may not be the first universe to exist; scholars have concluded there may even be parallel dimensions with the same events unfolding." Beauchamp could see how pale Malachi had gone, "Anyway, as each world falls to either Heaven or Hell, it is taken out of this plane of existence forever. For the planets where evil is allowed to flourish, this ultimately means *Hell on Earth*; an unceasing suffering for the enjoyment of the denizens of Hell. Other worlds who reach a state of profound enlightenment are taken into the loving care of God and they live forever in bliss. Ours is engaged in the same battle, with the forces of good and evil fighting to herald the new order. There are millions, if not billions of planets just like Earth going through the same horrors."

"I have seen some of them! I thought they were just dreams but it has been mentioned they are actual occurrences," Malachi said with animation, "And did you say God was a lady?"

"All the information we have gathered points towards a female deity, but no one has any solid proof. We aren't even sure they can be attributed genders. As for your dreams, they are all either events that have happened, are happening, or will happen in the future. At present you are like a caveman trying to understand satellite television, frantically changing channels and seeing scenes from multiple sources with no idea what they mean. In time, you will be able to turn them on and off as easily as a switch."

"So all that murder and horror was real?" Malachi felt sick.

"I'm afraid so."

"You're telling me the creatures I have seen actually exist?"

"Yes, but not in this plane of existence."

"Then how do you explain what happened to me tonight?"

"The orb you escaped from is made of concentrated demonic energy. Clarence has the ability to gather his power and summon a portal to Hell, but thankfully it takes many months of recuperation otherwise we would be dealing with a daily massacre. Once triggered, the sphere allows beings commensurate to the size of the summoning to pour through. It may have seemed big, but it was only large enough to encapsulate your apartment building. I understand the creatures that attacked you were insectoid in nature, and about two feet long?"

Bile rose in Malachi's throat from the memory of the screaming horrors and their infantile features, "Yes... but their faces..."

Beauchamp reached over and patted his leg, "I know, my son. I have read of the beasts in scriptures. They are the children born into hatred and squalor, taken before their time by neglect and violence. Their souls never knew love and they spend eternity yearning for revenge on the human race that abandoned them."

Malachi was outraged, "How can any being that claims to be benevolent allow babies to go to Hell? I thought the others were evil, but you are all just as fucking bad!"

"Malachi, please calm down. I don't claim to understand how they think, or why something so abhorrent is possible. What I do know is that every child on this planet is in danger of a fate literally worse than death if the forces aligned against us prevail."

"And where do I fit into all this shit?" Malachi's defences were up and it would be a long time before he trusted anyone again. Everyone he had met in the past couple of weeks had an agenda and the secrecy and lies disgusted him.

"Your powers have come about by a series of incidents that seem unrelated, but culminate in an awakening of divine strength. Would you mind if I ask you a few questions?"

"Do what you want," Malachi huffed.

"You are an orphan, correct?" Beauchamp asked with genuine sorrow.

Malachi nodded.

"How was their relationship?"

"They loved each other if that's what you mean," Malachi bridled.

"Did they fight? Was there ever any occasion where you felt unsafe?"

Malachi could see where this was going, "Never anything serious, in fact I can't even remember a squabble if I'm honest. Even though we were dirt poor, they always worshipped one another."

"Interesting. Have you ever hurt anyone physically?"

"A few people," Malachi replied, satisfied he had shot the first hole in the cardinal's theory.

"Have any of them been unprovoked?"

"Well, no, but it felt good when I was doing it. Does that sound divine?"

"Retribution in itself isn't evil. If you sought to hurt them beyond the deserved punishment, then it becomes an act of malice. Was that ever the case? Did you inflict pain just for the thrill?"

Malachi looked at the passing wall, "No."

"There is no easy way to ask this next question," apologised Beauchamp, "Are you a virgin?"

Malachi sighed, "Yes."

"Really? That is surprising as you are an extremely attractive young man," Beauchamp said with a bemused look.

Malachi couldn't mask a chuckle, "Are you trying it on?"

"Oh my goodness, no, I was merely articulating my disbelief." It was the cardinal's turn to blush. "If I hadn't taken a vow of celibacy, my predilections lie with the fairer sex."

"Sorry, I couldn't resist," Malachi smiled.

"I suppose I could have worded it better. I understand you were injured in a fracas recently?"

"You could say that."

"Would you mind explaining the incident? It may be the final piece of the puzzle."

"If I must," Malachi hated the whole episode, "I got stabbed trying to stop a woman from being raped by three men."

"Really? Would that have been Chloe?"

"Yeah. I met her at Desmond's bar and scared her away so it was my fault she was even put in danger. Not much of a hero, is it?"

"Nonsense. You put yourself in mortal danger to save her which is truly heroic."

"Great, another fan." Malachi leaned forward, wagging a finger, "Listen and listen good. I was shitting myself the whole time, I always do when anything gets physical, but no one else was going to do it. I got knifed and bled out in the hospital. It was only the work of the amazing nurses and surgeons that brought me back from the dead. So stop making out I am this fearless warrior sent by God."

The cardinal went wide eyed, "You actually died?"

"For several minutes. I even thought I saw my parents in a bright tunnel of light, but that was probably just a hallucination."

"So in essence you sacrificed your life to save hers." Beauchamp was on the edge of his seat.

"No, otherwise I wouldn't be here, would I?"

"It doesn't matter that you were resuscitated," he said with excitement, "You crossed over, don't you understand?"

"Obviously not," admitted Malachi with a frown.

"It will all become clear soon," Beauchamp assured him. "I also understand you had a subsequent reunion with your attackers?"

"Who the fuck told you that?" Malachi was on the defensive again. He had been promised that it would never be mentioned.

"Some of the... gentlemen, that saved you have talked to Michael. They are sure you are a shaman, or angel, or both."

Malachi folded his arms and scowled. Was there no one left he could trust.

"Please, Malachi. This is vitally important," Beauchamp pleaded, "Did you really forgive the men who killed you? Who tried to rape your friend?"

Cheeks going a deep shade of red, Malachi replied, "Are you trying to call me a coward? Well maybe I am."

"No that's not what I meant at all," Beauchamp exclaimed, "I wanted to be certain of the purity of your heart before I made a final judgement, that's all."

"Then judge me, because right now I wish I hadn't woken up in the hospital. Maybe it was my parents in that light, maybe not, but at least I would be at peace."

"You mustn't talk like that," he scolded.

"Walk a mile in my shoes, then come and tell me how I should be feeling," Malachi sneered.

"I can't even begin to imagine what you have been through, my son," said Beauchamp, "But things are in motion that can't be avoided. I pray we can convince you of your true value to us, nay to the whole world, before it's too late."

Malachi looked at the folded picture of his mother and father, "What am I?"

"To understand that you have to think of yourself as a lump of clay. Everything you have been through has moulded you into the man sat before me today," Beauchamp started to explain, "A couple of the awful tribulations could have made you a gifted individual, but when you add all of them together you have a perfect combination of circumstances. You come from a house of unadulterated love and compassion, and you too have adopted the traits of your parents. You are chaste, but humble. You have boundless forgiveness in your heart for those who don't necessarily deserve it, and you gave your life to save the innocence of a stranger."

"And?"

"And it means that you are an individual with tremendous power. Given enough time and training, you will be more powerful by far than Clarence and the darkness which fuels him."

"What training? What if I don't want to fight?" Malachi asked, waiting for the mask to slip and reveal that he was just as much a prisoner with the church as he was with Drake.

"Then that is your choice. We will keep you safe until your dying day when you will be reunited with your parents."

"You won't force me?"

"Of course not."

A mixture of thoughts and emotions raced through Malachi's head.

"Will I have to kill people?"

"Yes."

"Will I have to go against monsters like those in the orb again?"

"Yes, and the child demons you fought are nothing in comparison to what is coming. If the enemy gains in power the demon spheres will grow in strength and size until you are facing Hell's mightiest leviathans and the Demon Lords who command them."

"And you seriously think I stand a chance?" Malachi laughed sickly.

"I wouldn't ask you to join us if I doubted it," stated Beauchamp with absolute certainty. "Your capabilities are in their infancy and with our help you will be able to unlock your full potential. You will have the power to lay waste to the demonic legions who seek to enslave our world."

Malachi stared directly at the cardinal, "They have hurt me and the ones I love. I have seen the suffering they inflict on the innocent for their own sadistic pleasure."

"So you will join us?" asked Beauchamp, barely able to suppress his relief.

"I'm going to crush them all," growled Malachi vehemently. "Let's go to war."

AUTHOR BIO

Ricky Fleet has been a lifelong horror fan ever since he was (almost) old enough to watch the original Romero trilogy. Those shambling horrors gave birth to an insatiable appetite that has yet to be sated. After spending years in the plumbing trade, he then decided to start teaching, passing on his knowledge to the next generation of engineers.

Born and raised in the UK, cups of tea are a non-negotiable staple of the English life and serve as brain fuel for his first love, writing.

Today he shares his time between his real life students and the students of the zombie apocalypse in his first series: Hellspawn. At least the fictional students do as they're told. Most of the time anyway.

For upcoming news about future books, info about contests and prizes, or if you just want to chat, please follow me on my Facebook page at:
www.facebook.com/authorrickyfleet
and on my publisher's page at:
www.facebook.com/optimusmaximuspublishing
or on Twitter at @AuthorRickFleet and @Optimaxpublish

CHECK OUT THE OMP WEBSITE FOR
A COMPLETE LIST OF OUR TITLES

WWW.OPTIMUSMAXIMUSPUBLISHING.COM

BOOKS ARE AVAILABLE IN BOTH PRINT
AND ELECTRONIC FORMATS

RICKY FLEET
HELLSPAWN
SERIES

10.35 AM, September 14th 2015. Portsmouth, England.

A global particle physics experiment releases a pulse of unknown energy with catastrophic results. The sanctity of the grave has been sundered and a million graveyards expel their tenants from eternal slumber.

The world is unaware of the impending apocalypse, Governments crumble and armies are scattered to the wind under the onslaught of the dead.

Kurt Taylor, a self-employed plumber, witnesses the start of the horrifying outbreak. Desperate to reach his family before they fall victim to the ever growing horde of shambling corruption, he flees the scene.

In a society with few guns, how can people hope to survive the endless waves of zombies that seek to consume every living thing? With ingenuity, planning and everyday materials, the group forge their way and strike back at the Hellspawn legions.

Rescues are mounted, but not all survivors are benevolent, the evil that is in all men has been given free rein in this new, dead world. With both the living and dead to contend with, the Taylor family's battle for survival is just beginning.

Book 1 in the Hellspawn series.

Kurt Taylor and his family have battled the living and the dead and now find themselves on the run, their home reduced to ashes. With unimaginable horror lying in wait around every corner, the onset of winter and the plunging temperatures only add more danger to their precarious existence. They decide to forge ahead and try to reach the protection of others who have hopefully survived the zombie apocalypse. If this fails, their only choice would be to try and reach an impregnable fortress, a sanctuary that has stood for a thousand years.

Standing between them and salvation are the villages and cities of the damned, a path that will test their spirit and resilience unlike anything they have faced before. More companions are rescued from the jaws of death and join them in their perilous journey. Mysterious attacks befall the group and it becomes clear the dead aren't the only things that lurk in the darkness.

Tempers fray and personalities clash. The group starts to fracture and Kurt is forced to commit acts that cause him to question his own morality. Can they survive the horror of their new existence? Will they want to?

The Hellspawn saga continues.

BALLYMOOR, IRELAND, 1891

Patrick Conroy, a young American student of medicine in Dublin, decides to take a break from the hustle and bustle of the big city and spend a month in the quietude of the wild and beautiful Glencree valley, County Wicklow. However, surrounded by local legends and myths, he is soon dragged into an ancient mystery that has haunted the village of Ballymoor for centuries. Set on the background of the tumultuous years preceding the War of Independence, and colored by Irish folklore, the Haunter of the Moor is a ghost story written in the style of Victorian Gothic novels.

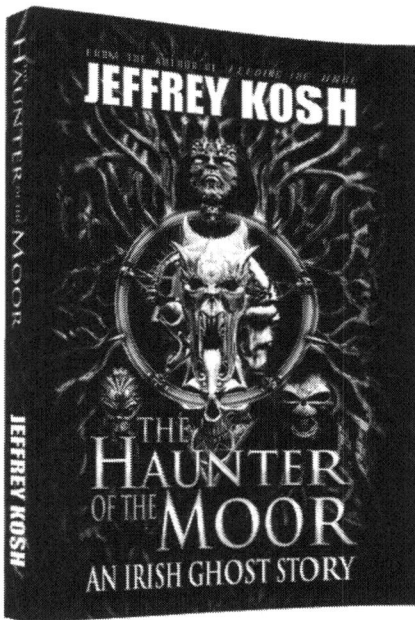

To Fight Evil with Evil

England, 1392.
As the Black Death quickly spreads through the kingdom, the little hamlet of Blythe's Hollow suffers under the yoke of a sadistic Lord. Desperate, the villagers decide to seek out the magical help of a local witch, causing the wrath of the Church. Torture and murder befall on those accused of being in league with the Devil, adding more sorrow to the beset folk of Blythe's Hollow. Yet, one man will rise against the tyranny; a man willing to learn Black Magick to fight back.

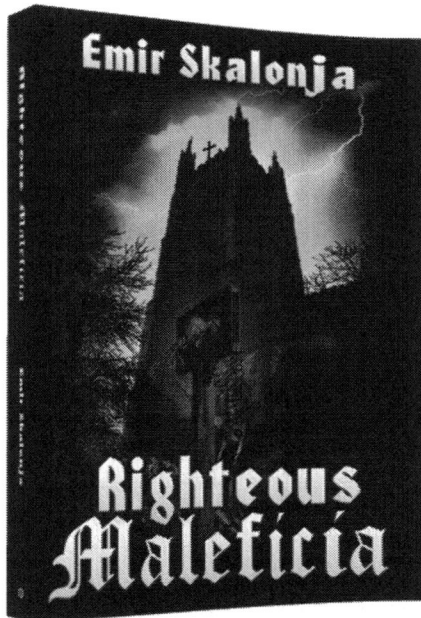

A modern dark urban fantasy, telling of two powerful families who uphold a secret duty to protect humanity from a threat it doesn't know exists.

Though sharing a common enemy, the two families form a long-standing rivalry due to their methods and ultimate goals.

Forces are coalescing in a prominent Central European city criminal sex-trafficking, a serial murderer with a savage bent, and other, less tangible influences.

Within a prestigious, private university, Lilja, a young librarian charged with protecting a very special book, finds herself suddenly ensconced in this dark, strange world. Originally from Finland, she has her own reason for why she left her home, but she finds the city to be anything but a haven from dangers and secrets.

Book One in a planned series.

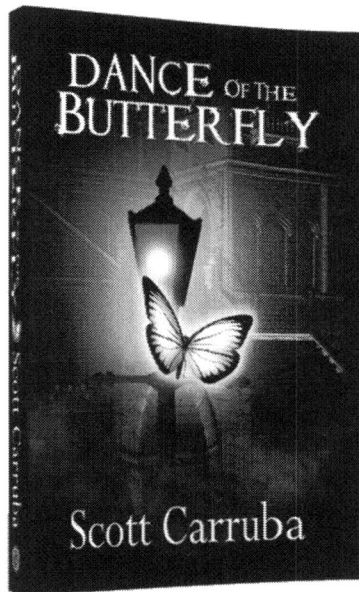

DANCE OF THE BUTTERFLY

Scott Carruba

Meet Mason Ezekiel Barnes, former NFL tackle turned successful author of the naughty ninja adventure series Mia Killjoy. Mason is obsessed with winning a Pulitzer and is thwarted by his fellow author and nemesis, the twerpy little gnome Conrad Bancroft.

Perk Noir is full of comedic relief, pop culture, NFL, jazz, a little touch of romance, and flashbacks of Lightning and his family during both the first half of the 20th century and later during the Civil Rights movement. Mason and Shelly and their adventures is a fun filled thrill ride that will appeal to all readers, there is something for everyone at the Perk.

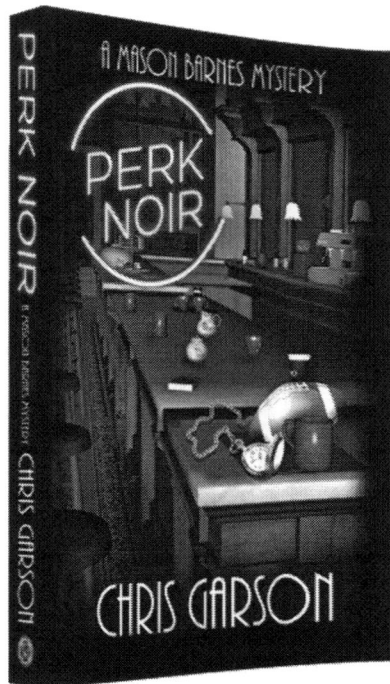

PERK NOIR

A MASON BARNES MYSTERY

PERK NOIR

A MASON BARNES MYSTERY

CHRIS GARSON

CHRIS GARSON

Two hunters pursue the same prey.

Fate has forged the slayer, Trey Thomas and the Sandrian vampire, Adalius, two natural enemies, into an uneasy alliance against an evil more powerful than either have ever faced. Only together do they stand a chance of defeating Anna; if they don't destroy each other first.

As they pursue Anna, the apprehensive Lycan watch as a confrontation looms on the horizon between vampires, the New Bloods and the Old Guard, which threatens to plunge the vampire world into civil war and trigger an all-out supernatural conflict which in the end could destroy them all.

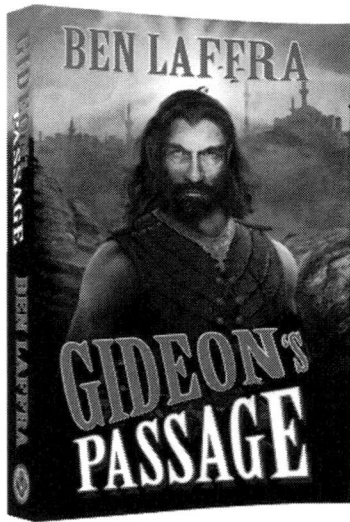

Killing is the sole province of the religious fanatics, an axiom as true today as it was some five hundred years ago; and no nation, region or person is immune.

Europe had clawed its way out of the Middle Ages with the dawning of the renaissance, only to be plunged once more into darkness, as the dogs of war circled to destroy its resurgence during the 16th century. The Islamic successor to the Roman Byzantines, the Ottoman Caliphate, flexed its muscles to conquer much of Western Asia, North Africa and South-Eastern Europe. Christian Europe shuddered when the once invincible bastion of the Knight's at Rhodes were defeated; and now trembled as the Ottoman army rattled the very gates of Vienna. No Christian army, it seemed, could withstand the ferocity of the Azabs, the Akıncı, the Sipahis, the Janissaries, and ruthless Iayalar's of the all-conquering Islamic hordes.

This then is the cauldron into which Gideon de Boyne is unwittingly thrust with his small army of dedicated Christian warriors. On the hostile island of Crete, at the doorstep of the Ottoman Empire, Gideon must face not only the overwhelming force of Muslim warriors but his own inner conflicts of the futility of war and his very Christian beliefs.

Will he succeed and come out of it unscathed?